PRAISE FOR
WEAPONS OF THE MIND

The action alone would have kept me turning the pages...but Greenwald and Kivelson, in their seamlessly blended and masterful prose, add real moral and emotional depth to the action. Their obvious care for this fully realized world becomes the reader's.

> —*Michael Macrone, author of* Brush Up Your Shakespeare! *and* Up Your Mythology

Kivelson and Greenwald have composed an elegant love letter to everything we love about space opera; the sprawling galactic civilizations, the strange alien cultures, governments and beliefs—and the humanity that they all share, even if most of them are not human. Their joined prose is a joy to read, their vision both familiar and wholly new, and the technology is expertly imagined—and the action-packed battles—and the humor—and the forging of friendships—and the woeful plight of heroes. . . Climb aboard the starship *Aquilon* with Tala and crew and get ready to believe in space wizards all over again.

> —*Michael B. Koep, Award Winning Author of the* Newirth Mythology *and* GIGMENTIA

An exciting, full-throttle romp through an imaginative new science fiction universe.

> —*Jonathan Fortin,* author of Lilitu: The Memoirs of a Succubus

Paul Kivelson and Owen Greenwald have crafted a space opera that is not only a thrilling adventure but also a thought-provoking exploration of the complexities of human nature. *Weapons of the Mind* is a masterfully written epic that sets the stage for what promises to be a remarkable trilogy, and it is a must-read for fans of the genre who crave a richly layered narrative filled with moral dilemmas, suspense, and unforgettable characters.

> —*Demetria Head, "A Look Inside", book review blog and podcast*

BOOK ONE OF THE RENEGADES TRILOGY

Weapons
OF THE
Mind

PAUL
KIVELSON
OWEN
GREENWALD

PAUL:

For my father, who read the book almost as many times as I did and without whose help both it and I would not be half of what they are.

OWEN:

For Jenna, my most devoted fan and biggest supporter, who has always believed in me and championed my dreams.
For the newer half of my family, whose love, kindness, and generosity made all the difference,
And for Kid. He knows why.

TABLE OF CONTENTS

CHAPTER ONE

THE INDIGO TRUTH

Officially, Athrumir Station didn't exist. No map or star chart marked it. Its only footprint lay in coded transmissions, off-the-record whispers, and the telltale blank space of redacted words. That hadn't stopped Arcus.

The station's hangar was empty, a silent memorial to livelier days. More tomb than waypoint. The only movement was automated, like the three-pronged landing claw guiding Arcus's ship into place. Flatscreens —monitors with no holographic functionality—lit up as they detected his arrival, long rows of light in the pitch blackness of the abandoned station. Nothing but stillness awaited him here, stillness and stale air.

The ship twisted in the claw's grasp, sending pale floodlights flashing across the far wall. Dust hung thick in the air like a shroud, swirling with agitation at the disturbance. Through the haze, Arcus could see several large, wide-mouthed hoses suspended from the ceiling by a network of wires. He wondered idly if they still functioned.

Having oriented the ship, the claw retracted with ratcheting clunks that reverberated through the hull. Centimeter by centimeter, the ship eased into place—and the deserted station lapsed once more into silence.

Arcus observed from his padded chair at the ship's main console and factored the station's disrepair into various inferences and hypotheses, weighing their probabilities one by one. Another piece of data that, when placed in sufficient context, would reveal Athrumir Station's many mysteries. Among them, why no navigational chart he'd come across acknowledged its existence, or why it was the final destination of four Wonders (*possibly more*, he acknowledged; there was no guarantee he'd discovered them all). But those mysteries were idle curiosities next to the greatest mystery of all, which had stripped him of everything he'd worked toward, and guided him here: *What is happening to us?*

There was a lick of white-tinged emotion at the thought, ninth-shade but barely a thread, burning itself out as fast as it had come. Almost on cue, the ship responded, as though its systems had been linked to the errant feeling—the engines began powering down, the docking process completing itself. The gaunt siari rubbed his temples with two arms, leaving the other two on the controls. Fourth-shade olive light flashed across his bluish skin as he discarded the groundless thought. There was no room left for such turquoise notions as that.

A bright yellow indicator on the dashboard switched on, signaling that gravity had finished equalizing. So gradually had it had diminished, he'd barely noticed. It was when he rose from his chair that the difference in movement became like white on black. Each step was free as a dance, effortless as the wind itself. He leapt experimentally and felt himself soaring in the brief moment before his brain caught up to his new circumstances. Gravity caught him a decisecond later (for the station wasn't weightless, merely kept at lower gravity than both the Peramit standard and his own preference). When he alighted on the ship's metal flooring, he felt a faint hum as the landing ramp extended. The door next to the pilot's chair slid open too, dividing down the middle. Beyond that threshold, past the reassuring glow of the ship's lights, Athrumir Station awaited, cloaked in stubborn, inscrutable black.

Arcus took two steps toward the door, then frowned, turning back to examine a small equipment rack along the far wall. The station's external security had been easily neutralized, serving no purpose but to confirm that something on this station required defending. But it suggested the presence of interior defenses as well, for invaders who survived the opening firestorm. His eyes swept over the small collection of tools, each hanging from an individual harness, each potentially useful. A harpoon cable, a pulse ring, a cooling unit...

His fingers paused in front of a sleek, military-grade 86-Tilde kinetic pistol. Philosophy warred with practicality for several long seconds before the hand moved on. He compromised with a mono-field knife, small and subtle. With one last look at the 86-Tilde (the temptation had reached the eighteenth shade; he never should have kept it), he tucked the knife's empty hilt into a holster on the lower left of his four arms and headed for the ramp.

What little he could see of the station was all soft edges and the natural steely gray of metal that meant the interior designer hadn't bothered to recolor. Certainly, no siari had been consulted, or they would have commented on the shade of guilt that color inspired. That particular association was deep-rooted in the siari brain. Even on the cusp of middle age, he felt it as strongly as ever.

Blended as they were, telling the artificially induced guilt from the natural was not without difficulty. He had a vague suspicion that guilt was appropriate in his present situation, but he'd felt the shades more and more lightly of late. If not for the ubiquity of unpainted metal, Arcus might have forgotten the feeling altogether. *My true emotions are guiltless*, he concluded. *I am beyond such weakness.*

As he crossed the threshold onto the landing ramp, the door sealed itself behind him, a brief source of noise in a hangar devoid of any sound louder than the background hum of electronic systems. Arcus took a last look over his shoulder at his ship—a rotund pod with three curved, overlapping wings that wrapped the body in a tight hug. The station appeared deserted, but there was still risk in leaving the craft behind. Its sensors hadn't detected any other ships in the hangar. If something happened to this one while he was gone, he could be stranded. But he had unwound those spools of thought several times, followed each skein to its conclusion again and again. He had but one viable choice—and so he allowed his feet to carry him down the ramp and onto the hangar's metal floor, so cold he could feel it through his shoes.

No sooner had he done so than the protective shield across the airlock blinked out.

The air in the hangar fled past him toward the freedom of exposed space, howling in his ears and pulling him along with it. His feet left the floor as the wind buffeted him upward, toward the open airlock.

The suddenness of the vacuum had surprised him, but he was not without options. Within his brain were two great repositories of potential. His will and his understanding—of the universe, and all its component parts. The first gave purpose to the power he held. The second gave it capacity.

He withdrew into his meta-awareness and bridged the gap between will and understanding, drawing deep from the conduit he'd forged. Energy, pure and malleable—siphoned from the universe itself and now his to use, the privilege of an Enhancer. It swept through him, Enhancing his weight ninefold.

Almost in the same instant, he sucked in a quick breath before the last wisps of air were lost to space. Just one breath—but already he was sending the Enhancing energy into his alveoli and circulatory system, heightening their efficiency. As fast as he'd drawn it in, he released it. Full lungs would only tear apart under the stress of expanding air as the room depressurized. One breath would be sufficient for now.

His feet touched down again, the impact unnaturally forceful. A reminder that though he felt no different, he was much heavier than he had been only moments before. Enhancement handled the unintended negative consequences to his change even without his conscious approval. It was intelligent in that way, expending itself in myriad smaller Enhancements to keep him safe from the repercussions of his own wishes. Not that it couldn't harm—if directed properly, Enhancement could cause all kinds of damage, though in practice it was often less effective than more traditional methods. He had more energy in reserve, ready to be used if needed. And it *would* be needed, he decided, eyes flicking up toward the empty, howling hole where the station's airlock had been. That had been no simple malfunction. The station had occupants. Unwelcoming ones at that.

His field of vision grew dimmer the further he went from his ship's nimbus of illumination. He sent some of his leftover power into his lightlets—small rings that peppered his pale blue skin, trailed down his arms, and marked his cheeks in the V-pattern of his genus. Right now, they glowed the saffron of thirteenth-shade determination. As he focused the Enhancement, the glow deepened, the light spilling in an ever-expanding radius until it lapped against the corners of the wide hangar, orange flashing across the metal and warring with the native silver. The effulgent beacon that Arcus had become strode with new surety, empty lungs burning in his chest. Determination danced like torchlight along every wall.

Ahead was the door to the rest of the station, tightly sealed. It was a massive, circular affair made of plasticrete, with metal reinforcers placed strategically throughout. Not beyond his abilities to batter through—but that was a crude, blunt solution to a problem with a simple answer. He crossed the remaining distance to the door's main console with urgent steps. A brush of his long fingers activated the terminal. A floating navigation menu in translucent, third-shade coral pink sprang to life above the terminal's emitter.

All was as Vinda had told him. Arcus had heard truth in the dying councilor's voice as she weakened. It had been as clear as Seurral's oceans, as pure as a harpstring's single, reverberating note. As a Harmonizer, he'd learned to Enhance his senses to separate truth from falsehood, memorizing the tells of every species wealthy enough to claim a seat on the Galactic Congress. Vinda had given her secrets willingly before the end. Among them had been three security codes, each of which Arcus now entered, fingers swift and precise.

Access granted.

Hidden within the *emergencies* submenu was a failsafe in the event of an airlock breach. A number of possible traps flashed through the more paranoid parts of Arcus's mind, but he triggered it anyway. The hangar shook as a thick metal sheet extended across the hole in the ceiling with a low, mechanical whirr, slowly closing off the gap. Arcus counted down the seconds while atmosphere returned before taking a long, beautiful breath. His aching lungs sang with eighteenth-shade yellow. Only then did he let his Enhancements bleed away—all but what powered his lightlets and the constant, minor augments to his strength, reflexes, and senses—reclaiming the power for later use.

He entered a second command into the terminal. With a series of clicks, the hangar door spun open, revealing the lightless corridor beyond. A black pit, beyond which all manner of unseen threats might lurk. Siari had no particular connection with black, but the relationship between night and danger, as with most sapient species, remained. Arcus's primal instincts murmured warning, but he had conquered those long ago. He paid them no heed as he stepped into the doorway, his corona of orange light moving with him.

His eyes swept the shadows, scanning for irregularities in the pristine silver-gray walls (*the station's construction predates graphics modules*, he noted) that could indicate a trap. The ceiling seemed the most obvious place to hide something—it was a mess of pipes and tubing, crevices and jutting bits in an uneven tapestry of disrepair. He kept his eyes turned upward, save for the occasional glance down to ensure nothing escaped his notice.

But it was by smell, not sight, that he detected the first trap. A breath of acrid air was all the warning he got, and then burning torment splashed across his chest. He gasped and his throat filled with lancing, gurgling pain. Surely his chest was melting, shriveling with agony, collapsing as vital organs liquefied—

His lightlets faded, the power funneled away and back into his body along with all his reserves, Enhancing regulatory systems and tissue resilience and nine other basic avenues of defense. He kept each Enhancement at full strength until the burning stopped. The small vent at shoulder height from which the gas had come was easily visible now that he knew to look. He had almost paid full price for his imprudence. His windpipe felt like it had been scrubbed with sandpaper and his chest was one massive, tingling ache. Arcus bent over, head swimming, and retched all over the station floor, with a fresh stab of pain as the liquid passed through his damaged esophagus.

It took several decihours of calm breathing and accelerating his natural healing through careful Enhancement, but his respiratory system eventually stopped trying to claw its way out of his body. Enhancers were hard to kill. Arcus had estimated that with his power properly allocated, he could survive the brunt of a thousand-kiloton explosion. His estimates were rarely wrong.

Too much time had been spent recovering; he could spare no more. Trapping a grimace before it could color his muscle, he pushed himself to his feet and reallocated energy back into his lightlets, which now shone the cerulean tones of fifteenth-shade caution. The light intensified until he was glowing just brightly enough to bathe his next few steps in blue.

The corridor twisted about itself like the intestine of a vast, metallic creature, unending and featureless. Arcus kept his pace swift, the hem of his white longcoat brushing the ground behind him. His footfalls were a series of thunderclaps to his Enhanced ears, his heartbeat steady hammer blows. Aside from those, there were no other sounds. Yet the silence was not to be confused with safety. For instance, several paces ahead, a patch of metal lay barren of the dust that was so uniform elsewhere. That could mean any number of things, few of them good. An Enhanced leap carried him over it, and whatever potential for danger it held remained unrealized.

The solitude was comfortable. Familiar. He'd lived it now for almost three centralized years, consumed by a problem only he seemed to understand the importance of. Consumed by a chance to cure the disease once and for all, rather than sacrificing so much just to treat the symptoms.

Once, he would have recoiled from that shade of bitterness. Now he embraced it, wearing it like power armor as he stalked deeper into the heart of Athrumir Station.

Orange light had just begun to break through the blue when the next trap sprang. There was no warning. One moment Arcus saw nothing ahead but empty corridor, the next he was encased in a spherical shimmer scattered through with seventh-shade gold. *A simple shield,* Arcus hypothesized. Further investigation suggested that his first assumption had been correct. He tapped a slender finger against the shimmer, then ran that finger slowly along it, testing for weaknesses. He found none. *Inward-focused containment. No operational estimate. Kinetic, non-discriminatory tiling, likely airtight.*

His six fingers curled into a fist. Kinetic shields could be overloaded —a few shots from a decent gun would shut one down. The memory of the 86-Tilde on his equipment rack brought fleeting, violet-tinged regret, but only of the fifth shade. He'd been right to leave it behind. Temptation had bested him too often, of late, and the Tenet forbidding Enhancers from carrying weapons was most explicit in its command. It didn't matter. Enhancers were a weapon unto themselves, and Arcus needed nothing more than his hands to batter down even military-grade shields. Intensive daily conditioning kept his arms acceptably muscular, though being siari, he wouldn't be setting any records. Enhancement was multiplicative; the same amount of energy that doubled a weak sapient's strength would double a strong sapient's as well. For that reason, it was important to give your Enhancements the strongest foundation possible.

Power threaded down his arms and wove its way through his muscles. He squared his feet, pulled back, and struck the impossibly smooth barrier with his upper-right fist. It glanced harmlessly aside. A frown pursing his thin lips, Arcus struck again, and again. Seven punches he counted, before his knuckles started aching. The shield hadn't even flickered.

A golden streak swam through the translucent haze in front of him. Arcus half watched it, running the math himself. Seven Enhanced strikes should have put stress on even the most resilient shield. Power cells could only be stretched so far. Unless…yes, of course. It was obvious. The struts that served as the shield's focal points, partially obscured through the shield-shimmer, were visible now that he knew to look for them. They must have slotted out of the floor when the shield came up; he couldn't imagine failing to notice them otherwise. The diode-covered, centimeter-high cylinders numbered eight in all and were evenly spaced around him. And directly connected, no doubt, to the station's generator. The shield would be all but invincible, and given the size of his spherical cage and his own bodily needs, he estimated he had enough air for seventeen decihours of shallow breathing. Even Enhancers couldn't stretch a breath out indefinitely. It would be a slow, hands-off sort of death. Theoretically, at least.

Arcus had to admire the simplicity and effectiveness of the design. The trap had clearly been built for effectiveness against Enhancers. How embarrassing for the engineer that its first test had pitted it against *him*. Not even the Central Pillar himself commanded his level of expertise. He had plumbed the secrets of Enhancement to a level few took interest in and fewer still were capable of reaching. He had seen the potential of an art long stagnated, elevated it beyond what the Center's finest candidates ever dreamed of wielding. No force or law could hold him.

Arcus summoned the fullness of his power. This time, instead of Enhancing himself, he sent it into a patch of air between two shield-struts.

The air resisted, of course. Gasses were among the most difficult substances to Enhance. One's own body was easiest. The deeper the connection between Enhancer and subject, the stronger the Enhancement, and the faster it took hold. Connection took many forms: similarity of structure, intellectual or emotional familiarity, even physical closeness. Scientists could not explain why this might be so. In fact, scientists who tried to make sense of Enhancement invariably threw up their hands—or equivalent appendages—and admitted defeat. They'd learned many "hows," but the "whys" were more elusive.

Whatever the explanation, an Enhancer at Arcus's level could compensate for such deficits with more power.

He forced his will upon that small patch of air, shoving his energy through the thin, imperfect conduit into the molecules themselves. It took almost six seconds for the Enhancement to take, and then the air began shimmering. If not for the shield, Arcus would have felt the sudden heat wash over him. The struts had no such protection. Their metal slowly reddened as the Enhancement persisted, their interior electronics overheating and failing. All at once, the diodes on the left strut went dead. The right strut followed only seconds later.

Arcus released the Enhancement and turned toward the next strut, but further action was unnecessary. Reducing two struts to dead metal stubs had rendered the shield unstable. Large cracks formed and smoothed over and reformed as the generator tried vainly to cover the original area. It flickered twice, one final flash of power, and dissipated.

And Arcus walked on.

Despite the danger, he found himself feeling eighth-shade excitement at the thought of the next obstacle. The station's gauntlet had become a battle of will and intellect between Arcus and its creator. He'd never enjoyed watching gauntlets, but perhaps if he'd known how it would feel to run one himself, he would have made time.

The sophistication of the traps only made stranger the relative ease he'd had with the exterior defenses. They had been so straightforward, so lacking, compared to the maze he'd found within. Yet it was the latter that the modern age had swept aside. Interior defenses meant less when fortresses and garrisons could be bombed from orbit and stations vaporized piece by piece. Even his ship, small as it was, could have annihilated the station without his ever needing to land. The state of the station's defenses suggested it was guarding something that could not fall into the wrong hands under *any* circumstances—but also wouldn't be missed if it were destroyed. The question then became, why had it not already *been* destroyed? It would have been the safest option. Even the best defenses were no guarantee of safety, as he was currently demonstrating. Truly preparing against an Enhancer of his skill was impossible, so why take the risk?

Such speculation was pointless. Every step moved him closer to the station's heart. He could feel the answers awaiting him, the information he'd been missing to stitch the rest into clarity.

The traps started coming closer together, but he'd the rhythm of the place now, a feel for the creator's mind. He spotted the tripwires, disarmed the mechanisms, avoided the false paths. There was a desperation to these tactics, subtlety giving way to brute force. He moved through it all, calm observation guiding his steps.

When a thick sheet of metal dropped into place behind him, he was ready. He dashed forward on Enhanced legs, hoping to escape the trap before it could spring. Another barrier slammed down in front of him, too fast to slip beneath. He tried anyway and ended up hitting the barrier at top speed. It didn't hurt much; he kept his body durable as a default.

The cautious glow of Arcus's lightlets deepened to the seventeenth shade, tinting the impromptu prison. He waited for something to happen, but seconds passed uneventfully, each feeling like a full cycle. If this was a simple cage, his disappointment could very well reach the twenty-first shade.

He sent a surge of power through his muscles and shoved against the barrier with all four arms. He might as well have blown on it. Brute force was out, then, but there were many other ways to—

A wall of blistering heat crashed over him like a tidal wave. Arcus gritted his teeth as the temperature intensified, feeling a shade of worry for the first time. Enhancers didn't deal with heat well. They could not diminish, only magnify, and "cold" was merely an absence of heat. To make himself warmer was trivial, but the reverse was impossible—as whoever had designed the room must have known. Enough heat could kill even a Torandian, boiling away their vital fluids right through that famously durable tubing.

His lungs felt like they'd been dunked in magma, but he didn't dare open his mouth. Bright red was bleeding through the blue of his lightlets. His thoughts were red too, fifteenth shade, in a swirling, unproductive panic. The room grew hotter and hotter, the walls and floor glowing in ever-deepening shades. The air itself swam before his eyes, so he shut them.

The brain, he felt himself think. *Before it's too late.*

Ah, but his subconscious could be crafty. Never until his desperation reached the sixteenth shade did it suggest the ultimate taboo, knowing that if he stopped to think about it, he'd be dead before he reached a conclusion. Thrice before, he'd broken the first Tenet, in situations so dire as to rob him of all other choices. A true Enhancer would have gone to the grave before entertaining the notion.

He'd left that part of himself behind years ago.

It was as fast and simple as a thought to turn his power onto its source, to Enhance electrical signals and chemical reactions and each individual synapse. He felt his brain clock into overdrive as for the fourth time ever, the power settled in. Time slowed like a rock hitting the water's surface. His whole scalp buzzed. Despite the pain frying every nerve in his body and the knowledge he'd made a mistake of staggering proportions—though a part of him wanted to believe it hadn't been, that the reported ill effects were Center propaganda designed to keep Enhancers easier to control—he felt a smile stretch across his swelling lips.

Heat-metal-safety-fear-cold-escape-sabotage.... His brain kaleidoscoped, a panopticon of fragmented concepts that each contained entire ideas—entire arguments—all instantly refining themselves or collapsing beneath their own inadequacy. Possibilities narrowed, solutions converged to...one.

It was astonishingly simple; how could he have missed it? A location capable of generating such intense heat was a safety hazard, particularly on a space station. Prudent design would necessitate coolant tanks as an emergency precaution. Though his eyes were still shut, he could recall the corridor as if it were a holoimage in his mind, down to the small, perforated tubes on the ceiling designed to distribute the chilling gas. He'd seen them and dismissed them as unimportant—a foolish mistake.

For obvious reasons, heat alone wouldn't trigger the emergency system. There had to be another mechanism. *Time,* his rapid-fire brain reminded him. Ah, yes. He was crisping. No time to test conditions. *Valves.* Perfect.

The coolant tank had to be above him. But where? His brain hummed at the challenge, flashing through tens of station schematics like a holo set to fast-forward. *One point seven meters up, zero point four meters over,* his brain supplied, and there was no time to second-guess it. Less than a second had passed since he'd started truly *thinking,* but his condition was worsening rapidly. He seized a portion of power, imbued it with a visualization of nitrohydroxiphane—by far the most common gas-based coolant—and the command to Enhance pressure, and sent it blindly into the area logic told him the tank had to be. There was no accompanying reduction in his available power and he knew he'd been wrong.

No panicking. His brain about-faced back to his calculations with frenzied efficiency. *One point fifty-five up, one point two over.* This time, the Enhancement took hold. As with the air, the understanding wasn't quite there, not the way it was when he Enhanced himself. His will was vast enough to force the issue.

There was a loud popping sound followed by the most comforting hiss Arcus had ever heard. He gasped with relief, then snapped his mouth closed as cold spread across his burning skin. The safety valves preventing corrosive concentrations would be broken, and while Arcus's Enhancements could keep his skin intact, he felt only third-shade certainty that his insides would prove sufficiently durable.

The cocoon of chilling chemicals enveloped him, replacing searing pain with a tenth-shade-yellow-by-comparison itching sensation as the nitrohydroxiphane ate away at his outer epidermal layer. He drew power away from his brain to bolster his skin, wincing at the disorienting shift back to slow, sludgy thoughts. It was like being allowed to fly for a decihour and then being dropped into a pit of tar. No, worse. Like lowering *yourself* into a pit of tar, knowing that the only thing keeping you from the sky was yourself. Given the option, who wouldn't choose to soar?

He knew the costs, but it felt so academic beside the all-encompassing truth that the galaxy had arranged itself into during those brief, beautiful instants of effortless thought. He cast around for a distraction, something to occupy his plodding mind. He found it in the growing numbness creeping up his limbs.

Thankful for something to focus on, however insignificant, Arcus stoked his body temperature. He allowed heat to radiate and spread, pushing back against the coolant's chill, maintaining a semi-equilibrium until he heard the two barriers receding. They scraped roughly over the cooling floor, enough time having passed to ensure an intruder's death. Arcus waited for the nitrohydroxiphane to disperse before opening his eyes. That motion alone hurt.

He had no desire to wait and see if the trap would trigger again. Ignoring a mushiness in his feet, he took off down the corridor. A few steps past the open door, the mushiness had turned to acute pain, so he stopped, sat on the refreshingly cool floor, and pulled his half-melted shoes off in chunks to assess the damage.

His feet were a mess of open blisters that wept blood and serum in streaks across the metal floor. He prodded one and let a grimace pass through his muscle onto the skin. Healing such an injury would exceed the time he'd allotted himself for optimum chances of success. Instead, he deadened the pain receptors in his feet with some strategic Enhancement and pushed himself up. There would be a price to pay for that, but he wouldn't be paying it now. He limped further into the station, leaving the blood-soaked scraps of his shoes behind.

He kept his senses Enhanced, anticipating more defenses, but there was only the ever-present hum of unseen equipment behind the guilt-inducing walls. It seemed he'd run Athrumir Station's gauntlet and emerged triumphant. Still, he did not relax his vigilance—not in the deserted chambers, or the interchangeable corridors, or the emergency-lit lift that refused to move, forcing him to break through the bottom and drop for almost eleven full seconds. He hit the floor below with a loud thud and pried open the safety door without pausing to recover, feet throbbing painlessly.

The door opened into a room larger even than the main hangar. The walls ascended into darkness deeper than Arcus's eyes could penetrate without further Enhancement. The room was bisected by a meter-high drop. On the lower level were signs of unfoldable landing claws. A secondary hangar, most likely, for those who didn't want to traverse a corridor of deadly traps upon arrival. It hadn't occurred to him to search the station exterior for a hidden entrance. Negligence such as that was inexcusable.

The room was empty of both ships and sapients, giving Arcus a clear line of vision to the other side. The far wall was dominated by a solid eberium door—more bulwark, really—that stretched six meters wide. When he closed the long distance to the door and pressed against it with his fingers, there was something hard and transparent between his hand and the metal. Another shield.

The door's command console was dark. Lifeless. Closer examination revealed several exposed wires along the back that had been dug out of their casings and slashed into pieces. One look was enough to conclude that repairs would be impossible.

Confident his Enhancements would protect him from shocks, he ran a finger along the exposed wiring. Still warm. The sabotage had been recent, fewer than four decihours past. The culprit—likely the same who'd initiated the hangar's flushing procedure, or at least a member of the same group—had meant to close off the station to him beyond this point. Arcus had not encountered anyone between the two hangars, and his hearing was sharp enough to notice even the quietest ships, had one taken off. That left one possible place for the mysterious sapient to be: behind the impenetrable door.

Yet the sapient's own act of sabotage had unmasked their ruse. Once the door had been sealed off, how had the station's defender retreated behind it? For that matter, the shredded wires seemed almost *too* prominently removed from the console, their innards hacked apart with exaggerated enthusiasm. It did not give Arcus the impression of hasty, desperation-fueled destruction. No, this was a tableau—every object a set piece arranged to convey a message. To signal hopelessness in the face of an insurmountable obstacle.

Not the sort of message worth wasting effort conveying, unless the obstacle wasn't actually insurmountable.

Arcus gave the room another sweep, this time slow and careful. Something to the left of the wide door snagged at his attention—an irregularity in the otherwise smooth metal. It turned out to be a small panel that, when manually slid aside, revealed an embedded omnipad and DNA scanner. Arcus's lightlets glowed a prideful sickly green of the ninth shade.

Now that he was standing right by the wall, more, subtler imperfections stood out like joy at nightfall. Microscopic seams outlined what was almost certainly a small door—a door absent the other's protective shield, as several prods confirmed.

It was fourteenth-shade doubtful both that his previous codes would work again and that his DNA was authorized for access, but those constraints mattered little to an Enhancer. Arcus's shoulder met the door with the force of a Surol avalanche, and it was the door that gave way.

He tumbled through the hole he'd made, muscles tingling with suppressed power, mind cooling as he settled into the Enhancer's battlecalm. He'd already settled into a defensive stance before he noticed that the sapient within didn't appear hostile.

It was a ctasil—old, judging by the droopiness of its features and the blackening of its rubbery mauve skin. If not for its natural stooping, it would have been as tall as Arcus, but it was easily twice as broad. Large, round, pale yellow eyes studied the intruder, staring out from a face that held only sadness and resignation. Though clearly a noncombatant—a scientist, most likely—its single arm held a long, sleek gun with a pronged barrel, pointed conspicuously at the floor.

Keeping one eye on the ctasil, Arcus scanned the room. It was smaller than he'd expected, judging by the size of the main door, and covered in open wires that snaked along the ground, dangled from the ceiling, and wrapped around pipes. 3-D images of different species' brains rotated above holoprojectors while flatscreens flashed with data. Devoting his full attention, he might have made sense of them. The armed ctasil was a higher priority, though, even if it hadn't yet done anything but stand there with that weary, violet expression.

Finally, Arcus spoke. "I'm looking for answers."

The ctasil nodded slowly, as if mentally balancing two very great weights. "I know," it said. "And I will not give them to you."

"I've come a very long way," said Arcus, taking a step. He unsheathed his mono-field knife and switched it on. The second-shade coral blade, an atom's length in thickness, snapped into existence above the small hilt. "Too far to leave without them. If I must, I will take them from you."

The threat tasted unfamiliar in his mouth, but he kept both skin and muscle aligned in hardened resolution.

"You will find me unreceptive to your methods. Today, I have sentenced the culmination of my art to death. I can imagine no greater torture than that."

"Elaborate."

"There was always concern that one like you would find its way here. A mad Renegade seeking revenge."

Arcus's mouth twisted before he could catch himself.

"We had protocols," the ctasil continued. "Which I have mostly followed. I have alerted Congress, and they have dispatched a vaporization team. The work of a long, full life, forever lost."

The ctasil breathed several long, shuddering breaths—its species' equivalent of sobs—then gathered itself.

"They wanted to destroy it long ago, but I fought them. Year after year, I argued. Now you are here, and so I gave them what they had been waiting for. An excuse."

"You did your duty." Arcus's voice was flat, not quite covering contempt fourteen shades dark. His words prompted another bout of shuddering from the ctasil.

"Not even that," it murmured once its shoulders had stilled. "Only what I could bring myself to do."

Its gaze alighted involuntarily on a lit monitor by the wall.

"You were told to purge the system," said Arcus. "But you didn't. You gambled that you could stop me instead."

"I couldn't," whispered the ctasil. "I *couldn't*. It's the only beautiful thing I ever created."

"I understand more than you might think," Arcus reassured. "You devoted yourself to something for so long, it became more important than the rest of the galaxy. So important, that you betrayed those you'd pledged to serve, hoping vainly that it could be saved."

Yes, it was all too familiar. The sensation of being pulled apart, knowing that the only possible response to the pain was embracing it and staying the course you'd chosen.

"If I had killed you, my work would have been safe," said the ctasil. "Please forgive me."

"I would've done the same."

"I have considered raising this gun and shooting you. But you would not die, would you?"

"Probably not."

"No, you would not," the ctasil agreed, and violet radiated from its features. "I have failed, and my life is over. Whether by you or by them, all I have done will be destroyed."

Too late, Arcus realized what was about to happen. The ctasil whirled toward the glowing monitor, lifting the gun. Without any conscious thought besides twentieth-shade desire to *save that data*, Arcus Enhanced his arm into a blur of motion and hurled the mono-field knife overhand, point first. Still too late to matter.

But the elderly scientist's thick finger stalled on the trigger, unwilling to destroy a lifetime's worth of creation. In that moment of pause, the knife's projected blade found its target, just beneath the creature's single shoulder. A fatal blow to a ctasil, but it neither twitched nor cried out as it fell—there was only a soft, accepting sigh as its eyelids shuttered.

How dare it, Arcus thought, eighth-shade anger coursing like blood through his veins. *How dare it try to destroy what I came for?*

He closed the distance to the creature's still body, glaring the whole time. Then he bent and ripped his knife free. Blood the color of wine leaked from the wound onto the floor in a slow, steady dribble. With a snarl, Arcus brought his arm back down, piercing the dead ctasil through the center of its broad chest.

Something raw and uncontrolled burst within him, a crescendo of instinct and violent purpose once content to murmur in his mind's deepest recesses and now brought into the forefront at last. Again and again the blade arced, a frenzied loop of down and up and back down, accompanied by sprays of murky fluid. Through a white haze, he half watched the knife repeatedly puncture the corpse, mutilating it beyond recognition, as if the arm that rose and fell belonged to another.

It was only later—how much later, he could not say—that he came to himself again. He stood crouched low over the mutilated ctasil scientist. He stared down at his victim expecting to be swept away by a polychromatic whirlwind of emotion, but his lightlets had shifted back to resolute saffron. There was no disgust, no remorse or confusion. Only that empty silence.

Arcus didn't consider this important. Naturally, negative emotions would be pushed aside in the triumphant ending of a search years in the undertaking. It was time to excise the last few knots of confusion from his understanding. He stepped over to the monitor that the ctasil had failed to destroy and looked at the lit screen. The truth was only a submenu away.

At first, he didn't understand what he was looking at. It was a jumbled schematic and words that, while separately familiar, together became eldritch. But the longer he stared, the more it came together. Slowly at first, then all at once, in a conflux of shock, disgust, and raw, bitter betrayal.

CHAPTER TWO
AN EXERCISE IN DISCIPLINE

No matter how still she kept her body, Tala's mind refused to stop fidgeting. Her eyes were closed tight, her legs crossed in meditative repose. Each slow breath in, she focused on safeguarding her thoughts from her room's numerous distractions—to no avail. Her attention kept straying downward, toward the soft clicks of an insect traveling across the floor.

She cracked one eye open a sliver. The insect was an ant with a bloated orange body, roughly a finger's length. Its four long antennae darted back and forth, as if trying to flag another unseen insect's attention. Its small legs struggled to keep the rest of itself aloft, a frenzied barrage of movement, flailing desperately for every centimeter of progress.

Surrendering to the distraction, Tala opened both eyes with a murmured grumble—though whether directed at the ant or at herself, she couldn't say. She uncrossed her legs and swung her feet off the glass bubble that topped her bed. It made a poor seat from which to meditate, but that was the price she paid for warmth. Modellus's nights got cold for a Central Cluster planet, and a temperature-controlled bed was a comfort deemed acceptable within the guidelines of the twenty-eighth Tenet: *When luxury becomes necessity, excess and waste follow.*

Tala opened the bottom drawer of her squat, metal desk and retrieved a box filled with old knickknacks. Each bauble had been given to her by Anora—a collection of mementos from their missions together. Tala removed them from the box one by one, placing them tenderly back in the drawer.

She spared a quick glance up at her room's only decoration—a riddle masquerading as a painting, projected above the desk. *Flowerbed*, it was called, originally painted by the famed artist Duna. It depicted an armless man, serene and peaceful, crouching in a field of windswept orange flowers. The image had been gifted to her by Frael, the Central Pillar, during one of her stubborn moods that had been so much more common in childhood. He'd implied the wisdom within the painting would help her somehow. Just about every Initiate had a story like that; even with his duties leading the Enhancement Corps, Frael managed to spend an impressive amount of time walking the Center's corridors, pinpointing troubled young Enhancers and nudging them back into harmony with the Tenets. Yet for all her study, *Flowerbed* remained as opaque as it had been the day she'd first projected it onto her wall.

She was expected to set a good example for the Initiates, yet she struggled with the most basic mental exercises. Control came so much more easily when she was moving, fighting, or working her power on something tangible. Her thoughts fell into place, mind locking onto the task at hand. Without actual purpose, success eluded her—so every day, Tala devoted an extra hour to practice. As Exemplar Scratch had told her many times, failure was just proof she wasn't done yet.

Perhaps once she'd learned to master herself, she'd be worthy to stand beside him. Here she was, a full Agent with seven successful missions in her engine-trail, and not once had she worked with her mentor in the field. Yes, Scratch was...*different* in that regard, but it still felt like a slight. Like if her control were a little tighter, her meditations more focused, the Tenets better internalized, he'd bring her along on one of his solitary hunts. They'd pursue the Coalition's enemies together, out on the edge of space.

"Switch from Meditation Room Three to Preset Two," Tala commanded as she stepped toward the scuttling bug, box in hand. The bare white walls around her shifted, colors surging as they returned to Tala's default choice of appearance. Worn wood spread across them, complete with a large window above the bed. Beyond the window, a grassy field met a wispy stretch of river. Several times, Tala thought she'd glimpsed a small, bushy-furred creature darting about the field— though animals weren't included in the window module's list of features. Perhaps she was imagining things, or perhaps the animal was a surprise coded in for the observant procrastinator.

The orange ant had traversed barely half a meter since she'd stopped meditating. It hadn't noticed—or simply hadn't cared—when the walls around it had morphed from white into a well-weathered, wooden veneer. With a scoop of her hand, Tala swept it into the empty knickknack box. It would likely be sucked up by the Center's vacuum bots if left to fend for itself. While her meditation was unsalvageable, she could at least improve a poor ant's prospects.

According to her omnipad, she was due to meet the others in the refectory. Still, it wouldn't take long to drop by the gardens on the way. She could deposit the ant there. She spread her palm over the box's open top, though not before waving her door open.

The Center's hallways were broad and welcoming, designed to be comfortable for all species. The corridors stretched a minimum of three meters wide and a towering five meters high. The sweeping design could easily accommodate even a Surolian's icy girth, or the height of a skeletal Torandian.

The corridor's current module displayed smooth, gray stone, broken up by bay windows. Not real windows—the mountain that the Center was carved into didn't have much in the way of views—but projections, programmed with all manner of distant landscapes. Tala preferred more natural vistas, but whoever ran the Center's modules clearly loved cities. Every day, a different city from a different planet could be seen through the windows' flat depths. Sometimes, she recognized certain landmarks: the oblong palace of an alvear hivemother, the floating, symmetrical Sorabul corporate headquarters over Amul-Banal, or even the flowing, rough-topped towers of the Legislatorium on Peramit. Today, they showed a city built upon a thick, rainy marsh. Up and up the buildings rose, past bloated, smog-laden clouds into a green sky.

But whether cityscape or pastoral splendor, she appreciated the glimpses of the broader universe, even if through a projected window on a digitized wall. She wasn't a prisoner—she could leave for missions and the occasional home visit—but the bonds of responsibility limited her travel possibilities nonetheless.

She'd gotten but two steps from her room when a rectangular segment of wall shifted further down the corridor. The stone façade faded to pale pink as it slid aside to reveal a room of diaphanous colored cloth and exotic plants that had grown, uninhibited, to cover every surface. Tala caught only a glimpse before Anora filled the doorway, emerging with a boisterous bounce.

At two and a half meters, Anora dwarfed most other nordok. Her skin was the color of baked clay, a ruddiness that contrasted with the ivory curtain of segmented bone cascading from her scalp and brushing just past her knees. The nordok, whether through a quirk of fate, astronomical coincidence, or divine intervention, had a genetic structure almost identical to humans. Though incapable of crossbreeding and possessing entirely different genesis planets, the two species were nonetheless almost indistinguishable at a genetic level.

Seeing Tala, Anora dashed down the hallway, arms wide, projecting her usual rolling confidence. She bent and cocooned Tala in a tight hug, her forearms' exoskeletal casing digging deep into Tala's back. The plates of bone, roughly two centimeters thick, covered not just Anora's forearms but a large portion of her chest and calves.

Tala wasn't a small woman—almost two meters tall, with the broad physique that can only be earned through demanding physical activity. But despite her stature, she always felt tiny within her friend's crushing, exuberant hugs. Her close-cropped brown hair was pressed tight against Anora's gray shirt and the ridge of bony plating underneath.

"So good to see you!" Anora boomed, picking Tala up and spinning her about. The large arms wrapped about Tala's head muffled the greeting.

"You too," Tala mumbled into Anora's shirt. "It's been what, three whole hours?"

Keeping a firm grip on the wooden box, she gently extricated herself.

Anora took a step back—a small step, but a step nonetheless. "Let's walk over together?"

"Sure." Tala stepped aside so a frazzled Acolyte could rush by. The young, red-haired human clung desperately to a tall stack of swaying omnipads. He ran with the alacrity of someone not merely late to something important, but in danger of missing it entirely. "Wisdom frowns on haste!" Tala shouted after him.

Anora shook her head, bony locks clattering off each other like the flailing limbs of an ancient spindly creature. She glanced into the box as they started walking, Tala falling in beside her. "I see you picked up a friend there. We taking him outside?"

"Yeah, I thought he'd like it better in the gardens. If you don't mind the detour."

Anora took a closer look as the ant explored its small enclosure. "I think we can spare the time for this little guy. Best hurry, though, if we want to catch lunch with the others before midday contemplation."

She started briskly toward the gardens, leaving Tala surprised at her speed. The pale outlines of doorways marking the quarters of Enhancers and their Vanguard lined the corridor, almost invisible to the un-Enhanced eye, separated by more false windows.

As they passed the turnoff to training halls four through eight, Anora launched into a string of chatter about her newest plant. Anora collected plants—in fact, she gave them free range to grow about her room as they pleased. Where she found the time to keep them all alive and healthy, Tala had no idea.

"The Mythcan orchid only opens up for water for half a decihour every six hours," Anora explained. "It's not easy, finding someone who can make time—*exact* time—to water it every day. A couple days isn't a problem—I know a sapient or two willing to take up the task. But when we've got to go this far afield, it makes things a bit more complicated."

Lacking good advice, Tala allowed herself to be distracted by the ant. "You're almost home," she whispered as they reached the door to the gardens.

Anora just chuckled, letting the matter drop and waving the door open.

Stepping out into the cold light of the morning sun, Tala tilted her head in greeting to the two lawkeepers stationed at the entrance. It was impossible to tell the lawkeepers' exact species, as both were covered top-to-bottom in reinforced protective gear. Their faces were hidden, entombed in boxy, standard-issue helmets. Both were armed with automatic guns: long, bulky things, equipped with high-impact microexplosive rounds. The letters EJL were emblazoned across their chests in black, marking their clearance status. The lawkeepers guarding the grounds had always been an enigma to Tala. It seemed to her that anyone foolish enough to attack the Center would meet more than enough resistance from the thousands of Enhancers who made the complex their home.

Sprawling and spacious, abundant with exotic fauna, the gardens occupied a large space at the Center's core. They spread outward from there before curling back around the outside of the facility. Land was expensive in Central Cluster, but as the Tenets had first been written within nature, the Center had dedicated a swath to capturing the beauty that had so inspired Mitra all those cycles ago. There was even a statue of him reaching his four hands out in supplication to the flowers and the trees. The gardens were a stark division of chaos and order; rows of neat, differentiated plants separated by oddly shaped islands of eclectic and intermingled botanical life. Hovering among the plants, metal pods drifted in slow rotation, spraying clouds of water from rings of concentric nozzles.

"Maybe it's just the arctic backwater I come from," said Anora, taking in a lungful of fragrant air, "but seeing all this…we really are lucky, aren't we?"

As Tala looked out over the garden, how could she do anything but agree? Thousands of different plants from hundreds of worlds, each with their own atmospheric and nutritional demands. Yet here they were, happy and healthy. "It's beautiful."

"I bet *their* Mythcans never miss a watering."

Tala didn't need Harmonizer training to sense the envy in her friend's voice. She gave Anora's arm a light squeeze, aiming away from the bone-plates. "You're the best mom a plant could ask for. Not your fault you don't have a cohort of Aides speeding up growth and Enhancing the soil."

She pointed to a cluster of bushes spilling over with pink, bell-shaped flowers. A Serdin sat among them, short and thick-limbed, hairy enough to pass as a bush himself. His dark bristles lay flat against his skin, a bodily manifestation of his calm. Tala felt a pang of jealousy unrelated to the quality of the Center's plants. Enhancers were expected to master their emotions, but Serdins could (and often did) shut them off at will.

They stepped past the Serdin to a line of small trees with trunks like ropy masses of vine. Would the Aide be alright with Tala's addition to the ecosystem? Either way, his eyes were shut, so this spot seemed as good as any other. She gently upended the wooden box, sending the ant into a yellow hedge that curved in and under and around itself, forming an interwoven set of concentric shapes representing the Enhancer's three levels of awareness: skin, muscle, and mind. The shapes interlaid with each other—but never were they allowed to meet.

"How do you think it got in?" said Anora. "The little critters don't usually make it past the cleaners."

Tala shrugged, watching the ant crush the grass beneath its hefty midsection. "However far we advance, nature can't be completely denied. Doesn't matter how many walls we put in its way."

"That a Tenet? Or did you get that one from the Exemplar?"

"Just an observation, and a silly one at that." Tala nudged Anora's shoulder playfully. "Of course, as your squadleader, I must point out that you should know all the Tenets from memory."

Anora's face was painted with faux indignation as she rubbed her shoulder with an exaggerated wince. "Assaulted both verbally and physically by my squadleader. I may have to resign my position as Vanguard One."

"Who's resigning from what?" Approaching them was Dorian, the only other human in Tala's squad. His broad face and narrow shoulders made his neck seem small and his head loom large. Most striking were his wide eyes. They were a hazel so light they looked almost orange, flecked with amber and gazing with rare affection on the universe around him. His skin was the color of singed lyptus wood and his hair was rusty, blending into black at the roots.

Tala greeted him with a wave. "Anora's stepping down. Ferric just might cry tears of joy."

"Nah," said Anora. "Changed my mind. I forgot he was next in line. Vanguard Two suits him."

Dorian gave one of his easy smiles. "Keeps him humble."

Anora gave Dorian an impish once-over. "Mighty suspicious, running into you like this. The garden's not really on the way."

"I, ah—" Dorian frowned, suddenly shy. "I thought—"

"Take a breath," said Tala. "We can talk as we go. Ferric and Vigdis are probably waiting."

Anora and Dorian followed Tala closely as she left the gardens, making double-time for the refectory. Dorian still looked oddly embarrassed. Tala's Enhanced ears could hear his elevated heartbeat, a light, concussive throb that blended with his other bodily functions and mingled with the small sounds of the outdoors. Even just walking with her friends, Tala's subconscious ran a host of Enhancements, her strength and senses pushed above human possibility. The struggle for Enhancers wasn't drawing on their power, but using it with intelligence and responsibility.

"Truth be told," Dorian said to Tala, "I thought it might be nice to walk over together. I must have just missed you. Luckily Pathmaker Dovis had seen you heading for the gardens and took pity on me."

A brilliant pink blossom sailed by, petals stuck out in every direction. Like someone had gotten overzealous with a stack of flowers and a stick of glue. "And what about me?" Anora asked. "You were just gonna leave me behind?"

"You know that's not what I meant," said Dorian, knocking aside another drifting bloom with a wave of his hand.

The group passed two more heavily armed lawkeepers guarding the Center's east wing. "Thanks for the thought," said Tala. "I like spending time with you too. I'm sure Anora agrees."

There were several paths to the refectory from the gardens, but the eastern route passed by the extreme environment training facilities. Not that Tala wanted to use the underwater training tanks or spend time in triple gravity, but she thought she might check the pit for Exemplar Scratch. It was her mentor's favorite training tool, and he had little competition for its use. Whenever Tala had to find him, she looked there first.

The east wing reflected a philosophy of open and free contemplation. Its walls were dotted with numerous small simulated windows, and each doorway was left open and inviting. It was a short walk through that section of corridors, past classrooms filled with young Initiates and their Vanguards. Holoprojectors beamed out personalized lessons from adjustable desks, drawing from a carefully curated curriculum. "So," Anora said as the group passed the last classroom, "You two packed for Neea?"

"I've been putting it off, but I guess I'd better get started," said Tala. "Either of you want to stop by tonight and help?"

"I can't," said Dorian, speeding to stay abreast with Anora and Tala as their pace quickened. "I already promised I'd help Ferric pack that stupid powersuit of his. Boxing up all those little parts will take forever."

Tala gave a sympathetic wince.

"Well, *I* won't abandon you," said Anora. "We all know your sense of style needs a guiding hand."

Tala laughed and Dorian joined in. The extreme environment facilities came into view as they rounded the corner.

"Looking for Scratch?" Dorian said, following her gaze.

"I wanted to check in before we left."

Tala waved open the door and the trio stepped inside. Dorian's eyes were even larger than usual as he and Anora took stock of their surroundings. Vanguard didn't have many reasons to visit this room. Tala stepped around the flooded glass box used for underwater training to find, nestled in a corner, a trapdoor with *Perceptual Deprivation Module* painted across the top in broad, clear letters. The trapdoor opened into a pit so dark that even Enhanced eyes were all but useless. Not too unpleasant, but for the training darts that shot at high speeds from the walls. Every dodge, deflection, and impact was recorded and tracked.

Seeing no pink light indicating use above the console, Tala sighed. "Guess I'll have to try and find him later."

Anora clapped Tala heavily on the back. "Don't sweat it. I'm sure you'll track him down before we ship out."

"I hope so," said Tala. "I've been feeling in need of some guidance. I just hope Scratch has the time."

"Oh, Tala." Anora gave her a weary look, "You're one of the best combat Enhancers of our generation, and considering you're human, that's saying a lot. It's Scratch who should feel blessed to teach *you*."

Tala didn't know what to say to that, especially in the face of Dorian's enthusiastic nodding. She settled on a halfhearted "thanks."

The corridors got more crowded the closer they drew to the refectory. Corvids with curved beaks and dull clothing over bright feathers, a knot of six-armed, insectoid alvear, and even a few other humans passed the group on their way to their midday meal. Food was offered throughout the day, but the refectory was always busy—not to mention loud. Thankfully, tight organization kept the potential chaos at a minimum. Tables were plentiful and evenly spaced. Adjustable compact benches served as seating. Against the far wall, three industrial-sized synthesizers churned out smooth, olive-colored flavored pastes into small metal bowls. Once someone entered a food or flavor into the synthesizer, the machine would deposit a paste matching the user's selection and nutritional profile. For those less fond of synthesized pastes, the Center's kitchens had a daily rotating menu accessible via omnipad.

Stepping into the refectory, Tala did a cursory scan of the room and spotted the last two members of her squad, already seated at their own table. Ferric and Vigdis sat opposite one another, breathing heavily, faces screwed up in concentration. Each was struggling to push the other's arm down onto the table's surface.

Vigdis was the taller of the two nordok, with a long, wiry body and sharp features that looked perpetually focused. Ferric was tall too, but with brawn to match. At that moment, he wore a wide grin as he pushed Vigdis's hand down and down. Ferric was always pushing himself toward something. His drive had led him to excel as the Vanguard's technology expert while maintaining top physical ability. If not for Anora and her effortlessly record-setting physical performance, he would almost certainly have been made Vanguard One—and he knew it, too.

"That makes three in a row for me," said Ferric, leaning back in triumph.

Vigdis gave him a skeptical look. "I don't understand. I've been working my hand up your palm just like that Connect article said. It had lots of notes, so it must've worked for someone."

Ferric flexed and mimed driving an arm onto the table. "Clearly not for you."

Vigdis's face broke into a smile as he noticed them. Tala smiled back, aware that most of Vigdis's greeting was meant for Anora. Inter-squad romances were generally frowned on, though not forbidden—a good thing too, or the galaxy would've missed out on the cutest couple Tala could imagine.

"Sorry we're late," said Tala, sliding onto a free patch of bench. "I had to run an errand in the gardens. Picked up these two on the way."

"We've amused ourselves sufficiently with the time." Vigdis blinked owlishly. "With a few more attempts, I'll get the technique down."

"Any place, any time," Ferric replied.

"I don't know," said Tala. "I think Viggy would've won if I hadn't been helping you."

"You..." Ferric stared down at his arm, looking appalled. Fair play had always been important to him. But then he laughed. "You thrice-cursed liar."

"Lies go against the Tenets," said Tala, expression as neutral as if she'd plunged herself into her battlecalm. "That was more of a joke."

At the distance she'd been, any strength she could have passed to Ferric would have been negligible anyway. Still, she *had* pushed a bit of power into him. Not enough to do anything, but merely holding Enhancement in his body as she'd been taught. A protection from foreign interference—Enhancement didn't interact well with itself. As long as she was already Enhancing them, another Enhancer's attempts wouldn't be able to gain purchase. She wasn't expecting any hostile Enhancers to attack the refectory, but against Renegades...

Someday.

"We had a nice walk," said Anora, taking the seat next to Vigdis and wrapping an arm over his shoulder. "Worth being late for. You should've joined us."

Vigdis tapped his order into his omnipad. "Perhaps I should have, at that."

"I rescued him," Ferric said. "I swear, he was just staring at the wall. Not meditating, mind—staring. Had to drag him out of his room."

"It was a thought experiment." Vigdis's eyes had taken on a faraway look. "I was imagining what shape my life could have taken if Tala had chosen another discipline. A Pathmaker, for example—it could have been interesting, exploring the universe. Harmonizer, Aide...actually, they'd *all* be interesting. Not that I'm complaining, mind you, but I'll admit to some curiosity. Why an Agent? I never asked what drew you to it."

As Tala formulated her answer, Ferric wasted no time preempting her. "No shame in working to your strengths. Tala chose the discipline that came easiest to her. It's just good sense."

Anora let out a long sigh that was half exasperation, half relief. "I just remember all that moping you did about making the right choice."

"I was a mess," Tala acknowledged freely. "I let it go right up to the deadline with no clue what discipline I wanted to try for. I don't know how many times I shook you all down for advice." Pausing, Tala tapped out her own order. "But it was actually Dorian that helped me choose."

"Really?" Dorian said with genuine surprise, his heart rate elevating again.

"Yes, really. I was pacing around my room muttering to myself at that point. You forced my door open, took a seat, and told me I shouldn't worry about what I wanted to do, because it was more important what I wanted to *be*. After some more thinking and another round of pacing, I realized I wanted to be someone who solves problems directly. Who does what needs doing."

"I shouldn't claim too much credit," said Dorian, smiling. "It was all plagiarized from what Mom said when I first shipped off."

"And of course, the years of smacking you guys whenever you deserved it meant I already had a bunch of free hand-to-hand experience."

Anora leaned forward. "I'm just glad you aren't a Pathmaker. I'd have died of boredom. Yeah, adding new gates and expanding our borders, blah blah blah, but how do they stay sane sitting in the same little engine room for years on end? No offense, but if my whole life was watching you meditate and bringing you meals thirty-one hours a day, I'd take the first airlock into space."

Ferric opened his mouth, but whatever he would've said was lost to the rasping voice of Exemplar Scratch himself. "Tala," was all he said, but it turned many diners' heads. He'd Enhanced the greeting such that it echoed through the refectory.

Scratch was a Torandian and that alone was a rarity among Enhancers. Like the rest of his skeletal species, he lacked both flesh and conventional muscle fibers. Only a thick mass of pale blue tubes ran up his limbs, serving the triple purpose of vein, sinew, and condensed muscle, with the strength and durability to bend steel and blunt knives. The tubes met in the center of his chest cavity, knotting in a dense ball of intermeshed veins around a protected sac of organs. His ears were small holes on either side of his skull, though he lacked a visible nose—along with a decent sense of smell. His pupil-less eyes never stopped swiveling, suspended as they were in lidless sockets by a network of thin veins, every bit as durable as the tubes upon his limbs. Those same eyes, orange as dying suns, bored into Tala from the refectory's wide doors.

"Exemplar," Tala said, switching from Universal to Torandian, as was customary. "I was looking for you, earlier."

Torandian had been tricky for Tala to master—though in fairness, Universal wasn't much easier. Even the galaxy's common language had been constructed to be easily understood by the Torandians, who spoke mostly by clicking their thick, meaty tongues within their toothless mouths. Toothless in a literal sense only, of course. Of the species that made up galactic society, Torandians were the most economically powerful—and therefore, the most politically powerful as well. Despite the supposed authority of the Galactic Congress, it was the Torandians, in all their ageless efficiency, who could truly be said to run the galaxy.

Scratch strode through the refectory with purpose, stopping in front of their table. "And so we have found each other."

Scratch's straightforwardness was almost unheard of amongst his species, but more striking than his personality was his appearance. He'd been an Agent for almost half an eight hundred-year cycle, and his body reflected that service in its patchwork of scratched, scarred bone.

Lifting his left hand, Scratch spread his four needle-tipped fingers wide. Tala knew what he expected; it was an old ritual between them. As she stood, she reached out with a concentrated mental push to each individual muscle and bone in her arm. Every Enhancer conceptualized their power differently. To Tala's mind, it was a vast swarm of dim lights in an endless void. Each light was another object to be Enhanced, a speck of potential awaiting permission to flare. Strengthening and reinforcing her arm, Tala punched Scratch's open palm with every milligram of power she could muster. It was a blow that would have gone right through almost any sapient, but the Pillar of Justice took it without moving, or even a sign of discomfort.

Eyes rotating down to her hand, Scratch lowered his palm. "Good. Every year, you grow stronger." He shifted his gaze upon each of her Vanguard in turn. "I can tell that you have grown with her. You all look well, if a bit undisciplined."

"You honor us, Exemplar," said Tala, reinforcing her words by running her fingers across their opposite wrists—a Torandian gesture of respect. "I strive to meet your expectations, both in training and in the field."

Scratch chuckled, a string of hissing breaths. "It's not me you must impress, Tala. The spirits are always watching, and in watching, learning. The wise learn from them in turn."

"I'll have to meditate on that," said Tala. Scratch's spirit-focused philosophy was unique in her experience; it certainly didn't come from Torandian beliefs. Though disentangling his metaphors often took some thought, real wisdom was buried underneath.

"I came to wish you success on your upcoming mission, but my other duties have left me with little time. I've been tasked with hunting a Renegade."

"Which one?" Excitement had crept into Anora's tone.

"Viron. We have a tangible lead at last."

Tala suppressed a shudder. Even among Renegades, Viron had a particularly dangerous reputation. The length of time he'd lasted without being apprehended—well, *killed*—since casting aside the Tenets' guidance was extraordinary, as was the body count he'd left as he worked his way across various edgeworlds. A remorseless killer. His cold, empty stare gave that much away, even just what the holo in the Center's files had been able to capture of it. There was something unsettling swimming in those dead eyes, something about the confident tilt of his jawline more frightening than his bulging frame. When Renegades got that dangerous, there was only one Agent the Center called upon, and it gave Tala no small pride to call that Agent her mentor.

And maybe someday, they'd call on her too. Even if she struggled with the more sedate parts of her discipline, she was still a powerful combat Enhancer who'd learned from the best there was. She should have been shipping out tomorrow to help fight Viron, not track down some rogue Fiurn Hult cell. But try convincing Scratch of that—he didn't even work with a Vanguard, much less other Agents. He was unique in that aspect as well.

"Good news indeed." And then, before she could stop herself, "May we accompany you?"

Scratch held her gaze for a long moment, considering. Did he know —no, he *had* to know how dearly she held this wish. She hardly made a secret of it, and the Pillar was more perceptive than most.

"It is a privilege I have offered to very few," he said. "And you have been given your own responsibility. Recall Tenet fifty-five: *From each acorn its own tree, from each tree its own fruit.*"

Tala gave a small, accepting nod, holding her disappointment back from manifesting on her skin.

"But when you are done...yes." Scratch's tongue tasted the air. "Should you prove yourself on your current mission, it is my judgment that you and your Vanguard will be ready to join me in the *hunt.*"

The word "hunt" rang out particularly loudly, Enhanced so that it would carry across the refectory.

It was no small thing he'd offered. Renegades were the Center's greatest shame, Enhancers who had failed to uphold the Tenets and had lost their minds as a result. Deaf to Mitra's teachings and deadly in their insanity, there was nothing left to do but put them down for good. Every Enhancer was intimately familiar with the threat Renegades posed, for it was a threat both external and internal. The Tenets outlined the one safe path by which Enhancers could avoid that fate, and as such were inscribed upon the soul of the newest Initiate and the wisest Pillar alike. Yet revered as the Tenets were, the Center lost several Enhancers every year, Enhancers that had given in to murderous rage. Tala had never fought one outside training sims, but it was grave business—the final acknowledgement that the Center had failed.

But even after all she'd hoped for such an answer, could she truly say she was ready to join him in the field? Dreaming about it was one thing, but now it was close enough to feel *real*. Perhaps she ought to...

No. She wouldn't run. Not from this opportunity, nor this challenge. "Exemplar, thank you. I will not let you down."

"You have yet to prove my trust unfounded," said Scratch. "I will be heading out soon and—spirits willing—you will join me upon your success. For now, Frael has summoned me."

"Then if it is not a burden, would you share my greetings with the Central Pillar?"

Scratch's only response was a loud tongue-click of acknowledgement. There were no proper farewells in Torandian; the species preferred to end conversations when there was no more to say. Without another word, he left, stopping only to grab a cup of synthesized blood. One of his fingers dipped into the liquid to feed, blood traveling up his veins as he walked.

Anora's own hand found hers and gave it a gentle squeeze. "We've got this," she said.

The others piled on, offering their own encouragement, but Tala barely heard them. This was the chance she'd always wanted. Yet in her head was a litany of all her failings, every little thing that should disqualify her from this honor.

The guilt built as she recalled her abandoned mid-morning meditation. Distracting as the bulbous ant had been, it was no excuse for shirking her obligations. She knew the thirty-fifth Tenet: *Responsibilities postponed are weeds well-watered.* She could practically hear the Central Pillar chiding her with his soft, worldly voice, see his jowls droop in a disappointed frown while his tail twitched halfheartedly. The thought of that frown was enough to get her moving, resolved to maintain her meditation this time. Scratch may have been the Pillar she needed to impress, but she'd given Frael enough cause for disappointment and had no desire to do so again.

CHAPTER THREE
PREEMPTED STRIKE

In Dorian's experience, space travel mostly involved sitting and waiting. He liked the quiet of it, the languid stretches of time with nothing that needed doing. Unfortunately, his leisure time was about to come to an end—Neea was now only decihours away, and his empty schedule had suddenly found itself packed with pre-mission duties.

Their ship—the *Chollima*—hungrily ate away at the remaining distance. It was sleek; built for speed in interstellar and atmospheric conditions alike. Its exterior was a soft orange color, stained with a thick, waxy finish. The interior wasn't much prettier; humble and austere save for a single luxurious guest's quarters—which none of the squad were permitted to use.

The *Chollima*'s bridge was a broad circular room acting as a hub, common area, and mission prep site. The rest of the ship branched off from it, like fingers from the palm of a hand. It had been designed such that a shipboard Enhancer would be positioned equally near the engines, generator, and other vital systems, maximizing the power of their Enhancement. Tala at that moment sat directly atop the thin section of floor separating her from the engines, bolstering their energy with her own.

Dorian reached back, adjusting his tac-helmet's strap. It was probably the seventh or eighth time he'd made that same motion in the last couple decihours. He couldn't seem to get the strap to tighten properly. Blasted thing always dug deep into his neck.

Although the *Chollima* had begun the final approach several decihours before, not everyone was fully geared up yet. Nominally, they were tasked only with performing an orbital scan, but regulation demanded they be deployment ready should the situation demand it. Ferric had his gloves off, hands deep in the ankle joint of a hollow metal leg. The foot rotated in a slow, deliberate circle, held aloft by a short clamp. Vigdis still had his tac-helmet resting beside him on the bench. He at least had an excuse. The *Chollima*'s long-range scanners had started sending data on Neea to his omnipad, and it was his duty to examine and analyze it.

Tala was Enhancing the scanners, of course—same as the engines. Military-grade scanners backed up by a skilled and powerful Enhancer like Tala could pierce even the most advanced cloaking technology. She sat quiet and motionless on the floor, directing her energy and meditating —or at least trying to. When some sapients were quiet, it was menacing. Some just gave an impression of dullness. Tala, though, cultivated a noisy sort of silence, a silence overcrowded with competing thoughts.

He'd probably been staring at Tala a little too long. As he glanced back at his own boots, Anora shouted through the cockpit's sealed doors. "We're nearing the planet. Tala, cut Enhancement to the engines, if you would."

"Just make sure we come in smooth," Ferric called from his table. "Last time, the bouncing almost made me cut a wire."

"Well, excuse me!" Anora bellowed, somehow doubling down on her already-impressive volume. "That Wonder was generating some crazy headwinds! Made things a bit more challenging!"

That was a contender for the understatement of the year. Dorian wouldn't soon forget the towering hurricanes Anora had threaded, sheets of wind battering the *Chollima* from all sides, all produced by a single small machine. And some Wonders could do much more extreme things than control the weather. Inverting gravity, attracting insects, producing unending streams of water from nothing...whoever or whatever had brought Wonders into existence, they didn't seem keen on repeating the same design twice. Just Dorian's luck that the first he'd encountered could have shredded their ship between storms like cabbage in a blender.

"You won't have to worry about turbulence this time," said Vigdis without looking up from his omnipad. "Neea's atmospheric conditions are calm on all fronts. Not that it matters, as you're supposed to be checking the scanner data with me, not working on personal projects."

"HA! You tell him, bright eyes!"

"Can you all quiet down a bit?" Tala asked. "It's hard enough tuning out the universe around me without said universe blasting my eardrums off."

Things were more relaxed under Tala than most Agents allowed, but Dorian liked to think their dynamic worked. The squad had grown up together, as was mandatory. Familiarity was one of Enhancement's two overriding constraints. The more familiar Tala got with something, the easier Enhancing it became. That principle applied to their gear, their weapons, even the ship they flew. After almost nineteen years together, the squad had grown familiar indeed.

Tala released her Enhancement and the *Chollima* slowed. There was no tangible change, no gradual slowdown—the ship instantaneously transitioned from ninety-three percent light-speed to just under twelve, smoother than the refectory's meal paste. Vigdis loved to rant about how many natural laws this tossed out the airlock, and his ranting only grew more impassioned when the subject turned to going *past* light-speed, which of course should've been impossible. All those brains and he hadn't worked out what made intuitive sense to Dorian: "impossible" just meant something different to Enhancers. Propel something fast enough—roughly seventy percent light-speed—and physics simply stopped mattering, leaving the Vigdises of the galaxy to throw up their arms and grumble into their drinks. One day, they'd learn to take off their skeptic visors and enjoy the view like he did. The stars elongated in the front viewport even as they outstripped the starlight behind them, leaving the rear view a solid, unbroken black. It was nothing short of magnificent.

Dorian couldn't imagine why Enhancing worked differently at high speeds, but it did. The moment Enhancement stopped, on the other hand, standard reality reasserted control smoothly and seamlessly.

"Hey," Dorian said to Vigdis. "I can go over the data with you. I really don't mind."

"I'll send you the access program," said Vigdis.

Dorian was happy to step in. Like a good piece of adhesive paste, he liked to think he sealed up the squad's gaps. As he logged into the program, Tala opened her eyes and stood. She made a sharp chopping motion, triggering the ship's exterior cameras. A large flatscreen descended into the center of the room, upon which Neea's horizon loomed large, curved and broad.

Transmitted through the *Chollima*'s etherway speaking tubes, Anora's volume was far more reasonable—a rare show of restraint from their pilot. *"Welcome to Neea, everyone. Host to some very interesting botanical life. The original Pathmaker team's report was fascinating. Did you know the trees here are potentially capable of rudimentary communication through controlled chemical releases into the soil? Of course, we can't confirm anything until they get around to sending a follow-up team."*

"Anora wishes she was on the tree-studying team instead," muttered Ferric.

The ship slowed as it dropped toward Neea's surface while Dorian studied the data appearing on his screen. Not quite done with her announcements, Anora activated the etherway again.

"Bringing us to a stop and switching over to hover."

The switch from cruising speed to a stationary float was nearly as smooth as their earlier deceleration. In this case, it was more due to the counterthrusters and military-grade inertial dampeners than any unexplained phenomenon. The only real marker of their sudden lack of movement was Anora emerging from the cockpit.

"All right," Tala said, giving everyone a once-over. "We're above the target zone. Vigdis, Dorian, what's your assessment? Does the reported facility exist?"

At Tala's mention of his name, Dorian remembered he should've been focusing on the data necessary for that assessment, rather than watching the others. Refocusing on the omnipad, he saw that Vigdis's files had finished uploading. The screen displayed an extensive underground network of branching pathways linking small clusters of rooms—and several much larger chambers. Dorian ran a finger down the screen and the diagram spread into three dimensions, projected above the omnipad as a hologram.

Vigdis cleared his throat dramatically. "Oh, there is a facility on Neea. And it's even bigger than intel originally suggested."

Dorian sensed an opportunity to add to the conversation. "Not only is it bigger, it's got some insanely heavy-duty transmission shielding. Most of what's coming through our detection software is based more on what we can't detect than what we can. Tala's the only reason we're getting anything at all."

Vigdis hummed his agreement. "Insurrectionist outposts are well shielded, but this is several steps beyond their normal precautions. I'd say this strongly corroborates current intel regarding this facility's purpose."

"It's true, then," Tala said. "Fiurn Hult's experimenting with autonomous weaponry."

"Technically unconfirmed, but we should proceed under that assumption, yes."

"Makes sense." Ferric stood with a tired grunt and stretched his arms out to the sides. "Enough combat drones could make Fiurn Hult a real threat overnight. Not hard to understand why they want this place hidden."

Tala started pacing back and forth across the ship's smooth, off-white floor. A handful of small, dome-shaped cleaning bots wheeled out from under her approaching feet, spraying and polishing with their miniature arms as they went. Collision avoidance was the extent of their simple programing. They could react, but only linearly—an important distinction, when it came to their software's legality.

"The first part of our mission is already a success," Tala said as she paced, restless as ever. She looked like a stalking panther, or an apatrex closing in on—Dorian gave his head a quick shake and banished the thought from his mind. "We've confirmed the existence of a shielded facility. We can assume the rest of the intel was accurate—that this is a Fiurn Hult outpost devoted to the research and production of illegal robotechnologies. We could wait for backup, but we're days away from the nearest outpost, and Ferric's right. Our window of time before their scientists make a breakthrough is small and shrinking. At this point, it's us or nobody. We've handled Fiurn Hult before. I believe we can do it again."

Anora slid on her tac-helmet and turned on her optics overlay with a forceful click. "Finally, some action. I say we go in heavy, and not just because I like going in heavy."

"We'll need to erase their data core," Ferric mused, drumming his fingers against his chin. "I'll drop in separately. Take a more stealthy approach. Long as you keep the locals busy, I shouldn't be noticed."

"Oh, we're choosing our own assignments now?" said Anora.

Ferric just shrugged.

"Thanks for volunteering," said Tala. "Remember, the GIAB will want a copy."

"I'm sure they do." Ferric gave a loud, amused snort. "Problem is, that data shield's strong enough to block anything we try to send. Even our tac-helmet feeds won't be able to punch through. But they should have a comm array. Something with a strong signal, or just a built-in bypass. So before I wipe the core, figure I'll use their own comms to send a copy over."

"Sounds reasonable enough," said Tala. "But if our helmets aren't uploading, that means no open channel. Once we split up, you'll be on your own."

"Don't worry about me. I can handle something this simple."

Anora plopped into a seat next to Vigdis, giving him a little wave. He smiled back, before returning his focus to the briefing. "Our scans also picked up a small escape vessel parked near the target zone. In fact, it's barely cloaked."

Dorian often wondered how Vigdis was able to read through endless amounts of data *and* follow the thread of surrounding conversations without falling behind.

"Sloppy to leave their vessel in the open," Ferric commented, fingers still drumming away at his chin.

"Sloppy is a good sign," said Tala. She came to a sudden halt, some internal thought reaching its conclusion. "As the on-site Agent, I'm calling it. We're going in heavy."

"Does Anora realize we'll be landing on top of her precious talking trees?" Dorian said it in Upper Concordonese—one of humanity's most widespread languages, and one he knew only Tala could understand. There was no reason to learn other species' languages (well, besides Torandian) when everyone knew Universal.

"Not like there's a shortage of trees here," said Tala, the Upper Concordonese rolling off her tongue like a native's. "She won't even notice. Still, best not to remind her."

Small, meaningless exchange it may have been, but having a secret that was just his and Tala's to share made him happy. Ferric, perhaps feeling the same, muttered something in a language Dorian didn't recognize. It got Anora chuckling.

Shrinking and tucking away his omnipad, Dorian pulled his bag out from under his feet. He holstered his gun and hung an electroprod at his hip. Next came his heavy boots. The boots were metal, alternating between light and dark blue in color, but had a soft leather interior. Each boot was equipped with a large heel that spread out from the base, giving them the appearance of thick snowshoes.

With his boots strapped on, all that was left was to arm his personal kinetic shield. It was a small disc, sandwiched between two circles of raised metal with an X-brace that strapped securely onto his back.

Activation was as simple as firmly pushing the top. Even military-issue shields couldn't take much punishment, but the difference between stopping a couple bullets and being hit by them was enough that Dorian and the Center considered it worth the cost.

The squad was well-practiced in the quick motions of mission prep, and it wasn't long before the others were armed and ready. They stood at attention, weapons strapped to their backs, shields primed. Tala didn't have a weapon other than her fists and feet, as was Mitra's way. It made their fights closer, more personal—and therefore, the moral mathematics of taking lives were calculated all the more carefully.

Their silence was meant to be solemn, appreciative of the power they were about to receive—but the atmosphere was more impatient than anything else. Dorian waited, watching Tala closely. She spoke softly once they'd waited the requisite time, eyes affixed to the flatscreen. "Enhancing strength, muscle, bone, and skin density to phase three. Lung capacity, oxygenation, reaction time, vision, inner ear durability, and spinal control to phase two."

And with that, Dorian felt the rush. His muscles felt tight beneath his skin, like a thousand elastic bands stretched to their limit. He could hear the pounding of his teammate's hearts beating faster in their chests. It was like someone had bottled up a hurricane and given him a hearty swig.

Tala continued, oblivious to the feelings her power had birthed. "Enhancing kinetic shields and repulsion mesh fiber density." For the nonorganic Enhancements, Dorian couldn't feel the changes, but he had complete trust in Tala's abilities.

They were supposed to stand in solemn, contemplative silence for at least ten seconds following primary Enhancement, meditating on the nature of power and the responsibilities inherent to that gift. Anora lasted all of two.

"Woooooh!"

If Dorian had thought her loud before, it was nothing before the gale buffeting his Enhanced eardrums. He could certainly understand the sentiment, though. The buzz he got from Enhancement always left him wondering what Tala felt. Lack of familiarity limited Enhancement's effectiveness—receiving it was a transformative experience, but it was a bare fraction of what Tala maintained on herself.

The airlock was a short walk from the central room. Dorian's steps were light and controlled, making the familiar stretch of ship feel strangely spacious. The airlock's broad double doors slid open at their approach. Air fled the ship in a roaring cascade around them. It tugged at Dorian's Enhanced frame, drawing him out toward open sky.

Neea's atmosphere was a deep golden hue, splashed with shifting clouds. He could barely make out the trees below: tightly packed, with a few ruddy leaves clinging stubbornly to bulbous branches. The air had a strange metallic quality to it, just noticeable enough to be unpleasant. Dorian found himself wishing their tac-helmets sealed.

Ferric jumped first. He shot out of the ship at a run, pausing long enough to give Anora a slightly smug look before he leapt. As gravity drove him downward, he angled his body into a line. The weighted guidance system in his heavy boots would take him where he needed to go.

Dorian went next, following Ferric over the edge and into the whipping wind. As he left the ship's temperature-controlled interior behind him, the full brunt of Neea's stratosphere enclosed him in an icy fist. Cold air buffeted him as he fell, and despite the thermal suit he wore under his repulsion mesh, he couldn't suppress a shiver. He flattened his body and rotated himself around, knifing his legs downward. If he strained his neck, he could still just barely see Ferric, on a collision course with the ground. Ferric's flightpath would take him to his own breach point—isolated, but near the likely location of the data core.

In all the years Dorian had known him, Ferric had always insisted on jumping first—and he'd known Ferric a long time. The volunteer age when entering the Vanguard program was seven (in centralized years) for humans and nordok both. With the Vanguard program, starting young was necessary to breed as much familiarity as possible. Constant Enhancement during their growth period had other, more permanent effects as well—there was a reason the whole squad came in on the tall side for their species.

Dorian's choice to apply for the Vanguard program had been mostly parroted. His dad hadn't liked having another mouth to feed, and his mom had trouble caring about anything beyond her immediate field of vision. He still saw them occasionally. They asked after him, but mostly as a matter of routine.

From the tender age of seven, he'd been trained to do what was needed for the good of civilized society. However, as the ground approached, he wondered—as he often did—what he'd say if asked to volunteer again.

Dorian gritted his teeth. The ground was coming up quickly. He liked the falling part well enough—the landing was what made him wish Tala opted to use the *Chollima*'s dropship just a little more often.

Squeezing his hand into a tight fist, Dorian primed the landing mechanism in his boots. They were built to absorb shock, taking the force of an impact landing off a Vanguard's body. Tala didn't need them; she could smash into the ground at terminal velocity without complaint or injury.

Dorian crashed through the topmost branches of the tall, twisted trees, shattering them into shards of wood that slid dully off his shield. With a crunch, he hit the ground feet first. The boot's shock absorbers compressed and absorbed the impact. Crisscrossing metal sprang up his legs, bracing him and keeping his body from flipping forward. Even wearing the boots, that maneuver would have turned his bones into jelly without Tala's Enhancements. "Going in heavy," they called it. Not a subtle approach, but it did make a statement. Besides, it was a lot harder to shoot someone out of the sky if they never slowed down for landing.

The squad landed almost simultaneously, just as they'd practiced. Waves of dust blasted outward from the multiple impacts, clouds of splinters raining down from above. Dorian's legs were bent slightly, as much as the braces allowed. Then his shock absorbers triggered again, this time releasing their stored kinetic energy downward, directly into the ground—which exploded beneath him. Soil shredded and the layer of metal beneath ruptured as Dorian blew his way into the facility below.

A plasticrete surface broke his fall. Dirt and metal fragments rained down around him, covering both him and the floor. The others landed hard, with Tala just moments behind them. She touched down on all fours, knees bent, fingers splayed. Even she would have had trouble breaking through into the facility unassisted, so she'd let her Vanguard—and the heavy boots—do the hard work.

Dorian unclenched his hand and the braces released their hold on his legs, retracting into the lips of his boots. The walls and ceiling of the slanted corridor in which he'd found himself were smooth—where they were still intact—unadorned with holoprojections or more conventional decorations. Further on, beyond their ruined entry point, a seemingly endless row of artificial lights gave it a sickly blue glow. It was like he'd fallen into a well-lit pipe.

Dorian drew his gun. Speed was their priority now—going in heavy meant stealth was out. Anora was already shooting, somehow having already drawn and lined up her targets. Four square cameras, mounted high on the corridor's walls, crumpled beneath her carefully placed bullets. Neea, Carrophan, Serd 04—whatever the mission, Anora was always one step ahead. As he clicked his safety off, the comms jumped to life with Ferric's voice.

"Vanguard Two reporting. I've made a clean breach. Going dark. Good luck, everyone. See you on the other side."

"Copy," said Tala. "Luck be with you."

Vigdis was scanning the corridor, eyes darting curiously about. Tala looked glacially calm; she always did in the field. Anora, as usual, had undergone a stark transformation the moment her boots touched the ground. She kept her eyes locked ahead, sharp and piercing. Even stranger, she was *quiet*. It was like something ate away all her normal cheer, leaving her focused and empty.

They ran together, tightly packed, silence broken only by quick bursts of gunfire whenever they encountered more cameras. Anora was so fast on the draw, she shot them down before they could fully swivel around.

Destroying the cameras wouldn't hide their approach, but it would limit the information available to their enemies.

The corridor seemed to continue forever, an unbroken slide into Neea's depths. On and on they went, the last bits of natural sunlight mingling less and less with the cerulean glow of the lights above. The heavy boots felt like large platters strapped to Dorian's feet.

After another half decihour, covering ground at speeds no un-Enhanced sapient could hope to reach, the corridor ended without warning in three plasticrete doors—long, gray rectangles, each bearing a mud-green number painted in the upper right-hand corner. The middle door was labeled across the top in big, bold letters. *SECTION SIX.*

"Right," said Tala, moving toward the rightmost door. Wasting no time, the squad took up position directly behind her. With a quick lash of Tala's foot, the gray door crumpled inward.

Fragments of the doorframe pinged off the bulky food processing unit stationed against the opposite wall as the Vanguard filed in, guns ready. A combination cleaner—standard model, capable of handling clothing and cutlery alike—rumbled softly against the wall as it processed a stack of cups. Chairs were scattered about the room in the vague vicinity of a small circular table that was missing a large chunk. But the room's most striking aspect was not the hefty cleaner, or the freshly-scratched food processing unit, or even the table lying broken in the center of the room. That honor went to the destroyed husks of three combat drones, strewn about haphazardly as if tossed by a bored child.

Dorian's chest prickled. The debrief had mentioned combat drones, but it hadn't prepared him to see one up close. *Autonomous killing machines.* He swallowed. The horrors of the old wars whistled through his mind. Entire planets scoured of life. Weapons that were their own masters, moving from massacre to massacre with grim, relentless efficiency. Cycles ago, before the Galactic Accords. Before society had known better. Dorian thought about what kind of sapient would want to resurrect that dark era of history and found himself gripping his gun a little tighter.

The largest of the three was quadrupedal, bisected horizontally across the middle. The other two sported ten angular legs that sprang out from a circular, swiveling base. From the upper portion of their bodies sprouted six limbs, four of which ended in compact cylinders—likely automatic weapons, Dorian decided. The non-weaponized appendages were equipped with four long, narrow fingers, which at the moment were clicking open and closed in a series of synthetic spasms. Identical round holes were blasted cleanly through their middles. An unidentifiable milky fluid dripped from the exposed machinery, forming small puddles around the empty chassis.

Dorian let his gun dip as he took in the room. "Strangely," he said, "I don't find this reassuring in the slightest."

"I'll consider this confirmation of our intel." Vigdis tapped his tac-helmet twice, activating his electromagnetic optic overlay. "No active signals. Whoever—or whatever—did this, they did a good job of it."

Worry was starting to crack through Tala's enforced calm, but her voice was even. "It's hard to imagine Fiurn Hult dismantling their own drones, but we can't rule out the possibility that they had their reasons. If something else is responsible, we need to identify it. It goes without saying that this technology absolutely cannot fall into unknown hands."

There were hushed murmurs of agreement. They retreated back into the long corridor. As a group, they moved toward the left door, preparing to breach. The Vanguard hung back, giving Tala room. Another swift kick later, they poured in through the broken doorway. Dorian sucked in a breath, gut clenching.

Blood. A fanning spray across the far wall. Flecks dotting the room's many dark, deactivated flatscreens. Dark splashes staining a wide desk, over which slumped the limp body of a decapitated siari female. The room's lighting gave the corpse a baleful glow, like blue fire was slowly burning it up from within. Of her head, there was no sign.

Dorian had killed before, in the field, but walking in on death always felt different. Something about the aftermath unsettled him. Perhaps his own powerlessness in the face of an outcome long decided. Gritting his teeth, he tore his eyes away from the body. By the desk lay two more of the quadruped drones, each with holes in their midsections that dripped viscous whitish goo. A particularly large puddle had pooled around one of the desk's legs. The desk itself was bare, other than the shattered pieces of the siari's omnipad.

"This happened recently," said Vigdis. "Three decihours at most. Look, the blood isn't even evaporating yet."

Tala walked slowly around the room, examining the many dead flatscreens. "The cameras we shot probably linked back to here. Dorian, Ferric's not with us, but could you bring their surveillance system online by yourself? Maybe it caught what happened."

"Maybe. Easier with a keyed-in omnipad, and hers doesn't exactly look recoverable." Dorian was still trying not to look at the siari. "I'll do my best, but whether I can or can't, trying will take time."

"Don't bother, then," Tala said with a grunt. "We can assume the existence of a second hostile force, motives and capabilities unknown. Pack the parts up. Let's see what's in section six."

Vigdis moved over to the desk, gingerly avoiding the wreckage. From the front pocket of his repulsion mesh vest, he produced a small, clear maglock bag, into which he deposited the broken omnipad's pieces. Dorian kept his eyes on the blank screens. Packing the omnipad didn't take long and nobody wanted to linger when it was done. One door remained: the door to section six. It loomed tall, almost seeming to warn the squad from entering.

"Hear anything on the other side?" Anora asked, her voice low.

"No," Tala said. "If this is the factory floor, it's running silent. That, or it's a trap."

She held up three fingers, a quiet countdown. When the second finger dropped, Tala pulled back her foot. The door was half again as big as the other two. A large door for a large factory—at least, that was the assumption.

Her foot shot out, kicking in the last of the three doors. Either because the door was bigger or because her kick had a little extra Enhancement behind it, the door didn't just crumple. It exploded forward, bouncing with reverberating thuds before settling at least six meters away on the newly revealed factory floor.

Past the small patch of light Tala had created by kicking in the door, the factory was practically unlit. The dim, lavender-tinged emergency lighting was enough to make out the indistinct impressions of massive machinery, but further detail was lost to the gloom. Like the overhead lights, the machines were dead—frozen and silent, wherever Dorian looked. From the ceiling hung rows and rows of massive ovoids. Dorian could tell they were made from eberium by the way they absorbed the meager light. Many were fixed in various stages of splitting apart from the bottom into four distinct pieces, and from these leaked the same pale fluid that had dripped from the damaged drones. Several had unfurled to the point that they resembled curved crosses. When Dorian strained his eyes against the dull purple glow, he could make out robotic limbs dangling from their centers.

Beneath the dripping pods rested lines of completed drones. They stood at attention on long, padded conveyor belts that wound deeper into the factory. The belts hadn't been spared from whatever power outage had hit the rest of the factory, and the drones they carried were equally motionless. Dorian hoped they'd stay that way. There were hundreds of lifeless silhouettes, dozens of different shapes and sizes. Etched into the chest piece of each was a symbol: a torch with stars for sparks, held aloft by the vague outline of a hand. Fiurn Hult was building itself an army.

Tala stepped inside, motioning the squad forward. Dorian braced himself as she crossed the factory's threshold, half expecting every drone to wake up simultaneously. He held his breath as he moved into the room, but they stayed motionless. Still, whenever he took his eyes off one, he got a feeling it was sneaking up behind him.

"Enhancing lights," said Tala, voice echoing in the cavernous room. Before the echoes had fully died away, the glowing strips of lavender brightened, leaving the factory fully lit.

The light also revealed the splatters of carnage streaking the floor.

Further into the factory, past where their sight had ended, the floor was a sea of broken combat drones, spent bullets, shattered electronics, and entire severed limbs. Bloody bodies were peppered among the wreckage—Dorian marked five, though there could easily have been more.

"Spread out," said Tala. "Check for survivors."

From the state of what bodies he could see, Dorian could already tell they wouldn't be finding any survivors. His mouth was opening to relay that when Tala tensed. Her head jerked to the side, attention snapping to a door against the factory's far wall.

"Gunshots," she said, motioning the Vanguard to follow her. "That room."

Almost simultaneously, another door to their left slid open. Dorian caught a glint of hazy purple reflecting off moving metal. Then came the soft clicking of dozens of spidery limbs spilling out onto the factory floor.

CHAPTER FOUR

DEVOTED TO THE END

Tala's legs became a blur, sending scraps of broken drone into the air with every step. She was halfway to the intruders before Dorian could process their existence. Like the rest of her body, her reaction time was augmented beyond human capacity.

The drones didn't respond. They didn't seem to have noticed the squad at all. Instead, they kept scuttling forward, eleven in all, mechanical bodies rigidly angled toward the far door. The door from which Tala had heard gunshots.

Whatever Dorian had imagined seeing their empty husks, seeing them in motion was worse. They moved as one unit, their many long legs rising and falling in tandem. Like eleven sets of arms on the same body: separate, but working in perfect concert.

A71B2 flashed across the periphery of Dorian's visor. A tactics code sent by Tala via a series of controlled eye movements. His body responded immediately. See a code, follow the order; the practice had been drilled in until it was second nature. A71B2 meant pinning the enemy down from behind cover while the Enhancer engaged.

The nearest piece of cover was a partially built drone. It was fractured and crumpled, no doubt due to a fall from the construction pod above. Dorian slid into place behind it. Even with Tala less than a meter away, the drones didn't break ranks or change their focus.

Tala jumped toward the closest drone and crashed into it fist-first. Her arm sank elbow deep into its chassis. With a crack, a cascade of luminescent pale fluid burst out of the hole. As one, the drones halted, bodies swiveling. Whatever had occupied their attention, Tala seemed to have diverted them.

Sliding into a low crouch, Dorian stuck his gun out from behind his impromptu cover. Bits of metal dug into his stomach as he leaned in close, firing off a burst toward the drone on the far right. Lacking a clear understanding of its design, he aimed for the guns. Whatever defenses they possessed, they'd have a much harder time killing the squad without working weapons.

The gun's counterweights kept it perfectly level as he fired. Each bullet connected with a flash of flame and an explosive roar that mingled with the cry of ripping metal. One went wide and detonated against the far wall, but the rest of Dorian's microexplosive rounds shredded most of the drone's limbs. Fragmented and ripped wide open, the barrels and guts of the guns were left smoking in the empty air. Undaunted, its one remaining weapon opened fire on his position. The bullets tore into his cover, sending pieces flying. Sensing his weakening position, another drone joined in with all four of its appendage-mounted guns.

As the already-damaged drone that made up his impromptu cover began collapsing under the concentrated barrage of bullets, Dorian slid lower and lower. Neither drone let up. Every so often, a shot would penetrate the rapidly deteriorating barrier and flatten against his shield. Dorian flicked his eyes in a specific pattern—a request for Enhancement. His quickening breath grew loud in his ears as his visor started flashing a dire warning about his shield's remaining strength.

A new message splashed across Dorian's visor—an ocular reply from Tala in the affirmative. Not a moment too soon. More bullets bit into his cover, and this time, thanks to Tala's Enhancement, it held. Dorian let out a small sigh of relief. He'd really caught their attention. Not his original plan, but he was still alive and his squadmates were hopefully taking advantage of the opening.

He risked a peek out from his cover just in time to see six bullets slam into one of his attackers' head attachments. One after another, they detonated across the three, long cylindrical tubes that probably served as ocular sensors. The concentrated stream of fire bored right through the machine's plating, cracking the otherwise-smooth face. Wires and fluid poured out like air from a punctured balloon.

The source of the well-aimed burst was making a beeline for Tala. Moving in erratic zigzags, Anora let fly with bullet after perfectly placed bullet. She had to have requested more speed—her movements were far faster than a phase two Enhancement would have allowed. A drone swiveled to meet her, but almost at once collapsed in a smoking heap, now shedding heat. Tala's work. She must have been already working on that one.

Many drones had gathered around their squadleader, who darted through them like a needle through cloth. Bullets bounced off her skin with fleshy pops. It would take more than light gunfire to bring down a fully trained Agent. As Dorian watched, she leaped two meters straight upward and kicked out, taking the head off a drone. The decapitated machine let out a loud grinding noise as its limbs spasmed, while its head flew with Enhanced speed right into another drone. Both went down with deafening crashes.

Dorian focused on providing suppressing fire while Tala and Anora engaged the drones at close range. They seemed almost as synchronized as their metallic foes, movements controlled and efficient. Microexplosive bullets and empowered punches struck with destructive results.

By the time Dorian had to reload, only three drones remained functional and firing. Tala took out the first with two rapid blows, one flowing seamlessly into the next. Anora's continuous fire sent another crashing down, mantled in smoke.

Together, they turned to the last drone. To Dorian's surprise, it chose to disengage, scuttling headlong toward the far door. It took all of five steps before Vigdis dropped from one of the many construction pods directly into the fleeing drone's path. How he'd gotten up there in the short amount of time since the fight had started, Dorian had no idea. The drone didn't have time to react before Vigdis blew it apart. It thudded heavily against the ground, the sound of its fall echoing across the factory.

Despite the holes ripped through its frame, that final drone still tried to move forward. Its legs twitched, unable to carry its weight, while its arms sank listlessly. All but one, which struggled to remain aloft, stretching out toward the far door. Its pronged fingers shook as they opened and closed, grabbing desperately at the air for something just out of reach. Then the long, segmented digits seized and that last rebellious arm fell slowly to the ground. Vigdis lowered his gun and took a few steps back.

Tala appraised her Vanguard, cocking her head. Dorian sent an all-clear to her helmet. He couldn't spot any injuries on the others, to his relief. With the number of bullets that had been flying, it could easily have been worse.

"Form up," she said, shaking a large, viscous globule of pale fluid from her hand. "We're not done yet."

With her words, Dorian's visor highlighted the factory's far door in a pinkish glow.

"The shots," said Vigdis. Behind his visor's overlay, Dorian was sure he was frowning. "What else did you hear?"

"They didn't stop during the fight, I can tell you that." Tala motioned the Vanguard forward and they fell into a V formation, marching double-time around robotic husks and piles of debris. "Heard some muffled screaming too. Everything's quiet now, but it hasn't been too long. Even if those responsible have fled, we should be able to catch them."

"It's looking like an internal conflict to me," said Anora. "There was a large-scale battle here, but the only casualties are bots and techies. They must've torn each other apart."

"Agreed," said Vigdis. "A schism of some kind. The drones we encountered were intended to reinforce one faction. Hopefully, the survivors have answers."

"Wouldn't mind thanking them, myself. They did a lot of our dirty work for us." Dorian felt guilty the moment he'd said it. For some reason, his mouth tended to malfunction in high-stress situations. His gaze snagged on a gutted corvid, all three eyes gazing blankly. He mouthed a contrite *sorry* to it, hidden as he was behind the visor. Nobody else said anything, which made him feel even worse.

Tala stepped up to the door, three fingers extended. "Be ready," she said. "I want us in there as soon as this door comes down."

Three fingers and a kick later, the door was free of its frame. Guns up and ready, the squad poured into the room.

Smoke slid past them through the empty doorway, rising from several small, sizzling electrical fires. It hung low, bluish beneath the room's lighting. With it came the coppery smell of blood, harsh and thick and almost overpowering. His initial vision was hazy until he switched his visor's settings, filtering out the smoke. Immediately, he wished he hadn't.

The room was full of corpses. Not tossed about as they had been in the factory, either—stacked in a macabre pile almost a meter high, their blood still wet on the floor. There must have been twenty at least. Corvid, nordok, human, siari…

Near the back of the room was a slender pillar surrounded by computers and a tangle of wiring. More terminals lined the walls, filling every centimeter of space. By the pillar stood a single sapient. A siari. Despite the smoke dancing about the room, his glassy, opaque eyes were fixed right on them. The skin of his face was stretched tight with at least seventy years of age; a thin smile plastered across his mouth, a sanguine glow to his cheeks. He was clothed in a neatly pressed, but faded, gray longcoat. One of his four long, thin arms lightly gripped a mono-field knife, another a small pistol of the Tilde line. Both weapons were pointed groundward—though given his proximity to a large pile of bodies, that did little to set Dorian at ease.

Before Tala could order the siari to drop his weapons, he spoke, his voice precise and clipped. "They weren't monsters, you know."

An order to hold flashed across Dorian's visor. He did so, gun tight in his hand.

"I hope you don't mind my seeing to them," said the siari. "Bloody work, but necessary."

"You're saying you did all this?" Dorian blurted, half disbelieving, half shocked.

"I ended the lives of these poor, unlucky sapients, if that's what you mean. In that sense, I alone am responsible." The siari's smile grew tauter. "Though it's worth considering that when one incites another to murder, the guiding hand is charged along with the finger that pulled the trigger. My crimes are not mine alone. They bear the handprints of a specific few, and the countless many."

Beside Dorian, Tala sucked in a breath. She took two slow, stalking steps. "I know you," she said. Then, as if catching herself, "But you're dead. You've been dead for years."

"I was as dead as I needed to be. The trick, of course, was dying convincingly enough."

"Stay clear," said Tala with new urgency. She hadn't taken her eyes off the stranger, but Dorian knew she was talking to them. "He's a Renegade."

Dorian's breath caught; his blood stilled in his veins. Squads were equipped for most threats, but a Renegade was not something to be handled without backup. The Renegade Protocols called for a coordinated assault by multiple Enhancers, with soldiers armed with Irradiators on standby in case things went poorly. Without the threat of insanity leashing them, Renegades pushed not just their bodies, but their minds.

On the bright side, the only sapient dangerous enough to ignore those protocols and hunt Renegades on his own had been Tala's personal mentor for over a decade. Dorian had a lot of faith in his squadleader. Besides, she'd always done well against Renegades in the training sims. Better than most other active Agents, in fact.

Vigdis muttered something triumphantly that sounded like "Arcus," which the Renegade acknowledged with a polite tip of his head. It was the first time he'd moved since they'd entered. His body was unnaturally still, gun and knife stationary at his sides. That he held weapons at all was a bad sign. It meant he'd shaken off the last of the Center's traditions. Renegades clung to them sometimes, at first, having known nothing else all their lives. Particularly the prohibition of weapons. If this Arcus was using them, there was nothing left holding him back.

Tala's voice was steady. "On your honor as an Enhancer, and in accordance with the discipline you once followed, I give you the opportunity to surrender."

Arcus's stillness was becoming unnerving. It was like looking at a statue, a living head growing out of lifeless rock. "I wouldn't," he said, eyes locking onto Anora. "I see your pupils dilating, your finger tensing. I hear the blood pumping through your veins. I can smell every fluctuation in your body's adrenal levels. I assure you, if you try to shoot, I will kill you. Your finger will not reach the trigger."

Anora didn't react, but Dorian knew her well enough to believe she'd considered taking her shot. A clean hit, while there was still enough distance between Tala and the siari to be sure of hitting her target, might have been worth the risk. Protocol dictated the Vanguard retreat if they could and stay back if they couldn't. The speed of a duel between Enhancers made their weapons as good as useless. More likely to draw the Renegade's attention than anything else.

Tala replied in Anora's stead, fingers tightening into fists. "Your fight is with me. You can trust that my Vanguard will follow protocol."

"We'll get to that," said Arcus in the same calm voice. "Protocol once seemed so important, but then, that was a long time ago."

His opaque eyes fixed on Tala, catching stray firelight between their lids. "It starts with a compromise, you see. That's all it takes to get the engine running. That single compromise. You'll make it too, someday. I see it written across your skin in lines too deep for the Center to flatten out. There will come a day when you look back upon where your choices have led you and realize you've become just like me."

"Tala would never break the Tenets," said Anora. "She's worked harder to learn them than any Enhancer I've met, and she still pushes herself to be better. I trust her with my life."

"Tala, is it? It speaks well of you to have such a faithful Vanguard. Mine tried to kill me the moment I was named Renegade. I regret that it took more than their loss to teach me the price of mixing friendship with duty."

A sweep of Arcus's hands indicated the corpses stacked against the wall. "Killing them also came with its share of regret. Our thoughts held common colors. The current paradigm of warfare is primitive and foolish, needlessly costly in flesh and blood. We send our young to fight and die in droves, while forbidding the use of machines that could fight and die *for* us."

"The galaxy has seen what combat drones are capable of," said Vigdis. "One sapient with enough production capacity could declare war on the whole galaxy and see it all burn."

Arcus laughed softly. "Such sensible justifications they have. I learned them young, same as you. But they're a mask over the truth: it was never about protection. It's about culling the weak. Immortal as they are, the Torandians have always relied on outside forces to do what time will not—and nothing better trims the excess than a savage, bloody war."

"I'm not here to debate civics," said Tala.

"None of this is up for debate. Our government has been shaped at every level to appease Torandian tradition. And so—" The gold of Arcus's lightlets intensified. "It is beyond salvation. Based on a flawed design from the onset, and only warping further beneath its own weight with every cycle. Easier to destroy it completely and start again from nothing."

"Yeah," said Dorian before he could help himself. "You seem pretty good at that."

But Arcus didn't seem offended. "I am," he said. "And I am willing to stain my hands for the good of the galaxy. My next victims, faith willing, will be more deserving than these."

He tilted his head gently to the side, examining the carnage of the lab. "I respect what they tried to accomplish here. Their battle against cycles upon cycles of wasteful precedent. Their ambitions extended further than any of you can fully appreciate. Perhaps they would find some solace in the knowledge that their sacrifices, though involuntary, will further Fiurn's Hult's goals more than they could ever imagine."

As still as he'd been before, it was all the more surprising when he moved. Three staccato, measured steps back, stopping as abruptly as he'd started. Something about the unnatural smoothness of his motions made Dorian uneasy. "Your deaths as well will play a part," Arcus said, lightlets stitching dull violet across his skin. Dorian felt a large weight settle across his shoulders at the frankness with which he spoke. "Cold comfort, perhaps, but I can offer no more. Fate can be cruel—if you believe in it—and my flightpath's been set for a long time now." His lightlets darkened, bleeding to burnt vermillion.

"Easy to judge a sacrifice necessary when you're not the one making it," Dorian said.

"I suppose you're right. We all have things we tell ourselves when the truth becomes a source of shame. The compromises only get easier, even for me. I shouldn't glamorize such messy business as this. Thank you for the reminder."

He took a long, slow breath, his narrow chest expanding and contracting, then shifted his focus back to Tala. "Forgive me. I was once a scholar, and long-winded self-indulgence still colors my words all these years later. I fear I've rambled on too long. I am a Renegade, after all, and you an Agent. Though I wish it were otherwise, there can be but one outcome to our meeting."

Tala glanced behind her, making sure Dorian and the others were a safe distance away. Like water from a glass, the energy poured out of him as Tala reclaimed it. His vision worsened, his lungs shriveled, his muscles grew lethargic and heavy. He'd never gotten used to coming out of battle Enhancement. It was less a return to normalcy than a feeling he'd lost something precious and transcendent.

"If you're so sorry about it, you could always surrender." As Tala spoke, the battlecalm settled across her features, leaving them empty of anything save for the fight.

"I cannot, I'm afraid. I came here for a purpose, and I will see it done."

Arcus's body blurred, faster than Dorian's unassisted eyes could follow. Just as quickly, Tala launched her body to the right, twisting in midair to orient herself toward her attacker. Before she'd landed, Arcus whipped his knife toward her face. It sliced the air as it flew, a flash of steel and pink that was just a blink from striking home when Tala's hand moved to intercept. A backhanded strike swatted the knife out of the air.

Arcus was right behind it, closing the remaining distance to Tala with a series of almost instantaneous steps. Tala landed lightly, just in time to meet his opening salvo of punches. The exchange that followed was so fast, Dorian couldn't begin to track it. The only thing he could identify was a grunt of pain from Tala. Around and around went their dance, interspersed with dull thuds that marked successful blows. Dorian's whole body ached to give the Renegade fighting his friend a face full of microexplosive bullets.

Arcus disengaged first, taking a half step back to reclaim his mono-field knife from the floor. Tala took advantage of the distraction to send a spinning high kick toward his head, forcing the Renegade to give ground. Before Tala could press her advantage, Arcus's gun fired. For a compact model, the noise was deafening. The floor below Tala's feet ruptured, launching dust and shards of metal into the air. Almost immediately, the debris accelerated, endowed with Enhancement to dangerous speeds. A few particularly large pieces flew far enough to score cuts along Dorian's arm. The damage would have been worse, but for his repulsion mesh absorbing the brunt of the shrapnel.

They exploded from the dissipating cloud of rubble. Arcus had caught Tala's fist, but she was using that same leverage to force him back. A long, thin gash marked her forehead, though no blood flowed from the wound. She'd likely sped up the clotting, a tricky piece of Enhancement. Arcus broke free and the rapid rain of punches, thrusts, and kicks began anew. Blow for blow, Tala held her own, even wary as she had to be of Arcus's weapons.

Then it happened, so fast Dorian almost missed it. One moment, Arcus's arm was low, at his side. Then his hand was wrapped around Tala's throat. Tala didn't even have time to register surprise. He yanked her by the neck, flinging her past him into the ground. Her head hit first, and the sound was loud and terrible, a hollow crack as her tac-helmet came free in three different pieces.

Seeing Tala fall, Dorian's finger tightened on the trigger. There was no time for conscious thought, only reflex. He wasn't alone either—the rest of the Vanguard had opened fire too and the whole room rang with the sound. But while Dorian had often trained against Tala, it hadn't prepared him to hit something as fast as Arcus. He almost seemed to vanish, leaving three streams of bullets to tear through the space he'd just occupied. They exploded with roaring pings against the far wall, laying waste to holoscreens and computer systems.

Anora broke position and charged, heedless of the spate of bullets hurtling past her. She kept her head down and her gun up, maintaining her fire as she made for her squadleader.

Tala stumbled to her feet. Blood dripped from her nose in a steady trickle, gathering at her chin. Dorian kept firing as Arcus swept toward her, knife poised to strike. His finger was pressed so hard on the trigger, his knuckle felt like it might pop free of his skin.

Arcus's personal shield lit up as several shots detonated against it. Fire swept over the quasi-invisible barrier, but still the shield held. Likely Enhanced. The Renegade flowed around the rest like liquid steel in a processing foundry, deftly intercepting Anora's charge.

Arcus's hand curled around her wrist and angled her gun toward the ceiling. Then came a sound like the bellow of a ship's engine, raw, yet carefully contained, as Arcus fired his pistol at point-blank range. Dorian shouted a warning, but far too late. The Enhanced bullet ripped right through her chest. His friend's rent body fell gracelessly to the floor. Someone screamed. It might have been him.

Tala's face was a canvas of captured horror. Shouting something unintelligible, she launched a string of punches at the blood-splattered

Renegade. Dorian kept firing; he didn't think he was even capable of stopping. Two more shots caught Arcus's shield, to no visible effect. As he sidestepped a low kick from Tala, a hand went to his hip and pulled free a small, circular device.

He twisted the disc's top and hurled it at Vigdis. Dorian's whole world went up in a flare of piercing red light. A wave of heat caught him, slamming him forcefully into the wall. His eyes burned, his ears rang, and his vision swam with spots. As everything shifted back into focus, he caught sight of Tala's prone and smoking form. Of Vigdis, only what had been under the thermal suit remained. The rest had burned away. At the epicenter of a blackened ring, Arcus stood unmarked and unmoved.

Arcus met Dorian's eyes and gave an apologetic nod that settled across his chest like a shroud. He tried to move his arms, to lift his legs, but they weren't responding. Nothing was. Arcus seemed to slowly slide across the room, drawing ever closer. He almost didn't even see the arcing blade. It was a coral-colored flash, nothing more.

His hands finally moved, but without thought or control. They grasped at his throat, struggling to hold it together. His screams were coming out as low gurgles. Above his head, the ceiling spun faster and faster. The lights spun too, a dancing blue inferno. The motion was too much. He shut his eyes, but the blue light followed him.

Through the colored darkness, Arcus's voice sounded murky, almost underwater. "You needn't die today," he was saying. "The choice is yours. Try to get up and I'll kill you. Or stay down. There's nothing you can do for them anymore. Fight or yield. Live or die. All that's left is the compromise."

Fight. Dorian latched onto that word, clung to it. He had to try. Tala needed him. But the blue grew darker and the spinning faster, and he *knew*. Hazy, half-formed images flickered across his eyelids, like his life was trying to flash before his eyes, but it was all jumbled together. Churning and seething, around and around. One big, indigo swirl.

CHAPTER FIVE

THE PRECIPICE

Get up, Tala told herself, not for the first time. It would have been easy, if her injuries were all that kept her down. She lay among bloodstains and shattered equipment, head pointed floorward, face and heart twisting with the knowledge of what she'd see when she rose.

Arcus's measured voice echoed in her ears, telling her to stay put, and she hated herself all over again for listening. The massacre replayed itself, inescapable, upon her closed eyelids. Screams, shots, the dull thuds of falling bodies. Then soft footfalls, fainter and fainter, followed by silence—and still she lay unmoving. Perhaps she wouldn't get up again.

She couldn't quell the turbulent storm the inside of her head had become. The placid mind was an Enhancer's first priority, for without it, all choices were suspect. Tala didn't feel very placid. She felt like the child she'd been when first admitted to the Center, ruled by her emotions instead of the other way around. It had taken private tutelage from Frael himself to settle her mind into the right patterns. Those well-worn mantras meant to quiet the mind were suddenly hovering just out of reach. Surely this turmoil, this sick ache in her chest, was the *right* response? What would it mean, if she felt nothing for the best and only friends she'd ever known?

Dead. Every last one.

If only she'd spent their last decihours aboard the *Chollima* on something more meaningful than bickering. *No more bickering,* she realized, and the thought was ice down her spine. Post-mission keepsakes from Anora, Vigdis's sappy poetry readings, the reassuring squeeze of Dorian's hand before mission prep…her squadmates had lit her personal horizon like comets across the night sky. It was impossible not to respond to the sudden darkness with feelings of some kind. Perhaps that made her a bad Agent—well, she knew *that* already. She'd let her worst nightmare come true, paralyzed by her own shock and fear. However easily he'd overpowered her, she could've still gotten up. Could've given it her all.

You'll die with them, she'd told herself, but right now, that didn't sound so bad.

There were footsteps now, just outside the door. Too heavy to be Arcus coming back to finish the job. Tala considered getting up, but couldn't quite muster the desire. "Who's there?" she called, but her bruised throat flared as she tried to speak, and it came out barely more than a whisper. "Who's there?" she said again, Enhancing the sound so it would carry to the intruder.

Instead of a response, the footsteps stopped. Then came a subtle click. A finger pushing slightly against a trigger, preparing to fire.

"Don't move," came a voice, low and rough, like a boulder being dragged across broken glass.

Tala knew that voice.

"Ferric," she breathed, but found she couldn't form any more words, caught as she was in the middle of an emotional battleground. Relief that one of her friends still lived, guilt at briefly forgetting his existence, and a complex mix of hurt and anger and bewilderment that her last friend in the galaxy had her at gunpoint.

"I'm supposed to give you the chance to surrender, but I don't think you'll take it," Ferric said. "Maybe you think I'll have trouble pulling the trigger. I can promise I *won't*!"

His voice had risen to a yell, and he took a quick, fierce breath before continuing. "Maybe you think you can survive a few bullets, and maybe you're right. But that's a whole lot of maybes, and I'm a damned good shot, just as good as Anora was. At this range…"

He was still talking, but Tala wasn't listening anymore. *I'm supposed to give you the chance to surrender*, he'd said, and that one sentence said it all. It was the same chance she'd offered Arcus.

It took two repetitions, but with a standard breathing exercise, she composed her skin, muscle, and mind. Only then did she trust herself to speak.

"I'm not a Renegade," Tala said. "I'm not sure why you think I am. I'm going to get up and turn around now, so we can talk about it." Her voice was low and raspy, and the words had a coppery taste to them. Blood from her broken nose must have dropped into her mouth. Even with Enhanced healing, Arcus had left his mark.

The words were wrong, she *knew* they were. They sounded too much like what a Renegade would say. Nonetheless, Ferric didn't shoot her, not even when she lifted her body into a crouch and eased into a standing position. As she did so, she got a proper look at her friends' bodies for the first time.

Anora lay closest in a pool of blood, face frozen in a horrified grimace, almost torn in two by the shot that had killed her. Vigdis's half-incinerated body was almost unrecognizable. Dorian had fallen against the wall, throat slit. He was still cradling his gun close against his chest.

Her hands clenched into fists before she could regain control of herself. Blind grief would not serve her in this moment, not with Ferric watching her for any sign of deviance. Even knowing that, it was hard to douse her fury. One long, slow breath, and she turned to face Ferric, face carefully composed, though beneath her muscle the storm continued to roar….

Ferric's gun was leveled unerringly at her chest. Beneath his tac-helmet, his face was a mottled orange-gray and knotted with grim fury.

He had the haggard look of someone who saw his likely death approaching, but refused to flinch away.

"They're gone," she said, forcing away a tremor. "I watched them die right in front of me. I failed them, Ferric. But I'd never hurt them."

She searched for a sign of belief in the jagged golden shards of his eyes, but they were inscrutable. He moved one hand to his belt, other arm straining to keep the gun level, and ran a finger along the screen of the omnipad clipped there. The screen lit at his touch and projected a moving image into the air at his waist. A video feed of the room, captured from a vantage point above. Tala watched the squad enter the chamber. Arcus wasn't anywhere to be seen. Instead, a small group of scientists were backing against the wall, looking terrified. Her own mouth moved, and Anora turned to engage her in conversation. Their voices were too soft to hear, but anyone could see from the set of their shoulders that the words being exchanged were heated.

"This isn't what happened."

The holographic simulacrum with her face struck without warning, slamming its fist into Anora's chest. Wearing a wrathful snarl, it pounced forward and grabbed her around the throat. Tala had to close her eyes, fighting back a wave of nausea. Blanking her vision sometimes helped her do the same with her emotions.

None of her training had taught her how difficult it would be when every part of your life crashed down around you.

"That didn't happen," she repeated, a little louder.

Her closed eyes did nothing to block out their pleas or the sound of their bodies being torn apart. The scientists were next. It was savage, yet efficient killing. The watermark of a Renegade.

Opening her eyes again took real effort. Existence was so much easier to cope with blanketed in darkness. The holo was gone, but there was no escaping what she'd watched herself do. The back of her throat felt hot and itchy. *It isn't real.* She repeated that to herself like a mantra, giving the thought its own rhythm.

"All the facility's cameras feed into the data core," said Ferric. "When I sent the contents to Information and Assessment, that bit of footage was one of the first things they got. I couldn't believe it—"

"You shouldn't. It's a fake."

His reply, when it came, was tired. "They've declared you Renegade, Tala. I can't take that risk."

The proper response—but then, Ferric always had been a model soldier. He knew the established protocols; Tala had learned them right alongside him. *Heed not the Renegade's devious lies. The Tenets will guide you true.*

He couldn't trust anything she said, but he also couldn't argue with proof. "Check the tac-helmet footage," she said, but even as she said it, she noticed Anora's helmet. Several paces from her best friend's body. Crushed beyond repair.

In fact, the only intact tac-helmet in the room was Ferric's. The rest had been dismantled, incinerated, or otherwise rendered inoperable—including her own, which had come apart when Arcus had slammed her head into the ground. And the helmet camera's automatic upload to the *Chollima* wouldn't have penetrated the facility's data shields. A deep, burning frustration welled up inside her. She freed it with a deep exhalation.

Could Arcus have left any genetic material? She replayed the fight again in her head, trying not to linger over her insufficiencies. He hadn't so much as bled—not that siari blood stayed liquid for long. Still, that line of thought, painful though it was, had given her an idea.

"The bodies," she tried. "The scientists. Gunned down. Check the wounds."

Ferric's eyes flickered toward the corpses in question, so quickly she almost couldn't tell he'd taken his focus off her at all.

"Microexplosive rounds don't make holes that small. Whatever gun made them, it wasn't one of ours."

She swept the room, making sure there were no such weapons in the immediate vicinity. As she did, something else caught her notice—the column of compressed datatubes surrounded by computers that had likely housed Fiurn Hult's drone control network. It had been scored with multiple cuts from a mono-field knife, and there was a hole where the network's core should have been.

"And what about that?" Her finger jabbed toward the column. "Something's missing from that framework. Someone took it, and it wasn't me or any of them. I know you can't trust me, but you can trust yourself. You can trust evidence. Someone else was here, Ferric. Please, you have to listen to me."

For the first time, she could sense his resolution wavering. "This footage didn't show up out of nowhere—"

"Which camera caught it?"

"Excuse me?"

"Which camera?" repeated Tala, gesturing toward the ceiling. Something resembling a theory was starting to stitch itself together, and the shape of it was dire indeed.

"Oh no. If you think I'm gonna stare up at the ceiling so you can—"

"*Vanguard Two.*" Despite everything, there was still enough steel in her voice to command. Ferric responded instinctively, lapsing into a reluctant silence. "There's no camera at that vantage point. At least, not one I can see."

"Must be a hidden one, then."

"Surely not beyond your capabilities to find."

Ferric chewed at his narrow tongue. His hand went back to his omnipad, cycling through menus and displays faster than Tala cared to track. He worked through muscle memory alone, never taking his eyes off her and keeping his weapon ready. Then the omnipad buzzed reproachfully and his face jerked downward for a brief moment, surprise stamped across it.

"Wouldn't you know it," he said. "I'm not finding any cameras at all."

No cameras. She held onto that for a moment, reaffirming the evidence of her own senses. The footage had come from somewhere else, though she couldn't imagine how. Holos that perfect took *time* to doctor, time Arcus simply would not have had. Even with specialized equipment, even with a full team behind him, even breaking the first Tenet and Enhancing his brain, such a forgery would have taken days. It *could not* exist.

Yet it did.

"Look at my face, Ferric." She held his gaze, doing her best to keep projecting strength. It would all crumble if she couldn't convince him. She needed someone to watch her—to watch her back. "You've seen my bruises when Scratch forgets to hold back during sparring. You know what those wounds look like. No gun broke my nose or grabbed my throat, and not even Anora would've tried to trade blows with an Enhancer." Saying her name caused more pain than she'd expected, but she ignored it. It was too important that Ferric believe her.

"Tell me what happened," he said, as if standing on the edge and heavily considering the jump. "Your version."

She told him. Starting with the facility breach, then the run through deserted corridors. The carnage that was the factory. Discovering Arcus. Fighting him and what happened after. Here her rasping voice grew hollow and heavy, and none of what she tried to say came easily. She trudged on anyway, shutting her emotions behind skin and muscle. Ferric listened without commentary, and when she was done, he was quiet for a very long time.

"Arcus," he said at last, tasting the sound. "I've heard that name before."

"The *Fountstar* raid," Tala supplied. "The stolen Initiates."

"Right, that's the one. He died on that raid, though. That part I remember."

"I can assure you, he didn't." Tala gestured at a nearby upturned cabinet, and when Ferric nodded his assent, she sat. "He was the Pillar of Devotion before Dalion. Went Renegade about, maybe thirty years back. He'd been mentored by Frael himself. They remember him as a cautionary tale now, a warning against growing too obsessed with Renegades. He wrote multiple studies on them, kept going even after he became a Pillar. I guess the moral was, *attempt not to understand Renegades, lest you become one.*"

"That a Tenet?"

"No," she said. "Maybe it should be."

It was so, so hard not to acknowledge the burning anger she was feeling. To stay equable while surrounded by everything she'd lost. To not shout at the walls until her voice was hoarse that the dead had no rights upon the living. How easy it would be to Enhance her cries until they rumbled through the whole damned facility, reverberating off of every wall until the planet sang with the sound of her loss.

Five years ago, she might have. She'd grown since then, learned to trust the Tenets. They would not look favorably upon an outburst. Even Scratch, with his unorthodox beliefs, would have chastised her—right after he finished chastising her for failing so utterly in her duties. Shouting would not turn back time or bring them back or give Arcus the justice he deserved, as much as admitting that made Tala want to throw the cabinet she was using as a chair across the room.

"You know what's scary?" she said, trying to fill the silence. "The *Fountstar* was hit just a few years before my initiation. If he'd lasted longer before turning Renegade, if my parents had met earlier..." She let the thought trail. "They never found those kids. I could've been one of them."

"*Stumps,* but I want to believe you." Ferric swore, letting out a breath and lowering his gun just a fraction. "I wish I could. But..." He gestured at the havoc-streaked room, at the bodies of their friends.

It hit her then. She staggered beneath the weight of the knowledge that her life was truly over. To the entire galaxy—to Scratch, to Ferric, to Kiav and Martic, to her *parents*—she was one of the monsters she'd trained her whole life to fight.

They're wrong. A surge of anger accompanied the thought, but with a deep breath, she banished it. *Quiet. Calm. Neutral. The Tenets will guide you true.*

"You can't risk helping a Renegade, I understand. But there's one Renegade you'll be helping if you can't trust me."

Ferric's jaw tightened.

"To the galaxy, he's dead," she said. "A Renegade is bad enough, but one that isn't in the Index anymore...imagine how much damage he could do. Nobody looking for him, nobody trying to stop him. I know the truth, but if even you don't believe me, who will? They'll dismiss it as a Renegade's ravings, and when Arcus makes his move, he'll—well, I'm not sure what his plan is. We need to figure that out too."

The blue panels flickered, light and shadow warring for dominance across Ferric's skin. He stared at the empty column of datatubes, at the scientists' bodies, even up at the ceiling. Finally letting his gun fall to his side, he unhooked his omnipad and tapped at it pensively, frown deepening. "What are you saying, then? He knew we were sent here? He had this video ready and waiting in the data core for me to find?"

She hadn't even considered that explanation. Such a thing was at least *possible,* unlike falsifying an entire holo in under a decihour. How it could have happened, she wasn't sure. *Why* was an even bigger mystery. But it made a warped sort of sense, which was the only sort of sense Renegades ever made. Tala had received cursory training in seeing past a Renegade's mindset in order to better combat them—while their plans tended to be less meticulous in execution, every Renegade's delusions were unique. She'd never heard of a Renegade operating successfully for two decades, but Arcus had managed *that,* so "predictable" had already been jettisoned out the airlock.

"I don't have all the answers," she said. "There's a lot that doesn't add up. Renegades burn themselves out, they don't just go on hiatus for twenty years. They don't usually use weapons against Agents either. And he didn't kill me, even though I'd seen him alive. I'm not pretending any of it makes sense, but that's how it happened. One thing I know, though. That craft we detected outside wasn't a Fiurn Hult ship. I'd bet my life if we went out there, we'd find it gone."

She met Ferric's eyes, and something gave. With agonizing slowness, he holstered his gun. His fingers peeled off the handle one by one, hand hovering near his waist like he was waiting for some excuse to take it up again. Tala didn't give him one.

"I'm not dumb," he said. "I know if you wanted to, you could've killed me already. Stupid to pretend that gun was making a difference. Maybe you're pulling some insane Renegade scheme and I'm going to regret this moment until my first descent, but you're right. There are too many unanswered questions. So here's what we're going to do. We'll search this place for solid evidence of Arcus's presence, top to bottom. If we find it, we'll present it and clear your name. If not…"

But he didn't say anything after that. Tala wondered what he could have said.

After a moment's hesitation, he sat next to her. Together they stared ahead, surrounded by bodies they refused to look at. To look would only remind her of her failure. They hadn't even been supposed to go planetside. *She*'d made that call. They'd followed her lead because they trusted her, and now they were dead.

Ferric had no reason to blame himself, but he would anyway. Competitive as he was, he was always first to rebuke himself for any perceived failing. Perhaps their thoughts had turned down similar avenues, but the centimeters separating their bodies were vast beyond physical truth. An inseparable, howling chasm lined with jagged spires and mantled in so fierce a blizzard that she could only occasionally glimpse the farther edge.

"Ferric?" she said, unsure what exactly she could say. The sound only barely cleared her throat and did nothing to fill the space between them. "I'm so sorry."

He said nothing, but his hand closed into a tight, frustrated fist.

Of the second ship, they found no sign.

Another useless bit of evidence in a facility filled with it. The bodies were still there, organic and robotic alike. The cavity in the column of datatubes was as empty as ever. None of it would be enough for the Tribunal. No other living witnesses remained to confirm her story. No tac-helmet footage existed that could prove they'd found the scientists already dead.

Tala had considered asking Ferric to lie for her; claim he'd seen what had happened—but only for a second. He was still wary, never taking his eyes off her. Whatever remnants of trust had moved him to lower his gun wouldn't survive such a request.

Footage originating from nonexistent cameras should have been a titanium-solid case. However, a closer investigation of the ceiling revealed that cameras *had* been installed, and only recently forcibly removed. Ferric had snorted under his breath when he'd discovered that. That was the moment she'd realized their search was hopeless.

There was no footage of Arcus in the data core's files. No genetic material of his among the bodies. No proof the ship had belonged to anyone but survivors fleeing the massacre, carrying a precious piece of their drone system with them. No other surveillance records that could have offered a competing version of events.

Wishing for water brings no rain. That was the ninth Tenet, one she turned to when she felt like punching a hole through the nearest wall. Life moved only one direction and that was forward, like it or not.

So as Tala limped through the bowels of the facility, her thoughts had been set on what "forward" would look like. Her future wasn't difficult to parse. With no proof to the contrary, she was a Renegade in the galaxy's eyes. That meant a lifetime incarcerated if she surrendered fast enough, death if she didn't.

Unless...

That whispered *unless* had suggested itself in a moment of frustrated weakness, after the facility's alternate access door showed no signs of forced entry. She'd put it out of her head at once, only for it to slither back in all the louder for its temporary absence. In that moment, the allure of it had shocked her.

She'd constructed barricades of argument and logic, then, to bar the errant thought from gaining further purchase. It had worked for a time, but she'd found herself actively tearing them down, countering and second-guessing and justifying, until these new thoughts had eaten away at her defenses and seeped through the barricades like smoke.

Unless. Still she refused to voice the thought that had taken root, but she could deny the sense of it no longer. It was the right choice, and not just because it was the only one she had left. With every step, her certainty grew. With each breath, her resolve strengthened.

Ferric waited ahead, in a small chamber off the main factory they'd repurposed into a temporary base of operations. He sat on a crate of power cells, hunched over his omnipad, but straightened when he saw her. Alert. Tense.

"The facility's alarm has an external log," he said.

"Let me guess. One recorded intrusion, matching our entrance through the ceiling."

It was hardly a risky prediction, and Ferric didn't bother responding.

"Your assessment of the alarm's security?"

"Sophisticated." Ferric shrugged. "Nothing's unbeatable, of course. What did you find?"

"The access door was sealed," Tala admitted. "I'm running out of ideas."

"We can keep looking until the Agents arrive—"

Tala imagined Agents emerging from the Center vessel, ordered to apprehend or kill. Martic, or Jiav, maybe even Kenna. She'd been friendly with all of them. Not that it would matter.

"No," she said, blinking away a wave of fatigue. "There's nothing to find."

Ferric's face resembled nothing less than a frozen crag, merely the right impetus away from a full avalanche. "Then we wait. There'll be a full forensics team inbound. Maybe they'll find something we overlooked. I can explain the situation, make sure they do a thorough job."

"We're not waiting." She used her squadleader voice—low, even, and reassuring. "It's time to leave."

It should have been harder to say, but the words tumbled free like any other.

"Absolutely not," Ferric said, looking like he'd been tazed with enough volts to down a Torandian. "You can't. Why would you even—"

"We aren't voting. I'm your squadleader, and I'm—"

"You're a—" Ferric clamped his mouth shut. Tala waited, the unspoken, awful word hanging in the air between them. It was Ferric who looked away, shaking his head. "Where would you even go?"

"That's the easy part. After Arcus."

"There are some," said Ferric, unspooling every word through a tight-lipped little frown, "who'd say seeking revenge is a sign of—"

"Believe me, I know what the Tenets forbid. Twenty-two does so explicitly. Three, thirteen, thirty-seven, and seventy-two by inference." Revenge was too small, too petty. The Tenets were right to forbid it. But to pursue something else…

"But nobody knows Arcus is out there. How many has he killed in all those years of obscurity? How many more will die before he's discovered?" She leaned forward. "This isn't about revenge. Innocent lives are at stake, and we're sworn to defend them. We're the only ones who can."

Every word was one she'd told herself, a tiny link in the chain that formed the greater argument. *Surely* Ferric would see, as she had.

"Tenet forty-four," she said. "*The decision to allow suffering lies within every observer.* Tenet sixty-one: *The weight of inaction carries as much force as any choice.* Tenet one hundred-three: *Hesitation is the enemy of necessity.* The path is clear, and my conscience with it."

"Arcus might not even *exist*," Ferric shouted. "You could be leading me off a cliff, with all we've found. Now I'm supposed to trust you enough to just let you escape?"

Like you could stop me. "You trusted me enough to help me try to clear my name. I'm asking you to extend the courtesy just a little longer. Help me hunt down the biggest piece of evidence of all."

"You know what it'll look like if you run."

"It won't tell them anything they don't already believe."

"Darkest Hell, Tala. Let forensics do their job. We can sort everything out right here, then chase Arcus without the GAF tanning on our engines."

He still didn't understand. She'd faced these arguments already. She'd made them herself.

"We've got nothing but dust and shadows. I hate to admit it, but it could be argued I had the capacity to fake everything we've found so far. If I go before the Tribunal without anything stronger, I'm leaving in electrobindings. You *know* this. If something here can exonerate me, great. But forensics will find it whether I'm here to meet them or not. If they can't find anything…well, I'll still tell everyone I can about Arcus, but I can't see them listening." A wry shrug. "Suppose they do get me, one way or another. How hard would you try to make sure the galaxy's ready for whatever he's planning?"

He wouldn't meet her eyes. That was answer enough.

"There, you see?" she said softly, letting a sad smile through to her skin. "There's no one I can trust to stop him but me. I *am* going, Ferric, and I'm going now. Will you join me?

For a moment, she heard herself through his ears, rejecting the judgment of the institutions they'd pledged themselves to. Refusing to trust the process. Resolving to chase down a long-dead Renegade she blamed for the crimes she was on camera committing. If she'd heard another Enhancer say those words, she'd have named them Renegade before they were halfway finished.

"If I don't?"

"I'd understand. But that wouldn't make it any easier to leave my last friend behind."

Ferric's eyes flicked toward the room their friends had died in. He drummed his fingers along the butt of his gun, perhaps wondering whether to draw and take his chances.

"Right then," he said. "Let's call down the dropship."

The *Chollima*'s pilot chair was designed for comfort, but Tala couldn't shake how wrong sitting in it felt. Like any moment, Anora would start shouting that someone was stealing her seat. The controls felt wrong, lumpy in all the wrong places and slow to move, like she was dragging them through tar.

She'd never used a flight console before. That too, she was trying not to think about. She had the requisite ninety sim-hours required to legally fly, though it was a little late to worry about legality. Ferric had more, but she didn't trust him not to reprogram their flightpath right into a GAF base, so she'd put him in charge of inventory instead.

The cockpit's viewscreen was still trained on the planet's surface, where their reconnaissance had guided them to jump. Directly in the center was the hole they'd made punching into the insurrectionist facility turned mausoleum. Tala absentmindedly fingered the *Chollima*'s laser turret control, imagining melting the whole base into a puddle with a relentless beam of heat. Her friends deserved to have their bodies properly vaporized, not left to rot. She didn't, though. There was always a chance the Center's forensics team could find something important. Get some key figures in the investigation asking the right questions. Her friends would have to wait a little longer for the rest they deserved.

The thrusters kicked in with a slight lurch. Perfectly avoidable; the kind of wobble that wouldn't have happened with Anora at the controls. They rose rapidly, approaching the thermosphere. Neea shrank beneath them and Tala wasn't sorry to leave it behind. If she never returned, it would still be too soon.

They'd chosen Ipwaan as their destination, mainly because it was the closest habitable world. Even better, it was in the opposite direction they'd arrived from. Tala hadn't heard of it before consulting a map. A peaceful planet, reportedly, if a little rough around the edges. Too far from major gatelanes to merit a significant GAF presence. Too poor to afford a planetary shield, which would have blocked them from landing covertly.

By the *Chollima*'s navcalculations, the flight would take four days. Slower than she was used to, but the cockpit hadn't been placed to optimize engine Enhancements, so some of her power was bled away, lost to distance. Four days was right on the edge of how much time the GIAB would wait before she was officially added to the Index. Their business on Ipwaan would not go smoothly if the whole planet had just been sent her full-body holoimage alongside a flashing warning. Standard protocol, though, was to hold off the announcement to prevent widespread panic, until the chance had been lost to deal with the new Renegade discreetly. The GAF would still believe—probably correctly— they could contain the threat she presented. That was mainly due to the code constantly being transmitted by the *Chollima*'s computer, providing GAF High Command, the Center, and every lawkeeper in the galaxy sanctioned or otherwise with her real-time location. Ipwaan's garrison would be tracking their approach, with reinforcements inbound. Wherever the *Chollima* fled, Coalition forces would pursue.

Keeping the *Chollima* was therefore not an option.

They left the last traces of atmosphere behind in favor of the all-encompassing grasp of open space. Somewhere, hidden among innumerable identical points of light, was Ipwaan's sun—Tala didn't know where, but their computer did. The autopilot made constant course corrections as the engines gathered power, preparing the transition to full thrust.

The shame returned in a wave when she took her hands off the controls. She was back in that blue-lit little room, head throbbing, tasting blood, immobilized by her own fear. Her hands remembered the grittiness of the floor, the way small chunks of broken drone had dug into exposed skin. Her throat still felt as dry as it had when she'd seen her Vanguard engage, already knowing what would result.

She hadn't protected them. Hadn't done much at all, really. The Tenets she'd quoted to Ferric drifted back across her mind. *The decision to allow suffering lies within every observer. The weight of inaction carries as much force as any choice. Hesitation is the enemy of necessity.* For all her justifications and ornate arguments, she'd violated those same Tenets by staying down, thinking only of her life while Arcus made his exit.

It starts with a compromise, he'd said. His words rose unbidden in her memory, as did his mocking smile, his pale eyes like empty mirrors. *There will come a day when you look back upon where your choices have led you and realize you've become just like me.*

Perhaps she deserved her new label after all.

A flash from the flight console caught her focus. Above it, a small red vortex had formed, pulsing larger with each swirl as if pulling mass from the air. Now that they'd started moving, someone was contacting them. Someone from Modellus, according to the signal ID. Swallowing her dread, Tala accepted the connection. The holographic vortex picked up speed, resolving into a familiar face. Despite her emotion training, Tala couldn't help but flinch.

The face looking down at her was not an angry one. It was not sad or hateful or even disappointed. There was nothingness in his unblinking stare, detachment in the set of his skeletal jaw. His needle-like fingers were splayed at his sides, unexpressive. It was total cessation of emotion itself, and terrifying to behold. The Enhancer battlecalm.

She'd flinched as much from the implication as the surprise. Enhancers did not enter battlecalm for training exercises. It was a shield against hate, fear, bloodlust, and any other emotion that could become dangerously inflamed during live combat. Seeing it here, in the eyes of her old teacher, confirmed to her heart what her brain had already known. To him, she was now only another enemy.

It stung like a slap to the cheek, but Tala masked her hurt behind all three levels of neutrality: skin, muscle, and mind. She would be the model Enhancer, adhere steadfastly to the Tenets, and present herself calmly. She would give Scratch nothing to find fault with.

"Hello, Exemplar," she said in Torandian, brushing her fingers softly across opposite wrists.

"Renegade Kreeth." The vacuum of feeling in those two words tore at her soul. "In the name of the Galactic Coalition, the Galactic Armed Forces, and the Central Pillar, you are requested to surrender. Refuse and we will not attempt to take you alive."

Tala swallowed involuntarily, trying not to imagine facing her mentor in battle. Torandians were fearsome physical combatants, Torandian Enhancers even more so. Add the weight of several hundred years of experience and Scratch—Exemplar Scratch, Pillar of Justice—could probably take her apart in his sleep.

She could surrender. It was a choice she'd already rejected on Neea, but this moment felt different. Though she'd chosen, she hadn't truly *committed*. Perhaps a choice wasn't truly made until taking one path closed off all others. Like committing to a discipline. She'd known this offer was coming, just as she knew now that she wouldn't get another. It shouldn't have made the decision harder, but it did. Especially when the offer came from the sapient whose approbation she prized above all.

Two futures loomed wide before her, one final crossroads set at opposing trajectories.

"I cannot," she said at last, and she knew it to be true by the weight of it against her tongue. "The Tenets guide me onward."

"I see." Scratch's face did not even twitch. "As they do me. They urge me to destroy the thing you have become and free the spirit within. And Renegade, I do not fail."

"You've been assigned to me?" Tala covered her shock, but with difficulty. It wasn't technically disallowed for an Agent to take on a new assignment before completing the old. Nor was it done under any less than extreme circumstances. "Even with Viron—"

"This failure is mine to erase. I petitioned thusly, and the Pillars agreed."

"You haven't failed. My mind is my own." However slim the chance he'd believe her, she had to try. "Pillar, please listen. Arcus Boral is alive. We encountered him on Neea. He murdered my Vanguard. He orchestrated all of this."

Scratch clicked his tongue in the negative.

"I fought him." By the disciplines, it was hard to keep her voice level. Her well-rehearsed argument had fragmented, spilling out in a jumble. "He set everything up. He killed the scientists. He faked his death. I don't know what his plan is, but you need to add him back to the Index. That video in the data core was faked."

"Do you believe that video is all that marks you Renegade?"

Tala's spine prickled. "What do you mean?"

But the meaning was clear.

"We have received further evidence," Scratch said. "Inarguable evidence."

"Tell me."

Scratch hesitated. "Some things are not to be spoken of."

For the first time, a flash of frustration breached Tala's mind. It died before it could break through to the skin. "Then I may not argue against them."

"I did not come to hear your arguments. Only your surrender."

"In that case, Pillar, I must disappoint you yet again."

Scratch turned his head to someone outside the holofield's range of replication, saying something she couldn't hear. Tala turned her attention inward, grasping for something, anything that could convince him. She was still thinking when his impassive face shifted back toward her, bringing the full force of his emptiness to bear. When he did not immediately speak, Tala took the initiative.

"I'm going after Arcus. I'll stop him, just as you taught me. I won't let anything in the galaxy keep me from doing what's right, and Exemplar, that includes you."

"Doing what's right," Scratch repeated softly. "Betraying your Vanguard and your oaths. Fleeing judgment. Disregarding the Tenets."

"Ask yourself if those accusations match how I'm speaking to you right now. If they fit the sapient you know."

"The Tala I knew is dead, and you will follow shortly."

Without warning, the hologram dissolved from the center outward, stray wisps forming into the words *Communications Ended* in the Universal script. Tala slumped back into the pilot chair. The tension she'd been damming up over the conversation flooded into her body at once. With it came a deep, heavy disappointment that weighed at her limbs and closed around her heart like a vise.

She'd never really had a chance of getting through to him, regardless of their connection. She hadn't thought otherwise, though she'd made the mistake of allowing herself hope. None of what she'd imagined had prepared her for the reality of standing in the path of that merciless, unfeeling, indomitable will. For being so easily dismissed by the sapient that had all but raised her.

Among the day's many tragedies, it had been on the smaller side. Still, as with an ancient tree, there came a point where the weight grew too great to bear. She probed at her chest for the next half hour, but the pain that had nested there remained.

CHAPTER SIX
THE DUTY OF THE LIVING

The *Chollima* was sized for up to eight passengers, but Tala's squad of five had always made it feel full. Now she found it vast and cavernous, made up of wide, empty expanses and vacant chambers. Increasingly, her quarters were the only bearable choice. There, isolation was expected. Ideal.

Even then, she wasn't safe. The scuffmark on the doorframe had been left by Vigdis's boot. The low cupboard by her bed had been installed at Dorian's recommendation. The corner closest to the door was where Anora had always tossed her coat whenever she'd barged in.

The laboratory's sterile, sticky smell refused to leave her nostrils. She tried lying on her bed, staring at the ceiling, and reciting the first sixty-seven Tenets. Then she did it again, grappling with the meaning behind each one. It didn't help. Not even the Tenets could lighten the weight of her loss. Nor could they shield her when despair and loneliness and trepidation nipped at her thoughts. When Agents lost squadmates, the Center placed them on leave, lavishing on them whatever resources they required to overcome the emotions that slipped in when loss unsealed the door. Tala had none of that.

Worse, she couldn't stop dwelling on the fact that the galaxy's most decorated Agent was hunting her, and not Viron. The human had proven a remorseless killer many times over, and the reassignment of his case only abetted his butchery. More innocent lives on her hands, more needless deaths. It was enough to drive any Enhancer past the lip of madness.

That first night in the *Chollima* found her cross-legged in the main hub with her omnipad and a wide sheet of scrawl, struggling to formulate a plan of action. As she worked, the fog that had spread into every recess of her mind started clearing. Her heart no longer felt like a lodestone in her chest. The sound of the gun that had taken Anora's life wasn't scattering her thoughts before they could coalesce. Equal parts relief and guilt followed the realization, but sleep now seemed attainable—albeit not before her omnipad shifted to its morning display.

Though the heaviness had returned by the time she awoke, it retreated again as she revisited her notes. The clarity of strategic planning wasn't quite the calm, centered state she'd been taught, but it was close.

So her self-assigned mission became a refuge. She furnished plans, honed them, picked them apart and discarded them as useless. She outlined objectives, strategies, and fail-safes. She considered and reconsidered each action point as many times as it took for the despair to pass her by. Purpose gave her the means to continue.

(Deep within and only barely acknowledged was the naked fear of what she might have become had she not been framed. Whether she could have been even half as strong left bereft and purposeless, adrift in bitter solitude).

Ferric sometimes sat in on her planning sessions, but never for long. In those brief spells, she felt the mantle of his discomfort thick against her skin. He must have felt the loneliness just as she did, though he'd never have admitted to such weakness. Still, it wasn't quite enough to overpower his suspicion. He kept to his own quarters, for the most part. When he did emerge, it was usually just long enough to slap a meal patch on his arm and make sure she wasn't converting the *Chollima*'s engine into a thermonuclear device.

On the second evening—or what would have been evening on Peramit, the standard-setter for galactic time—she asked how he'd been keeping busy. The answer wasn't altogether unexpected, given that he was at that very moment intensely focused on a Maestervolt holo.

"Working on the suit."

She'd been waiting at the food synthesizer when he walked in, watching its three slender nozzles assemble her supper to her precise specifications. They reminded her of Torandian fingers.

"I'm not going to let myself be helpless," he added. "I *will* avenge them. Even if I have to fight a Renegade."

She smiled, pretending she hadn't noticed the subtext his tone had made evident. Those little digs came standard-packaged for any interaction with Ferric, now. All she could do was put on a brave face and try not to show how much they hurt. She tried to think of them as penance for her failure on Neea. While that didn't dull the pain, it did give the pain a purpose. Which helped, in its own way.

After that, Tala started noticing signs of Ferric's work. Disturbed wall paneling, a stripped briefing table, intermittent life support failure in the *Chollima*'s nonessential chambers. His onetime hobby turned to obsession, he'd begun repurposing the ship for parts, taking it apart as it flew its final mission. It truly sank in, then: the four days to Ipwaan would be her final four days aboard the ship she'd grown up with.

Remembrance is the duty of the living, she recited time after time, both out loud and in her head. Applying the ninety-eighth Tenet to an inanimate object felt silly, but she couldn't deny the comfort it brought, just as it had when remembering her squadmates. So long as she held the *Chollima* within her mind, it would never truly be gone.

But her memories carried unseen danger; separating thoughts of her friends from those of their killer proved impossible. The Tenets were clear that remembrance was her duty, but equally clear about the hatred it provoked within her. In the end, unable to reconcile the contradiction, she turned to practicing cognitive partitioning during her daily meditations. The fault doubtless lay in her own mental weakness, as it so often did.

By the final few decihours of their journey, she'd made something akin to peace with the ship's loss. Soon, they'd enter Ipwaani space and encounter the planetary defense fleet doubtless watching their approach. It wouldn't be large, not for a planet like Ipwaan, but how Tala dealt with it would affect how soon the general Renegade alert was pushed out to every omnipad in the cluster. Thus far, no such alert had been issued. That would ideally stay true a while longer.

Ferric was cursing up a storm across the hall. It seemed his powersuit-in-progress no longer fit the magcase he'd brought it aboard in. Looking about her own spartan quarters, it was hard to muster sympathy. The most essential gear (rations, armaments, shield units, fuel cells, heavy boots, etc.) had been packed away earlier that morning, leaving only personal possessions. Tala, having followed as best she could the fifty-sixth Tenet (*freedom from objects is freedom from hindrance*), could fit her belongings into half a luggage case.

Packing took less than a decihour, and half of it was spent contemplating *Flowerbed*. If answers hid behind the paint—or holographic representation thereof—she needed them more than ever. All she saw—all she ever saw—was that same meditative, armless human among orange flowers, beneath a sea of stars. Frael had been confident she could tease forth what meaning the image held. Though she trusted his judgment implicitly, today clearly wasn't the day he'd be proven right.

She packed it last. Its projector came loose with a light tug, sending the painting dancing across the floor. Into the half-full case it went, atop the raggedy stuffed koala her parents had given her the day she'd departed for the Center. The thought of them seeing her featured in a Renegade alert made her stomach clench before she could quiet her muscle, as it had the other hundred-odd times she'd pictured it. As always, it was followed by the stinging feeling that she should have treated them better. Visited more often. Judged less harshly.

Paying no heed to Ferric's continued string of nordok invectives, she lifted the case one-handed. She took one last look around her empty room before sealing the door behind her.

The fingers on Tala's left hand tingled with energy.

She focused in on the dim light that represented them in her mind— well, *five* lights, really. Each light was made up of countless smaller ones, representing skin, bone, blood, muscle, and all the other aspects that defined each finger's existence. Those lights were made of even more lights, in an endless cascade downward. It was a complex interplay between mind, energy, and body. A melding of purpose and reality, with herself at the intersection.

The experience was wholly unique to her. She'd discussed it with her fellow Initiates and found no evidence to disprove the old truism that there were as many ways to perceive Enhancement as there were Enhancers. There was only one common aspect: the feeling of incompleteness that accompanied each attempt at explanation, no matter how thorough. Her own description of how it felt to access her powers was accurate enough, yet it was missing...something. If there were words to describe *what*, no Enhancer—not even Mitra, wisest of them all —had found them.

The tingle spread to her palm, and then up her arm. A simple control exercise for Initiates, designed to build awareness of their power. Tala had long progressed beyond such exercises, but she still found them calming. Energy retreated from her hand and flowed upward, past her shoulder blades to concentrate in the center of her back. Inhaling deeply, she held it there, power without purpose.

The dropship hatch slid open. Tala straightened in her chair, letting the energy dissipate. Ferric gave her a precise, economical salute that held more mockery than respect.

"Ready," he said.

Tala eyed the two bulging luggage cases next to him, then the magcase floating behind. "Sure you've got enough gear there?"

"We can't all be living weapons." With a wave of Ferric's hand, the magcase slid neatly over the threshold, nestling into a corner. Ferric kept an eye on it until it had stopped moving—it contained his most precious possession, after all. When it had settled, he lifted one of the other cases. Grunting, he heaved it in as well. "Trust me. If we run into your Renegade, you'll be glad I brought all this."

Rather than responding, Tala elected to look pointedly at her omnipad. Ferric had cut it close; the countdown time until they entered Ipwaani territory had barely half a decihour left. Not that he seemed to notice her displeasure.

"Program ready to go?"

"Triple-checked." Tala took another deep breath. *Gently beats the content heart.* "If you want a look..."

"Pass." Ferric pulled in the last case and the dropship went from cramped to packed. "It's all in your hands."

The bridge was empty. Systems had been either shut down or left on autopilot, all administrative function ceded to Tala's omnipad. She'd programmed her commands into one sequence, waiting on a single prompt to begin. Flying the *Chollima* remotely from its own dropship was the ridiculous kind of stunt Anora would have loved. Even thinking her friend's name was enough to send a sharp, icy stinging across her chest. She wondered if that pain would ever dull, or if she wanted it to. It was Anora who should have been flying. They'd limped this far on autopilot, but anything more complicated than open space would overwhelm it.

Ferric resealed the hatch and plopped into the copilot's seat. The timer ticked down bit by bit and she found it hard to look away. Every second that slipped by was one second lost with the *Chollima*. It would soon be another casualty, another piece of her life that Arcus had ripped away. Again the brutal images ripped through her mind, blood and bodies falling—

She dislodged the memories with a violent shake of her head and wrenched her focus back to the countdown. Ferric gave her an odd look, and she wished miserably that she could have found comfort in his proximity instead of tension. The last seconds drained away in what seemed like an eyeblink. The *Chollima* slowed as it passed the arbitrary line designating Ipwaani space, roughly a thousand kilometers from the planet's surface. Right on schedule, a hard, crisp voice filled the cockpit.

"Agent's vessel Chollima, *this is Commander Eklukas of the Galactic Armed Forces, representing the Ipwaan Volunteer Defense Fleet. You are instructed to power down and initiate boarding protocols."*

The transmission, directed at the *Chollima's* bridge, had been rerouted to Tala's omnipad. Commander Eklukas doubtless didn't expect his overtures to be obeyed or even acknowledged, but she respected him for trying. A less principled commander might have opened fire without warning. Against a Renegade, he would even have been lauded for it.

"It's time," said Tala. "Sequence starts in three. Two."

"*Chollima, power down—*"

"One."

"—or we will open fire."

Tala hit the button and the *Chollima* went to full thrust.

Preemptive Enhancement shielded them from the worst of it, but the acceleration still hit like a meteor. Tala's guts felt like they were trying to force their way through her spine. Ferric let out a strangled gasp. Still, they were both conscious, so Tala marked it as a win. Helped along by Enhanced engines, it took only four seconds to reach Ipwaan's far hemisphere. It was unsettling, flying blindly along a preprogrammed routine. The only sign they were still moving was the dropship's muted rumble. The only way they'd learn something had gone wrong would be as abrupt as it would be fatal.

A Renegade in your sphere of responsibility was the sort of threat best responded to with a fleet. For a planet as far-flung as Ipwaan, that meant the entirety of their defense force and the unspoken knowledge that it wouldn't be enough. They'd come expecting a fight—a true Renegade would have exulted in tearing their ships apart one by one, punching holes in their hulls and slashing fire through their bellies. Instead, Tala had fled, faster than any un-Enhanced vessel could hope to respond. She'd put a planet between them and her. For now, they were blind.

Tala withdrew her energy from the *Chollima*'s engines. It was already slowing of its own accord, following its coding to the letter. There was a soft ka-chunk as the dropship detached and floated free, drifting on its leftover momentum. Peach-colored and blocky, with an auburgine "rim" circling the bottom, it looked nothing like the *Chollima*. Tala had always thought they'd been designed by separate committees.

Goodbye, she thought, watching her ship for the last time as it pulled away.

As she'd thought, this section of Ipwaani space was empty. It would not remain so for long. The dropship's engine kicked in and Tala helped it along, sending the tiny craft hurtling planetward. Ipwaan filled the viewports, a rubescent atmosphere smothered by thick, gray clouds. Small gaps in the cloud cover revealed dull violet oceans washing up on blackened beaches, and patchy vegetation of orange and brown. Billowing particulate matter interposed themselves between, dark specks drifting in coils along air currents and darkening the planet's blazing sun. Tala aimed the ship toward the thickest cluster of clouds, hoping to obscure their approach.

Behind them, the *Chollima* slowed to a hover. It had instructions to draw attention, evading enemy fire with its limited autopilot. After it had sustained enough damage, it would flee the system at top speed toward the next closest planet, making Commander Eklukas think he'd driven her off. The ruse wouldn't fool GAF High Command for long. Hopefully she'd be off-planet in a new, untraceable ship before they figured it out. Then the hunt for Arcus could begin in earnest.

"Landing point?" said Ferric.

The ship slipped into the clouds and her view became nothing but roiling gray. Atmospheric pressure shook the tiny craft, leaving Tala struggling to compensate. Anora's dropship landings had always been so smooth. The dashboard rang with multiple collision warnings that stopped as their forward-mounted laser burned the incoming debris to cinders. Barely a moment passed when it wasn't shooting at something. Ipwaan's atmosphere was unusually crowded.

Clearing intersteller detritus was the laser's main purpose. Energy shields were powerful enough to negate even the strongest laser cannon, making them useless in ship-to-ship combat. Against unshielded targets, though, there was no better tool.

"Hundred-fifty kilometers out from the closest city should be enough." On such a recently colonized planet, the population wouldn't have spread too far from the colonizer ships' original impact points. "We can run that, no problem."

She leveled out their descent, keeping to the cloud cover while chasing the evening line around the planet. The clouds darkened around them, slowly giving way to churning black. Only when the darkness was thick and heavy did she send them back into their descent, breaking free of the clouds—for all the difference it made. Ipwaan's night was absolute, unchallenged by artificial lighting. It felt like flying through a massive sensory deprivation chamber, with only the navcomputer's measurements to guide her. She'd turned off most of the dropship's scanning systems to avoid detection, leaving only brief bursts of sonar to keep her from giving herself a premature burial. First flying remotely, now landing blind. Tala couldn't help but hope that somewhere, Anora was angry to be missing this.

A 3-D topographical rendering of Ipwaan's surface floated above her omnipad, interfacing with the dropship's sonar to approximate their position. They rocketed over dry riverbeds and barren plains, squat hills and stubborn forests, cracked outcroppings and wide swaths of sand. At the hologram's edge floated a small number, rapidly decreasing—altitude.

"Colony Four two-fifty kilometers out," said Ferric. "Mountains in eighty-seven. Good spot to land."

Tala had already clocked both locations near the edge of her holographic "map." "Mountains" was generous; "hills" was more accurate. She adjusted their trajectory with a twist of the dropship's yoke. On her omnipad, the small dot representing the dropship veered left. Large or small, a chunk of planet between the dropship and Colony Four —or Asur, as the locals called it—would help stymie whatever scanners they had available. Almost two decihours later, they'd reached the mountains' shadow and Tala judged it safe to activate the dropship's powerful forward beams. Tiny dark flecks swirled and danced in the two shafts of light, brushing across the cockpit's viewports.

She chose a small valley tucked into the center of the range and brought them to a shaky hover just above it. Steep inclines surrounded them on three sides, a perfect nook in which to hide.

"Brace yourself," she said. "We're about to land, but I can't promise much more than that."

So saying, she punched in the landing sequence.

Touchdown was never an enjoyable experience. At its best, it was slow and boring: a reputable shipyard guiding you to your hangar with sophisticated machinery. At its worst, it was existentially terrifying, knowing that even with Anora's expert hands on the controls, you were one botched calculation removed from grounding the ship permanently. Even with the flattest, most favorable site, natural terrain was a nightmare to land on. The valley Tala had chosen was neither flat nor favorable.

With brittle slowness, they approached the ground, whipping up clouds of earth and rock that pinged off the dropship's hull. She flooded it with energy, noting a stubborn resistance that hadn't been there with the *Chollima*. She'd never spent as much time familiarizing herself with the dropship, and it showed. The landing struts met the planet's surface with individual vibrating thuds and an agonized scraping sound, sending the dropship swaying from side to side before bouncing to a halt. With an electronic hum, the hatch slid open, letting in a wave of heat and ash-scented air.

The valley outside was rough and rocky. Parts were glassy, glinting in the dropship's light. Others were covered by rusty, broad-leafed vegetation. Beyond the light's reach, Tala saw nothing but darkness. Even the starlight was trapped behind Ipwaan's perpetual clouds.

Ferric undid his harness, hunching to keep his head from brushing the ceiling. He put a hand on the hatch's guardrail and hopped out onto the planet's surface. His magcase followed, sliding gracefully across the dropship's lip and into place behind him.

"We'd better get moving if we want to beat that Index update," he said. "Nice landing, by the way. Give me a hand with those cases."

"Fine," said Tala. Her fingers flowed across the dashboard, initiating a total shutdown. "But you're taking the extra one. It's yours, after all."

Ferric gave a sigh of pure suffering, which Tala ignored. It was his own fault for overpacking.

The mountains gave way to barren knolls, which in turn leveled out into a wide, pebbled steppe. Tala's power sustained them along the way. The cumbersome luggage cases were nothing to Enhanced muscles. They ran mostly in silence, brushing bits of floating ash away from their faces. Only the piercing white light of Ferric's omnipad kept their path illuminated. Tala's still displayed the local topography, now zoomed in to match their current situation. Asur was still far, but they were making good time, and it would be a while before they needed to stop.

She kept her mind sharp by trying to remember everything she'd briefed herself about Asur. It was the second smallest of Ipwaan's six colonies, so there hadn't been much. It had been established earlier this cycle to harvest the native jandrofyls, weird little lizard-things with backs that looked like moss. They secreted something important, but she couldn't remember what. It hadn't seemed relevant.

"Remember, the locals don't say Colony Four," she reminded Ferric. He grunted an ambiguous reply. That was all they said for the next four kilometers.

The sky started to lighten not long after, the muted gray of pre-dawn. Gradually, the clouds bled to a hungry red as the sun spilled its light over the horizon. Above them drifted the ever-present ash, black against the ruddy coat of clouds. As the unseen sun drifted higher, the clouds took on their natural gray once more. While night had been uncomfortably warm, the daytime heat was almost intolerable.

They came to a wide trench, the last evidence of a long-vanished river, and followed its curving course for a good half hour. The air was dry, blowing forcefully across Tala's face and through her close-cropped hair. She took a long sip from her canteen. Three-quarters drained already, and it wasn't refilling. There simply wasn't enough moisture in the atmosphere for the bottle to leech.

"Little more in the lower back, please." Ferric was starting to flag. Tala upped the Enhancement to his back, which supported one of his two massive cases.

"Thanks."

Ferric straightened, steps falling back into their steady, rapid beat. The magcase followed like a second shadow. Early on, he'd tried balancing the other cases on top of it, but hadn't been satisfied with the precarious result.

Trees began to dot the rocky plain. Bottom-heavy, gnarled trunks peppered with small holes, through which leaked a slow trickle of light yellow sap. Wide, thick orange leaves drooped sadly from spindly branches. As Tala ran, the trees became more frequent, though never closer than sixty meters apart. They stopped in one's shadow as the air began cooling, hunger pangs finally beyond Enhancement's power to eliminate. Ferric pulled some nutribars out of the case on his back and passed two to Tala. She washed hers down with shallow sips of warm water from her depleted canteen.

"Something tells me we aren't going to find a Rensens dealership in Asur," she remarked between bites. "Or anywhere else on this miserable planet."

"Does it matter? We couldn't afford their prices anyway. Your account's been locked by now, and mine's probably flagged."

"True," she conceded, "but a new ship's only half the problem. The easier half at that. We need a pilot too, and Rensens doesn't carry those."

"You got us here just fine."

"You mean autopilot did," said Tala. "We're lucky nothing came up it couldn't handle. The trip from Neea to Ipwaan took four days. In galactic terms, that's a decihour-long stroll. One debris shower would've ended us. Autopilot can't handle that. _I_ can't handle that. If we get in a dogfight, if an essential system blows, you'll notice the difference real quick."

"But—"

"Besides, you're officially MIA and I'm about to be added to the Index. Our faces are no good. We need someone to handle supply runs and checkpoints for us. A pilot's the natural figurehead."

"Exactly," Ferric said tightly. "Our faces are no good. What pilot's gonna aid a Renegade? That's not just illegal, it's stupid. Even if we do find one before the Index updates, we'll only have them for as long as it takes the alert to go out. Then we're stuck on a ship with a hostile."

"Maybe we can find one that's willing to work with us, even given the circumstances."

"Anyone who would, I wouldn't trust enough to fly with."

"Maybe they're blind?"

"A blind pilot."

"Selectively blind. You know, face blind."

Ferric's deepset eyes narrowed.

"You're being unrealistic," he said. "Of course it would be great if we found some perfect pilot. Just, under present circumstances, it's looking a little," he chewed his tongue pensively, "impossible."

"You're really fine with risking your life like that?"

"Of all the most likely ways my life could end on this mission, a flight mishap doesn't even crack the top three," said Ferric. "If it's an asteroid, a pilot, or...well, I suppose it's all the same in the end."

He rose with smooth nonchalance. Quips aside, his original concerns weren't invalid. Yet he of all people should have been thrilled to welcome a pilot aboard. An ally in the wings, if he decided the Renegade aboard needed to be...contained.

Her eyes lifted skyward, toward the impenetrable bank of clouds. Arcus was somewhere beyond that barrier. The longer it took to find a ship, the colder his trail got. A pilot was a risk they needed to take.

Ferric strapped the heaviest case onto his back, grunting with exertion. "Hey, Tala."

"I know," she said, getting up. "I'm coming."

"Not that. Just wondering where you're planning to look first."

"Not sure," she admitted. "Though I have some ideas."

Just because Arcus had been thought dead for almost thirty years didn't mean he hadn't been active. If she sifted through the right data, she knew she'd find something that didn't add up, some mystery that solved itself once Arcus was put into the picture. It wasn't much, but anything was better than a galaxy-sized search space. More immediately...

"I think we should start with how he died. Examine every record, figure out how he faked his death. There's something there, a piece everyone else must've missed. If we can prove he's still alive, I could even clear my name. Then—"

"I meant for a pilot."

"Oh." Tala coughed to cover her embarrassment, knowing he wouldn't be fooled. It was an unproductive emotion, so she let it drain away like water on parched ground. "Does Asur have a flight academy?"

She didn't remember one in her brief. She didn't remember Asur having much of anything. Nothing except—

"I'd be surprised if *Ipwaan* has a flight academy," Ferric snorted. "Might as well go door-to-door."

"You know what we will find in Asur?" She spoke slowly, hesitant to even share the idea. It wasn't something she would have considered before. Then her Vanguard's cries welled up in her ears and she felt the ache of her injuries, and there was no longer any room for hesitation.

"I assume you don't mean the gauntlet saloon—"

"The biggest gauntlet saloon in the cluster."

Ferric's lips curled. She'd expected as much; he'd never made his distaste for those places a secret. In truth, she felt much the same. Anora had dragged her there once, promising a fun night out. The experience had left a lingering disquiet. Tala lived a violent life, but it was for a purpose. The blood that flowed that night had been shed for nothing but entertainment.

"You know places like this are where gauntlets get really bad, right?" he said. "This isn't Modellus. Laws are looser out here."

He wasn't wrong. The farther you flew from Peramit and Central Cluster, the rougher the galaxy got. Of course, "farther" was a relative term when you could fly through a gate and pop out eleven parsecs away. The mechanics of gate placement didn't care about spatial distance. Gates followed natural fluctuations in the fabric of space-time. When one was found near a large enough concentration of terraformable planets, a gate was built and the Coalition added a new cluster. The more gates between a cluster and Peramit, the harder enforcing the Coalition's laws became.

"If it's bad, it's bad. It won't get worse because we see it."

"No, that's when we're supposed to act. That's our job. Hells, that's our duty. I enlisted to shut down places like this, not patronize them."

Tala brushed at the ash that had settled on her shoulders. "We're not going there for drinks and a wager. We need a pilot."

"And we can't do that anywhere but a gauntlet saloon?"

"Where else would they be? You read everything I did about Asur. It's a third-tier colony on a fourth-tier planet. But that saloon's a pretty major rest stop for a planet this close to the edge. I can't vouch for the quality of the pilots, but the quantity should give us some choice at least." She sighed. "Don't think I *like* this. If you've got an alternative, I'll happily hear it."

"I thought my door-to-door idea wasn't bad." Ferric wouldn't meet her eyes. Instead, he was a little too focused on fiddling with his straps.

Tala closed the distance to him and put a soft hand on his shoulder. A polite intrusion, giving him no choice but to look up.

"By algorithm, you'd like them," she said. "Sapients striving to prove themselves. Displaying their potential. Honing their skill. I feel like you could get behind that."

"There's a difference." Ferric took a step forward, letting her hand fall. "You know what kind of sapients gauntlets attract. Is that the kind of pilot you're looking for?"

There was that guilty feeling again. She'd known, when choosing to leave Neea, that her future would not be simple or easy. But the sort of sapient her mind conjured up at Ferric's words sickened her to the core. Slavers. Thieves. Pirates. Grifters. *Company kept is the most truthful mirror,* said the thirty-eighth Tenet. It didn't *forbid* her idea, but nor did it cast her in a good light for indulging it.

It's all to stop Arcus. All to stop a Renegade and whatever dark plots he's woven.

None of this turmoil reached Ferric. She contained it with practiced ease behind blank eyes and neutral lips. Just as the Tenets demanded.

"One cannot crawl free of darkness without exposure to light," she quoted. "We do them a disservice by shunning their company. The proffered hand can be stronger than the clenched fist."

Skepticism was writ large on Ferric's face, but he just lifted his second case. "Let's get going."

Tala was all too happy to let the conversation die. She sucked down a few drops of water, lifted her case, and broke into a run, Ferric at her side. They were in a race against time, and while the omnipad on Ferric's belt had been silent so far, they couldn't count on their luck holding indefinitely.

Her feet slapped against the rocky, uneven ground in a steady rhythm. The scenery flew by, trees and escarpments and jutting stone "fingers" that pierced up from the ground. However, there were no living creatures to be seen. Not even as much as a sun-bleached skeleton. The silence was strained but absolute, haunted by unspoken words and feelings.

As twilight fell, the clouds shifted back to dull red. Long streaks of deep crimson splashed across them like claw marks left behind by some massive beast that had lacerated the sky until it bled, standing out vividly against their more muted backdrop. It was beneath this sky that they came upon the first landmark of civilization they'd seen upon the silent panorama: a stone causeway, stretching as far as Tala could see. It was wide enough for ten sapients to pass abreast, and down the center ran a podpath of gleaming steel. The continental thoroughfare.

A driving pod whizzed by, a squat egg painted pallid green, with four spherical wheels stuck to the bottom that left a swirling trail of dust in its wake. Tala looked on enviously, imagining its air-conditioned interior. Her Podcaller account was certainly flagged by now, and using Ferric's would lead to scrutiny. Instead, she tapered off her Enhancements, gradually—and reluctantly—returning them to a speed that wouldn't draw attention. The difference hit her almost at once, a wave of fatigue and sore muscles built over the course of their nonstop run. Ferric groaned beneath the full weight of his cases.

"Not much longer," said Tala. With her reclaimed reserves, she Enhanced her vision threefold. A small blur on the horizon resolved into a tiny settlement—Asur, Colony Four. Buildings lit up window by window as the day waned, setting the village twinkling with sharp light. It was among the smallest settlements Tala had ever seen, barely as large as some of Modellus's districts—in fact, it could have fit inside the Legislatorium with room to spare. "It's just ahead."

"Great," Ferric panted. "So, what's this gauntlet place called, anyway?"

Tala cleared her throat awkwardly. "The Blunted Cleaver."

By mutual, unspoken agreement, they returned to their uneasy silence.

CHAPTER SEVEN
A BIRD IN THE HAND

Even from a distance, finding Asur's gauntlet saloon wasn't hard. It towered forebodingly over its neighbors, almost four stories tall in a town where the next highest building barely reached two. Asur's other buildings weren't just small, they were unregimented; scattered freely around the colony as if by artless hands. It was entirely unlike the carefully planned blocks of Modellus's teeming megacities. The overall effect was strangely peaceful. There were no packed crowds to push through, no endless streams of driving pods zipping to and fro, no cameras tracking every movement for abnormalities. The last was especially comforting.

As they drew closer, Tala realized the saloon might have been the ugliest building she'd ever seen. Its exterior was lumpy, as if built by stacking rocks in a cylinder and flashpainting the result a glossy black. Three small contained fires burned above its arched wooden doorway, illuminating a metallic orange plate into which words had been hammered: *The Blunted Cleaver*. The sign shimmered with an attention-grabbing hologram overlay—sparks danced along the edges, occasionally exploding into miniature fireworks. The definition of subtlety.

Outside the door stretched a line of sapients—long, but moving quickly—which Tala and Ferric joined. The walkway was made from the same rough stone as the building, and lined with black, corvid-style lanterns. The fire was artificial; heat was already at a surplus.

"Remind me how we're paying?" said Ferric.

Tala stretched her shoulders, feeling the deep ache that had gathered there over their day-long run. "Same way I paid the couriers."

They'd dropped their luggage off with Asur's courier service and received a small pink chit in exchange. Lugging their valuables into the saloon was a bad idea—and besides, they needed the break. A growing proportion of her Enhancement was tied up in pushing back fatigue. They were due a calm, multi-day rest. Ferric had been concerned about payment, so Tala had handled the matter discreetly. He wouldn't be a fan of her solution. Probably suspected as much, given that he kept badgering her to explain how she'd paid.

"Not really an answer."

"I've got it covered," she assured him. "Don't worry."

They reached the front of the line soon after. The Blunted Cleaver's doorkeeper was kirtian—a short, furred species with beady eyes and sagging jowls. Other than his round little belly, he reminded Tala of

Central Pillar Frael. He gave them each a once-over through a heavy squint.

"Welcome to The Blunted Cleaver. Watching or entering?"

"Watching," said Tala. "Table for two, please. Nothing too open."

"Three stars even."

Her account being frozen, Tala would have to make do with less conventional units of currency. She reached into her chest pocket and pulled out something rectangular and turquoise-tinted the size of her thumb. The power cell for her personal shield.

"Military grade," she said casually. "Worth four times that, at least."

The kirtian squinted at that too. Tala hoped barter wasn't too uncommon here; it thrived on edgeworlds where not every sapient had an omnipad and nobody wanted their transactions registered. Or, for that matter, scrutinized by the GIAB—the Galactic Information and Assessment Bureau. She held the cell out for him to examine, letting him snatch it with a clawed hand. Ferric's eyes were fixed stubbornly on a lavender driving pod further up the podpath. It seamlessly threaded two buildings and vanished down a sideway. Ferric looked like he wished he could do the same.

At last, the doorkeeper pocketed the power cell and tapped his omnipad. "Third floor. Follow the green light."

Tala tugged gently on Ferric's arm. Reluctantly, he followed. "That was government property," he muttered plaintively.

Tala shrugged. "Not anymore."

"Wait, what did you give the couriers—"

The kirtian waved the door open and all hell broke loose.

Shouts, hoots, roars, and thuds, each trying to drown out the others. Every shady, illicit, or restricted substance in the known galaxy mixed together into one acrid scent. Flashing neon, holoscreens and flatscreens at every possible angle, colors further along the spectrum than human eyes were normally receptive to. And settling over it all, an oppressive, murky light chosen for its ability to wash out stains. Tala released the constant, low-powered Enhancement she maintained on her senses, and her world immediately got about fifteen percent more livable. She diverted the extra power into her spinal column, and did a quick breathing exercise.

It felt like she'd walked into a combat zone—and in a way, she had.

Species she'd never seen in the flesh crowded around the tables, consuming exotic meals through their preferred orifices. The floor shone with guiding paths of light, covering most of the common spectrums. One path, a green the color of the refectory's pastes, led to a set of dingy lifts. A sign next to them noted that the floor above had arena seating along with the gauntlet itself, while the top floor boasted the balcony view. The sounds and sights were overwhelming; everywhere she looked were holos of a Surolian pushing their way through a tangle of razorwire. The big show: a contestant challenging the gauntlet.

Razorwire was deadly, but it had been designed to stop flesh. The three-meter mass of rock and ice thundered forward on four broad, blocky legs, ignoring the small nicks that resulted. Tala's eyes went to the bottom of the holo, where a progress meter read *52%* and odds were displayed at 1.2-to-1 against.

She might have watched a little, had something else not yanked at her attention. A table of bedouks, seven in all. The small, lumpy, olive-skinned sapients weren't common in Central Cluster—this was the most Tala had ever seen in one place. But that wasn't what had drawn her gaze. It was the sleek injector filled with turbid gray liquid that one bedouk had just inserted into his nostril's right skin flap. A kalisser synthesizer. The ultimate designer drug, capable of reading a sapient's biological makeup to create a blend of personalized euphoria. At first. Over time, most species developed a resistance to the synthesizer's compounds. To reach that perfect high, the synthesizer would raise the dose until you died with a smile stretched across your face.

She took a step toward the table. Just one, before reality stopped her cold. It wouldn't make a difference. A confiscated synthesizer would be replaced. A trip to the detox clinic wouldn't scrub an addiction that ingrained. Nothing would, short of following him around, keeping him from using until his tolerance receded. She couldn't put one life above her mission when so many others were at stake. The math didn't add up, as much as she ached to intervene.

It was so hard, admitting she couldn't save everybody. Even blessed with a gift most sapients could only dream of, she was limited. Powerless. She could only watch as the next bedouk took the synthesizer from a shaking paw.

Several steps along the green line, Ferric was waiting. His lips were so thinly pressed that his mouth was in danger of vanishing altogether. The set of his jaw told her he'd surmised everything she'd just thought, and wasn't happy about it.

But he didn't push past her and confront the bedouks himself.

She allowed her feet to follow the green glow. Every footfall betrayed her principles anew. Behind her, a sapient pumped poison into his body, slowly drawing closer to his final dose. Ahead, the line ended at a run-down lift.

"What's that thing you always told us?" said Ferric, just loud enough to be heard over the saloon's clamor. *"Every action has its cost, but a good deed is beyond price?"*

It was the twelfth Tenet, and one of Tala's favorites.

"Confronting them isn't the right answer," she said. "They wouldn't have given up their synthesizer without a fight."

"Then you should've been prepared to fight. You know what it's doing to them. How can you—"

A nordok stumbled into Ferric and dropped his drink, sending pungent froth spilling across the floor. He looked up at Ferric's towering frame—partly natural, partly the side effect of an Enhanced metabolism all through childhood. Whatever he'd been about to say, he thought better of it, vanishing back into a gyrating mass of sapients.

"See how unpredictable this place is? Any fighting could spread out of control. Much better to let the authorities handle things."

The lift jerked open at their approach, revealing a siari and a corvid. The corvid was running a slow claw down the siari's orange lightlets, but they came apart as soon as they realized they had an audience. They moved past, eyes locked, arms almost touching. The sight pulled at Tala's chest as she stepped into the lift. After a moment's hesitation, Ferric followed.

"You can bet the authorities here look the other way," said Ferric as they rose. "It's in Asur's best interests not to drive away customers. This place is probably keeping the whole colony alive."

The third floor was less populated than the first, and blessedly less raucous. Tables of varied sizes and configurations were spread around a wide hole in the floor. A thin railing protected patrons from a four-meter drop into the second floor and the gauntlet itself. Wrapped around the walls were a series of covered booths closed off with burgundy curtains. It was to one of these booths that the green line led them.

Tala drew the curtains shut behind them and slid onto a squat, padded stool. Their table was polished metal, far nicer than those she'd seen on the main floor. Like the other tables, the middle was devoted to a holographic Surolian taking on the dangerous series of challenges that comprised a gauntlet. Currently, they were swatting at a flock of leather-winged kraeliarrk, smashing one from the air with a grace that belied their bulk.

"I hate this place," said Ferric, placing his omnipad on the table. Its display had automatically transitioned to The Blunted Cleaver's menu. Several prominently placed "daily deals" wiggled enticingly. "Lousy ambiance, barbaric entertainment, and I can't even order anything."

The last kraeliarrk died, crushed between the arena wall and the Surolian's clublike fist. Ferric harrumphed and turned off the holo.

"Shouldn't have let a Surolian compete." It was probably a bad idea, but Tala couldn't resist teasing him a bit. The way she always had when everyone gathered around a table. "Seems kind of unfair, right? They negate half the gauntlet by default. Ruins the spectacle."

"I'm *not* having this talk."

Their waiter arrived impressively quickly. He was a short, dark-haired human with a round face and a smile so permanent, it could have been carved on. It didn't even flicker when they declined to place a wager. He took their twin orders of water down on his omnipad with impeccable cheer, and swept back toward the lifts, following a bright pink line and humming a tune Tala recognized as *She's Got a Supernova Smile*. She watched his back cautiously until he disappeared from sight behind a table of slender, leaf-adorned affajans.

Ferric got up and pulled the curtains closed again. "You know who would have loved it here?"

"Anora," they said in unison, and for just a moment, the shared anguish that bound them together was stronger than anything else. But almost as quickly, Ferric let out an exasperated grunt and turned away.

"Didn't mean to bring her up. I know there's no point."

"It's fine," said Tala a little too quickly, trying to swallow the sudden swell of sadness that had pushed its way up into her throat. "Don't apologize for remembering them."

They deserved a place in her thoughts. Now and forever. No matter how it hurt, she'd bear it.

"That's not—never mind." Ferric was now examining a particularly clean corner of the table. "I really don't like being here. How can I get us closer to leaving?"

"Want to ask the barkeep if he knows any dependable pilots? If you can scrounge up a list, we could use that as a starting point."

"You're really going to trust someone who frequents this place."

Tala hesitated. "I don't know," she said, with complete honesty. "All I know is that we're dipping low on options. I promise I won't let my guard down just because we're desperate. If I can't trust them, we won't hire them."

"That's the thing," said Ferric, with the simmering hostility born of an argument well treaded. "Nobody you *can* trust would agree to fly a Renegade."

Perhaps recognizing the shape of the coming conversation, he rose from his chair without pressing the point. With a respectful dip of his head, he swept the curtains aside, almost running into their waiter, who was returning with two tankards of water the size of Ferric's upper arm. Ferric muttered a hurried apology, took a tankard, and drained it in one long gulp.

When it was empty, he cleared his throat—dislodging the last of Ipwaan's dust—and set off for the bar, cup still dangling from his hand. The waiter, whose smile had not budged through the encounter, handed Tala her own cup and retired, closing the curtains behind him. After giving the water an Enhanced sniff and deeming it both unpoisoned and acceptably clean, she took a sip—and realized just how thirsty she'd been. Before she knew it, half the cup was gone.

She spent the next few decihours alternating her attention between the tankard and her omnipad, scrolling through the planetary marketplace's spaceship listings. They were just as sparse as she'd feared. *Wishing for water brings no rain*, she reminded herself, and let the disappointment pass through her without holding onto it.

Nothing in the *Chollima*'s class was available at any price. Even if there had been, it would have been an inferior replacement, lacking decades of built-up familiarity. Her connection would be anemic, her Enhancement impeded. Next to a properly Enhanced Agent's vessel, even a Pavise battlecruiser looked slow, weak, and vulnerable.

With a victorious fanfare, her table holo turned itself back on. Her eyes darted up on reflex to see the gauntlet completion percentage at eighty-six, with the Surolian gauntlet-runner advancing across a narrow bridge that trembled ominously beneath their weight. Outside, the saloon had gone unnaturally quiet. Slowly, the Surolian edged closer to solid ground...

An angry shout came from outside the booth, followed by a squawk of pain. Tala whipped open the curtains. Locating the noise was easy— the whole room was looking right at it. Beside a nearby table, three nordok stared down a small, green-and-black-feathered corvid, faces contorted in malign intent. The tallest of the three had the corvid's wrist in a tight grip. As the corvid struggled to pull free, a second nordok wound up and punched her in the abdomen. She let out another squawk and almost fell, but the tall nordok was still holding her upright.

None of the onlookers did anything. Only half were still watching. This was probably a common story here. Stopping the fight would be left to security, whenever they felt like getting to it. Maybe fast enough to save the corvid. Maybe not.

Except this time, there was an Agent present. Someone to be the line between peace and chaos, as Central Pillar Frael taught. A sapient was in need. To respond was her duty. Her purpose. One leap, and she'd be in front of them. She tensed to spring, power dancing down her legs—and held position.

Involving herself in a saloon brawl in front of a capacity crowd of witnesses was the opposite of inconspicuous. All it would take to endanger her mission was being brought to the wrong sapient's attention. Fights broke out here daily; jumping to one corvid's aid wouldn't change that. Just like confiscating a bedouk's kalisser synthesizer wouldn't keep them from tomorrow's dose.

Tenet twelve, she reminded herself. Ferric's rebukes weren't undeserved, and his suspicion and disapproval had grown no weaker in her memories. This time, she couldn't help but wonder whether it was justified. A shiver passed over her as she remembered Exemplar Scratch's empty gaze in their last call. Pitiless, implacable, and certain; the harshest rebuke he could have meted out. Had they seen something in her besides the power of the label she'd been given? If there was even a chance he had, she couldn't afford to slip or stray. She was an Enhancer of the Agent's discipline. The line between peace and chaos. The Tenets lived within her, and her every decision reflected their truth.

Energy pulsed beneath her skin and down her spinal column, a technique she'd learned from Scratch to Enhance her reflexes without directly touching the brain. Mind given over to the battlecalm, she wove across the saloon floor at a sprint. The nearest nordok turned, face transitioning to naked shock, and she sent him to the floor with a blow to the sternum. Even without relying on superhuman strength, she knew how to hit hard.

She could do this, she told herself. Play the part of a concerned citizen who just happened to know how to fight. Nothing strange, in a place like this. They'd never know the true nature of who they faced.

The other two whirled on her, but to her Enhanced reflexes, they moved as if through dense liquid. She danced forward, allowing one to graze her shoulder. A glancing hit, but she drove a fake wince across her face.

She moved between them, catching another blow and pivoting to use the attacker's momentum against him. As he stumbled, she yanked the tall one forward by the collar into the other's path. Both fell in a tangle of limbs. One tried to rise, so Tala kicked him in the side, augmenting her strength by just a hair so he'd stay down.

They stared up at her in shock and pain. Tala rubbed her shoulder like it stung, glaring down at them in a low combat stance. "Fensul's teeth," the one she'd kicked mouthed, through what looked like a broken rib.

As she emerged from her battlecalm, she could see herself through their eyes. Just shy of two meters tall, in utter control of the fight from the moment it began, dismantling their attack with brutal effectiveness. Like her friends must have seen Arcus, before...

The adrenaline drained away, leaving her tired and slightly nauseated. "That's enough for one night," she said. "Go home."

There were pained groans of assent. Their acceptance must have signaled something to the remaining onlookers, because the tension filling the air deflated at once.

A flicker of motion caught her attention and she whirled around to meet it. Her hand closed on a feathery shoulder.

"Hi!" said the corvid she'd rescued, beak open in a smile. Her voice was loud and unrestrained, each word carefully articulated.

Tala released her at once. "Sorry," she said. "They didn't hurt you too much, did they?"

"I'm fine," the corvid chirped, heedless of the bloody patches on her face where feathers ought to be. "Thought I was flightfodder. Thanks."

"No thanks needed." Tala reached out to brush the corvid's comb— their equivalent of a handshake. "It was the right thing to do."

The corvid replicated the gesture, running the claw at the end of her wing through Tala's hair. The sensation wasn't wholly unpleasant, but

Tala was glad when it was over. "*That's* something you don't hear often in a patch-job like this. You sure you're in the right place?"

As the corvid spoke, her eyes never stopped darting around the room. Tala couldn't blame her after what she'd just been through.

"Long story short, no," she admitted. "I'm Veeney Rathers. Nice to meet you."

The corvid gave a squawk in return that Tala assumed was her name. Corvid names had never really made the transition to phonetics that could be mapped to Universal. The best approach was to be consistent in your approximation and hope that particular corvid wasn't easily offended by alien tongues butchering their name.

"Well, Quarack..." Tala paused, looking for a reaction. Quarack didn't react, so she continued. "Do you think they'll come after you again?"

But somebody interrupted from behind before Quarack could reply.

"I see you've reconsidered your stance on starting fights in gauntlet saloons," said Ferric. "What happened to 'alert the authorities and let them handle things'?"

Tala took a single calming breath and let her consciousness float outward with it, as she had so many times in the Center's meditation chambers.

"I didn't start this one," she said. "I ended it. And if I hadn't, she could have been killed."

"It's true," said Quarack quickly, wings outstretched to signal honesty. "I was in big trouble. Where's the wind blowing today?"

Ferric ignored the traditional greeting, opting instead for a steady glower.

"A sapient was in need. I acted. Where's the issue?"

Ferric's neck tightened with the effort of holding back a litany that Tala assumed couldn't be said in public. Instead, he turned to Quarack. "A question, if you don't mind. How many omnipads do you generally carry?"

Tala frowned, confused by the non sequitur. Beside her, Quarack was trying to shrink out of her field of vision. Then it clicked. Tala's hand snapped out and gripped the corvid's shoulder again, digging her fingers in tightly. Now that she knew to look, she could see Quarack's many pockets bulging with rectangles of various sizes that were almost certainly former property of The Blunted Cleaver's patrons.

"I helped you," said Tala, feeling slightly ill.

Quarack wrenched hard against the hold, flapping her wings in Tala's face, but it was like tossing meteorites at a planetary shield.

"Hold her."

Ferric wrapped his arms around Quarack's wings, forcing them down. She squawked indignantly, and Tala realized with some chagrin that they were drawing attention again. Quarack must have noticed too, because she quieted at once.

"Would it help if I said they deserved it?" she said in an undertone. "No? Well, a couple upstanding sapes like yourselves seem like just the type I'd be happy to work out some sort of deal with."

Tala ignored her and slid one of the omnipads out of Quarack's tunic.

"Hey, that's mine!"

"This one, really?" Tala looked it over. "Little odd that the shell has Norvik writing on it. And these others, they're all yours too?"

"In every way that matters."

"Somehow, I doubt the Cleaver's staff will share your perspective."

"C'mon. Don't call this in. I'll make it worth your while."

Tala opened her own omnipad's scanner program and held it to Quarack's arm, right where the wing tapered off into the wrist, ignoring the three-eyed glare boring into her. After a few seconds, a high-pitched chime sounded and information started scrolling across the screen.

There was a criminal record. A long one.

"Veeney." It was Ferric's voice, gentle, but insistent.

With a sweep of her finger, she moved on to Quarack's employment history. The list of jobs was almost as long as the list of indictments, starting with a delivery job at XCo six years ago (Tala checked the year twice; corvid ages could be hard to estimate, but Quarack was twenty at most). Now she was a registered freelancer. A pilot.

Nobody you can trust will agree to fly a Renegade, Ferric had said. Quarack didn't even clear that bar. Her criminal record proved as much —though despite the long catalogue of run-ins with the law, larceny was overwhelmingly the most frequent charge. By freelancer standards, that was almost *spotless*...but she burned that thought down before it could develop further. Hiring a pilot was a desperate move. Taking on a thief was several gates beyond that.

"Veeney."

This time she met Ferric's eyes, indicating receptiveness.

"Let's hand the corvid over to security and go. We're drawing eyes."

"Fine," she said. "Did you at least get some names out of the barkeep?"

"Better. He made me a list with—" Ferric frowned at his empty hand and reached into his pocket again. "Darkest Hell, it was right here."

He saw the list at the same time Tala did—held tightly in Quarack's clawed fingers. Two of her eyes were watching them in amusement. The third was focused on the rumpled sheet of scrawl.

Power swirled in Tala's body, awaiting direction.

"Give that back," Ferric said, with soft menace.

"These are..." Quarack tried to slip free of Ferric's grip and failed. "These are all pilots. You two looking for a pilot?"

Ferric dragged his hand down Quarack's wrist, fingers tightening. She twisted to the side, still reading.

"I hope this wasn't your first patch of soil." Quarack's feathers shook with distaste. "If *Hani Qar* is on here…"

Tala couldn't help herself. "That bad?"

"Awful. Can't fly her way through—" she jerked her hand out of Ferric's grasp. He caught it again immediately, but she'd maneuvered him a few centimeters further from the list. "—an open field. Doesn't help that she insists on flying an alvear-made ship with only two arms."

"We can determine that for ourselves," Ferric ground out. "Tala, there's no reason to trust any of this."

Quarack squawked indignantly. "I know what I'm talking about. I owe you for pulling me through the snapweed, so I'm giving some free advice. Though if your bony friend thinks he's too high-plumed—"

"Let her talk," said Tala. Like a persistent headache, the notion from before was back. It was the same breed of idea she used to have, the ones eighteen years of discipline instilled by the Center had quieted but not quite stifled.

Being held as she was, Quarack missed Ferric's skeptical look. "Araem?" she said. "Bribed their way through their mastery exam. Has some native talent, but they'd rather sit than soar, if you catch my meaning. I don't even *know* this name, not a good sign. Oh, Golranisabul Sinavecelomere. His ship hasn't passed its safeties three years running— besides, you'd be trusting a bug. Colavel's not too bad, if you don't mind living quarters that smell like engine leakage. Keep telling her to get those vents fixed, and don't get me started on the kitchen…."

Tala let the corvid talk, only half listening as her finger moved across the omnipad's screen. On a whim, she accessed Quarack's service record.

"—last client is over at that table, actually. You can ask them—I mean, *anyone* can tell you…"

It was crazy. Maybe her worst idea so far. The kind you pointed to when the situation exploded in your face, to say *this was our first mistake*. But the more she tried to dismiss it, the more strangely appealing it became.

"Pause," she said in her best command voice. Quarack cut off at once, which was far more gratifying than it should have been. "You really made the Orion-Jukali intercluster trip in nine light-days without an onboard Enhancer?"

Quarack blinked at the sudden change of subject, but then her eyes lit up. "Eight point two, by my computer," she said proudly. "I usually have a healthier respect for event horizons, but I was dipping low on options."

Even Ferric looked impressed. Tala sent him Quarack's file with a swipe of her finger—then, as his hands were busy, held her omnipad in front of his face. The service record was longer still than the criminal record, and near the bottom, a small entry had been highlighted in rich, verdant green: *Ritji Blockade: Runner (uncompensated).*

Tala had followed the incident at Ritji closely, devouring the Universal News Broadcast's reports as quickly as they'd been put out. It had been two years, but the holos were fresh in her memory like she'd seen them yesterday. Three fleets of dark warships hovering directly above Ritji's major population centers, dispatched to cut the planet off from galactic trade and starve it into submission. Gunvessels littering Ritji's atmosphere like leaves, trailing smoke and fire. The blockade had lasted eighteen centralized days before the GAF had broken it. Eighteen days that Ritji had needed to survive without a functioning supply chain.

It would have been worse, UNB reports had stated, save for the efforts of a number of freelance pilots, who had risked their lives to slip beneath the blockade and provide what little their ships could carry.

The balance within Tala's head shifted.

"We need a pilot," she said. "According to your service record, you're capable enough. Are you available?"

Ferric made a choking noise. Quarack's three eyes met Tala's two, suddenly all business.

"Could be," she said. "Gotta say I'm a *much* better choice than these shellfeathers." She twisted her neck around to look at Ferric, who still held her in a death grip. "Can you pay?"

"We're prepared to pay what's fair," said Tala evasively, wishing she still had access to the Center's bottomless accounts, or even her family's holdings. She just hoped she had enough barter to get them to another planet. "But you'll need to give the omnipads back."

To Quarack's credit, she shrugged without the slightest chagrin.

"Wait, hold up." Ferric looked like he'd swallowed a sporefruit whole. His eyes swiveled back and forth between Quarack and his list of pilots, which he'd managed to snatch back. "You're being serious right now? You actually want to hire *her*?"

"Well, 'want' is a strong word," said Tala, with more certainty than she felt. An Agent's role was to apprehend criminals, not work with them. "Problem is, I don't think we're going to do better than her."

The Center would never have signed off on such a thing. But it was to the Tenets she'd sworn her oath, not tradition. There were hard lines never to be crossed, but surely she could accept help from a dubious sapient or two without opening the hangar doors to full Renegadehood.

Besides, if she had to rely on a thief, she could do much worse than one who'd run the Ritji blockade.

CHAPTER EIGHT

THE ΛQUILON

A small, smoldering fear had crept its way into Tala's chest and rooted itself there, refusing to be dislodged. It had manifested as soon as Ferric was out of sight, a persistent whisper that he was the only one left. He wasn't far—merely too protective of his powersuit to trust the courier company with its delivery. Perfectly safe. At least, that's what Tala kept telling herself. But it was one thing to say, and another to listen.

She and their new pilot had continued on to Asur's small hangar complex. Based on what Tala had gleaned of Quarack thus far, she'd expected to find her ship docked in some secret underground shipyard, staffed exclusively by shifty-eyed characters who took pay only in surreptitiously distributed bribes. Reality was more mundane; even the walk to hangar forty-nine was short and uneventful.

The hangar door was an intimidating rectangle cast in plasticrete with the number splashed across it in faded yellow paint. At a jaunty wave from Quarack, it slid upward with a soft, grinding sound, old machinery straining. Her wing's motion continued, stretching in a grand flourish toward the waiting ship within.

Tala did her best to be impressed and failed miserably. The ship's lilac-painted prow was large and bulbous, like a ring adorned with a precious stone too big to be anything but unwieldy. It tapered off briefly before widening again into the main body of the ship. There was heft to it, like it had bloated itself on cargo, stuffed full until it was forced to expand to its current, squat proportions. An old model. Cargo cruiser, fifth tier. It would be winning even fewer races than beauty pageants.

"There she is," Quarack declared with an auctioneer's enthusiasm. "The *Aquilon*."

Tala stepped inside the hangar, ducking under one of the *Aquilon*'s long thrusters. The walls pressed in close, struggling to hold all twenty-seven meters of ship. What little space remained mostly belonged to the three-pronged docking control mechanism.

Quarack tapped a taloned hand along the hull. "She's outfitted with all the tech you'll need for any sort of business, legal or otherwise. With me at the helm, we'll outrun or outfight whatever your mind can conjure. Of course, it does depend a bit on what your mind is actually capable of conjuring. I'm speaking under the assumption your imagination is somewhat lacking; you seem a bit stuffy—no offense."

Sadly, Quarack's chances of outflying what plagued Tala's mind seemed slim. She didn't fear what might happen to her, but rather what she might do to others.

"Well," Tala said, "if you fly even half as well as you seem to think you can, the job's as good as done."

Quarack scratched her beak side to side in agreement. "See, I knew there was a reason I offered you the opportunity to fly with me. How about we take this to the next level and I give you a look inside?"

She ducked under one of the large triple port burners that formed the ends of the *Aquilon*'s two broad, stubby wings, motioning for Tala to follow. The corvid moved with an extra spring in her step as she rounded the ship. Coming to a particular patch of hull, she darted forward, contorting into a position beneath the ship that made it seem like her legs were trying to start an intimate relationship with her face. "The best part is down here! Exterior switch should be..." she felt around blindly, "right around, here-ish! Whoops, that's not it. Just a scratch in the hull— pecking asteroids. Gimme a sec."

While Quarack groped around, Tala eyed the ship speculatively. What might Quarack have installed, to warrant such a grand introduction? Beyond extra plating for impact protection, ships didn't get much built into their hulls. Even dedicated bombers fired from front-facing launch ports these days.

Quarack cawed in triumph, then quickly scrambled away. A thick, rectangular block of gray-blue metal shot out from the bottom of the ship, ringed by four mechanical clasps. Lurimite. Known for its remarkable durability, efficient sublimation of force, and stubborn resistance to even the most expensive fabrication methods. Also for its unpleasant smell, redolent of burnt plastic dissolved in ammonia.

Nose wrinkling, Tala stepped back. Quarack seemed unperturbed by the stench. "My pride and joy! Custom high-impact landing gear, optimized for any and all open terrain."

Whatever Tala had been expecting, it wasn't that. It took her a few seconds to sift through the implications before she found her voice. "Gear like that's the dangerous kind of illegal—for good reason. You could completely circumvent port facilities. No customs, no registry. Total freedom of movement."

Tilting her head, Quarack tapped her beak in laughter, "Well, *yeah*. That's kinda the point."

Tala's hesitation must have shone through (and been heartily misinterpreted), because Quarack hastily added, "And I know plenty of mods are slapped together with half a fish and some cooking oil, but this is the real deal. Field-tested it myself more times than I'd care to admit without a full sweep for listening devices. I've got a sape who handles these things for me. It's why I'm on this rust heap of an edgeworld— Sobeik likes his anonymity."

Tala cast a look around the hanger, feeling a jolt of reflexive panic as she noticed, again, that Ferric was missing. "So they've done more work for you beyond the landing gear?"

"Oh, I've got the works here. Whatever mods I could afford to stuff inside this old junk heap. If you wanna see more, follow me."

Tala's mind jerked into a nosedive, spiraling through various illegal modifications and dangerous weapons. Most of the worst were ruled out by the *Aquilon*'s size alone, but there was still a worrying list of possibilities. Still, she'd already decided her need was enough to warrant turning a blind eye to many things that would have driven her to action in the past. There was no harm in seeing what the corvid had to offer.

"All right," Tala said. "Let's see it. Once we're inside, we can talk payment options."

"Options, eh?" Quarack rested her head on her right shoulder. "I've dealt in barter before. In fact, most of my work is in goods I've personally appropriated. Keep that in mind—I'm pretty good at eyeballing what something's actually worth."

They passed under the other wing to reach the cargo bay doors. Stopping in a pocket of space between the ship's front section and one of the rear thrusters, Quarack dropped the entry ramp with a tap on her omnipad.

The *Aquilon*'s interior was surprisingly dingy. For someone who'd spent so much time on expensive mod work, Quarack had put little care and effort toward basic ameneties. The bulbs above were bright but spotty, one in three dark or dim. The walls were metal, without projector screens. Even the air inside had a stale taste to it, like it had been kept stewing in a bottle for a few lifetimes before being uncorked.

"So," Quarack said as they entered, "what can you offer?"

Tala had expected that question eventually. She had only one thing worth enough to charter a ship for any real length of time, and no amount of guilt would change that. She shifted from foot to foot, testing her bearings. The ship's floor was smooth, almost to the point of slipperiness. Her answer came carefully, a balancing act of sticking to the truth and avoiding suspicion. "My partner and I, we've been trying to get off-planet. It's only recently that we got our opportunity. We came across," she hesitated, trying to really sell it, "a dropship. Military-grade. A bit damaged, but mostly intact. Whatever happened, nobody's coming for it —if they were, it would be gone by now."

It wasn't often she envied her family, but she would have given a great deal for their talents now. Barter was in her blood, going back five generations. It had made them wealthy, extremely so, trading mainly in fusion core generators of all types. Her mom, dad, and sisters could sell you the sweat off your own brow—at a good markup. She loved them, but in an abstract way, born more of thought than feeling. Though they hid it well, she imagined they felt the same. It was hard to maintain a deep wellspring of emotion for so long, over such distance.

There had been visits—brief ones, during which they'd always been kind. But they'd never quite grasped that Enhancing was to be used only for the good of the Coalition, and not for personal gain. Her powers hadn't been granted her to help expand her parents' already thriving businesses. They'd met her refusals with equal parts confusion and determination. How could they understand? Though Tala's power had been hers since birth, there was no genetic component to it. Her family had never felt the weight of the responsibility they came with.

Quarack squinted at Tala for an uncomfortable amount of time, leaving her wondering if she'd made some small mistake; somehow let too much truth bleed through her words. But the look of scrutiny vanished almost as abruptly as it had arrived. "I should be able to work with that. Sobeik would do some pretty humiliating things for that type of scrap. If it is military, it'll have a scanning scrambler. That alone would be a tidy profit. Odd for the GAF to leave a transport unclaimed, but I suppose we are in the hinterlands—all the competent officers probably left for Central Cluster long ago."

"How long could two passengers fly for, on salvage like that?"

"Here's how we'll do this," said Quarack, "I'll step out for a sec and comm Sobeik. He'll send some sapes to check your info. Supposing the lead pans out, he'll give me a price, and we'll fly for as long as the money holds."

That plan involved more trust than Quarack deserved. If just one of the sapients involved decided to take the ship and run...

"Don't worry." Quarack blinked all three eyes. "Sobeik and I have a long working relationship. He wouldn't short me for some quick profit."

"You trust him, then?"

"Don't know if I'd break out the T-word, but he's not dumb."

Tala let out a long exhalation. Time and options were tight, and if she was going to go for broke, she might as well do it by betting on a sapient's better nature. "Fine," she said. "I'll send you the coordinates. It won't be hard to spot."

She input the numbers into her omnipad's short-range messenger. A noise like a ravenous bird of prey sounded as Quarack's own omnipad received it.

"Got it," said Quarack, not turning as she walked farther into the ship. "Feel free to wander. I'll be back in two taps of the beak. Just keep clear of my quarters and don't break anything!"

Without waiting for a reply, she vanished down the corridor to the right. Tala stared at her omnipad, hoping she hadn't made a mistake. Every decisecond this Sobeik spent checking for the ship increased the risk of a poorly timed update to the Index.

Tenet sixty-eight, she reminded herself, shaking away her misgivings. *The choice is yours to freeze or tend the flame.*

Tala waved open the first of the corridor's two doors. Sleeping quarters, cramped but well furnished. An ancient-looking bed capsule with a clouded glass dome and a small stack of self-inflating pillows took up most of the room. A low, plastic-alloy table and a sonic shower unit covered what remained. The projector screens were set to a simple, solid drab green, but the occasional small flicker confirmed that the color was indeed simulated. The room was serviceable, if not luxurious. The sort of room someone on a tight budget would squeeze into as a compromise for life in an expensive city.

She didn't linger long. Across the way was another unmarked door. Tala waved her way inside, hoping she wasn't wandering into Quarack's quarters. It was, in fact, a room much like the first—with one notable exception. Projected across every wall was a corvid, very clearly male, in only the barest suggestion of attire, swaying and strutting across the walls. For the first time in recent memory, Tala found it impossible to even form a thought. She stood slack-jawed, waiting for her brain's backup generator to kick in.

"Oh good, you found it." Quarack had returned. "Saves me the trouble of figuring out how to warn you. I haven't bothered to fix the projectors yet. It's always worth a laugh."

"It's, um, it's something," Tala managed. She finally tore her eyes away from the oddly mesmerizing scene. Quarack stood in the doorway, claws folded around her omnipad. Her eyes darted between Tala and the screen.

"There are three more berths, counting mine," she said. "So there's some flexibility there—unless this one ignites your interest."

Tala, not knowing how to respond, and wanting to leave before the projections took up permanent residence in her subconscious, just nodded in reply. She followed Quarack back into the corridor. From there, the corvid continued her tour, eyes never straying far from her omnipad.

After exploring the last berth, Quarack led Tala on an expedited tour of the ship's bow: sealed cockpit doors, a run-down kitchen with open bags of carbon concentrate formula stacked beside a food synthesizer that wheezed like an alvear on life support, a washroom Quarack made sure to mention was human-compatible, and another room marked only by the words *KEEP OUT* in dripping red paint. From there, they moved down the ship's spine to the rear.

"Primary turret's up there," said Quarack as they passed a narrow ladder. "Now that's special, got it off a scrapped Torandian Desolator-class. Some bigshot War-marked's private warship. Custom job, so planetary security never notices just what I'm packing."

Tala made a noise she hoped conveyed the appropriate amount of interest. Quarack preened.

The shield generator was next, dense clusters of worryingly time-worn wire bent tightly into a compressed spire. From behind the thick, glass-paned door, it looked like a small castle of steel and filament. They didn't linger long, as the sharp crackling of current made for an unsettling dissonance of sizzles and pops.

"It works fine," was all Quarack said to Tala's questioning look.

Next stop was the engine. A bulky older model, all stacked boxes of insulation shielding and hefty hydrogen processing pipes. The engine itself looked like a standard deuterium-based fusion model, with glowing plasma caught in a whirling magnetic prison. Of everything they'd viewed so far, the engine, while old, appeared the least distressed. Nothing was as dangerous on a ship as a bad engine—if the safety features failed, it was basically a high-powered explosive.

Though the location was less than ideal. The *Chollima* had been designed to keep Tala near its engine at all times, but the *Aquilon*'s was tucked in the back, away from the quarters. Not a huge distance, but every centimeter lost them a bit more efficiency. She'd have to find a closer room to occupy.

Quarack wasn't paying much attention—either to Tala or the engine. In fact, the fervor of her taps had only increased. The clack-clack-clacking was the only noise coming from her guide, so Tala interjected. "Where to next?"

"Ah, just in here. There's a lot of ship left." Quarack beckoned her down a cramped pathway, winding into the *Aquilon*'s guts. The passage opened into another small room, a maze of clustered cables and tubing that wobbled perilously. Several tubes vented ominous black smoke.

"Life-support modules," Quarack explained without stopping—or commenting on either the smoke or the grim, sulfurous smell.

Near what must have been the very edge of the ship, Quarack came to a halt. The corridor ended in a small chamber dominated by a large metal trapdoor. Probably the entrance to the cargo bay, though given everything Tala had seen, it could just as easily have led to something dangerous and/or illegal.

Quarack ran a claw down her beak. "Cargo hold's through there, but as usual, the important part's what you can't see. If you need to move anything sensitive...well, let's just say the floor isn't the bottom of this particular crab can."

"Shielded?" Tala said. It had not slipped past her that Quarack's compartments might work just as well on more humanoid cargo, should the need arise.

"Scanproof, lead-lined, fully sealed. The works." Quarack stretched her neck, slowly rotating her head in a full circle, then compressed her omnipad and clipped it to her belt. "Well, that's all the interesting stuff. Shall we call it here?"

"I'd prefer to see the rest, if you don't mind," said Tala, hoping to come across as more interested than dubious.

"We can take it slow, if that's how you'd rather play it."

Quarack shrugged her feathered shoulders and wheeled about the way they'd come, this time taking a different path. Agitation was leaking from her posture; there had to be something bad about the ship Tala hadn't seen yet.

"So, where do you want me to fly you?"

"The plan hasn't quite taken off yet," said Tala. Not for lack of trying on her part; she'd been working out a destination since she'd left Neea. Just as with Frael's gift, she'd made a frustrating lack of headway.

"As you like. Aimless drifting works for me, but you're paying the same rate either way."

Quarack lapsed into a rare silence after that, even while showing Tala the *Aquilon*'s energy coils. The flow of current was sharp and bright; a vivid blue corona clinging to interconnected strands of tightly curled glowing metal. Although it was behind a protective screen, the effect was eye-searing.

"Ocular shielding seems a little lackluster."

Quarack didn't answer. For someone who'd been loudly boasting half an hour ago, she'd gotten strangely quiet.

"And the coils are fully functional?" Tala prodded.

"Right, the coils." Quarack tapped her beak noncommittally. "Could use a tune-up. They'll be fine for now."

She was already walking toward the engine room. Tala scrambled to keep up, blinking away the dimness that followed turning away from that intense, burning light.

"You're an odd one, you know that?"

The suddenness of Quarack's remark caught Tala off guard. "I could say the same," she replied with more confidence than she actually felt. She'd never done undercover work, but a GSB operative she'd once shared a shuttle with had divulged a few trade secrets. Among them, that confidence was often the difference between being believed and being shot.

"I suppose you could," said Quarack. She was walking faster now; they'd swerved around the engine room entirely and somehow found themselves back in the main corridor, near the ship's entrance. "I," she continued, "am odd in ways that make sense, when taken together. My eccentricities tell a story. A nonstandard one, perhaps—more storage in there, it's boring—but perfectly understandable, given context."

"Is the implication that I don't?" Tala asked warily, as they reached the string of corridors leading back out of the ship.

"Not at first." Quarack motioned her toward the exit and Tala complied. "But I think I've a better sense of you now."

Ferric still hadn't arrived, Tala noted upon emerging into the hangar. Shaking that thought off, she leaned sideways into the hangar wall. She made an effort to keep her posture straight—while it wasn't a Tenet,

Scratch had always said a slumped back was a symptom of a slumped mind.

Quarack stopped a moderate distance away. "So," she said, "shall we dispense with the pretext, then?"

"What pretext would that be?" said Tala carefully. She cast her mind inward to that endless tapestry of light, not drawing on her power, but holding it expectantly.

"Your eyes are a little too quick. Noticed it right off, the way you swept the room. Took in the action. Like a practiced thief, or maybe a veteran lawkeeper. Course, you don't seem like a keepie. Most of them have a certain look to 'em. With enough practice, you can pick 'em right out of a crowd. I'm damned good at it." Quarack's talon slipped slowly, deliberately, to her omnipad. She tilted her face downward, obscuring part of her expression from view. "Didn't think much of it when we met. But then you said too much. And *then* my cameras got enough material for a facial scan. From there, it wasn't hard."

Tala forced herself to keep breathing evenly, mouth suddenly dry. Her mind spun like wheels in a swamp, searching desperately for traction.

"Can't imagine I'm big-time enough for an Agent to handle personally, so I figure you're after a bigger beak. Someone I've got dirt on, maybe, or who you think I can lead you to. So, who is it? And where's the rest of your Vanguard hiding? No sense in them skulking about now."

Quarack still thought she was an Agent. Of course—her public information hadn't changed yet. She could still salvage this. Her thoughts began to organize, and with them came options. Lies were an unacceptable recourse; so said the Tenets. It wouldn't be hard to knock Quarack out and flee, but that would mean starting again with a new pilot. That left a third option, a dangerous option. Even more dangerous was the part of her that had begun warming to it. But would the corvid listen? Would she even believe such a story?

Did she care either way, given an opening to be done with the subterfuge? To finally, for the first time since she'd met Arcus, just be *heard*?

"Well?" Quarack sounded remarkably calm for someone who believed herself surrounded by the galaxy's most elite peacekeepers.

"I…" Tala began, stalling for time. Time she urgently needed to think. "I, um. What was my mistake?"

"The dropship. Corrupt and inefficient as the GAF may be, they don't leave their toys sitting around for days at a time. A lost and unclaimed dropship? That payday had my beak itching for a bite. But when something looks too good to be true, it's usually worth taking stock. Shame, really. I was starting to kinda like you. Rare to see someone so earnest keep a bit of fire under the skin."

How ironic, after all her doubts the dropship's value would be enough to see them off-planet. It had been too rich a trove instead. There had to be an explanation Quarack would accept, but Tala's focus was divided. *Where's the rest of your Vanguard?* Quarack had asked. The question had sunk cold ripples past her muscle, dangerously deep.

If only they were with her. If only she'd been dispatched here as an Agent, her friends awaiting her signal to swoop in and arrest their target.

But she hadn't and they weren't. That part of her life was buried and done, and she couldn't keep holding onto it. They were worth more than that.

A rushing torrent of words tumbled out of her as if a dam had been broken, well ahead of her thoughts. "There's nobody here but me, and I'm not here for you. I hadn't even heard your name until you gave it. I'm working outside the Center's authority, and—I'm showing you far more trust than sense. I hope you'll hold your judgment until the end."

The story came loose like thread from a spool: tightly wound to start, but coming freer the more she pulled at it. Her meeting with Arcus. The deaths of her friends. The crimes she'd been accused of, both known and unknown. Quarack never broke her stare or let her claws drift away from her omnipad's surface. She reacted once only, when Tala acknowledged her new designation: a three-eyed blink so fast that Tala would have missed it altogether if she hadn't been expecting it.

When she was done, Quarack stood silent and still for a long time. Then, she answered with two soft beak taps. Once in acknowledgment, once in surprise.

"So that's your story, huh?" she said, finally letting her hand fall. "Not the type of thing most would just out and say. It *does* drop the last few ingredients into what was a very confusing dish. You're either a terrible liar or the best I've ever met. Believe it or not..." the corvid squinted, then made a strange choking sound. "I'm inclined toward the former. Don't worry, we can work on that. If you're on the run, you can't just blurt out your life story the moment someone looks at you sideways."

Tala's body was tight with the tension of conflict deferred. "Did you just...volunteer to give me lying lessons?"

"I'm charitable like that," said Quarack—a likely demonstration of her qualifications.

"What about blasting out an emergency alert?" Tala prompted. "Following the Renegade protocols?"

"I could still do that. How about I let you aboard instead?" Quarack tapped out a chuckle on her beak. "I know some things about running when your whole universe throws empties. Claim it as a victory for sentiment, or just general greed—that dropship *is* tempting, now I know it's safe—but I'll bet on you."

Tala let a smile brush her lips. "Thank you."

"And if you *are* lying and planning to murder me, let's be clear. I can handle you. It's not all overconfidence."

Quarack turned her omnipad around, revealing a remote targeting program. Readouts and controls for a primary turret system—the *Aquilon*'s, presumably—stitched their way across the display, each gun primed and locked onto Tala.

"The photon drill's a little overkill, even for an Enhancer," Tala said. The sheer volume of ordinance pointed in her direction should have made her feel threatened. Yet the knowledge that Quarack wasn't blindly trusting her, that she had an actual understanding of the threat a Renegade might pose, brought more relief with it than anything. Their new pilot was a few notches more discerning than Tala had estimated. More likable, too. Despite Tala's misgivings, Quarack's brazen irreverence was strangely charming.

Her Enhanced ears picked up a familiar rhythm from outside the hangar. Footsteps, weighty but soft, with a slight irregularity between the right and left. The sound alone was enough to give her a shot of calm. Ferric had come back.

Two other distinct rhythms accompanied him, along with the telltale creaking of a transport trolley. They stopped in front of the hangar. "Ferric's here," Tala announced.

"Quite the set of ears," Quarack acknowledged. She turned her omnipad back around. "Of course, if you're wrong, I'm gonna mock you."

"Thanks for the warning," said Tala, chuckling despite herself. It had an unfamiliar taste to it. Not unpleasant, merely using machinery that had spent too long in storage. "Don't open it yet. Let the couriers leave first."

There were three separate thuds of unloaded luggage, the low murmur of conversation, and then the two unfamiliar rhythms retreated with their trolley. Tala nodded to Quarack, who jabbed at her omnipad. The hangar door rumbled upward again. Ferric stood outside with the luggage, magcase floating beside him. As soon as he saw Quarack, his eyes narrowed.

"Hi," said Tala, stepping forward to lift the first case inside. "Good to see you."

"It's been what, an hour?" Ferric took in the *Aquilon* with a long, appraising stare. His expression didn't change. "So this is the ship. Does it actually fly?"

"So I hear."

"And how are you paying for...you know what? Forget I asked." He grabbed a second case. Quarack pointedly did not offer to help with the third, so Tala went back for it. Once everything was inside, Quarack shut the hangar door. Between the ship and the luggage, there wasn't much space left to stand. Tala found herself squeezed up against Ferric, who was still glowering over her shoulder at their newfound pilot. If Quarack noticed, she gave no outward sign, beckoning them to the ramp with a curved, black-tipped wing.

Tala's omnipad vibrated, shaking against her hip with forceful urgency. It was accompanied by three violent, ear-catching dings. Quarack jumped, flapping to keep her balance, and her wing struck the *Aquilon*'s hull. Her omnipad was doing the same. Ferric's too. Every omnipad in the galaxy would be receiving the same message, every hologram dispersing and reforming into the same revolving image: a scowling reproduction of herself, highlighted in red.

After the third burst of noise, a stern, emotionless voice cut in, carefully modulated to avoid suggesting any particular species. *"Uni-News galaxy-wide alert: Active Renegade Index updated."*

She'd expected this. Anticipated it. It still hadn't prepared her to hear that condemnation blasted across the galaxy. It was like dumping buckets of ice into a mountain stream: cold as the water was, it could always get colder.

"Well then," said Quarack.

Ferric's breaths were coming shallow and fast. Tala laid a calming hand on his upper arm. Bad as she felt, it would get a lot worse if Ferric took drastic action.

"Relax," Quarack said, waving a claw indifferently. Her other talon was pointed at Ferric's right hand, which hovered a half-centimeter above the pistol at his side. "Tala told me everything. As long as things stay as they seem, we have an accord."

Ferric had that look again. The one he got when he had something to say, but wasn't going to say it. "Kind of you," he said at last. He was fighting to keep the sarcasm out of his voice, and losing.

"Yes it is," Quarack beamed. She unhooked her omnipad, minimized the emergency alert, and opened what appeared to be a game. Bright balloons floated through a forest, bursting apart into showers of crystals when Quarack popped them. Below, a small, basket-wielding rodent tried to collect the gems before they hit the ground. "You're lucky I'm the magnanimous type. On that note, do you have new omnipads yet?"

"I ran an isolation subroutine—" Ferric tried.

"That's a no, then. Not a bad trick. It'll keep you safe for ten days or so, longer if the law isn't actively trying to put your signals together again. It's not a permanent fix. You'll want these instead."

She produced two omnipads from a fold in her coat. Frowning, Tala took them. Quarack and hidden omnipads were a combination that still didn't sit right with her.

"They're completely clean," said Quarack. "I'll throw them in for free, as an investment into our working relationship."

Tala handed one to Ferric and slipped the other into her pocket.

"Thank you, Quarack," said Quarack, in a passable imitation of Tala. "You're so generous, Quarack. You didn't have to save our ungrateful, featherless hides, but you did, Quarack."

"Are you done?" said Ferric.

Quarack clacked her tongue against her beak. "I suppose I'd better be. We don't have much time. Some sapes are probably looking at that emergency alert and realizing they saw that Renegade heading for the spaceport. The sooner we can leave this dirtball behind, the better. Now I know you're still working on a destination, but we gotta head somewhere."

"We need information," said Tala, stifling a grimace. "Everything there is to know about the *Fountstar* raid and Arcus's supposed death. A lot of that will be classified; we need Information and Assessment files. So, we'll have to go somewhere important enough for a GIAB base, but minor enough that we can still beat their security."

"Security!" said Ferric, voice blowing across her like a gale. "What's your plan, here? Storm a government facility?"

His face contorted with suspicion, but Tala knew she was only glimpsing the shadow of a much larger beast. "No. I don't know. Maybe."

"Maybe," Ferric repeated, grinding the word between his teeth until it was tortured almost beyond recognition.

"We're dead in space right now. If there's information out there that can point us right, Information and Assessment will have it. We need to find something."

"Not like this."

There was a sound like someone blowing a glitter-filled harmonica. It took Tala a few seconds to figure out that Quarack had unmuted her game. The sound repeated twice more as she popped balloons, followed by a whistling clatter as crystals fell into the rodent's basket.

"You need to pick *something*," said Quarack, not looking up from her omnipad. "Preferably before the keepies bust in here, guns blazing. Maybe you big military types don't mind that so much, but I'd prefer not to get shot. Especially since I haven't done anything to deserve it this time."

There was a squeaky, triumphant "*Basket blitz!*" from the omnipad.

"Listen," Quarack continued, "what about Tarous? It's out of the way, it's got a facility, and I happen to know a sape who works there. Owes me a favor, you could say. With the right leverage and a decent sob story, she'd probably be happy to slip us the info you need. No break-ins, no hacking. Not too far, either. Half a deciyear, if that."

Tala glanced at the *Aquilon*'s engines, running a few quick calculations. "I can bring that down to twenty days."

"Strike my feathers from my comb, I'd forgotten about that," murmured Quarack. "Oh, this'll be *fun*. I've never piloted an Enhanced craft! What'll it be, Grumpy?"

Bit by bit, Ferric eased his hand away from his side. "It's not perfect," he said, "but I think I can live with it."

Quarack squawked in excitement as flashing green letters spelling *Frenzy Mode!* splashed across the game's hologram. "Then it's settled," she said between frantic jabs. "I'll warm the engines. You two, load that heavy-looking gear into the hold. Incidentally, how long can your species go without food again?"

"We prefer not to," Ferric said warily. "Why?"

"Oh, no reason," said Quarack. "I just hope you enjoy classically synthesized corvid pastes!"

CHAPTER NINE
THE EMPTY PLAN

Ferric frowned at the tangled wires beneath his fingertips, twisting his lower lip between his teeth. His powersuit was resisting again, testing his skill and patience both. Five years he'd worked on it, and it hadn't yet learned he had plenty of each to spare.

Such a minor problem, to eat up four full days of work. He'd successfully integrated parts stripped from the *Chollima*'s anti-infantry underturrets into the suit's left arm. He'd even managed to sync the gun with a rudimentary targeting system in the visor overlay. That should have been the hard part.

Instead, he'd discovered he couldn't fire the thing for more than three seconds without cooking his arm Serdin-style. The gun had been designed with a shipwide cooling system in mind and no body-mounted system could keep up. Normally, he would have moved on. Three seconds on the other end of a vessel-class gun was enough to reduce just about anything to pulp.

"Just about anything," though, didn't include Renegades.

The suit had started as something to keep him focused between classes, and later, missions. Too much free time left him tense and listless, struggling beneath the weight of something as immeasurably large as it was intangible. He'd figured he could improve on the Center's standard opsuit design. Earn a commendation or two. But the pastime had erupted into full-blown hobby when he'd discovered the Volter Central Resource.

Ferric didn't like to think about what question had frustrated him enough to turn to the Network for help—in fact, he deliberately tried to forget his former ignorance. His search had led him to the Network's largest community of powersuit enthusiasts, followers of the celebrity engineer Maestervolt. He'd found more than an answer to some silly question there. He'd found an unending parade of sapients with their own suits, specs, and goals. He'd found deciyearly engineering contests and bountied design challenges. The suits he'd seen shared there had humbled the junker he'd thrown together from retired Center tech.

It had only honed his determination to excel.

One iteration after another, he and his suit moved ever so slightly toward that classically unattainable goal: perfection. The thrill of progress had settled into his bones. It kept him tinkering long past curfew hours and through training, coaxed him into bringing the suit on missions just so he could use the travel time productively. And a good thing, too—when the world had caved in around him on Neea, the suit had been waiting for him. It could have been under maglock at Modellus's Center, leaving him defenseless. Dead weight.

Ferric had no illusions as to his abilities compared to a fully trained Agent, particularly one with Tala's power. Enhancers were born with a connection to something unknown and he wasn't; he had to make up the difference in other ways. The suit was a mere passion project no longer. It was insurance.

Just like that, his mind was back on Tala. Trying to peer past her eyes to the thoughts beneath. Wondering if he'd be better served fighting his way past Quarack and activating the *Aquilon*'s self-destruct. Because sincerity could be faked, and Renegades were cunning and unpredictable and used your heart against you. Just because she hadn't dropped the act and killed him *yet* didn't mean she wasn't planning to once he'd outlived his perceived usefulness.

She was probably lying. But the situation was odd enough, the risks of disbelieving her high enough, that he'd found himself caught between two versions of reality. In both cases, though, two things held true: First, a Renegade was on the loose. And second, staying near Tala kept him in a prime position to do something about it. Regardless of what he wanted to believe, his duty to the Coalition came first. Always had.

A twist of his thumb and forefinger rewound the holo he'd been referencing. An elderly human—Maestervolt himself—jerked back into place.

"Notice here," he said again, pointing to a small pink circle on the inner casing of an ML-140 power cell. His voice was calm and orderly, with gravitas worn smooth by time. *"I like to mark where I've removed a diode, so I always know what's been where. Good work takes time and a careful eye. If you don't perceive the human color spectrum, I recommend asking a friend to point out the mark I've made here."*

He was short, even for a human, with long, delicate fingers like spiders' legs that danced across machinery with a master's cadence. His cheeks were sunken, but his eyes shone as if marked by distant moonlight. His mustache, which must have had more hair than his scalp at this point, drooped over his upper lip like twin waterfalls, threatening to brush against the wide collar of a jet-black tinkerer's apron.

Ferric watched him remove the offending diode with loving fingers, trying not to feel the slight twinge of jealousy associated with witnessing another sapient's talent. There was no reason to compare himself to *Maestervolt*, of all sapients. The man was a genius, with a galactic following of almost ten billion. It was rumored he'd been brought in for consulting on the suits worn by the Dauntless Guard, the mysterious soldiers that served as the Legislatorium's last line of defense. The Argent Warden, the Sentinel of Oblivion, and the Sable Vigilant—or so they were called, their true identities kept hidden behind their disparate masks. They numbered only three. Three was enough.

"We're swapping in an older model," Maestervolt was saying. *"Something of an antique—but you can sometimes find them in relic shops, or reenactments. You want it manufactured between eight-sixty-one cycle six and thirty-six cycle seven. In thirty-six, they added inhibitors as a safety measure. Good for general use, bad for our purposes. You can remove them if you can't find the right antique, but that's a little more complicated. If enough Volters share this holo, I'll make a tutorial for that."*

"Volters" was Maestervolt's nickname for his fans, one they'd embraced wholeheartedly. Ferric tentatively considered himself a Volter, though he didn't attend the conventions or apply for apprenticeships. He did enter contests when he could, and regularly submitted his schematic to the forums. That was more than most Volters did. The majority didn't even own a powersuit. What bound them together was their common obsession and a challenge from Maestervolt himself: to innovate, create, and learn all they could.

The workstation he'd set up in his new "quarters" (and he used the term loosely) had turned the room into a minefield of loose parts and stray tools. The clutter clashed with his favored wall projection—a pale salmon color with a few subtle perspective tricks to give the illusion of depth. A melding of the complex and the tranquil.

All he had was what he'd taken on the Neea mission and everything he'd salvaged from the *Chollima* before evacuating. In his hunt for useful parts, he'd stripped their former ship down to the frame. He still felt some residual guilt over that, but what had the alternative been? Letting all that tenth-tier machinery go to waste? No. The *Chollima* would have preferred it this way; he was sure of it.

The holo ended with the usual reminder to subscribe, and an invitation to show Maestervolt your powersuit in his laboratory on Peculain. Ferric restarted it.

"Welcome back, Volters. Today, I'll be moving on to part two in my series on power cells..."

As Ferric reached for his soldering stylus, his omnipad chimed an alert. He straightened and wiped the sweat off his forehead. Lunchtime. Without an alarm reminding him when to eat, he'd work right through mealtimes. Today, he'd made do with a breakfast patch on the upper arm through the morning hours (something he'd often been reprimanded for on Modellus) but they weren't meant to replace real food. A pity, given the state of the *Aquilon*'s synthesizer. He sometimes thought he'd rather go hungry. He'd brought a few meal canisters from the *Chollima*, but those were long gone.

Ferric crossed the small chamber on tiptoe, weaving through loose piles of equipment. The door slid open at a wave. He hopped over a small box of welding tools into the *Aquilon*'s central corridor, which was almost as cramped as his room. He did his best not to look at the opposite room, which Tala had taken. She wasn't there now; she spent her waking hours as close to the engines as she could get without frying herself. Vanguard protocol stated that in such situations, it fell to him to anticipate and attend to her needs. It didn't cover the unlikely situation that your squadleader was in the Index, and so Ferric had elected to ignore it.

Such a paltry thing, this half-condemnation. Two possibilities existed: Either Tala was telling the truth (in which case she needed his full and unquestioned support), or she was lying (and killing her was his responsibility). There was no noncommittal middle ground, where proper procedure was to turn a cold cheek while grudgingly acceding to whatever course she charted. His was a comfortable kind of idiocy, thriving on uncertainty and wearing its groove deeper with every repetition. Leaving him in an indefinite holding pattern between the cup and the knife, keeping both options open by committing to neither.

Quarack's contact would end his temporizing, he'd decided. If the facts didn't support a reasonable scenario by which Arcus could have survived his own death, he'd do what needed to be done. It would sit with him forever, but he was a soldier, and he knew his duty.

He wouldn't have to wait much longer—the ship's readouts were registering point two past top speed already. While her fine control needed practice, Tala's connection to the raw power of Enhancement was among the strongest of her generation. It was no accident that she'd gone to Modellus, rather than one of the smaller enclaves.

He reset his meal alarm, then started up a game of *Target Acquired* before he could stop himself. An old habit from a more leisurely time, when every decihour not spent improving his suit *hadn't* potentially meant the difference between life and death. He'd taken to indulging himself while walking—between ship chores and suit work, that was the only time left.

Ferric's omnipad was bright beneath his fingertips as he tapped out a steady rhythm that kept his character's defenses up as it gunned down holographic ships in droves. The effect was surprisingly calming; the rules were simple and nothing was expected of him but victory. All was as it should be.

The last ship nosedived toward the screen and exploded while Ferric's character did a celebratory little dance. He shoved his character onto the tile that triggered the next level—

And collided with something small and feathery, which bounced off of him with a startled squawk.

"A thousand sorries," said Ferric, dipping his head politely toward the diminutive corvid.

"Hey, no worries." Quarack flapped twice, smoothing her feathers back into place. "I should've put the next step before the horizon, you know?"

"Nah, my fault. I was focused on the game."

He shifted awkwardly, searching for the fastest way to leave the conversation. Perhaps a few selfless acts in a long string of broken laws were enough to win Tala's trust, but Ferric had no such delusions.

It wasn't that Quarack was an obvious grifter and criminal, with a moral calculus often reserved for Serdin bureaucrats. That did make her untrustworthy, but untrustworthiness was twenty-to-a-crescent among freelance pilots. You could organize your schedule around it. No, what stuck in his throat with every swallow was her carefree flippancy when it came to Tala.

It would have been hypocritical to condemn the corvid outright for helping her when he himself had chosen the same. But he understood the debris he was threading. Quarack didn't seem to care. She danced around her ship quivering with barely contained mirth, only tearing her eyes away from her omnipad long enough to come up for air. She treated her Renegade passenger like an old friend, without a shred of concern. If she could ignore the danger so completely, what else was she capable of?

He waved halfheartedly toward the cockpit. "Shouldn't you be, uh, in there?"

"At full thrust? Nah. She'll fly herself just fine."

"Then what are we paying you for?"

Quarack's eyes glittered. "You trespass on my ship, you leave through the airlock. As long as you pay, you aren't trespassing."

She tapped her beak, all cheer and jollity, but Ferric hadn't missed the threat.

"How's everything so far?" she said.

"Fine," Ferric lied. Quarack had to be aware of the state of her ship, but some pilots got touchy when you pointed it out. He especially wanted to bring up his bed, which refused to read his omnipad's stored temperature setting. Each night, it defaulted to a temperature that left him shivering and required constant manual adjustment.

"Good, good." Quarack bobbed her head. "So, what were you playing?"

"*Target Acquired*," said Ferric. "It's a rhythm-based shooter with some tactical ele—"

"Played it. Pretty fun. Light on challenge, though."

"Yeah? You beat Planet Two's bonus level?"

"Ah." Quarack clacked her tongue. "Yes, that one was a little tricky. The secret is, you weft-thrust immediately after you clear the starting area—"

"Weft-thrust?"

"Oh, you don't know about weft-thrusting?"

Having basic concepts haughtily explained to him always made Ferric's bones itch. Somehow, Quarack made it so much worse.

"Okay," she began, unhooking her own omnipad. "So you know how you jump forward a bit as you accelerate…"

Quarack launched into her explanation, but Ferric was only half listening. He hadn't torn himself away from his powersuit so he could get lectured on game mechanics. Yet he found no pause in her endless litany with which to politely remove himself. He could only listen while she explained how his preferred watershower setting (just below scalding) impacted…something or other. He didn't need any of this. Games weren't meant to be trivialized with exploits. The challenge was the point.

Frustration and suspicion frothed and mixed below his scalp nubs as she began to demonstrate the art of "tapdodging" on her own omnipad. He was mindlessly *mm-hmm*ing whatever she said by then. With every casual snub disguised as advice, it grew harder to keep it all from boiling over.

"There, that flicker? That's when the i-timer kicks in. It's on a CD, though—"

"She's a listed Renegade."

He hadn't meant to say that, but it was far too late to take it back. *Clumsy*, he chided himself. He sucked in a calming breath and felt his irritation ebb, a process aided by Quarack's immediate silence. At least he'd finally gotten her beak shut.

Quarack's whole body looked tightly coiled, abuzz with kinetic potential. Confusing, then, that her attention wasn't directed his way at all. She was watching her holographic ship blast enemies apart above her omnipad. Curious, Ferric let himself settle into a more combat-ready crouch. Her body shifted slightly, confirming his suspicions.

"That doesn't mean anything to you?" he said, anger growing in the space her silence had left.

"You really want that airlock treatment, yeah?"

The holographic spaceship looped around and shot down another virtual enemy.

"A Renegade," said Quarack. "That human down in the hold, I'm supposed to be scared of her? I don't know who you're trying to fool, nestmate, but she couldn't even palm a Krukki token without recording a full confession and electrobinding herself to the nearest keepie outpost."

Mountains of contrary evidence flashed through Ferric's head—particularly the time Tala had *snapped* electrobinding.

"Plus, Congress is a briefcase full of wrapworms and they've got Uni-news in a jar on their—"

"A briefcase full of…"

"Wrapworms. Didn't they teach you *anything* in that temple you grew up in? Point is, why trust anything those lamers say? You know why the Legislatorium has all those aerial defenses? Because anyone with a glider could float in on all the hot air."

Ferric managed a courtesy smile. "Ha."

"Now, obviously, I'm not gonna fly a threat to the galaxy around. But you two are about as dangerous as hatchling belly fuzz. Why trust some *government* label over my own razor-sharp intuition?"

"Because that's how you're supposed to deal with Renegades." It came out a little sharper than Ferric had intended. For a moment, Quarack's beaked face bobbed up from behind the omnipad.

"Then what's your excuse?"

Ferric's teeth snagged at his lower lip. The question was a good one, and all the more annoying for it. Not for the first time, his thoughts drifted to Tala in the luggage hold, pouring every bit of power she had into the *Aquilon*'s engine. All her usual Enhancements would be gone, leaving only an ordinary—though well-trained and muscular—woman. She'd never be more vulnerable than she was in this moment. He turned the thought over in his mind like a flat stone, polishing it, preparing it to bounce across a lake infinitely wide...

"I don't know," he admitted, and the words didn't come easily. "Maybe I don't have one."

The *Aquilon* dropped out of full thrust over Tarous some thirteen days later, a full two ahead of schedule. That left them with almost three remaining deciyears of paid travel, according to Sobeik's itemized estimate and Quarack's own quoted rates. Ferric was pretty sure that either Quarack was ripping them off or Sobeik was ripping *everyone* off, but he couldn't prove anything either way. He just hoped that whatever they discovered on Tarous, it would be worth having handed over a military dropship to a scavenger.

His powersuit was already packed neatly into his magcase. It waited by the door to his quarters, floating a quarter-meter off the ground. He'd packed the suit first, but even with that distraction removed, the rest had taken a while. Fitting everything of value into one backpack had been an exercise in spatial efficiency. In the end, he'd managed, though the mesh grated out a protest every now and then, and not a single pocket was capable of fully closing.

Quarack cut through the atmosphere in a wide arc, keeping her distance from the planet's designated arrival points that dotted lower orbit. The maneuver never would have fooled more sophisticated planetary defense systems, but those were for important planets, not edgeworlds. Though Tarous was spatially a mere blip from the bright center of the galaxy, it was a longer trip than many other planets thousands of light-years toward the periphery. Gates didn't care about physical proximity.

Not long ago, it would have been Anora in the pilot's seat smoothing their descent while he fumed over her talent. *Vanguard One.* He shook his head, feeling his cheeks mottle. There were no excuses for his old pettiness, and no chances left to make amends.

With a single mighty heave, Ferric lifted his pack, which contained everything he'd brought aboard that their shifty-eyed pilot might be tempted to steal in his absence. Extra power cells, collapsible DL-80, unregistered Network interface, and enough ammunition to stock a midsized outpost. Better to have something and not need it than vice versa, though if he ended up needing all that ammo, they'd have bigger things to worry about.

The ship slowed as it passed beneath a large, pinkish cloud—not gradually, not a deceleration, but with jarring immediacy that left Ferric disoriented however many times he experienced that particular phenomenon. In defiance of the galaxy's natural laws, part of the craft's velocity simply *vanished.* A startled squawk came from the shipwide etherway, and then: *"Am I crazy? Someone come tell me I'm not crazy."*

Ferric sighed. That old classic, abruptly-end-Enhancement-without-warning. Most Enhancers left such pranks behind alongside childhood. Tala had kept it clipped to her belt, ready to use whenever her Vanguard got too complacent. An unsuspecting target like Quarack must have been too tempting to resist.

Childish and a little mean? Yes. Enough of a deviation from Tala's expected behavior to count as evidence that she had, in fact, gone Renegade? Not quite.

He bid his cramped quarters a sharp nod farewell and made his way to the exit hatch, dragging his bag behind him. Now if the landing gear could only keep from suffering catastrophic failure and killing them all—

The ship buckled, sending Ferric sprawling to the floor with a shout. He went one way, his pack went another, and his omnipad somehow ended up beneath him, jabbing at his frontal bone-plate as he landed. Thankfully, it didn't seem damaged. Neither did the magcase, which had automatically adjusted its antigrav settings to keep itself a comfortable distance from any collision.

"Passengers, we've arrived on Tarous," came Quarack's voice, suffused with sadistic glee. *"Please excuse the bumpy landing. I forgot to warn you."*

Ferric got to his feet, rubbing his bone-plate. Leave it to Quarack to respond to a challenge to her childishness in kind.

"Guess I should've seen that coming."

Ferric whirled at Tala's voice, a little too quickly. If she was offended, her face didn't show it. Unlike him, she carried nothing but a small satchel. As she passed Ferric's pack, she lifted it with one hand and tossed it to him. He staggered beneath its weight as he caught it, only barely managing to keep from toppling back over.

"You overpacked again," she said. "If you listened to Tenet fifty-six..."

"Trust me, nobody's listening more than me," said Ferric, trying desperately to remember how that one went. "This is all indispensable."

Tala didn't look convinced. But then, neither did she look unconvinced. Her training precluded such displays.

With a loud hiss, the floor in front of them lowered. A thin strip extended outward from the farmost edge until it touched the ground. Before the process was finished, Tala had already started down the ramp. She'd always been eager to touch solid ground after long flights. Bittersweet memories of better days collecting in his throat, Ferric followed. The ship continued to hiss and sputter around him, little complaints filling his ears from all sides as it settled. Gases vented from several points in the hull. Ferric wondered how many of those points were by design.

They'd landed a fair distance from civilization, in a grassy field—or what had been a field before the *Aquilon*'s landing gear had worked its concussive brand of destruction on the surrounding landscape. The gear worked by redirecting the force of the landing outward rather than letting it be transferred into the ship itself, and that much kinetic energy left its mark on the terrain. The landing had created a shallow crater roughly thirty meters in diameter, interspersed with pulverized torica trees. Past the crater's lip, the mangled landscape gave way to tranquil, two-pronged purple grass and a horizon that was only beginning to darken.

The air filling Ferric's lungs was dry and sweet, with a slight breeze to it that played at his bone-stalks. Stars mantled the lavender velvet sky, shining with soft strength despite the pale yellow sun's best efforts. The effect was that of a gemstone-studded bolt of cloth stapled into place above him. Flies with four wings and bodies like grapes cavorted and somersaulted, trilling their mating calls to the evening. The calls grew louder with each passing second, as if they'd been interrupted by the *Aquilon*'s arrival and were only now starting up again.

"We made it," he said, partly to fill the silence and partly in genuine disbelief.

Quarack chose that moment to emerge, hopping down from the ramp in a motion she'd probably intended to look acrobatic. Her talons dug into the landing-tossed earth and she let out a loud hum of satisfaction. Ferric waved her over wearily.

The lanky corvid glared back at him. "Where I'm from, that's an obscene gesture."

Ferric had his doubts, but didn't care enough to argue. "Sorry. Now get over here."

"Seriously. You're lucky I'm even still talking to you. Normally, we wait a full local day to acknowledge anyone who does that. And even then…" her voice dropped theatrically, "they must perform *the penance*."

She turned back toward the ship and watched the ramp slowly retract while Ferric ground his teeth. Sections of reflective foil unfolded outward like a parachute to coat the lilac hull. Only when every system had powered down did she finally approach, dragging her claws with exaggerated slowness.

"All right, here I am. Who's the party for?"

"We're an hour out from Filtik," said Tala. "We should probably give your contact some warning, right? This 'Silvia'. Or were you planning to show up at her door unannounced?"

"My contact." Quarack's gaze shifted to her feet, one of which was tapping at the ground like it was sending a coded message to some subterranean creature. "Yeah."

"You've been putting us off all trip," said Ferric. He waved toward her again on the off-chance that it actually *was* offensive somehow, but she didn't seem bothered. "It's time. No more stalling."

"But of course." Quarack spread her wings wide, a bright smile on her beak. Her leg was still tapping away. "Nothing would make me happier. Only, I may have misrepresented slightly the nature of my relationship with her."

Ferric snorted. "What a surprise."

"What's the issue?" Tala said.

"Well." Quarack shifted beneath their twin stares, trying to worm her way out from under them. "There's the matter of that favor. Technically speaking, she doesn't owe me a thing. Actually, as long as we're speaking technically, I'm not really her friend either."

"So how are you planning on getting her to give us the files?"

"It's gonna be tough." Quarack clucked sadly. "Really tough. I'd say impossible. Because she also doesn't exist. I made her up."

"*What?*"

"I probably should've led with that, yeah."

"You lied." Tala's voice had taken on a brittleness Ferric had only ever heard after the disaster on Neea. That minor association was enough to make his breath come shallow and fast, fingers curling. Quarack's claws were twitching too, though with barely restrained mirth.

"Maybe a little. Who doesn't?" She paused, taking note of their stony expressions. "You have to admit it's kind of funny, at least."

"This isn't a game," said Tala. "We're hunting a Renegade. We can't afford to waste time on jokes. I thought you understood that."

"And I thought you'd understand that we needed to leave Ipwaan as soon as the alert went out instead of getting into a squawking match with your musclebound friend over there," said Quarack. "I guess sometimes we expect too much from each other. Under the circumstances, I think a well-intentioned lie was more than called for."

"There are no well-intentioned lies," said Tala. "Just the truth, and those too lost to speak it."

Ferric cleared his throat, and Quarack, perhaps looking for an excuse to change the subject, latched onto it.

"For clarification's sake," he said, "You do not, in fact, have any contacts at the GIAB outpost on Tarous?"

Quarack waved a wing carelessly. "Don't much want to, either—probably a really uptight bunch."

"So you tricked your own clients into chartering a flight to a planet neither of them had previously shown interest in. A more cynical sapient might conclude that you'd intended to waste eighteen days of our time. Running up the bill, so to speak."

"I had no intention of—"

"Then you'll be happy to waive the cost of our travel so far."

"I—" Quarack choked on whatever she'd been about to say.

"That sounds only fair to me," said Tala. Her voice was back to normal, neutrality falling across her bearing like an old jacket—somewhat worn, but comforting in its familiarity. "The seed begets the harvest, after all. Tenet seventy-four."

Quarack's head bobbed to and fro between them, searching for leniency and finding none. Her neck gave an odd little shudder as she swallowed. "Fine. We'll reset your ledger to a hundred-thirty days."

"And no more lies."

"Might as well ask me for all the oceans of a cluster's worlds gathered together in a single flask."

"No more lies," Tala insisted.

"No more lies," agreed the corvid grudgingly. A bald-faced lie, if he'd ever heard one. "As long as you stop quoting Tenets at me. I'm done with cheap platitudes. Didn't need them from my parents, and certainly not from you. Deal?"

"Deal."

"Great." Ferric practically growled the word. "Glad we worked that out. Let's get offworld and put together a real plan this time."

"Actually," said Tala hesitantly, "I don't think we should leave quite yet. This planet *does* have a GIAB outpost, after all. We might not have time to put a new plan together."

"Sure we do. Quarack said she'd refund us."

"Time before Arcus strikes again, I mean. It could be a year from now, or tomorrow. It's safest if we find him sooner."

"We don't have anyone on the inside."

Tala's voice was low and stubborn. "I know."

Despite the evenness of her breaths, Ferric felt a tingle of apprehension. More than a tingle. It was bleeding into full-on hopelessness as the full spread of Tala's intent took form. The jut of her chin seemed harsher now, her shoulders more set.

"That's not an option."

"If I thought asking nicely would work, I'd try that. And maybe there's some way to find Arcus that doesn't involve classified intel, but I haven't thought of one yet and by the disciplines, I have *tried*. So yes, it is an option. It's the only one I have."

"A break-in," Quarack surmised, clacking her beak. "I love it. That's what we're talking about, right? Because I'm in."

"The other option would be a direct assault, which we don't have the firepower for—*not* that that would be an acceptable tactic," Tala added hastily.

"A direct assault?" Ferric snapped. His voice was starting to climb the register. "Are you listening to yourself?"

Tala didn't flinch. "I understand how it sounds."

"Do you? Because it sounds like you really want access to those files. You want it so badly that you're willing to betray everything you know to be right in the process." Ferric felt cold metal against his hand and realized it had drifted to his pistol—for all the good it would do against an Enhancer. "What are you actually looking for?"

"Say it then," said Tala. "It's nothing I haven't been called by the rest of the galaxy—"

"May I formally submit that she's making the most sense she ever has?" Quarack said, flapping her wings twice to draw attention. Ferric had almost forgotten she was there. The green-plumed corvid stepped jerkily forward and raised a wing, as if offering testimony to the Tribunal.

"You shut up," Ferric snarled, flashing his teeth. "You're a thief and a liar."

Quarack preened. "I wasn't sure you'd noticed."

Ferric looked deliberately away, at a small copse of torica trees that had survived the landing. Their leaves had been scattered to the first Hell, but the gnarled, honey-gold bark had barely suffered a mark. They must have been ancient indeed, holding vigil over the clearing for centuries before outsiders had landed a spaceship on their heads. Above them, the stars were growing brighter, emboldened by the fleeing sun.

"Nobody will be hurt," said Tala. "I'll slip in, retrieve the file, and slip out. You can decide what to do with me afterward."

Ferric focused resolutely on the toricas.

"*Please*," said Tala, voice cracking. "Ferric, I know I can prove he's out there. Just forward me a little more trust. I don't need much."

It would have been so easy to say yes. It was what you did, when a friend was in need. And whatever else she was, Tala was his friend.

He drew his pistol, the cold metal fitting perfectly against his palm. There was no reaction from Tala, not even a narrowing of those gray eyes. She'd known it would come to this, and she wasn't worried. Why would she be? He'd have to hit her, and even then, it wouldn't take her down.

"I can't let you do it. Raiding a government building goes too far." Ferric thumbed the safety and stared down the sights to the center of her torso. "If you can't see that, it tells me all I need to know."

"Don't." The word was half threat, half appeal. He'd never found either particularly effective. The tactical part of his mind—which ironically spoke with Tala's voice—was telling him that if it came to a fight, he'd already lost. A compelling argument, if a cowardly one. Ferric Untag was many things, but he was no coward.

"Whatever information you're searching for, you'll have to go through me to get it."

She could kill him with a thought. Her familiarity with him was enough to stop the heart in his chest in mere seconds. It would take a Wonder—more specifically, the Enhancement-disrupting energy field they generated—to give him even a fraction of a chance. That didn't change his willingness to fight if it came to it. He'd face his death straight-backed and proud. Like a soldier ought to. The breeze was pleasantly cool against his face. A worthy cause and a peaceful sky. There was dignity in that.

Tala still hadn't moved, her expression as unreadable as ever. He glanced at his magcase. All that tinkering, useless. It was far too late to think about putting the suit on. Would she even have let him trade blows with her if he had? He liked to imagine she'd have given him that chance at least.

"Do what you have to." The corner of Tala's mouth twitched upward, like she'd tried to smile and failed. "I wish you wouldn't look at me like you expect me to hurt you. I don't think I ever could. It'll be harder if they know I'm coming, but I need to try. Goodbye, and thank you for trusting me this far. I know it wasn't easy."

She gave a sharp, determined nod and took a tentative step back. Then another, and another, and still Ferric didn't fire. At last, she wrenched her eyes away from him, wheeling about on her heels to face the deepening sunset and the lip of the shallow crater.

He could call this in. She was too far to keep him from opening a channel with the local GAF base, even if she turned back now. With the planet on alert, she wouldn't even get close to the facility, let alone the files she was looking for.

She knew that. But she was throwing away her one chance to stop him anyway. Jeopardizing her own plan to the point of impossibility—for what?

"Wait."

Tala stopped at the crater's lip.

"You'd really set your chances on fire like that? Jettison any possibility of success out the airlock?"

"Of course. You're my friend." Tala's voice quavered slightly, so slightly that Ferric might have imagined it. "Whatever you think of me, that doesn't change."

"And you really think this will confirm your story?"

Tala did turn at that. Her eyes narrowed on Ferric's gun, which he reholstered. It wouldn't have done him any good anyway.

"I don't know. But I don't have any better ideas either. I'm hoping for at least a lead."

"You'd better hope there's more than that," said Ferric. "Because if I'm not satisfied with what you find, you're going to wish you'd left me on Neea."

Copper eyes met gray and they studied each other for a long, tense moment, neither quite sure what they'd found. There was only the chittering of the flies interspersed with the occasional odd noise from Quarack's omnipad. Ferric watched the reflection of the sun in Tala's gaze sink toward the horizon, casting shadows that grew longer by the second.

Tala broke the silence. "Are you really doing this?"

"I don't want to."

"Then don't."

Ferric weighed that, and decided she meant it. "Thanks for understanding," he said. "I know you'd rather not do this alone, but—"

"She will not be alone!" Quarack shouted. Once she'd made sure she had their full attention, she took several exaggerated, dramatic steps toward them, wings spread wide. "In your time of need, I will stand at your side. Though your friends desert you, I will stay true. I shall be the heartbeats in your chest and the updraft beneath your wings. As hope fades—"

"*Thank* you." To Ferric's relief, Quarack actually stopped talking when Tala cut across her monologue. The smuggler-turned-pilot blinked all three eyes, choking on whatever melodrama had been halfway up her throat. "I don't want to drag anyone else into this."

"Nope. Nope nope nope. If you think you can keep all the fun of raiding a government building to yourself, you're two hops and a broken wing away from sinking. I am *in*."

Tala crossed her arms. "And what exactly would you be contributing?"

"I'm so glad you asked. You really are lucky you hired me. Not only am I a pilot, I also deal in information. The GIAB's a tough seed. Even with special powers, you won't get far going in blind. I can give you building schematics and security memos for…well, you're broke, so how about I knock five days of travel off your total?"

"And you came by these things how, exactly?"

"Wouldn't you like to know?"

"Actually," Ferric said, fixing her with his best incredulous stare, "yes."

"I'm not at liberty…" Quarack squirmed under his gaze, struggling to avoid eye contact. "All right, all right. I don't have it. Yet. But I *do* have friends here, real ones this time. The type that can get you anything you need."

"Criminals?" Tala asked warily.

Quarack bristled, but Ferric didn't believe she was half as offended as she looked. "Businessfolk."

CHAPTER TEN
SKIARAWA

Flying as low as she dared, Quarack brought the ship to a small, deserted island off the Ceralie coast. By the time they'd landed, the horizon was just beginning to brighten. She would've preferred to fly a bit longer, following the rising sun around the planet, but the human had gotten grumpy when she'd set the idea aflight. Waste of a perfectly good prolonged sunrise, if you asked her. At least touchdown had been smooth. The new landing gear was worth every last crescent she'd paid. More, actually, since she'd haggled Sobeik so far down.

She watched through the exterior cameras as reflective paneling covered the hull, an extra precaution in case a Planetary Airborne Patrol unit happened by. "Sleep well, my wings," she clucked. She wasn't one for poetic flair unless insults were involved, but she made an exception for her ship. The *Aquilon* was the wings she'd never had, wings that evolution hadn't withered into uselessness. It represented flight in a galaxy determined to force you to ground.

It was almost enough to let her forget the rest. Corruption. Fraud. Betrayal in several different flavors—the kind that struck at the nest, that couldn't be tossed to Kra as *business as usual* in a slowly rotting galaxy. She hated this ship just as much as she loved it. It should never have found its way to her, but what would she have done without the cursed thing? That part of her psyche was a jumble of contradictions and disorder. Just like the rest of it.

Well, she wouldn't get rich dwelling on ancient history. She'd promised her passengers a floor plan, and by fire or poison, she'd find them one. Her pride was on the line—and more important, five days pay. She leaned back in the pilot's chair, stuck her feet on the dash (kicking away an empty snack casing in the process), and began composing messages to whichever contacts she could pull from memory. Text-only, as was respectful, and individually tailored to each recipient. Sapes responded better to that personal touch.

The Network was monitored—everyone knew that—but individual conversations could generally be counted on to escape notice among the storms of data flowing across the galaxy (Occasionally, this assumption proved false, and then you quickly found yourself before the local courts. Or, if you were really unlucky, the Tribunal). The real trick was avoiding the GSB's notice. That was easier on edgeworlds, where their resources were less concentrated. Even still, most sapes with a crooked bent wouldn't take your business without a preexisting relationship. As in the legal side of business, connections were Eternal.

Hours passed before the replies started rolling in. And what disappointments they were—cocktails of cowardice and small-mindedness, with notes of subservience that lingered bitterly on the tongue. Nobody wanted to make enemies of the GIAB. Dorniot even had the audacity to mock her openly. Seemed like just yesterday he'd been a flunky, nothing but an updraft beneath old Pejagal's wings. Now he was perched comfortably on the roost, already forgetting the friends who'd put him there.

An emptiness in her stomach fell upon her as if by ambush, demanding attention in a rumbling voice. She glanced at the clock, which gave the time in both local and centralized units. It was past dinnertime for her, even as the light of a new day broke over Tarous.

She'd earned a break. Dinner, then. Quarack swung her feet to the floor, noticing the ache in her muscles. Her wings unfolded to their full span, almost scraping the walls, as she stretched indulgently.

The kitchen was by the cockpit, right across from her chambers. Twelfth-tier design, that—all the most important places clustered together. She was soon settled at the table with a bowl of puréed qiarkaw, fishing out the lumps with one claw while alternating between messages and *Falling Fruit Basket Adventure* with the other. The fruit proved to be the more rewarding of the two. The messages were all negative; she was opening them more out of spiteful obligation than anything else. She'd just sent a string of virtual sporefruit spiraling into her basket with a graceful sweep of her claw when an alert chimed. Another response, this one from the Viscers.

Good hunt for my lesser friendling. With the matter laid for our table, we choose prudence to chase. Your inquiries deliver regret that we may not cross over. If your request would permit passing, our feet are burnt, yet recommend disappointment.

It was the best translation she could manage. The Viscers had pretended to be a Torandian front for as long as Quarack had been acquainted, but still hadn't found anyone fluent enough to fake the language. Real amateur stuff. She was almost glad she didn't have to work with them. Almost.

"Good thing I'm getting paid by the day," she chuckled.

"You say something?"

Quarack dropped her omnipad and scrabbled for cover, but it was only Tala. The tall human stood at the kitchen's threshold, breathing hard. Sweat beaded on her forehead, affixing stray hairs against her skin.

"Nope! You know me, not much of a talker," chirped Quarack, hearts hammering at her chest cavity like rats in a compactor. How did a slow, clumsy human keep blindsiding her? "Where've you been?" she said, asking the first thing that came out of her beak to give her mind another few wingbeats.

"Out for a run," said Tala. She made her way to the other end of the table and tapped it. A stool rose out of the floor and she sat without so much as an invitation. Quarack bristled with affront, but gave up when Tala seemed unmoved by her display. "I needed to think. Decide which goals are most important to me, and what I'm willing to do to pursue them."

It still unsettled her how easily Tala had taken her by surprise. The human wasn't even built for stealth: broad-shouldered and muscular, raised in a monastery with every need provided for her. That wasn't the kind of upbringing that taught you—

Something else struck her with all the weight and inevitability of a time-worn ruin that had finally given out. The *Aquilon*'s ramp was equipped with sensors to detect uninvited guests. Nobody should have been able to enter or leave unnoticed. Tala had done both, and the sensors hadn't noticed a thing.

It was easy to imagine the Enhancement Corps as a congregation of stodgy fools only good for pushing ships around and grounding the odd existential threat. Easier still when one showed up and immediately proceeded to push your ship around in pursuit of some existential threat. But it would be dangerous to forget that Tala was more than that. Sure, she spent most of her time meditating in a storage room and spouting insufferable aphorisms. But she was strong enough to beat down three nordok without breaking a sweat and—evidently—quieter than a moonbeam on a still night. She wasn't *just* a human. The sooner Quarack internalized that, the sooner it would stop surprising her.

"You look like your tank just hit empty," Tala said, evidently mistaking her silence for drowsiness. "Find anything yet?"

"These things take time," Quarack deflected, injecting energy into her voice. "Less for me, of course—best-connected sape this side of Peramit."

Tala smiled at that, but immediately clamped back down into neutrality. Quarack found herself wondering if she could read minds.

"How about you? Find your answer?"

"Not sure yet," said Tala. She leaned back slightly, still perfectly balanced atop the stool. "There was always so much to learn at the Center. Starship classifications, chemistry, xenobiology, martial arts, and everything in between. Then they sent me out into the galaxy. Training exercises on Concordon B. Raids along the Btalf-Labryn spacelane. Even flew through a Wonder-generated hurricane. Everything I saw, I saw through an Agent's eyes. The way I was taught."

It could have been residual frustration at her task or a fledgling glimmer of actual respect, but Quarack was surprised to find the human's words had drawn her interest.

"It's still my first instinct to look at things that way. Like a line of empty squares waiting to be checked. This requires a different kind of sight. The galaxy I thought I knew so well, I don't recognize it anymore. There are traps and pitfalls I wasn't taught to watch for, and if I stumble…it's not just me who's left with the consequences. Sorry, I'm rambling. I should let you work."

"No, no, no, no," croaked Quarack. "I'm listening."

"I'm mostly done. I just have to decide whether I can navigate with a new set of eyes. And if I can, whether the benefit is worth the risk. If there's a right answer to be found in that tangle, I haven't found it. And I spared no effort searching."

"Couldn't you just…" Quarack hesitated, unsure of the proper terminology. "Enhance your brain until you—"

There was a sudden storminess in Tala's expression, though formed less of anger than distress. Like some dark thought had breached the surface of her mind and begun to uncoil.

"It's been tried," she said grimly. "That's where the first Renegades came from. They sought to make weapons of the mind, and in doing so, turned their power back on its source. Before all other lessons, we learn to never attempt it." Without warning, she stood. "Goodnight."

"I forgot. I'd never want—"

"I know." Tala's voice was showing the hour now. "I don't blame you. You were trying to help, and I appreciate it. But I think I'd better get some sleep."

Quarack wasn't sure she believed that, but she couldn't see a positive outcome of arguing the point. "Good plan," she said. "I could use some of that myself."

Tala saluted crisply. Quarack clucked and turned back to her omnipad as a new alert chimed, acutely aware of her error. What kind of shell-feathered fool was she, forgetting a thing like that?

This time, her claw hesitated, fighting the combined weight of fruitless past experiences. It would only take a few seconds, but reading was hard when she was already angry about what she'd see. Why not save time and skip the middle step altogether?

She looked anyway, of course. It was not at all surprising to see another perfunctory apology, followed by a flaccid excuse. She was about to close the message when her eyes fell on the next sentence.

She let out an exultant squawk, catching Tala on her way out and hopefully annoying the nordok.

"Told you I'm the best," Quarack said with pride that masked her relief. "I got us something."

Potentially, she qualified to herself, but that was hardly a distinction worth drawing attention to. Why taint the good news with inconvenient accuracy?

Thus far, the village of Renlon had avoided the tide of modernization that had transformed the rest of Tarous. Local fauna darted through alleyways and between boxlike wooden buildings. The podpaths were asphalt, lit by evenly spaced metal spires topped with glowing orbs. The word "quaint" more than came to mind, it bought property there and became a neighborhood fixture. Renlon had been chosen as neutral ground for the meeting, mostly because none of the locals seemed to care what happened in the wider galaxy. Tala was disguised, though a more technologically up-to-date city would have recognized her in deciseconds: an omnipad, sized down to fit against the back of her neck, was projecting a hologram of someone else's face over her own. Great for fooling casual scrutiny from passers-by. Not so great if someone poked her.

Good old Elmeton had come through again. Not personally, but he'd been able to point Quarack toward someone who'd been looking in all the same places with similar lack of success. They'd be meeting him at Talon Grab For Meal, the only corvid eatery in Renlon. The lack of competition hadn't done its customers any favors.

"This menu is grounds for war," Quarack groused. Too much of it was "corvid-inspired" fare for other sapes, completely removed from the real roots of the dish—not to mention any semblance of good taste. "I've never seen such prosaic choices. Tchakhara is a staple of our genesis planet! Why would you ever leave it off the menu unless you were *trying* to insult us?"

Her internal restaurant critic still spoke with Dad's voice, all these years later. Over countless meals, he'd taught her everything he knew—an observation here, a warning sign there. However unwanted they were now, they stayed with her. Hearing Dad still ruffled her feathers, but those lessons were ingrained in her psyche; too much a part of her to shake.

The moment I walked in, I could tell the tastelessness of the decor would carry over to the food, it said in that dry, professional tone Dad had all but patented. Under normal circumstances, she'd have avoided the Talon like her final nest, especially planet lagged as she was. But organizing clandestine meetings was as much a game as the meeting itself, and choosing a corvid establishment (or a butcher house calling itself one) would grant some home-territory advantage, despite it being neutral ground. Every minor edge added up.

She hadn't anticipated just how awful the Talon would be, though. They'd erected some holographic Corvaar-native trees, run "corvid music" through a search program, and commissioned art from someone who'd *maybe* seen a corvid once. Everything was painted in bright colors meant to evoke plumage, which was the most backward way of decorating she'd ever heard of. Her feet hadn't stopped drumming against the floor since she'd entered. There was no home-territory advantage to be found here—only regret.

I have had worse meals, though nowhere that's still open—thanks to the Galactic Health and Wellness Bureau.

Ah, but things had been different once. She'd gotten to sample purple affita off the fourth moon of Concordon A, and she still woke some nights with the taste on her tongue. She'd dined within a glass dome five thousand meters under Seurral's yellowest ocean while two meters away, her assigned chef tailored amuse-bouches to her taste. She'd enjoyed the hospitality of a day-long kirtian treetop feasting resort, where she'd eaten so much she hadn't been able to move the next day. All the top establishments had competed for Dad's attention—*still do*, she bitterly amended. They'd flown from planet to planet and meal to meal, billions clinging to Dad's every word. She'd seen the best of galactic cuisine. Perhaps it was only fitting that she now experience the worst.

Their steward, a stubby kirtian with long, flappy jowls, approached. Quarack turned her beak toward the ceiling, refusing to acknowledge him. "Your table has been prepared, friends," he said. "Your companion is already seated in the party room."

There was an awkward pause. Tala couldn't make the hologram's lips move well enough to talk, and Quarack was still counting cracks. A *kirtian* stewarding a *corvid* restaurant. Had they been unable to find any corvids? Or had all the corvid staff quit in protest?

The kirtian finally gave up on a response. "Please follow me."

Tala obeyed like the trained gibbon she was. For someone with mystical, physics-defying powers, she sure was happy doing whatever she was told. Quarack still wasn't sure what she was adding to the meeting besides risk, but she'd insisted on coming along "for backup." It was a sign of lingering mistrust, which Quarack couldn't argue against in good conscience. She didn't trust them either. Especially the nordok, who was sulking on her ship because something illegal was happening. Idiot.

She followed reluctantly, somehow making it to the room without throwing things. The kirtian waved the wooden door open, bowed low, and stepped aside.

Whoever Quarack had expected to see waiting for them, it hadn't been a lone alvear. Especially one who, if the dullness of his russet exoskeleton could be believed, was currently crossing the chasm between twilight and sunset of his species' unimpressive lifespan.

Her hindbrain prickled at the sight. Dealing with alvear had unique difficulties. They could communicate with each other instantly—much like an innate, alvear-only Network. They could broadcast your conversation to every alvear lawkeeper on the planet, and you wouldn't know until they blasted their way through the walls to arrest you. Seeing one was almost enough to turn her right back around. In her time on the underside of the law, she'd learned to never get an alvear involved.

Instead, she told herself not to worry three times until she was feeling good and convinced. Logically, *rationally*, there was no reason to worry. All alvear broadcasts had to be routed through a hivemother, of which there were mercifully few. While most major planets had one at this point, Tarous was far from major, and the range on alvear communication wasn't interplanetary.

Still, every year new hivemothers were born and exported, and the number of hiveless planets shrank. Someday—maybe even in Quarack's lifetime—there would be no safe havens from alvear omnipresence.

But at the moment, there was only one alvear she needed to worry about. He extricated himself from a truly hideous green-and-orange patterned hammock as they entered and straightened himself as best he could, mandibles twitching with irritation. Quarack didn't usually get that reaction until she opened her beak. There was a *lot* of self-importance packed into that withered, 130-centimeter frame. At his thorax was strapped a long handgun burnished with platinum, barely visible through its sheath. All three of her eyes zeroed in on the weapon's bulging power cell—a gun needed a pack that large for very few reasons, all deliciously illegal. Love at first sight. Her claws fidgeted at her sides. *Not yet*, she told them. *Patience sets the clouds afire.*

She repeated it twice more just to be sure they'd listen, then wrenched her gaze off of the marvelous weapon and looked their potential associate in the eye. Well, eyes. He had twice as many as she did, but she didn't let that intimidate her. "You're the one who talked to Elmeton?"

"I am he," the alvear said, spreading his six arms wide in a gesture of goodwill. The top pair were thicker and shorter than the others. The bottom pair were tipped with twisted hooks. "I must thank you for agreeing to this meeting. It is my hope that we can arrive at a mutually beneficial arrangement. Shall we begin with names?"

Quarack clucked indignantly.

"It was worth the ask." The alvear slid out from behind a table covered in starters, moving with a languid bearing he probably practiced daily in the mirror. "I don't suppose you would change your mind if I enumerated the many successful business relationships that have relied on trust?"

"Nope."

Names were out of the question regardless, but something about this strange, baleful alvear was putting her on edge. It wasn't anything concrete; just intuition, probably the way he moved like an aristo and talked like he'd swallowed a bottle of lacquer. But she'd learned to trust her feelings. The business with Dad had taught her that lesson, and *oof*, had it been a painful one.

Besides, she'd already decided to call him Bugboy.

Bugboy waved his lower arms erratically. "I'm grateful to meet you nonetheless. I had almost given up on finding someone on this edgeworld willing to assist me."

He said "edgeworld" like the very taste of the word had infected his mouth.

"I thought you were offering to help *us*, not the other way around."

"Elmeton intimated that you had need of a floor plan," said Bugboy defensively. "I have one, along with knowledge of their security measures."

"And just how did you get your grubby little—"

"That, I will explain later—and that's an actual *later*, not a scuttle. By the First Hivemother, I swear it."

Quarack and Tala looked at each other. "However you got it, we want it. What's your price?"

"Price?" Bugboy sounded surprised. "I didn't go to the trouble of obtaining a floor plan so I could sell it. It's Bureau files I'm after. Procure them for me, and I will consider it payment in full."

Quarack blinked. She'd been prepared to fight for the lowest price possible, but that sounded a bit too much like "free" in her expert opinion. If her years adjacent to the underworld had taught her anything, that meant a catch. The less obvious it was, the worse it would hit when payment came due. "And if we don't?"

"If you're asking what would happen if you successfully recovered the files that have attracted your interest, and not mine? I don't think they'd ever find your bodies."

Quarack tensed, and Tala's fingers curled into fists.

"Legally speaking, that's not a threat, I don't think," said Bugboy. His demeanor hadn't changed, but Quarack's skin was itching beneath her feathers. "As I haven't stated an intent to harm, but merely speculated on the ease of locating your corpses. No, no, I believe precedent is clear. Interesting, isn't it? That context can add my meaning around an absence of legal intent?"

He took advantage of their silent reply to pop an entire iarr into his mouth and chew thoughtfully, carefully extracting the bone with one of his middle arms. Quarack's internal restaurant critic—still sounding like Dad—thought it looked both mushy and rubbery, which she hadn't realized was possible.

"I seek information on Darfelatulaming Ceowogreffach, the galactic councilor for Hivemother Kitik's brood," he continued through a look of disgust that was directed at either the iarr or the councilor he'd mentioned. Maybe both. "I want every scrap of data that relates to him, however tangentially. Will that be a problem?"

"Not at all."

This was closer to familiar ground. Negotiation was language, skill, and art all simmered in the same pot, and she fancied herself quite deft behind a stove. She'd encountered three types of criminals, each requiring a different approach: the unexceptional thug types, the genuinely frightening toughs, and the effete, genteel sapes you'd swear were model citizens if you met them elsewhere. If you were smart, it was that last group you were most scared of.

But if Bugboy was serious about only wanting some councilor's files, Quarack was more than happy to hand them over.

"If you're gunning for a councilor, I'll even go through it and highlight anything that looks helpful," she said. "Bunch of useless fluffs."

There was real, uncontrolled vehemence in her voice by the end. In all the Coalition's clusters, there wasn't a situation Congress had improved—and plenty it had worsened, betraying the public interest it had nominally sworn to serve. Nothing set her tail ablaze like abuse of authority for personal gain.

So yes, it brought her fierce joy to know that whatever Bugboy wanted with the councilor's files, it almost certainly involved a politician going down in flames.

"Yes. Well." Bugboy shifted his weight uncomfortably. "As you so clearly know how the galaxy works, you should have no trouble securing my data."

"Hand over that info and you've got yourself a deal."

"My resources are not limited to mere information. I also commissioned several items of interest to help bypass bureau security. While I have since learned of their inadequacy, you may find them helpful."

"Let's see 'em."

"I'm afraid we haven't quite reached that stage." Bugboy's voice had *definitely* developed an irritated (and irritat*ing*) buzz. "I risked much to obtain them, and risk more by passing them along. If the raid were to fail, and it was then discovered that *I* had a hand in it... well, you can see how that would be inconvenient. So there is a baseline level of competence that I expect from anyone who—"

"Competence? Look here, Bugboy, I have competence coming out my—"

"*Bugboy?*"

Oops. That had been out loud. "It's a Corvaar term of endearment?" she tried.

A blank stare. "I ask that you keep any expressions of endearment to yourself."

He picked up another iarr. It took everything Quarack had not to slap it out of his hand. Her feet were starting to fidget.

"I was correct, as it turns out," Bugboy continued. "Three-four-two cycle fourteen. Veafa's third Tribunal address. A threat's two essential components are the promise of harm and the explicit involvement of either the originating party or their known associates. As that second component was missing, I think we can continue assured that I have *not* threatened you."

"Follow my beak. I don't care."

Bugboy clacked his mandibles, annoyed. "Even as an academic hypothetical, there is value in—"

"Do you want your files or not?"

"Don't ask questions you already have an answer for. Now, you were about to prove your competence?"

Quarack blinked, thrown. "We were what now?"

"I should like to hear your infiltration plan, if you please."

"Where in the nine winds are we supposed to pull a *plan* from when the whole reason we came to you is that we don't have a layout or security briefing? You want us to put together a plan without that stuff? Because that's impossible."

"I don't expect a point-by-point complete with illustrations, but I'm not about to risk my position by handing sensitive data over to someone who hasn't convinced me they can *think*. At the very least."

"And anyone who can *think*," Quarack mimicked the alvear's tone— well, as best as she could with a beak, "will tell you the same thing. Throwing around a plan without basic intel is a waste of time. And stupid."

"I don't believe you appreciate the precarious nature of my position. You're asking me to put my trust in you—"

"Yup."

"—without knowing how trustworthy you are, or what you're capable of—"

"Lots."

"—for all I know, you're a pair of dirt farmers who decided to try crime over drinks last night."

"You have literally nobody else," Quarack tried. "You came to meet us yourself. All your other contacts turned you down. You're desperate."

"Not that desperate. I am happy to wait another few deciyears for someone *capable* to come along."

Capable. It was that word that flashed through Quarack's mind like Kiraa, the wind of obliteration. Every feather on her frame vibrated with anger. She *was* capable. Best damned pilot she knew, and self taught at that. She'd run the Ritji blockade three times. She'd exposed the corruption of a food critic known throughout the galaxy and left in his ship before he knew what she'd done.

And she wasn't about to lose this deal over some misguided hunt for talent.

"You want capable?" she snapped. "You want something that sets us apart?"

"Why, yes. That's what I've been—"

"Fine. Madame Philosophy, I think it's time we introduced our friend to the sape behind the mask."

Tala stiffened.

"Trust me," Quarack said, not feeling trustworthy in the slightest. "We're gonna show this bug just what kind of special we are."

The element of corvid strategy Quarack had always instinctively understood was the art of *skiarawa*, which in Universal roughly translated to "swerve from nowhere." Thinkers, tacticians, and celebrities had recorded enough on the subject to fill a warehouse full of omnipads, but it really just boiled down to "throw something at your opponent that's impossible to expect and make your move while they're still trying to make sense of it." Corvid wisdom. Best in the galaxy.

"Yeah, this could backfire," she said over Tala's half-formed objection. "But think about what's at stake. You said it best, you don't know how much time we have. Isn't this risk worth it?"

It was a blind shot, cribbed mostly from what she'd overheard from Tala and Ferric's argument, but it found its mark. Tala's resistance crumbled, making her just as predictable as Quarack had pegged her. Her hand began its slow journey to the nape of her neck while Bugboy blathered along about his trustworthiness in sensitive matters and the experience he'd had dealing with "undesirable elements." The way he spoke made Quarack want to introduce him to some undesirable elements of her own—namely, polonium.

"Just so you know, she's innocent," said Quarack, not caring whether or not she was talking over him. "I think. Probably. She's not dangerous, anyway—at least, not to the general public. Try and remember that, yeah?"

"Heard it a brood of times." Bugboy waved his middle arms around. "I am remarkably adept at withholding judgment, so long as—"

The wide forehead and dark, ample cheeks of Tala's holo melted into nonexistence, revealing her true features. Bugboy's reassurances cut off with an odd little warble as his mandibles started shaking like midday club-dancers. He backed away until he hit the wall behind him, lifting his omnipad between them like a shield. Quarack jerked her beak toward the omnipad and Tala lunged, crossing the distance before Quarack could register the movement. Bugboy yelped, the omnipad hit the floor with a clatter, and the coppery alvear's arm was twisted safely behind his back.

"Please!" Bugboy's newfound shrillness warmed her mood considerably. "I'm much more valuable as a hostage, don't—"

"Sorry," said Tala. Confronted with Bugboy's reaction, her face resembled nothing more closely than an imploding star. It made Quarack want to brush a comforting wing across her forehead. She knew the feelings behind the face; she'd felt them herself for a long time after taking the *Aquilon*. "I didn't want to hurt you. Please just listen. The Index is wrong."

"Forgive me if I meet that claim with some skepticism. We—" Soft clicking. "*They* would not conceive of being careless with the Active Renegade Index in such a way. The process involves numerous checks across multiple governing bodies—"

"I've been flying with her for," Quarack made a liberal estimate, rounded up, then doubled the result, "more than three deciyears. As an independent observer, I'll vouch that she's harmless as can be. Girl wouldn't pick the nits off her own feathers. And just so you know," she cut ahead of Bugboy's scoff, "I am a highly reputable pilot! You think I'd work with a Renegade?"

"Given that you *are*, in fact, working with a Renegade, I'd say it's a fair assessment."

He tugged weakly against Tala's grip, perhaps hoping she'd changed her mind, but the broad-shouldered human held firm.

"If you truly mean me no harm, perhaps you'd be willing to allow me a brief recess so I can consider this new development with all the care it deserves."

"I think you'd best stay put for now," said Quarack. For an arrogant old blowhard, it seemed there was actually some courage rattling around Bugboy's graying exoskeleton. "We wouldn't want you rushing off and doing anything stupid."

"I know that isn't exactly helping our case," Tala said into his earhole, "but I'm telling the truth. I'm trying to get into that building to clear my name. If you can help me, I can," she forced down a swallow, an uncommon ripple of feeling that quickly receded, "get you your data."

"And if you *don't*," added Quarack, "we'll blast our way out of here, jump planet, and leave the whole mess for the keepies to sort out. They won't know where we are or where we're going. You might not be so lucky."

"I trust you're familiar with Coalition protocol regarding Renegades?" Bugboy drew himself up to his full, unimpressive height in an attempt to reclaim his lost dignity. "Largely the work of Master Thalix and later refined by the diplomat-professor Reein in cycle eight..."

A dry tedium settled over the alvear's speech patterns, interrupted only when Tala was able to break through a dramatic pause in what would certainly have been the full history of the Renegade Protocols.

"I'm no Renegade. I swore an oath to the Tenets, and I will keep it until my last breath."

"C'mon, don't you see how calm she is?" Quarack scuffed her talons against the floor. "What kind of Renegade wouldn't have already flown into a rage at how annoying you are? I mean, I'm not a Renegade and even I want to."

"Obviously, what you know about Renegades wouldn't fill a snack casing," said Bugboy loftily. "The sensational examples make for better newscasting, but many were more reasonable than you might think. Remarkably persuasive, too."

"If she's so wrong, why have you already made up your mind to help us?" said Tala.

"And how do you draw that conclusion?"

"I let go of your arm half a decihour ago and you didn't notice."

Bugboy's face rumpled in confusion as he brought his arm out from behind his back. He wiggled it like he was trying to confirm it still worked.

"You would have noticed if you'd been trying to get away, or alert the lawkeepers, or fight back. You didn't." Tala shrugged. "I think you might just be desperate enough to work with us."

Bugboy sank back onto the hammock with a long, rattling groan. His eyes darted to Tala and she stared back with a face deader than last week's dinner. Quarack wanted to reach over and shake that girl. Yeah, Enhancers were supposed to be boring, but would it kill her to at least *smile* at a potential client?

They had him, though. She felt it in her lower eye, saw it in his stance and every tiny, exasperated motion. He'd already made up his mind, he just hadn't admitted it to himself yet.

"We will help each other," he said at last, like it had been his idea all along. "And when we are concluded, I will call every bureau in the galaxy to hunt you down. I am not your friend, Tala Kreeth, but I will accept your help regardless. For you too, I think, are desperate."

Tala met his eyes without flinch or flicker. "If you think it right."

Something passed between them. Quarack felt it, the hardening of terms. The moment of agreement all further negotiation would be based on.

The broader strokes of the raid to come occupied the next few hours. Disagreements needed welding, downpoints needed sharpening, allegiances needed solidifying. Plus Bugboy's smug rundown of the "items of interest" he'd acquired—which, Quarack hated to admit, were actually pretty impressive.

Slowly, the beginnings of a plan folded together.

"There's one last piece of business," said Tala much later. Her disguise was reactivated, and its stationary lips lent her speech an unnerving quality. The suggestion that there was more to be done almost sent Quarack diving out of the hammock she'd sprawled into to throttle the offender. The starters were long gone, and the hours were tugging at her limbs. Oblivious to her fatigue, Dad was still shaping his scathing review.

I would happily recommend the Talon to a particular sort of masochist: one with an empty account and a diamond stomach.

When nobody seemed eager to ask what business Tala was referring to, she continued. "You know my name. We're at a severe disadvantage as long as we don't know yours."

"And I have no issue with that state of affairs," said Bugboy.

"What about the many successful business relationships that have relied on trust?"

Quarack almost spat bile across the table—yet if she had, it would've been an improvement on her meal. Did Tala think she was being smart? To sapes like Bugboy, "trusting" was just a synonym for "foolish." How artless would you have to be—

"Trust," said Bugboy slowly, rolling the words between his mandibles. "You seemed to spit on the idea before. Now that it can advantage you, you turn it right back around at me. I have every right to respond as you did." He raised a lower arm. "But an old friend of mine once told me "don't fear the truth, make it your own," and his advice hasn't led me wrong yet. I think I will embrace trust and secure this partnership."

Quarack's throat was making little squeaks she had no conscious control over. Bugboy glanced her way and chittered amusedly, which made everything that much more embarrassing.

"My name," he said, pausing for what Quarack took to be dramatic effect, "is Cernarvitalimun Teomonious."

He waited, all six arms outspread, for some sort of reaction.

"Huh," said Quarack. "Mind if we just call you Teo?"

Disappointment and indignation warred across Teomonious's face and agreed on a stalemate. "You most assuredly may *not*."

Quarack clicked her beak with relish. "Bugboy it is."

CHAPTER ELEVEN

THE OTHER SIDE OF THE LAW

The Galactic Information and Assessment Bureau's main branch on Tarous was an imposing alabaster edifice: three square floors stacked atop each other like supply crates. A two-meter gray fence ringed the outside, a barrier between the building and the sapients strolling along the city walkways.

In front of the facility, Filtik was bustling. But elsewhere around it, the city had receded somewhat, leaving narrow alleys lined with disused storefronts and littered with snack casings. It was to one of these alleys that Tala had directed her driving pod. Face hidden behind tinted glass, she scanned the podpath for passers-by, and found none.

A deep breath of the pod's cold air cleansed her body and mind. Pre-mission clarity had set in: the focus at the razor's edge, the pivot to parameters and objectives. A familiar feeling, from the days when she'd had a full squad of her friends at her back, and the resources of a galaxy-spanning civilization to muster.

Everything had changed, but in the end, it was the same as it had always been: a mission to complete, a wrong to put right. She'd spent her whole life training for it. Circumstances be damned.

"Thank you for choosing Podcaller," said the pod's crisp, synthesized voice as the side door slid open. *"We hope—"*

"Mute," said Tala. The voice stopped.

Being automated, a pod had been deemed the safest way to enter Filtik without being recognized—by either sapients or cameras. Their newfound alvear ally had grumbled bitterly about paying for it, but Quarack had put up such a fuss about the Podcaller logs being able to place her on Tarous that he'd eventually acquiesced.

The pod zoomed away as soon as Tala had exited, off to find another passenger. She was alone in the alley, barely a dozen meters from the facility's fence. A light breeze tugged at the plastic robe she wore. It would not do to linger here—this section of walkway had no cameras, but someone could pass by at any moment. The doubts she'd once found so weighty mingled with her thoughts like light mist: still visible, but unable to impede her.

Her left hand dropped to her side, where her robe was especially bulky. Hidden within the folds was an activation cord. Tala pulled it.

The robe was one of Teomonious's "useful assets." Tala had seen most of the GIAB's security measures before: metal detectors around the perimeter, thermal and visual scanners, the works. But while most security systems scanned for sound, the GIAB had opted for an experimental new technology called a sonar map—or so the alvear's stolen security memo had reported.

"Every centimeter of the interior is constantly being bombarded with sonar waves at a level no sapient ear can register," he'd said when giving her what he'd called simply "the cloak." "Once you're inside, your body reflects those sounds. This allows the computer to pick up your sound silhouette and build a model. But the computer doesn't track the individual sound waves in motion. It can't. It sees where the sound starts and where it ends up. That gives us an opportunity. We can alter those sound waves mid-flight."

Teomonious's explanation had gotten more technical after that, and Tala had gotten sidetracked wondering if Enhanced ears would pick up the high-frequency sound waves. The gist was that the cloak bent sound around it—a blind spot in the sonar map. There was only one issue: the cloak didn't work.

It had performed flawlessly in trial runs. Those trials, however, hadn't accounted for the metal detectors. The cloak needed a high-powered computer running calculations, but a proper computer wouldn't make it through without setting off alarms. Thus, Teomonious had commissioned one made almost entirely from plastic components.

This was where his original plan had foundered upon the limitations of science. A plastic computer was too slow, too inefficient, for the job. But when it came to Enhancers (as Teomonious had explained, practically floating from satisfaction at his own insight), the limitations of science were just another challenge to be overcome.

Tala reached out mentally until she brushed against the point of soft light that was the cloak's computer. An intricate machine, though flimsy —and entirely nonmetallic. It was still mostly unfamiliar to her, but she'd spent the last few days familiarizing herself with it, and her mental conduit was now at least adequate. She directed energy into the computer, pushing it beyond its inherent ceiling.

Assuming the device worked, that was the sonar map dealt with. She wouldn't have to worry about the facility's thermal scanners either. The cloak's plastics had been designed to fool those as well.

Her left arm felt a growing chill where the cloak's plastic electrodes were attached. She reached into her remaining pool of energy and Enhanced her body heat, stoking her arm back to warmth. The cloak's other complication was its power source. Lacking a battery, it was entirely reliant on the wearer's thermal energy for power. Teomonious had warned that using it came with significant health risks, but Tala was confident she could keep her internal temperature up. Enhancing the self was always easiest. Your flesh, your bones, your skin…nothing was more familiar than your own body. The Center's self-reflection exercises had only honed that.

They had no clever workarounds for the guards and visual scanners, not without drastically upscaling the cloak's computational and power needs. Teomonious had provided a detailed holomap of camera locations, patterns, and blind spots. Tala couldn't take the holomap with her, but she'd watched the cameras swivel about on the elderly alvear's omnipad until she could see them when she closed her eyes. It would have to be enough.

She approached the fence at a brisk walk. Her approach vector had been chosen after careful study of the holomap had pinpointed a permanent blind spot just past the fence. Security officers were concentrated around the building entrances, leaving the rest of the grounds relatively unguarded.

Just before the fence, she tensed and sprang, Enhanced muscles carrying her over the two-meter fence. As she crossed the invisible boundary, she braced for alarms, but the silence remained unbroken. Then came the shock of hitting the ground on the other side, right in the center of the blind spot. Or, what Teomonious's intel had identified as a blind spot.

Tala appraised her surroundings. She'd landed by a small non-holographic garden that extended to the front and back of the white stone building. Wide plots of colorful native flowers converged upon a single torica tree, which was shielding Tala from the nearest camera. She pressed herself against it. The golden bark was hard and gnarled, with natural crevices. Perfect for gripping. At least for now, the adhesive she'd brought wouldn't be necessary. She placed one foot on a jutting knot and began climbing. Easy work, even without Enhancement. Like all Agents, Tala dedicated at least four hours to exercise—though lately, she'd upped it to six. As the tenth Tenet said, *any Enhancement is only as great as its foundation.*

When she'd risen out of the cameras' cones of sight, she maneuvered around the narrowing trunk, placing the tree between herself and the building's front. The Filtik late-afternoon crowds would be just as much an obstacle as the cameras had been; once she cleared the fence, she'd be visible to them. The torica's trunk was thick enough to hide her for now, but dwindled to a point near the top. Soon, she could go no higher. She peered out through the leaves at the building's smooth walls. The tree left her short by almost two full meters. Unfortunate, but not insurmountable.

A trivial work of Enhancement opened her ears to the world. Sap moved beneath the torica's bark, the buzzing of the flies grew maddening, and thirty different conversations on the walkway below melded together into a chimera of sound. Quarack was down there somewhere, counting down the seconds before her planned distraction.

She didn't have to wait long.

"You!" The corvid's most attention-grabbing screech cut through the general cacophony, loud enough that Tala winced. "I *knew* I'd find you out with her! You promised you two were done!"

All around the epicenter of Quarack's tirade, footsteps were stopping. Tala had heard enough. She readjusted her hearing, then took in a breath and let it seep slowly through her lips. As the air drained away, so too did her focus on heating her body. Immediately, her arm's temperature plummeted. Another breath. She Enhanced the sturdiness of the thin branch beneath her feet until she was sure it would hold her full weight. The rest went into her legs.

A third breath. Her left arm was shaking now, and the chill had crept into her shoulder. She released her hold on the trunk and stood, balanced, upon the branch. When it didn't bend, she broke into a full run, putting one foot directly in front of the last and batting branches out of the way with her right arm.

Tala leapt, and realized at once it wasn't high enough. With how thinly she'd spread her power, the jump that should have carried her onto the roof had set her on a collision course with the wall just below. She swung her arms to grab at the roof, but her left didn't respond—

Impact. Five fingers dug into the rooftop ledge and found purchase. She dangled there, willing her numb left arm upward while her fingers screamed at her to let go. The taste of exertion hung heavy in her throat.

Her arm still wasn't moving, so she gave up on it. Instead, she poured energy into the one that could. The cold was ever-present, creeping down her shoulder and spreading toward her chest in dark, wintry spikes. But her fingers gripped the roof with new strength. Teeth bared in a silent roar of pain, she lifted herself until her chest cleared the lip and settled on the roof.

She wanted nothing more than to rest, but every second she stayed put increased the chance someone would see her legs dangling off the building and raise the alarm. Quarack's tongue-lashing spectacle could only do so much. So she pushed herself forward until her body was safely hidden, as the chill advanced deeper into her core.

Tala lay still for a full decihour, breathing deeply and stoking her body heat until the shivers stopped. She probed her useless arm, massaged it while it warmed, flexed each finger individually as their function slowly returned. A phantom of the chill she'd banished lingered, a cross between tingling and throbbing.

Once she felt ready to continue, she rose. The roof was flat, smooth stone, dotted with ventilation ducts and cameras pointed skyward. Tala gave the latter a wide berth, counting steps as she walked. At thirty-seven, she stopped. The map had indicated a small storeroom just below her feet—assuming she'd measured correctly.

Tala knelt and pulled a small bottle of water from her pocket, then turned her focus to the roof. It resisted, its light dim and guttering. She hadn't worked much with stone, much less this specific patch. But Tala could bring more energy to bear than most Enhancers, and stone was at least solid. It wasn't like trying to Enhance air. She flooded the roof with power, and though the result wasn't impressive, she could feel the stone become just slightly more permeable.

She tipped the bottle of water, maintaining the Enhancement even as she felt her arm cooling. Teomonious's report had indicated impact sensors meant to detect violent intrusion just below the sheet of rock. Once the moisture shorted them out, they wouldn't be detecting anything.

It was close to twenty seconds before the chill forced her to stop, but raising her body temperature again was an easy matter. She wasn't sure how long the water would take to short the sensors. Quarack had said it wouldn't take much moisture to disable them. She'd seemed the kind of certain that implied personal experience.

Tala counted each moment with the monotonous accuracy of someone who'd spent many meditations waiting out the chronometer. When she thought it safe, she dropped to her knees and ran her fingers along the damp roof, searching for imperfections.

After finding a suitable crack, she focused on her fingers and nails, making them harder, denser, and stronger. The roof put up little resistance as she wormed her fingers in and began the slow process of enlarging the crack, made slower by the need for quiet. In the twenty seconds before the chills returned, she'd managed a small hole, beneath which—to her frustration—a layer of metal was visible.

The process continued in the same pattern: stoke heat, Enhance hands, dig, repeat. Occasionally, she had to dislodge a shard of stone from beneath her fingernail. Blood usually followed, droplets falling into the growing hole. After several passes, she'd managed to work around the metal beam and reveal a hollow stuffed with insulation and dead sensors that ended in a polymeric layer. A hole large enough to accommodate her soon followed.

The polymer was segmented into square tiles, allowing for easy removal and replacement. Hopefully, the ceiling of her target room: a small storage closet. Tala peeled back one segment, biting back the pain in her fingertips, and peered into the room below. It was dimly lit and empty of sapients. She'd measured correctly.

Tala removed another segment and slithered through the gap. She landed soundlessly on the hard, paneled floor between two deactivated waist-high cleaning bots. After a quick scan, she pressed her ear against the door and Enhanced her hearing fourfold. A host of sounds rushed in to meet her: humming electronics, the murmur of disrupted air, the odd, crisp whoosh of doors being waved open. No footsteps, though. At least, not in the immediate vicinity.

Keeping her ear to the door, Tala withdrew three long strips of Enhancer's adhesive from her pocket. Aside from her opsuit, the adhesive was probably the most useful thing she'd salvaged from the *Chollima*. She applied it to her fingers and toes, taking care not to touch anything else. It was cold to the touch, and stung on contact with her fingers' many grazes. By itself, it would last roughly an hour, though Tala could Enhance its chemical reactions to render it inert before then if necessary.

Tala waved the door open and cast a cautious look around, reorienting her internal holomap. The corridor's walls were a dull off-white, etched with geometric patterns that crawled from panel to panel in regimented lockstep. There was a sterility to the air so strong you could almost taste the disinfectant. The central archive was some distance away, but breaching any closer would have been risky; camera coverage would only increase as she neared the archives. However, the cameras themselves were universally directed floorward. Tala pressed her fingers against the wall and began to climb.

Climbing demanded most of her concentration. The adhesive couldn't hold her weight by itself, so she had to give it a little help. Between that, keeping her hearing sharp, and maintaining her body temperature, her energy reserve had reached its limit. Complicating the matter, Enhancing the adhesive made it too sticky to pry herself free from the wall. Making progress meant dropping her Enhancement, moving the newly freed limb, reapplying the Enhancement, and repeating with a different limb. Over and over and over.

As she moved across the ceiling, navigating the cameras proved manageable despite their numbers. Movement was slow, though, and Tala was painfully aware of how exposed she was crawling along the ceiling like an oversized insect, gravity pulling at her limbs. Twice, she heard footsteps ahead and had to adjust her route. Once, they came too quickly for her to escape the corridor. She sandwiched herself against the wall above the doorframe, frantically reaching for an elusive calm as her heart pounded in her chest, loud as a bass drum. A blue-clad Serdin passed right under her, and only luck kept him from glancing back over his shoulder.

The lack of comms was disquieting. She was used to having an open channel, her friends' voices a constant comfort in her ear—however unprofessional they'd been at times. Now there was only silence, a silence that lured her thoughts into darker places if her vigilance lapsed. Even Quarack's voice would have helped; reminded her she wasn't alone. But smuggling an omnipad through the metal detector would have been impossible. The plan was to acquire one eventually, but the facility kept too close a watch on every corridor, every room.

Every room but one.

The generic green carpeting and off-white walls had started running together, making every stretch of building look the same. Doors and windows became points of differentiation, each an opportunity to check against her mental map. There was an increasing heaviness in her head. Once, she took a wrong turn (or had the building changed?) and a corridor ended in a kitchenette. She was forced to backtrack, hemmed in on all sides by the steady *thump-thump-thump* of nearby footsteps.

Her luck ran out just two rooms from the central archive: A door slid open with no warning as Tala was upside-down-crawling past it. She had no chance to run, no time to think, nothing to hide behind. All she could do was freeze and wait to be seen.

"Actually, hold up a moment."

The door finished opening. The sapient who'd been about to walk through, a short human woman with curls the color of red wine, was half turned, looking back into the room. She was clad in the blue uniform of GIAB personnel.

"While you're here, I might as well tell you that your assessments for Operation Cheswah are out of date."

"Already? I modified them an hour ago."

Tala knew an opportunity when she saw one. Counting on the conversation to mask the sound of her movements, she climbed toward the open door.

"They were out of date an hour ago too," said the other voice. This one was deeper, but not human. Nordok, perhaps? "Your work presupposes Eternal Panegyr's command, but Panegyr has been temporarily reassigned to the Haven scenario. Yes, I know," he continued as the human sputtered in surprise. "But there are twenty-three likely destinations for the Biostabilization Matrix, and only so many nearby fleets. Without Panegyr's reassignment, there's a chance we lose the Wonder for good. This is an important one, as you know."

"But—but his fleet! It won't be in position!"

Tala reached the door and tucked herself into the corner between the wall and the ceiling, as hidden as she could be given the circumstances. Her breathing felt overpoweringly loud but an Enhancement to her lung efficiency allowed for shallower, less frequent breaths. Though not an energy-intensive Enhancement, it still took more than she had available, so she was forced to reallocate some of what was currently Enhancing her adhesive. Praying nobody else would enter the corridor, she waited for the conversation to end.

"It's been in position for two deciyears and counting. The fleet cannot strike without a target to strike at—"

"Oh, you *cannot* blame that one on me."

"Of course not. If anyone's at fault, it's Jerus."

"Everyone's saying he's close."

"His investigation is in a perpetual state of closeness. Or so he tells the directorate." The nordok voice was dismissive. "The Praeters are elusive, but not even they can hide an entire planet."

A note of surprise traveled across Tala's brow. Few spoke of Praeters in such matter-of-fact tones. It was hard, after all, to hear reports of savage beast-sapes from the edge of known space and not see them as a rejected action holo plotline. Jiav had always maintained he'd fought one on Kennesor Three, but she'd never really believed it. Oh, they *existed*, of course, but she'd assumed the myths had grown larger on their journey inward.

If the *Galactic Information and Assessment Bureau* was taking them seriously...

"Jerus has a galaxy's worth of collected data on their movements," the nordok continued. "Hasn't it occurred to him to use it?"

A hesitant sigh, one that wanted to be more belabored than a superior's presence allowed for. "It must have."

With a soft pop, the weakened adhesive on Tala's left hand separated from the ceiling. Her whole body jerked as part of it tried to fall while the rest held it in place.

"You hear something?"

Swaying slightly, Tala clamped her hand back on the ceiling and fortified her adhesive. Her breath was frozen in her lungs. Her heart had become a jackhammer; surely they could hear it trying to jump up through her throat.

"Seals must be acting up again," said the woman. "I can put in a request with maintenance—"

"Don't bother. If they couldn't fix it the last three times, they can't fix it now. I'll call in a contractor and bill maintenance for it."

Tala closed her eyes in silent thanks.

"Where was I? Ah yes, the fleet-calc. That's right. Admiral Highwater petitioned the Advisory to take command of Operation Cheswah in the High Warmaster's stead. All aspects. That means intel work as well as fleetside. If Jerus doesn't hurry up, that arrogant narl's tooth might find them on her own. Think about how we'd look then. Keep that in mind as you proceed with your revisions."

"Highwater." Tala could practically hear the woman's brain ticking away, socketing this new information into place. "I'll have those preliminaries rewritten by end of day."

"Looking forward to it," said the nordok. "Gives me something to look through during *Displaced*. Semifinals tonight."

"No spoilers, please. I'm a few segments behind."

The nordok snorted. "Who you rooting for?"

"I like longshots, so Vijubb."

"You're fired." An awkward pause followed by a bark of laughter. "But seriously, see if you can find yourself some standards while you're sketching up the fleet-calc."

"Yes, supervisor." The woman's voice was tight.

"Dismissed. Now get back to work."

Tala watched from above as the woman stepped out from beneath the doorframe and waved the door closed with a halfhearted wiggle of her fingers. She was lost in her own galaxy, nose glued to her omnipad. Tala could have chanted all 154 tenets back-to-back in Torandian and she wouldn't have noticed.

The woman vanished behind another door. Tala was moving before it had fully closed, scuttling to the door at the other end of the hallway. She dangled by her feet to wave it open, taking care to barely brush the edge of its sensor range, and re-adhered her hands to the ceiling. The corridor beyond was empty. *Third door down.* With every meter of progress, her anticipation built.

The small antechamber beyond that third door existed more as a quirk of design than to fulfill any particular purpose. It was little more than three walls and a door of reinforced metal that dominated the fourth: tall and broad, with an embedded six-point security system flashing blue and orange across its face in timed intervals. The last obstacle between Tala and the GIAB central archive, and easily the most formidable.

"The door." She could practically hear the rustling in Teomonious's voice that had indicated embarrassment, back when they'd outlined the plan. *"I have no way through—you're hiveless."*

Tala and Quarack had examined his blueprints and determined that the door was impassable without triggering a lockdown. It was a full meter thick, blast-resistant, required authorized DNA samples (among other things) to unlock, and was watched at all times by the finest security the academy could produce. Pressure plates in the floor monitored the total weight entering and exiting, checking against the computer's estimate. Then, the visitor's credentials determined how much of the archive they could access. With every new detail they'd gone over, the problem had become more daunting, and Tala had increasingly found herself wondering exactly who Teomonious knew, to come by such detailed information.

Quarack had solved the problem within a decihour and spent the remainder of the meeting rubbing it in their faces.

At least hiding wouldn't be an issue, as the door Tala had come through was the only one. She flattened herself against the wall directly above it for what felt like the hundredth time. At least, she thought with a touch of humor, if she ever needed to Enhance a doorframe, she'd be set for familiarity.

Her joints throbbed, and what little blood hadn't already drained from her limbs was trickling into her torso. Though it was probably only a few decihours, it felt like far longer before the door opened beneath her. By some quirk of fate, it was the redhead from before. She didn't look up, engaged as she was in conversation with the hologram of another human.

"—yeah, but you already knew he's a dick," the holo was saying. *"He's not blaming you, right?"*

Tala was already moving, creeping along the ceiling like an upside-down ocelot.

"I don't think so? Hard to tell with him."

"Yeah, I guess."

"Hey, I'm at the archive so I'm gonna go. Thanks for letting me vent."

The woman reached the door. With a quick goodbye, the woman ended the hologram, resized her omnipad, and tucked it into her belt.

"Aleph-two-two-zero," she said, enunciating clearly. Then, more casually, with dramatic flair: "To foibles and follies both, my friend."

A long needle extended from the doorway. The woman didn't flinch as it rested itself against her upper lip.

The cameras' ever-present murmur didn't tell Tala their exact field of vision, so she'd charted a wide berth around the largest cluster. The path should be safe, by her estimates. Unfortunately, she wouldn't be in position when the door opened.

The woman touched the door with one finger, dragging it across the gleaming surface in a pattern Tala didn't try to follow. Light trailed in its wake, tracing its path before fading back to silver. When the woman withdrew it, the door parted. It opened diagonally across, each half sliding into its respective wall.

Arm. Leg. Arm. Leg. The door took less than five seconds to open fully. And Tala was still moving toward the target area, centimeter by slow centimeter. Below her, the woman passed through. The door began closing behind her. Tala was out of position with no time left.

So be it. This had always been the riskiest part of the plan.

There was no safe route past the archive door's security cameras. No blind spots, no way to tamper without triggering a lockdown, no security rotations during which nobody was watching. She'd always known she'd have to get in front of them—a step she would've preferred to take from a more ideal position, rather than meters short of it with a rapidly closing window of opportunity.

Tala concentrated on the humming of the cameras, affixed their positions in her mind, and pushed energy into them. They resisted, as unfamiliar objects always did. Next, she withdrew the Enhancement from her adhesive and ripped her hands free from the ceiling, pushing off with her legs into a half dive, half fall. She'd calculated her trajectory in a twice-clipped moment, substituted the calculations with guesswork, and taken the result on faith. The cloak she held tightly around her to minimize any flapping. She would only be in the camera's field for deciseconds, but those deciseconds were more than enough to scuttle the mission. If she'd mistimed...

Something *gave* within her mind and the Enhancement took. For just one crucial point in time, each lens's tint was magnified. Their monitors would be black, as if the system had suffered a momentary dip in power.

As the double doors ground together, she passed between them, twisting as she did to slap the lower door with an adhesive-wrapped palm. The Enhanced adhesive gripped the door and refused to be ripped free. Her momentum jerked to a halt. If she hadn't also been Enhancing her arm's muscles and joints, the maneuver would have dislocated her shoulder. Instead, she fell, arm swinging her like a pendulum back into the door. Grinding machinery covered the sound of impact as the twin halves slotted together into an impenetrable barrier. She hung there, gritting her teeth against the throbbing pain in her shoulder.

She couldn't hear any alarms. Presumably, that meant her trick with the cameras hadn't yet put the facility on high alert. Just to be sure, she twisted her head to confirm that the central archive hadn't been locked down.

The sum total of Coalition knowledge was a simple off-white, unadorned terminal with an upward-facing emitter. It stood by itself in the center of the otherwise empty room, far too small for the space it inhabited. Yet to her Enhanced hearing, it pulsed with a steady hum that echoed from beneath the floor. The central archive. Contained within its unassuming chassis was everything she'd been searching for. Information. Answers. Hope.

Looking at the terminal's smooth exterior, she couldn't keep a small current of resentment from drifting across her thoughts. At the depths she'd had to stoop to just to be here. At the blank terminal that even now stood cold and unwelcoming, unwilling to open its data banks to her....

The woman stood by it with her back to Tala. She placed her hand over the emitter, confirming her identity. That would be the extent of the room's security—there weren't even cameras. Footage of the archive's data was a security risk in itself. It was just Tala and the blue-garbed operative, alone with the galaxy's secrets.

The adhesive had outlived its use. Tala Enhanced it into inertness and dropped to the floor. She closed the distance quickly and quietly, the way Scratch had taught her. Even if the woman had been listening for intruders, she wouldn't have heard Tala stalk closer and closer.

Authentication complete, the terminal lit up, now projecting its interactive file navigation holo. The woman traversed it with precise gestures, flipping through directories until it expanded, reforming into a representation of Treos Cluster. Parts had already been highlighted in red.

The woman clicked her tongue pensively, unhooking her omnipad. As she lifted it, Tala struck. She cleared the remaining distance with an Enhanced lunge. One leg swept the woman's feet and a blow to the back of the head finished the job as she fell. Tala's other hand caught the woman's omnipad out of the air. *Speed-strength-speed.* It was a familiar Enhancement combat pattern, one Scratch had coached her in relentlessly.

To fuel those few explosive seconds, she'd redirected energy away from shoring up her body heat. Her left arm felt like she'd dunked it in ice water. While it warmed, she tried to look anywhere but at the woman she'd knocked out. It didn't do anything to soothe the guilt skittering through her stomach like a nest of roaches.

"Sorry," she muttered. The apology felt strange in her mouth. Forcing herself to look into the woman's sightless eyes, she tried again. "Sorry." It felt a little better the second time, but still somehow incomplete.

She didn't know how long she had. At any moment, someone else could try to use the archive. That didn't keep her from moving the woman to a sitting position against the far wall. As far as making things right went, it wasn't much, but it felt like something.

The omnipad lay where Tala had placed it, screen bright. It had been unlocked mere moments before Tala had taken it. She scooped it up and entered Quarack's frequency, audio-only.

"Feather, this is Cloak," she said into the emptiness where a hologram would have been. The corvid had insisted on codenames, and Tala hadn't felt like arguing.

"Channel open and secure, Cloak," came Quarack's voice, as carefree as if she were lounging on a sunlit beach. *"Took you long enough. I'm almost back to the ship. You in the archive room yet?"*

"I wouldn't be calling if I wasn't."

"Great! Told you my plan would work. Bet you're glad—"

"I'm currently undetected, as far as I know." Tala decided to get the conversation on track or she'd be there all day. "One," she hesitated, again feeling that crawling guilt, "hostile down."

"Let's do this, then. You got terminal access?"

Tala looked back at the clustermap of Treos and dragged her fingers through it, scattering and dismissing the hologram. The wisps of light swirled and reformed into a series of floating, silver-blue menus. An anticipatory thrill fluttered in her chest. "Accessed and unlocked."

"Grab the icon near the top, the one that looks like a sun made out of cubes."

Tala hesitated, hand halfway outstretched toward the *Renegades* menu heading. "Not seeing it."

"Look harder."

The *Renegades (Deceased)* submenu spread open in front of her, organized from most to least recent. She scrolled twenty-two years down…twenty-three…

"I'm not seeing a file on Arcus either."

"Did you go blind on me? I knew we should have switched jobs."

Tala took a deep breath to settle her rising frustration. How could Arcus be missing from the *central archive*? Had he somehow deleted his file? Furthermore, no suns made of cubes were anywhere to be seen. With a muted growl, she navigated to *Politicians* instead, then *Galactic*, then *Current*. Might as well see if *something* was where it should be. Each submenu selection made the hologram shift and squirm, new lists forming out of remnants of the old. None included Quarack's icon.

"I'm serious," said Tala, scrolling through a slew of unwieldy names. Halfway down, she found the name Teomonious had sent her after, *Darfelatulaming Ceowograffach*, and closed her right hand around it. "I can't find the icon. What submenu should I be looking in?"

"Shouldn't matter. Try Preferences, then Network Communications."

With a jerk, Tala ripped Ceowograffach's file free and shunted it away from the other names. It floated apart from the rest, near the top, bobbing slightly. She expanded *Preferences*. "I don't see *Network Communications*."

"It's right there, how...ah. Clever."

"Care to share?"

"I bet they've disabled file sharing entirely. Smart. Annoying, but smart. I could've handled simple precautions, but this..."

Tala's heart sank. She was so close, practically dying of thirst while waist deep in water. Free to browse whatever she wanted, but unable to take anything with her. Her hand trembled with the desire to *shake* the console until her data fell out. "Are you saying we can't get the data?"

"It sure limits our options."

"Run them by me."

Silence on the other side of the omnipad. Tala glanced furtively at the door, hoping it would keep closed. If it didn't, the whole operation would meet a messy end.

"Keeping individual facilities from infosharing would be shellfeathered," said Quarack slowly. *"There must be a way. Likely hidden, more secure. If I was there—"*

"Stop by if you like," said Tala. "They're really welcoming here."

"Yeah, yeah. Gimme a moment."

Tala didn't wait on Quarack's analysis to start thinking—she could do all sorts of tricks with Enhancement that Quarack would never think of. *Start with the personal.* One's self was the most efficient vessel for power, and therefore the first place to search for solutions. Her first idea was Enhancing her strength and running off with the entire physical databank, but that had so many problems that she dismissed it immediately. Still, something at the core of the idea spoke spoke to her. If she couldn't transmit the data, why not take it with her?

"I hate to admit it, but I've got nothing."

Tala looked down at the stolen omnipad. An organization as paranoid as the GIAB would never allow an unsecured device to remove files from their system. It wasn't even worth testing. If they didn't even have internal cameras for fear of sensitive data being recorded, then what—

Inspiration hit Tala like a meteor across the waking dawn.

"Got it," she said. "Stand by, Feather."

Ignoring Quarack's disbelieving cluck, she opened Ceowograffach's file and banished the rest to the far edges of the holo with a sweep of her hand. The files themselves were superfluous. Always had been. The *information* was the important part. She made sure the omnipad was set to record before turning her attention back to the terminal, and started scrolling.

"Fine, I'll ask. What's your genius idea?"

Knowing Quarack would have to hear herself admit defeat every time they played the recording gave Tala a smidge of smug satisfaction. "You'll find out soon."

Ceowograffach's file wasn't particularly long. Tala saved the recording, then frowned at the terminal. It seemed Arcus's file was above the security clearance of the operative she'd followed in. *Why* was unclear, but there was no question that the file was missing. While frustrating, the mission could still be salvaged. She already had the beginnings of an idea.

"You'd better say, or I won't tell you how to find info on Arcus."

"Look up related files that involve him and try and piece things together that way? Was that it?"

The channel filled with unintelligible corvid grumbling.

Tala pulled up the file on the *Fountstar* raid first. As Arcus was thought to have died there, it might give her a better idea of where to look. Or maybe she could spot how he'd faked his death. Holographic text materialized above the terminal, accompanied by a small video in the corner. Footage from the *Fountstar*'s bridge. Two small ships hung just out of firing range. One was an elongated diamond, black hull barely visible against the backdrop of space. The other looked spherical, partially shielded from view by its three wings that curved around the main body like rays of light circling a black hole. The *Fountstar* hailed them, but was ignored.

While the preamble to the space battle played out, Tala examined the writeup.

Ambush of Enhancement Corps Transit Vehicle 4084/5520-5 [Fountstar]

754 Cycle 16, day 128, hour 14—- 0-2-7-31 Albar Cluster, en route to Modellus Center

Full passenger list

Ambushed by Arcus Boral (Renegade), Amara Vert (Renegade)

Many words had a subtle glow to them, indicating the presence of subfiles—Arcus's name among them. Tala gave it a tentative prod, holding her breath as the databank's floating words once again rearranged themselves, the *Fountstar* raid fading.

Arcus Boral
Born 704 Cycle 16, day 373 (age 72)
Status: Active

More words followed, but Tala couldn't read them. Everything else had blurred into illegibility. Her brain had frozen, eyes flicking back and forth to read those two words again and again. *Status: Active. Status: Active. Status: Active.*

Not dead! She felt her face straining with the effort of keeping neutral, but whether it was laughter or anguish she held back she couldn't say. This whole time she'd been worried about proving Arcus was still alive, and none of it mattered. Because they already knew.

They *knew*. And they'd upended her life anyway.

"Quarack," she said. The omnipad was shaking. No—her hands were shaking. "Are you still there?"

"Who's Quarack? Nobody here but your friend Feather."

"I found Arcus's file. It's worse than—"

There was a sudden deep rumbling behind her. Tala looked over her shoulder, dreading what she already knew she'd see: the great diagonal double door sliding open. She'd run out of time.

With the opening door came calm. That came first for any potential engagement—and there was no way around an engagement once that door finished opening. No room for despair, for blame or worry. No time to wish she'd finished before someone else needed the archive room. There was only a worst-case scenario, and limited time in which to mitigate the outcome. It was as the ninth Tenet instructed. As her mind sank deeper into the battlecalm, she steadied the omnipad, still recording.

"I'll need to tell you later."

She poured energy into her hand, Enhancing its speed. It surged to life, scrolling through Arcus's file, opening two or three new subfiles every second. The omnipad's camera had just enough time to capture each image before she moved on to the next. In her infiltration, she'd smashed countless Tenets and cycles of Enhancer wisdom into shards. That couldn't be for nothing. She wouldn't let it be.

She spared another glance back. A squat corvid stood frozen, framed by the receding door, beak open in shock. Tala met his eyes, then turned back to the terminal. She could feel him staring, could almost sense his turmoil as he tried to process what he saw. When she finished recording, almost four seconds later, he still hadn't moved. Tala saved the video, stored the omnipad (in its smallest configuration) in her cloak pocket, and focused her willpower on the archive itself.

This wasn't part of the plan, technically speaking. But whatever information she'd gotten in her flurry of recording, letting the GIAB look at what she'd been interested in didn't seem like a wise move—especially after what she'd already seen.

Besides, all this information was backed up offsite. She kept repeating that to herself as she waited for the Enhancement to take. Then it did, and she felt the systems melt. Smoke curled up from the terminal through the space her holosession had just occupied.

That did it. The corvid wheeled around and bolted, shouting into his own omnipad. Tala didn't bother boosting her hearing—she could guess what he was saying. Instead, she made a mad dash for the door, which was already closing in an attempt to seal her inside. Legs saturated with power, she bolted through the gap with room to spare.

The alarms—three total—chose that moment to start screaming. All around her, the off-white walls turned a flickering red, with evac routes traced along them at knee height. The cloak was useless now; with no time to avoid cameras, it didn't matter whether or not the sonar map picked her up as well. She reclaimed the energy she'd been pumping through it, and by the disciplines, it was a *lot*. It wove into her muscles, her bones, her organs, sweeping her away in an invigorating rush of power that washed right up against the walls of her battlecalm. She spared some for the omnipad's frame, too. Above all, it had to survive.

The antechamber door barely slowed her down as she burst through in a shower of glass and displaced steel. Neither did the surprised security officer on the other side, who had just enough time to cry out before Tala's lowered shoulder caught him in the chest. His partner, a little further back, at least managed to level his sidearm. Tala slapped it aside and kicked him in the stomach. He fell, and Tala didn't let herself make sure he was all right. She gritted her teeth against the impulse to turn around. Against what was right.

Except that going back would mean throwing away her escape. Damn her, but that selfish desire for freedom was too deeply ingrained. Every mentor she'd ever had was shouting every word of wisdom she'd ever received, and it wasn't enough. She couldn't live up to the oaths she'd taken. So she ran—from her own shame, as well as from certain capture. Toward her best chance at stopping Arcus for good.

Didn't I warn you? It starts with a compromise.

The surprise almost made her stumble. That had been *Arcus*'s voice.

The choices compound, the lights bleed over, and the justifications only run thinner. Eventually, you notice them for what they are—wasted effort.

Despite the danger, she stopped, peering about the corridor. It was empty save for the two prone SOs, yet Arcus's voice echoed through her battlecalm, as scornful and taunting as it had been the day he'd turned her life inside out. She picked up the pace again, trying not to cast wild looks around. He wasn't here. It must have been her imagination's idea of a sick joke.

So take this step downward. Take the next, and the next, and the next as you pursue me. But when you look up and find that the pit you've crawled into is so deep that you can no longer see the sun, do not pretend surprise. It is beneath your dignity.

"Shut up," Tala snarled. To her great surprise, it seemed to work.

Now she wasn't sure *what* to think. Arcus's voice was gone, leaving only a crawling, itching feeling in her ear canals. As if the sound had defiled them, even though it couldn't actually have passed through her ears.

"Didn't say anything," came Quarack's voice from her pocket.

Right. The omnipad's connection was still open. Tala latched onto the distraction at once. "What's my exit plan?"

"Contingency three is looking good. Fieldsmith Airbase is running flight drills and lawkeeper patterns are holding. If you can get on base, you have a clear shot."

In her distraction, she almost passed right by the door she needed. She realized her mistake midstride, and had to throw herself sideways through it. It put up as little resistance as the last door had. "Any advice?"

Quarack's reply was half apologetic, half smug. *"Don't get shot."*

Several bullets caught her in the stomach.

Before she could recover, another round followed the first and the stinging pain in her abdomen spread to her chest and shoulder. Tala reflexively tried Enhancing her personal shielding unit, only to remember she'd left it on the *Aquilon* with the rest of her metal.

"Too late," she managed.

A makeshift barricade of riot shields blocked the narrow corridor. Gunbarrels poked through—either five or six. Tala couldn't take the time to count. Thankfully, they'd stopped shooting. Why, Tala didn't know, but the reprieve was welcome regardless. Her whole front felt like it had been crushed by a stampede. Before the SOs could decide to keep shooting, she kicked through another door and took cover within a side office.

"Cloak! Talk to me, Cloak! If you die, I'll—"

"I'm fine," Tala grunted, brushing glass out of her eyes. A bullet had lodged in her side. Not deep, but more painful than the glancing shots. "Durable, remember?"

Quarack gave a strange hiccup. *"Got it. Yep."*

By breaking through the chamber walls, she could get around the barricade without being shot. Maybe even grab one of the riot shields. Properly Enhanced, those would protect her from most of the GIAB's arsenal. She looked about the office and found a burnished iron light fixture. She lifted it one-handed, switched out her speed for pure brute strength, and smashed it into the adjoining wall base first. It took three heavy blows to make a large enough hole. She pushed through the remnants of splintered wood, crossed the office on the other side in three steps, and started on the opposite wall.

The office door flew open. Tala's Enhanced reflexes spun her out of the path of a stream of bullets that cut through the air she'd just been occupying. As the new arrivals' guns moved to track her, she slid beneath their fire, right into their midst. Five burly SOs wore expressions of naked shock.

Speed-strength-speed. Tala moved like the highwinds of Surol: too fast to predict, too unpredictable to brace against. A series of precise blows downed her opponents one by one, their efforts to subdue her either dodged or shrugged off. There was a rhythm to it, a dance that continued until only one foe remained. She caught a punch with her free hand and tossed the Serdin who'd thrown it into the wall, then swung her other without thinking—

She was still holding the fixture. Her arm froze midswing, the second Tenet swimming to the forefront of her consciousness: *A life taken by hand is a life taken out of necessity.* Enhancers *did not wield weapons*— and in her hands, the fixture qualified. She opened her hand like the metal had burned her and let it fall, bent beyond recognition.

The Serdin had recovered. But he wasn't shooting, or even getting up. Instead, he was talking into his omnipad.

"Renegade," he graveled. "She's a—"

That was all he managed before Tala knocked him out too.

A fourth alarm rose above the other three, mixing together in a discordant clamor that drummed relentlessly against Tala's skull. As she watched, the walls changed again, words appearing in the Universal script. Two words, repeated in flashing red as far as she could see: *ALERT. RENEGADE.*

Shoulder first, Tala threw her body against the weakened wall. It gave way with a loud crack, sending her tumbling into a third office. She had to be past the barricade by now, so she waved the door open and charged through.

She'd guessed right—she emerged behind the shield line. What she hadn't expected was for the barricade to be abandoned. Almost abandoned, anyway. In the center of the hallway was a small metal cylinder—a gas grenade. She turned and ran, holding her breath. That wouldn't help against high-tier gasses, but she trusted the GIAB not to deploy high-tier gasses on their own premises. A door stood in her way and she tumbled through, shattering the panes. Only when she was through the door did she allow herself another breath, and she made it a quick one.

One thing was for sure: her hope of picking up a riot shield had gone up in smoke. But that detail was asteroid dust to her present situation: wounded, deep in enemy territory, tracked wherever she went. There was still so much ground left to cover.

That meant it was time to abandon her infiltration route. There were shorter, more direct ways outside now that being seen no longer mattered. The facility's floor plan was still etched into her memory. She concentrated, drawing lines between herself and various windows as she ran, the bullet in her side pulsing with each step.

A small balcony on the second floor seemed like her best chance. The route was brief and straightforward—down the hall, through the lounge, around the office space, up the stairs, and full speed ahead. Preferably without getting hit by anything too high-caliber. Rivulets of power curled through Tala's muscles as she picked up the pace, making for the lounge at top speed.

A rectangular gunbarrel jutted from behind a side door, one thin, gloved finger already depressing the trigger. Tala threw herself out of its path. She landed well and was balanced again in a moment, but when she whirled to retaliate, the door had already slid shut. Tala eyed it warily, knowing every wasted heartbeat would make escape harder. It would be simple to ignore her assailant, pump some durability Enhancements into her back, and sprint for the lounge. Yet something told her it was a bad idea. A sense of danger had intruded into her battlecalm, putting her on full alert for a threat she couldn't place.

The door whisked open again. This time, Tala caught a glimpse of a tall, black-clad siari silhouetted in the doorway, lightlets aglow with the bright coral-pink of concentration. She flattened herself against the wall as he fired—noticing as she did what had set her instincts screaming caution. She'd seen the trigger pulled, but there had been no customary shattering of the air, no sound of impact. Not even a bullet's midflight whine.

Worse, she knew why, and the knowledge brought with it a chill due only partly to the danger she was in.

The siari corrected his aim, trying to get off another shot before the door closed. Tala reached out to it with her mind, Enhancing the door mechanism's rate of movement. The door slammed shut, catching the siari's arm between it and the frame with an awful crunch. There was a muffled grunt of pain from the other side and the door began to reopen. That was all the time Tala needed to close in and snatch the gun from the siari's hands. A closer look confirmed her suspicions. It was black and blocky, with no chamber, and a familiar small emitter at the end. Anti-Renegade ordinance.

Killing an Enhancer wasn't easy. That went double for Renegades, for whom no stratagem was too twisted to deploy. One inventive Renegade was a match for an entire city's defense force, and then some. Bullets, lasers, and even biological weapons had proven insufficient in the past.

The problem had gone to the Torandian think tanks and occupied the brightest minds in the Galactic Armed Forces' special weapons division, and Congress had funded their combined efforts with as many nova as they could get the votes to approve. The most successful project had been the Irradiator, a small handgun that—while still expensive—could be mass-produced and used intuitively by any sapient with weapons training.

Tala remembered reading the statistics on Renegade violence and how many fewer lives had been lost per cycle after introducing the Irradiator. She remembered being grateful for its invention.

The irony was not lost on her.

Gun in hand, she turned her back on the injured siari and kept running. She took the weapon apart piece by piece, scattering metal bits behind her like drops of blood. The lounge was meters away when three other doors opened in unison, each revealing a figure in black holding an Irradiator. Behind her, she heard three more doors opening as well. Gritting her teeth, Tala crossed the remaining distance in a single Enhanced leap, hurling herself through the lounge door.

Had she been hit? Tala wasn't sure—she couldn't even be sure if they'd fired. If one had tagged her, she was already dead and wouldn't know it for another few decihours.

The lounge was modest but well-furnished, with a skora gameboard projected against one wall and a chrome HeatSync box plugging away in a corner. True, the floor was covered in broken glass, but that was on her.

Outside, six pairs of footsteps were closing in on the broken door. Tala hopped over a particularly dense patch of glass and ripped the HeatSync off the wall. She hurled it bodily out into the corridor, where it smashed against the floor. Machinery and droplets of cyclohexasilane flew in all directions. It was the droplets she focused on, drawing from her hundreds of hours spent memorizing atomic structures. She wouldn't say she was *familiar* with it, but there was enough familiarity to serve as a catalyst for the power she commanded.

The cyclohexasilane pooled on the tile, inert. Not reactive enough to serve her purposes, but close.

So Tala Enhanced its temperature and it burst into flame.

The fire gathered strength as she fed it, warping air and flooring alike. Soon it was a wall of heat and hunger standing between her and her pursuers. The air shimmered and popped, but Tala kept a steady stream of Enhancement pouring into the flames, siphoning off the numerous minor Enhancements that added up to increased durability. None of them would matter against Irradiators.

Tala left the fire crackling behind her as a fifth alarm, shrill and insistent, joined the previous four. The lounge's other door opened with a clipped wave. Workstations on the other side had already been evacuated, consoles and holoprojectors powered down. She skirted the outer edge of the room, making for the stairwell door. Her ears couldn't detect any evidence of sapients on the other side, so she waved it open.

She took the steps three at a time, cloak flapping behind her. It hadn't been made to take this kind of abuse, and it showed. The stolen omnipad kept bumping against her leg, but she was just glad to know it was still there. It took only a few seconds to reach the second-floor landing, and two more to kick the door open when it didn't respond to being waved at.

Four decameters ahead, where several corridors converged, was a small square of light. It stood out like a beacon of hope against the backdrop of *ALERT. RENEGADE* that scrolled endlessly across the walls. Tala broke into an Enhancement-assisted run, then re-hardened her skin and muscles as an SO popped out of a doorway and fired. Regular, shelf-variety bullets, this time. The battlecalm filtered what would have been relief into a bland tactical optimism, even as several bullets found flesh. She didn't let the shooter distract her. Only the window mattered, and it was coming up fast. Tala redirected even more energy into sturdiness—she'd need it. Another bullet lodged itself in her back, causing her to stumble, but she focused through the superficial pain. The gun might as well have been a slingshot for all the power it had to stop her at this point.

Two paces from the balcony window, she leaped. As she did, a bullet streaked past her head and the window exploded into a thousand tiny splinters. Tala barely had time to close her eyes before the flurry of glass mantled her, scoring her exposed skin with dozens of minor cuts and leaving her robe in tatters.

But she was through. A light outdoor breeze played against her stinging cheeks. She opened her eyes to a star-speckled afternoon sky. Behind her, five—no, *six*—alarms still screamed disaster, but the noise was less overwhelming now that it wasn't coming from all sides.

Tala placed both hands on the balcony railing. She took a deep, steadying breath to reinforce her battlecalm.

Then, with a burst of strength, she vaulted herself over.

CHAPTER TWELVE
THE RIVER CONTINGENCY

There was nothing left to do but fall.

No shouting security officers, no gunfire, no life-and-death decisions. Just wind whipping against her ears, almost blocking out the clamor of the building's alarms. Just the echo of what she'd seen in the central archive, grabbing onto every free tendril of thought and dragging it down into the singularity in her chest: the crushing knowledge that proving her innocence had been impossible from the start.

Then her feet thudded against the ground, flattening flowers and leveling landscaping, and the maelstrom quieted. Into a dark corner of her brain it went as the rest came alive with the sole thought of escape.

She'd landed in a garden bed at the facility's front. Damp loam clung to her toes as she made a headlong rush for the fence. While the lawn had been clear, personnel were beginning to arrive from inside the building. Three had guns drawn—thankfully, the mundane sort. The crack of gunfire mingled with the flapping of plastic as bullets struck across her chest and arms, high-caliber enough to leave deep bruises.

Before any more SOs could emerge and open fire, she reached the fence. An Enhancement-assisted leap carried her to the top. Her toes curled around the four-centimeter strip of plasticrete, helping her find her balance.

Before her was crowded city. Though Tarous was an edgeworld, it had not been spared the touch of civilization, with the crowded walkways and brimming podpaths that came with it. Among the crowd, SOs moved with determined precision, directing foot traffic and herding civilians into side streets. The streets were still full enough that they had to have only just begun the process. Then the crowd noticed her, heads turning and eyes widening as she hopped down from the wall onto the pavement below. Murmurs built as their mouths opened, strolling gaits arrested mid-step. There were so many of them. Too many.

Even an agonizing death by Irradiator was preferable to the prospect of innocents killed in her escape. But she couldn't stop. There was nobody to put her faith in; nobody to take up the banner if she faltered. The weight of the omnipad in her pocket was reminder enough of that. Her mentor was Hells-bent on hunting her down. The GIAB had lied to the galaxy. Even Ferric had abandoned her.

She sprinted for the podpath. The civilians scattered as she bore down on them. Some of them were screaming. One kirtian had frozen in her path, jowls quivering like grass in the wind. She shoved him aside, using barely any force—just enough to send him stumbling away.

But not everyone was running. The SOs elbowed and bumped their way toward her, moving against the current rather than with it. They came at her like boulders rolling down a hill: fast and not caring who they knocked down in the process. Thick layers of repulsion mesh covered them from head to toe, and they were just as heavily armed. Tala Enhanced her eyes and zeroed in on their weapons. Just as she'd feared, she spotted at least two rectangular emitters.

Unbidden, her thoughts turned to that gnawing death, delivered without sensation or mark. A shaped ray of self-propagating radiation moving at near light-speed, well beyond even an Enhancer's ability to dodge. She wouldn't even know she was dead until the cancerous cells had spread to lethal levels. They'd shown her the end result at the Center: a Renegade's body, warped beyond recognition.

A few seconds of concentration and she could have disabled them—proper application of Enhancement could destroy most electronics. She didn't have a few seconds to spare, though, and trying would probably end with her getting shot. They weren't shooting yet, but at the rate the crowd was thinning, they'd start any moment. Not everyone would have waited. Collateral damage was accepted practice when dealing with Renegades.

Slamming her foot down hard enough to crack the pavement, she launched herself into the air, clearing the heads of the nearest three sapients. She landed right in the middle of the podpath. Pods diverted around her as the traffic grid's safety protocols instantaneously reacted to the new foreign object in their midst. Two couldn't merge into the new lanes in time and instead slid to a halt. One was an extra-large eight-seater, the other a compact model built for one. She pivoted against the smaller pod and ripped the side door from its moorings.

Tucked into the plush lavender interior was a middle-aged man with eyes like grapefruits and a mouth that opened and closed like a fish that had found itself hurled onto land. "Please don't—" he began, before Tala took his shoulder and sent him tumbling from the pod with a careful yank.

"I'm sorry!" she shouted—the terror on his face was all the harder to behold for its cause.

The pod turned on its own, carefully avoiding the sprawled civilian. Tala moved with it, keeping the pod between her and the SOs, and brought her leg down onto the hood with all the force she could muster. She must have hit something vital, because the pod's movement stopped —and not a moment too soon. The crowd had thinned enough that the SOs had decided they could start shooting. Bullets tore chunks out of the pod's chassis, but it wasn't the bullets she was worried about. She just had to hope the pod was thick enough to insulate her from Irradiator fire.

She kept her body low, letting a couple seconds pass without movement. A plan was starting to map itself out, but the SOs would need to close the distance before she could make her move. For now, a blanket of bullets and an uncertain amount of invisible Irradiator fire had her pinned. Of course, staying stationary for too long was a death sentence in its own right. She could disable the guns a few at a time, but the Renegade alert would soon call down the armed forces and every available lawkeeper, independent included. The SOs moving to flank her were a more immediate threat. Worse, reinforcements were arriving, both through the now open facility gate and from around the sides.

Around her, bits of the pod danced into the air, spinning like droplets from a sprinkler spraying metal instead of water. She drew a breath, first through the skin, then the muscle, then the mind. Harmonizing all three systems.

There was no time left—and if it was already too late, she'd find out later when she started vomiting up blood. She burst from cover in a low sprint, noting with some concern that the podpath was otherwise empty. A trio of SOs who'd gotten a bit too close didn't have time to react before she was among them, laying them out with blows to their helmeted foreheads. As the third fell, she grabbed his limp, unconscious body, confiscated his weapon, and swung him in front of her. It wouldn't necessarily stop the others from shooting, but the SO's body armor would protect her either way. It was tough enough to handle bullets, and more important, lined with a lead-based alloy.

She retreated back toward the center of the podpath. Nobody was shooting yet, but several SOs were breaking ranks and circling behind her. The abandoned pod still sat in the middle of the podpath, leaking fluid from multiple holes. One SO was trying to use it to shield his approach. She held the unconscious body close against the plastic cloak that clung wetly to her skin and prepared to run. If she could make it to an alleyway…

Then she heard it: the sound of a pod. It barreled down the podpath toward her, in defiance of the traffic grid's safety protocols. Her first thought was that the lawkeepers had arrived, but the squat, silver chassis was no lawkeeper's vehicle.

The SOs seemed as surprised as she was, so she took off down the podpath, hoping the silver pod would be distraction enough to help her escape. But she'd taken only five steps when the pod broke from its lane, swerving unexpectedly toward her—and the approaching SO. There was a moment when it seemed certain the pod would hit the officer head-on, but it skidded to a halt with a low hiss just a handful of centimeters from the startled sapient.

"Identify—" he began, before the silver pod's door flew open and smashed him in the face.

If the day's earlier surprises were like tumbling off a cliff, this one was the ground flying up to meet her on the way down. Within the pod sat the last of her Vanguard, with a face like he'd just taken a bite out of his own tongue. Ferric met her eyes and gave a brittle nod.

As the SO leveled his gun, Tala hurled the unconscious body at him and made for the pod at top speed. The officer flopped through the air like a gangly mannequin, limbs dangling, and hit the shooter hard enough to knock him to the ground. Before anyone else could fire, Tala slid through the pod's open door, over Ferric and into the seat next to him.

"Northeast," she said. Ferric didn't argue. He slammed the door behind her and spun the emergency manual guidance wheel as the pod jerked back into motion. Tala focused her attention inward until she'd found and brightened the metaphysical lights that were the pod's engine and chassis. She'd need every drop of speed and protection she could wring out of them.

A pool of wires festooned Ferric's lap, evidence of what he'd done to isolate the pod from the traffic grid and enable manual control. Some of them were attached to his omnipad. The other ends fed into large holes in the pod's inner paneling, through which Tala could see glints of metal.

Ferric twisted the manual steering, sending them careening onto a new podpath—and right into traffic. Other pods reacted at once, peeling away from an inevitable collision however they could. Some sapients lowered their windows and stuck their heads out, shouting obscenities or angry questions, an aural tapestry of shock and fear and miscellaneous noise.

The sounds filtered through her battlecalm, fading to nothing against the quiet backdrop of her analysis. None of her plans for disaster had included Ferric, but with access to both him and a driving pod, her options had opened up some. Assuming he wasn't here to bring her in himself.

"Why'd you come?" she said.

The podpaths had all but emptied at this point, pods clearing before them like dry leaves before a gust. The grid was adapting as best it could, moving its charges away from danger.

Ferric didn't answer her question. "Here," he said, handing her a clothing canister. His outstretched hand joggled as he turned them sharply past the entrance to a sprawling, eight-story megamall.

"Thanks," she muttered, trying to keep her eyes on the podpath while she ripped into the cloak. Even if Ferric hadn't seen her disrobe regularly during their training and field missions, any thoughts of modesty would have lost out to the desire to be free of its sweaty layers. The R&D had probably cost a couple nova, but she shredded it all the same. At least now, if she was killed, her corpse wouldn't be found drowning in plastic.

"One shot penetrated," said Tala, feeling the pain in her side flare up as she let herself notice it. The bullet would have to stay in a little longer; right now, it was doing a remarkable job of keeping her blood where it was supposed to be. "I got lucky."

She didn't mention the Irradiators. If she was dead, she was dead, and there was nothing to be done.

She gave the canister a test spray. The liquid fabric was a muddy green, the color and texture best worn while fixing pipes or rewiring a basement. Satisfied, she began crafting a jumpsuit with wide, efficient sprays. As she was finishing her legs, her stolen omnipad flashed to life.

"*EMERGENCY. Active Renegade last seen in a silver Mormont driving pod. The following districts must follow Renegade safety protocols immediately: Downtown, Rust Row, The Plaza, Industrial. EMERGENCY...*"

The warning continued on loop, calm and robotic.

They were moving fast enough that it wasn't easy to watch the sapients on the walkways, but Tala could see panic spread like a plague through the crowds. Some stared at their omnipads in amazement and disbelief; others wasted no time dashing for the nearest building. Several raised their eyes as they passed, gaping and pointing as their silver Mormont pod whizzed by.

Ferric raised his voice over the endless warning. "They're following us on city cams. Won't be long before we have PAPs on our tail."

Tala acknowledged that with a deep exhale. They couldn't do much about either of those facts. Between omnipresent camera coverage and the oncoming eyes in the sky, their every movement would be laid bare. Even pushing two hundred and fifty kilometers an hour, their fate seemed certain: boxed in and surrounded.

One last spray along the neck finished the jumpsuit. Tala retrieved the omnipad from the remnants of the cloak. "I suppose I owe you a thanks for the rescue too," she said, sliding the omnipad open. She dug in with her fingernail and plucked its data core free from a nest of chips and filament, silencing it for good.

"Don't," said Ferric. He made two drifting turns in quick succession that pushed the pod's Enhanced stabilizers to their limit. The further northeast they went, the narrower the podpaths became. At their current speed, the turns were getting razor-sharp. "I don't deserve or want it. Just tell me where to go."

Tala had come up with a number of contingencies in the outlining stage. Quarack had made her own enthusiastic contributions: semi-coherent plans for dealing with everything from spontaneous combustion to beetle swarms, and even something about parasitic mind control. Overall, Tala had preferred working with Vigdis. He'd always thought of everything.

Almost everything.

They could take two routes from here, both reliant on Teomonious's knowledge of the city. Despite his condescending tone, he'd proven to have both a remarkable breadth of knowledge about the area and the willingness to share it. He'd been a little *too* willing at times, settling into a dry lecture on the history of some unimportant building on more than one occasion.

The airfield was out. There was just too much potential collateral damage, and she'd endangered enough sapients for one day. That left one option, unpleasant as it was.

"Get back on Main and take the turn at Primus. Straight shot from there. Once we're in the tunnel, stop."

She hadn't spent as much time on the city's layout as she had on the GIAB facility's, but she'd done her best to affix a rough map to her memory. It would've been far easier to Enhance her brain until it could hold every detail after a single pass. Not that saving a few hours was worth the consequences.

Ferric grunted his assent and took a hand off the wheel to tap at his omnipad. It was perhaps the least bitter reply she'd gotten from him since she'd been labeled Renegade, but she wasn't exactly celebrating. He sounded almost lifeless. Where was her friend's quiet fire?

The pod slowed as they took another narrow turn. Tala spotted a school on the corner: rows of small, personalized classrooms with their own modular play structures. She hoped the children were safe and calm under the watch of their curriculum monitors. "You could at least," she said, a geyser of feeling bubbling up from the base of her spine, "do me the service of using words."

Ferric's brow wrinkled, a mixture of anger and regret. "I don't really know what to say."

"Fine. Then I'll talk instead." She knew it wasn't the right time. Even with his reflexes Enhanced, Ferric needed to keep the entirety of his focus on the podpath or they'd end up smeared across a storefront. But the words demanded release. They wouldn't be held up for even another second. "I have proof Arcus is alive. They knew it all along; they've known for years. It was right there. I can show you."

Ferric's grip on the emergency steering tightened, but his expression didn't change. "I guess that should make me feel better. I wish it didn't feel so convenient."

"What does that even—"

They skidded around another corner. Ferric winced as the whole pod rattled around them. The podpath was several lanes wide in each direction now, a gleaming ribbon of metal. Main Street. Hundreds of pods adorned the edges, all filled with anxious sapients whose day had taken a terrible turn. Beyond them were shopfronts and offices, flying by in a blur.

That was when, like a shot from the dark, the lawkeepers arrived.

Two vehicles sped out from an upcoming intersection: one from the right and one from the left. They consisted of four powder-blue ovular mounds segmented together into a wormlike shape. Each segment had its own set of wheels—and, Tala knew, its own independent engine as well. Their turns took them diagonally in a snaking sweep across Main. The three pods were set to converge at the tip of the arrowhead.

An attempted live cordon? A sacrificial play? Tala couldn't tell. At their speed, there was no time to think it over. Too late to swerve, too fast to brake.

Tala let it all drain away. Her body weakened, her senses dulled, and the half-formed bruises and bullet wounds she was keeping numb erupted along her skin. Everything she had went into the small light of the pod's engine until it flared inferno-bright.

At the same time—as she'd somehow known he would, through one of those strange moments of clarity that come with decades of friendship—Ferric pushed down hard on the accelerator, the first real hints of life stretching across his features.

They shot toward the rapidly closing gap between the serpentine pods. Before Tala could worry about whether they could make it, they were through—though she would have sworn she felt some paint scrape off the side.

Everything rattled again as Ferric tried to slow down. "Dammit," he muttered. "That was Primus."

Tala stopped a grimace at her muscle. "It's all right. Just take the next one."

She bled power from the engines and sent it into the wheels, hoping to keep them intact through whatever Ferric was subjecting them to. In the rear display, she could see the lawkeeper's pods reorienting to follow them. They were fast little things. Possibly as fast as their own pod, even with Tala putting her finger on the scales. She'd have to do something about them.

There were many ways to break a driving pod, most of them dangerous for their occupants. The wheels would be safest. Each one relied on several magnets at their center for pinpoint control. It was those magnets she focused on, one in each wheel, Enhancing their electric currents until they seized. Between the distance and the unfamiliarity, it almost took too long. But just before they crossed into shooting range, their pursuers skidded out of control, trying in vain to compensate for the impossible. With them shrinking away in the rearview, Tala felt her connection fade.

They needed to reach the tunnel before more joined in the chase.

"I was really hoping," said Ferric, "I'd never have to steal a pod again."

"I didn't—wait, *again?*"

"It's actually kind of funny. Sometimes, I feel like my whole life has been trying to atone for the first one."

"When *was* this?"

Ferric gave no indication he'd heard her. "Turns out I'm pretty good at justifying my actions when I need to. Who knows? Maybe next time, it'll be a whole shuttle."

"Either tell me what you're talking about, or focus on navigation."

There were echoes of the old squadleader in her voice, of commands used to being heeded. But she wasn't Ferric's squadleader anymore. That relationship had died the moment she'd abandoned the Center. Whatever this new thing was, it was still uncertain, still taking shape. Still, whether through habit or agreement, Ferric turned his full attention to the road and jabbed at the rear display with a bony fingernail. "Behind us."

High in the air, a good distance out but steadily eating through the gap between them, were the sleek, narrow shapes of three light reconnaissance cruisers. From tip to tip, they looked almost like the folded planes Tala had used to craft from the refectory's napkins—flat, triangular wings and narrow bodies ending in a needlenose cockpit. The Planetary Airborne Patrol had arrived, leaving bright, glowing propulsion trails in their wake.

"On the bright side, the lawkeepers should back off some," said Ferric, turning down yet another side street. "With aerial teams tracking us, there's no need to shadow us so closely. At least, until they can set up a full military blockade."

"Comforting."

"And hey, these PAPs don't seem to have missiles."

"They aren't firing them," Tala corrected. "Yet."

She sent an exploratory mental probe at the cruisers, already knowing the result she'd get. They were just too far away. Playing it safe after what she'd done to the pods.

One last turn and they were on Primus at last. The podpath was narrow, especially compared to Main. It was filled with the sort of shop that only the most dedicated tourists ever find: the off-brands, the specialty items, smaller family-owned eateries and luxury dining alike. And there, at the end of the street, a downward slope into a broad tunnel. Built under another megamall, the tunnel led to a pod storage bay, where hundreds of pods waited to be summoned.

Ferric floored the accelerator and they beelined down Primus, their airborne pursuers adjusting to keep pace. In mere seconds, they crossed the last stretch of blocks into the tunnel's mouth. Ferric hit the brakes and Tala Enhanced them, bringing the pod to a screeching, shuddering halt. Their flying escort was one reason Tala had chosen the tunnel—now that they were inside, the cruisers had lost their sightlines.

The interior was surprisingly bright, lit by strings of decorative coiled bulbs in plastic bubbles lining the walls. Along the sides were narrow walkways—presumably for maintenance or emergencies. Aside from them, the tunnel was empty. Active pods would have been diverted into the storage bay to wait out the alert.

This next part would require speed. The hover cruisers couldn't follow them inside, but the lawkeepers were under no such restriction, and Tala had seen how fast their pods were. She scanned the tunnel's interior for cameras. Destroying them would trigger an alarm and a locational ping, but Tala wasn't worried about that. They already knew exactly where she was.

Ferric looked toward her. "I see six."

How right it felt, to be working with someone who could anticipate her like that.

"I counted six too. I've got them."

She leaned back and turned her mind to the cameras' rotational mechanisms. This particular model had a motor in the middle that kept them swiveling. She targeted her focus on those. After a few seconds of concentration, she formed the connection and overclocked each motor simultaneously.

The result was like six small rockets launching via centrifugal force. The cameras' moorings snapped immediately, leaving them free to plow into the walls. Six crunches echoed through the tunnel.

Ferric raised an eyebrow. "Unnecessarily showy, but effective."

With a sweep of her hand, Tala plucked the clothing canister from the floor where she'd tossed it. Ferric started disengaging his omnipad from the tangle of wires in his lap, but she made a cutting motion with her hand. "Not yet. I want you to rig the pod."

"Rig?"

"Have it drive off on its own. Buy us a little confusion. Keep it going as long as you can."

Ferric tugged at a cord he'd just disconnected, trying to get it back to the omnipad. "Back the way we came?"

"Mmhmm."

The squint of concentration that settled across Ferric's face as he began tapping away almost brought a smile to hers. She *had* missed this.

Tala left Ferric to his task, retrieved the rest of her belongings from the plastic tangle formerly known as the cloak, and exited the pod. While he worked, she added to the jumpsuit she'd hurriedly sprayed on. She sprayed a pocket onto each hip (into the left pocket went the data core she'd retrieved from her stolen omnipad; she filled the other when Ferric wasn't looking), then finished with a large hood. It wasn't precise work, but canisters weren't precise implements. All the while, she kept her ears pricked for approaching sapients.

"Sounds like pods closing in," she said. "Four to six. They aren't here yet, but they will be soon. How much longer?"

Ferric stepped out of the pod, mouth quirking with poorly concealed satisfaction. "It's ready."

"Already? I was expecting—"

"A longer wait? Glad I can still impress you. One more tap and it's off. Should give them a bit of a chase. I've set the window tint to max, too. I mean, they'll probably scan it, but maybe they won't think of it right away."

Tala flipped her new hood forward. "Let's go."

They made for the right walkway at a run. Partway down the tunnel was a service hatch. Tala pointed it out with her arm and Ferric gave a small nod. As they approached the tunnel wall, Tala gave them a boost. They leaped up and onto the walkway.

"Send it out," said Tala.

She turned back for just a second to watch as the little silver pod powered up and did a tight U-turn. Then, spherical wheels grumbling, it was off. It accelerated swiftly up the gentle incline toward Tarous's relative daylight. Despite herself, Tala hoped the pod would survive its doomed mission.

With enough added muscle, Tala was able to rip the service hatch out of the wall, revealing a stairway just large enough to accommodate her broad shoulders. It was lined with chalky pale orange stone and smelled strongly of clay. The passage switchbacked steeply, lit only by old glow strips. It wasn't a long trek to the surface—they hadn't gone far down the tunnel. But air was feeling scarce by the time they'd made it to a small metal door that led to the outside world.

Tala couldn't turn around to see, but she could hear Ferric's shallow breath close behind. "Once we're through, we're just another two civilians moving to shelter. You head out first and block the way while I handle the cameras."

"Yeah, great, let me just get in front of you—"

Pressing her back against one of the corridor's narrow sides and her legs against the other, Tala began scaling the wall. The ceiling wasn't high, but by pressing herself almost against it, Ferric had just enough room to crawl under her.

She sent a surge of energy through his leg as he kicked the door. Something cracked—in the wall, thankfully—and the door tumbled open. Ferric stepped through to the street, hood up, hunching in an amateur attempt to hide his features. She followed in the blind spot he'd created, using it to focus on the nearby cameras. Spotting them wasn't hard; city cameras were often intentionally left visible. As much deterrent as security measure.

Their internal mechanisms were muted light in her meta-awareness. She reached out to them, taking the time to establish a connection. Destroying them would pinpoint their location, so instead, Tala Enhanced their focus. She made each lens zoom in to the point that all they could see were minuscule patches of walkway.

"We're clear," she said. Ferric relaxed.

They walked quickly, trying to look like normal citizens fleeing to shelter. The jumpsuit's pockets were heavy, and she tried not to think about their contents. Instead, she kept her focus on dealing with each new camera they encountered before they entered its line of sight. Like their pod's suicidal rush, the deception wouldn't last long; a hover cruiser or lawkeeper was sure to spot them given time. But they wouldn't have to press their luck much longer.

Something wet brushed her hand. At first, seeing nothing, she thought she might have imagined it. Then she felt it again, and this time, she noticed droplets of water beading on the podpath and dotting the walkway in front of her. A new scent hung in the raindrops' wake: that of rusted steel.

"I'm still surprised you came," said Tala. "I half expected you to be gone when I got back. Not that I'm complaining. Without you, I probably wouldn't have made it."

Ferric made a low noise in the back of his throat. It sounded almost like a fledgling chuckle. "There was a time it would've made my year, hearing you say you needed me like that. I..."

"What?" Tala prompted, when it became clear he wouldn't keep going of his own accord.

"I stole that pod before I joined the Vanguard program. That first pod, I mean. Only way I could think to make it to the spaceport. I was just a kid, scared out of my mind, running from everything I knew. The entire time, I told myself it was all so I could do my part, help the galaxy. But that was a lie. I had no way of knowing I'd get accepted."

Tala would have bet the data core in her pocket that Ferric had originally meant to say something else entirely.

"You asked," he said. "Now you know. The worst part is, I'm glad I did it, damn me."

He grew quiet as they approached a sapient sitting outside one of the mammoth boxy warehouses that dominated this precinct. A Surolian, icy body glinting in the rain. They didn't seem in any hurry to move—trust a Surolian to take an evac alert as a mere suggestion. Nor did they seem to have much interest in Tala or Ferric. Nonetheless, they gave the sapient a wide, quiet berth, and conversation did not pick up again after that.

They moved deeper into Filtik's industrial district, passing more warehouses as well as the occasional quiet factory. The rain was coming down harder, in heavy gray sheets. The weather made it harder to spot upcoming cameras, but on the other hand, it cut visibility for anyone searching for them as well. Another PAP unit flew by overhead, and Tala hunched down beneath her sodden hood. As if that would hide her.

Tala might as well have followed the water collecting in the walkway's gutters—they were headed to the same place. A brown-painted factory, seemingly assembled by gathering seven wide smokestacks and joining them together with roofed bridges. It was surrounded by a wire fence, and in that fence's shadow, a massive storm drain guzzled up the flow of muddy water. Grime and runoff mixed with the rain as it pooled around the drain, pouring in as quickly as the grated opening allowed.

Tala had floated the idea of escaping into the sewers, but Teomonious had taken that as an invitation to detail modern sewage practices until she'd relented. He'd kept going for a while after that, though, Quarack wiggling her fingers behind his back in increasingly exaggerated mockery the whole time. Filtik's sewers were vacusealed, pressurized, and far too narrow for a human to fit.

The alternative they'd found was an underground river. Filtik had been built over it rather than around, due to a strict interpretation of natural preservation bylaws that Teomonious had been eager to recite by heart. Several storm drains across the city fed into it, so Tala and Quarack had pinpointed which one would be easiest to get to.

Feet sloshing through the pool of brownish, metal-scented soup, Tala approached the drain. Her fingers wrapped around the cold bars of the grate. With a mighty wrench, she ripped it from its fastenings. Ferric waded out to join her. With the grate gone, water was pouring in faster. She eyed the dark, slippery opening with trepidation. At least it was impossible to get any more soaked.

"You said not to thank you earlier," Tala said. "But really, thank you." She looked down at the pocket where she'd tucked the data core, feeling it push against the skintight jumpsuit. "Because of you, I have a chance to figure out what's really going on."

"Congress," said Ferric. "You said they... did they really know?"

Tala's grip on the grate tightened as she nodded. So many little feelings she shouldn't be letting in.

Ferric took another step toward the storm drain's mouth. "Guess I'll see for myself soon."

"Why did you come?"

For a moment, it seemed like Ferric was again going to pretend he hadn't heard. Then he shut his eyes and let his head hang loose, water running down his chin.

"I didn't. I'd been waiting there the whole time."

The grate fell into the puddle with a heavy splash.

"I didn't know whether I was there to stop you or help you. I just knew I had to be there. When the alarm went off, that's when I realized I'd set myself up at a rigged table. Playing to lose. Didn't trust you, couldn't leave you, and trying to do both meant I wasn't succeeding at much of anything. So I made my choice. I chose what I could live with over what I couldn't."

While Tala was still working out how to respond, he took two steps past her and slid himself down through the mud and water into the waiting darkness.

CHAPTER THIRTEEN

CONCURRENT CONTEMPLATION

It was a common misconception, Teomonious knew, that the galaxy's lesser insectoids treated the alvear any differently. In reality, the fat, four-winged flies dive bombing his head displayed a remarkable lack of phyletic solidarity. ((An unwelcome distraction, particularly with two of his six distinct mental processes turned toward irrelevant activities. Some would call such an allocation indulgent, but in his experience, a varied thought pattern bred a more flexible spectrum of responses.)) [[Thus, one mental track focused on personal development]] ((while another stayed introspective and analytical.)) {{He even allowed his rawer emotions to sweep across and dominate a third. Those had their value as well.}}

((One brain processing six separate simultaneous strings of thought, bound together through their connection to the Di-ro, the alvear shared mind.)) ||Instinctively, he reached for it—the Di-ro. But there was nothing to find. Lacking a hivemother to connect to, his sixth mental track was unresponsive. The constant ebb and flow of memories between himself and the broader alvear collective had been replaced with a disconcerting emptiness.||

((Teomonious had done his best to grow used to the feeling, but it never got any easier to reach out to the Di-ro and find it dormant.)) {{With his stress compounding alongside the number of flies, the escape would have been most welcome.}} The buzzing creatures swarmed with a vengeance outside the metropolitan area's limits. The city's smells drew them in, but a high-pitched screech across every district kept them out. Though inaudible to any sapient ear, it worked wonders to keep the bugs at bay. As a result, they gathered away from the city in clouds so thick you couldn't wave an antenna without hitting one.

((Perhaps some other alvear's memories held a solution. But without the Di-ro, he could only examine the memories he'd retrieved before passing out of range.)) [[He instead chose an old memory of a spawn-day sibling of his. Ceplubadofalric Motaniloba read at a brisk pace and had impeccable taste in literature. Teomonious often stocked his memory with an assortment of Motaniloba's personal readings before leaving on any extended trips.

This particular piece of writing was a treatise on the growth and change of modern fair use practices. A moderately engaging topic with the potential to diffuse some calm into the tracks of his mind.]] {{But not so much calm that he grew complacent. Whether the Renegade returned or not, his next movements needed careful charting, with every possible escape vector considered.}} There were fewer of those than he would have liked. The pilot had parked her ship altogether too far from the city, among some particularly large hills carpeted in aubergine forked grass.

((The motive behind her choice of location was clear, but he would have appreciated being offered access to the interior of her vessel.)) Beyond the winged pests—large and small—the air was dry, irritating to his chitinous exoskeleton. ((He should have brought a chair; his current tense state did not excuse a lack of proper preparation. As the High Councilor Eternal often said, the moment you started letting your mistakes compound was the moment you started losing.))

{{Each passing second increased the pressure, like a hand squeezing steadily tighter around him. The Renegade alarm, muted but still insistent, kept his omnipad vibrating. Would the Renegade make it to them? More importantly, would she have his data?}} The sound of the pilot's long talons tapping away at her own omnipad felt like knives dropping directly onto his brain. Each click grew his headache, maturing it from childhood to full unruly adolescence. ((More aggravating than the headache itself was its needlessness. There was no possibility that game of hers didn't have holographic capabilities.))

"While I have never claimed to be a sapient of simple tastes," Teomonious said, looking over at where the avian pilot had perched herself on the grass, deep in the shadow of one of the hills, "I could suffer through a thousand inquietudes if you would kindly switch to the holographic interface."

The pilot was obviously trying to get a rise out of him. Every sentence from her beak had been crude and insulting. ((But he could be diplomatic if the situation required. He knew how to keep his temper level—at least as long as was necessary.)) {{Every member of this band would be handled eventually; the muck was too deep to let any of it stick to him.}}

She didn't respond to Teomonious's request. In fact, he was moderately certain she had turned the volume up. ((The noise was a distraction. The challenge was allowing the efflux of his thoughts to filter through it.))

[[The subject of legal history had always engaged his thoughts and imagination, so this book was of particular interest. A society's laws were the projected essence of its ethos.]] {{Good governance was just as much about working around laws as it was about shaping them.}}

[[Alvear brain chemistry, unique within the known galaxy, made for an interesting challenge to the proper application of the dense tangle of bylaws and Tribunal rulings masquerading as galactic fair use policy. The problem posed by the loss of revenue associated with the sharing of stored memories through the Di-ro had sent the Legislatorium scrambling. Such an impassioned debate had ensued that one Serdin councilor had called for the forced lobotomization of the entire alvear species.]]

"Have you ever," Quarack said, "disliked someone on a visceral level from the very moment you met them? Like, they could be replaced with a big pile of trash and you wouldn't notice the difference?"

{{The Renegade would take care of herself, given time. For the pilot, he'd planned to arrange detention for the foreseeable future. Plans, of course, could be changed.}} ((There was prudence in a more permanent solution; it would further minimize the chance of his involvement coming to light.))

Teomonious clicked his mandibles. "I have some experience in the political sphere. In that world, you learn quickly that inferences based on surface level observation are unwise. It is common for sapients to cloak themselves in a hive of misdirection and lies. Do not mistake me, I have felt my share of instinctive distaste, but I have learned to defer judgment."

((He'd always hidden a third layer beneath the second. The moment they thought they'd excavated your true face from the topsoil was the moment they stopped digging.))

"Oh, I don't know," said Quarack, with a lazy scratch along her beak. "I think you're giving most sapes too much credit. But then, what do I know, compared to such an august personage as yourself?"

{{So she knew.}} ((Not necessarily; she could be fishing for information. But the level of mockery, the choice of praise…she at least suspected. It wasn't a secret worth the trouble of keeping,)) {{but there was danger inherent in the criminal recognizing his value as a hostage.}}

((But a disaster only earned that name if you weren't ready for it.)) [[The first serious proposal had been floated by a Torandian councilor relatively new to his position and hoping to make his legislative mark—a simple blanket ban on all sharing of purchasable content through the Diro. This, of course, would have been unenforceable.]]

{{Had the pilot shared her suspicions?}} ((Though he'd studied the public records of both the Renegade and her accomplice, he was no closer to gleaning an understanding of the strange pair. The Vanguard he found hardest to read, partially because he'd barely encountered the nordok at all.))

He was spared the necessity of a response by the sight of two dripping blobs cresting the nearest hill. Brown muck covered them from head to toe, sloughing off as they made their way down the hill to the ship. {{Apprehension rose within him as the Renegade approached; his life was hardly a guarantee with her around. Greater still, though, was his excitement. Had she succeeded? Did she have the passkey to his grand resurgence?}}

"Welcome back." The pilot waved a wing. "Looks like you two had fun."

The taller of the two shapes let out a deep-throated grunt.

"I am, of course, thrilled to see you've returned." {{Subservience would appeal to the Renegade's mood. All he had to do was keep her pacified, prove he was worth more alive than dead, and then he could put this affair behind him.}} "I must ask, did you acquire what I requested?"

In answer, the shorter shape reached into a grimy pocket and retrieved an equally grimy data core. "Everything's in here."

Teomonious reached for the core with his middle set of arms—his manipulators—but the Renegade pulled it away, sending an arc of mud flying. "Our data's on there too. Got to separate it first."

He jerked his arm back to his side. ((The Renegade seemed in a good mood—relatively speaking—)) {{but there was always the chance lurking behind every misstep that she'd choose to cut short his life.}} [[An alvear's lifespan necessitated a speedy educational period built on the back of the Di-ro. It was Forbildinsorgalis Bartamitraxul, the legendary councilor, who had charted the appeasement of all concerned parties: an alvear-specific tax. In return, copyrighted material could be shared legally among spawn day siblings. As long as they paid their usage tax, Teomonious and his eighty-three siblings were considered by fair use law to be one sapient.]]

((The nordok was looking at the data core like a starving sapient trying to determine whether the meal before him was poisoned, and whether or not they'd passed the point of caring.)) {{He sympathized with the feeling. Now that he was so close, every second of waiting was practically crushing his thorax. ((He wasn't sure what he'd find, but if anyone had a hint of the secret Ceowograffach was willing to kill to preserve, it was the GIAB.)) {{He needed that secret more than he'd ever needed anything.}}

<<With a sliver of will, he repurposed a mental track from idle deliberation to his personal memory storage. The compulsion was there to relive that old failure.>> ((Perhaps it was a form of masochistic self-flagellation, but there was motivation to be found in the reaffirmation of his anger.)) <<The story had broken during the eighteenth hour, timed to be seen by all three of Peramit's shifts. The second shift, by far the largest, had been relaxing after their evening meal when it hit. An uncharacteristically deft move.>>

"I, for one, can't wait," the Vanguard said.

"There's a display terminal in the kitchen," said the pilot. "And honestly, any day I get to feast my eyes on classified secrets is a good one."

{{If he walked into that ship, he might not return alive. It would be all too easy for them to silence him. Then again, nothing particularly solid stood between himself and death as things were.}} ((*Keep yourself too valuable to be discarded.*))

{{Attempting to flee without his data wasn't worth considering. It was the fool's gamble for him, plunging deeper into the pit of failure hoping to find something that could pull him out. Whatever it would take to see the scales tipped right. If he died, he died, but he would not suffer irrelevance.}}

<<He still remembered how the bevari had tasted against the roof of his mouth. He'd been mid-mouthful, reclining on his favorite pouffe, when the report had splashed across the projector. Eyes wide, mandibles spread, he could do nothing but watch the UNB broadcaster launch into the exposé of the year.>>

"Excuse me!" Teomonious interjected. "I have far less incriminating places to be. If I could just extract what's mine and be off?"

The Renegade shook her head vigorously again, sending another spray of mud and water uncomfortably close to Teomonious's favorite hand-stitched red-and-green-patterned shirt. He scuttled back a few steps, trying to determine whether they had applied the grime as an unfortunate attempt at camouflage.

"Very well, I can wait—inside it is. Lead on, my sodden friends." With some effort, Teomonious kept his tone equable. ((The most valuable commodity was control. Even its illusion had power.))

{{The problem with illusions was that they only worked if everyone believed in them.}}

The ship's interior was every bit as slapdash as its pilot. Teomonious hoped his repeated harumphs were coming across as disapproving, but so far, the corvid had just asked if he had something in his throat. ((At least he was safe from the flies while they waited for the other two to towel off and change.)) {{More delays. It was almost intolerable.}} ((To that track, at least. And while some of its impatient rage bled into the rest of his thoughts, those had been tuned to a more rational course from the onset. He'd waited almost a year to see what was in Ceowograffach's file; the remaining decihours were immaterial.))

Upon being led into the kitchen area, Teomonious immediately moved to claim the nicest-looking seat. Its qualifications for the title were all the more damning for their scarcity. True to the pilot's word, there was indeed a holoemitter in the middle of the table—but was the kitchen really the only room on the ship that had one? {{It was like asking him to believe that their only comm system was in the wasteroom. This all seemed the leadup to an ill-advised prank.}}

The Renegade and her Vanguard joined them within the decihour, mostly purged of grime. The data core too was scrubbed clean—at least on the outside. ((Within, he hoped, was the accumulated filth of Ceowograffach's dealings.))

The Vanguard started interfacing the data core with the table-mounted display. {{The itch in Teomonious's exoskeleton was impossible to repress, bleeding over into his other tracks. It was time to see what seeds she'd pocketed. The rich soil of his curiosity was fresh and ready.}}

A lingering look of distress plagued the Renegade's face, despite her apparent success. ((Like her other odd behavior, her Renegade status would certainly explain that, but he'd told the corvid the truth earlier: Simple generalizations had never been Teomonious's style. One did not test a hypothesis by trying to confirm it.)) The Vanguard bore his own malaise, but it was made up of so many fractured specks of emotion, it was impossible to tell where one festering insecurity ended and another began.

"I'm running an image organizer," the Vanguard said. "This could take a moment."

((Teomonious wondered whether the two were lovers, or just ignorant of each other's personal space. Such trysts were not uncommon, given the genetic similarity between humans and nordok.)) Two taps from the Vanguard brought the display to life, words and pictures filling the empty air.

Darfelatulaming Ceowograffach
Born 757 Cycle 16, day 241 (age 19)
Councilor of the 4525th Galactic Congress, 775-present
Constituents: Kitik (Hive)
Succeeded by: <>
Preceded by: Cernarvitalimun Teomonious

Just like that, everyone in the room was looking at him. {{At last, the recognition he deserved.}} ((It had been inevitable that they'd learn—if not now, then when they saw news of his reelection in the holos. Withholding his name would have delayed this moment, but the trust its revelation had purchased was more than worth the cost.))

"You're a councilor?" said the nordok, the flesh around his nose wrinkling.

<<He hadn't even been done in by a frequent habit, merely an idle weakness he found pleasure in on occasion. But with that video, everything good in his life had died. They'd shown him sitting in his office, listening to hyperchord music. The isolation that particular strain of music carried with it, the way it severed his connection to the Di-ro— it had been an utterly foreign sensation, like dipping his mind in liquid nitrogen. The video hadn't played long, but it hadn't needed to. The broadcaster had followed it up with two "experts" who fell over themselves to gush about his dereliction of duty. His deviance. How no true servant of the alvear would cut himself off from his constituents. How such a degenerate chemical rush compromised the brain. All nonsense, but fear and superstition were powerful tools—and

Ceowograffach had wielded them with enough skill to elevate a middling scandal into an emergency recall.>>

"Former councilor," said Teomonious. "Though soon, I may—"

"*Oh* yeah," said the pilot. "How did you not know? Bugboy's got more politician in him than a Peramit highrise."

"Wait." That was the Renegade. "You knew? You didn't tell us?"

"Why are you mad at *me*? He's the twice-pecked councilor skulking around on edgeworlds—"

"I've got questions enough for the both of you."

"What about, oh, Tenet thirty-two?"

((The pilot had clearly plucked the number from the air)) but it seemed to work all the same. The Renegade took a slow, even breath, and Teomonious regained control of his twitching antennae.

((The pilot hadn't seemed the least bit frightened by the confrontation.)) Rather than deescalate, she turned her glare up a few tiers. "I figured you'd checked his name after the meeting. That's like backroom dealing basics."

"Not all of us are used to working with criminals," the Vanguard muttered.

{{As willing as he was to let his accomplices fight among themselves, Teomonious couldn't let that one pass.}} "I resent the implicit comparison."

"No one asked you," the corvid shot back.

<<He couldn't recall ever experiencing such unconditional antipathy.>> ((But he was no stranger to such things; Bartamitraxul himself had had his share of enemies.)) [[Teomonious reviewed portions of the inspirational alvear's memory daily. Other than the classified sections, Bartamitraxul had imprinted his entire life upon the Di-ro for historical posterity. And what a glorious life: one of struggle, of fighting on behalf of a fledgling species in an ocean filled to the gills with ancient behemoths ready to feed on the weak and the lost.]]

{{Lately, Teomonious's personal struggles had taken him down a far less grandiose path than his esteemed ancestor. Teomonious had been elected to represent the Kitik hive, touched the highest of highs, and championed his species' concerns in the vaunted and venerated halls of the Legislatorium itself. Now he was stuck in a dingy ship with the dregs of the galaxy. Left to hope that a deranged and dangerous criminal would deliver him a chance of salvation.}}

The Renegade was staring at him. Teomonious tried to shrink within his exoskeleton, but there was nowhere to hide. [[He searched his memory storage for similar human expressions, trying to divine her meaning, but found nothing. *Instinctively, he reached out to the Di-ro for a relevant memory.*]]

|| … ||

[[Failure.]] {{Now that was frustrating.}}

"You were a councilor," she repeated slowly, sharply. "I'd like your perspective on a few things, if you don't mind."

"I—I'm afraid I'm not—" ((With some effort, the flow of babble dried. Better to stay silent and invite speculation than reveal one's indecision to the world.)) {{But keeping resolute under her gray-eyed glare, that was a breeder-crucible all on its own. He needed to soften her anger before it congealed around his legs. And his curiosity, that traitor, pressed him toward agreement.}}

[[Possessing an inquisitive mind and a fervent love of history, Bartamitraxul had written dissertations on a score of subjects. Teomonious's favorite of his works examined the intricacy of Surolian trade customs. Surolians—or the "children of Surol," as they called themselves—were solitary by nature. They'd constructed their culture entirely around isolation and self-sufficiency, so the concept of trading was by its nature anathema.]]

"I cannot promise anything," were the words he settled on. "But I will listen, and perhaps I will share my insight. Consider it a favor."

"Like you won't talk our ears off for an hour no matter what she—"

"Not helpful, Quarack." The Renegade turned to her minion. "Can you skip to Arcus's file?"

Ferric double-tapped his omnipad, and his hated successor faded away. In its place was a siari, face pinched by the touch of age.

Arcus Boral
Born 704 Cycle 16, day 373 (age 72)
Status: Active

Though the name was familiar, Teomonious couldn't quite place where he'd heard it. Judging by the others' reactions, he was the only sapient in the room for which this was the case. {{Like all ignorance, his was a weakness. A threat yet to be unmasked was impossible to counteract. That was how Ceowogreffach had been able to grasp a chunk of chitin from Teomonious's exoskeleton.}}

<<His first thought, shooting to the forefront of all of his mental tracks simultaneously, had been how shockingly well planned it was. Ceowogreffach should not have been smart enough to keep such an inquiry quiet, much less parlay that middling vulnerability into an advantage.>> ((Most sapients were simple, comforting themselves with thoughts as ephemeral as their trivial lives. Occasionally, though, you found yourself surprised by what caverns coiled their way beneath a placid surface.)) <<As his indulgences were gleefully paraded across the holoscreen, a sense of dark certainty had filled him. Ceowogreffach could not have conceived of such a maneuver himself. Teomonious would have seen it coming. He'd had the grubling under surveillance since he'd first spotted the naked ambition in his thoughts.>>

The Vanguard's mouth pressed tighter and tighter, like someone was trying to wring what little juice they could from his features. ((He had not yet learned that the strongest of feelings are the best indicator that your face should close its borders.)) <<Watching the exposé of his own scandal, his countenance had remained as stone. A wall that the universe couldn't breach.>>

"How could they cover this up?" The Renegade was addressing him. ((*Cover-up. A conspiracy.*)) "You were one of them. How much do you know?"

<<Teomonious wrenched a track away from his grim reminiscence and into his library of stored memories. The name *had* been familiar, and —there it was. A defense subcommittee meeting he'd once observed. One of the nordok councilors had brought up a colleague who'd died at the hand of a Renegade named Arcus some twelve years previously. Yet they'd spoken as if the Renegade were deceased.>> ((The pieces practically came together on their own after that; this was the conspiracy they'd invested so much into uncovering. A Renegade's existence kept secret, not just from the galaxy at large, but from sapients of consequence.))

{{That, he was dismayed to discover, was interesting.}}

"I can only speculate," he said, eyes lingering on the holo. "Perhaps they were trying to prevent panic of some kind, or worried about informants." {{Even for spur of the moment hypotheses, those were weak.}} "It could be as simple as covering up someone's mistake. Never underestimate what sapients will do to keep their iniquities out of the public eye."

"I can't believe it," the Vanguard murmured. "They knew." It didn't seem aimed at anyone, and nobody jumped to engage him in conversation.

The pilot scratched her beak with what Teomonious's stored memories indicated was irritation. "Let's see how deep this goes. *I* knew she was telling the truth. I want all the juicy stuff."

{{Revolting as it was to admit, he and the pilot were in full agreement on that front.}} ((Not regarding the human's supposed innocence, but rather, curiosity at the nature of this conspiracy. Who had known? More perplexing, why had he not been among them? Secrets were like planets; they had a presence of their own, and tended to pull sapients into their orbit.))

"How does it matter?" said Tala. "How, when I can't prove anything they don't already know?"

"Who cares? Do it on general principle. But if I were you?" The pilot gave an easy shrug. "I'd still want to find him myself."

{{Ah, revenge. Now, there was a path wrought in the image of his own heart.}} [[The solution, of course, was plausible deniability—trade by way of strategic drops in designated zones. After a suitable amount of time had passed, a Surolian could "discover" the drop and leave their own trade goods behind. Arcane, technical, perhaps a little absurd. But all the best legal maneuvers were.]]

"I know," the Renegade said. "It has to be me. This information is a gift. But, just knowing there's no way back—"

"We'll find one," said the Vanguard. "No matter how long it is, we'll walk it together. If you'll still have me?"

"It's not a question. You're my Vanguard."

{{And just like that, this already protracted ordeal had become a bad holodrama. If they started shedding water from their eyes, Teomonious was going to find something large to crush himself under.}}

"Would it be too much trouble," he said, "to have a copy of these files sent to me? I work better at my own pace."

It was like they'd forgotten he was even there. All three of them turned as one, surprise hanging off their faces like a kirtian's jowls.

"I, um, don't see why not," said the Renegade, nodding to her Vanguard. "If you can help, you'd be doing the galaxy a great service."

{{There was plenty he wanted to say to that, but he still wasn't convinced the Renegade wouldn't up and murder him if sufficiently provoked.}}

He pulled out his omnipad and stretched it to a reasonable size, then opened his file delivery. There they were, neat little packages of data waiting to be unwrapped. The rest of the group had already moved on, back to their own display. He redirected one of his tracks toward listening in on their conversation. {{The corvid was speaking again. "This guy was a Pillar? That's a pretty big deal for you lot, yeah?"}}

It took him a few seconds to understand what he was looking at. The package he'd been sent was less a top-secret file, and more a *video recording* of a top-secret file. That recording had been sliced to pieces and strung together into a series of images, which the Vanguard's software had grouped together into a coherent order. The Renegade's blurred hand could be seen in many of the pictures, navigating the files even as she'd recorded. ((He was much more of a stickler for impeccable presentation than most, stemming from his time in the Legislatorium. Other species assumed that due to the Di-ro, the alvear valued uniformity in all things. That couldn't have been further from the truth. The Di-ro preserved and highlighted that which stood out; differentiated the remarkable few from the masses.))

Teomonious skipped past the initial images. Much of it was irrelevant to his purposes; the cover-up was the only compelling aspect. More specifically, how he had never caught wind of it. ((The best place to start would be the incident where Arcus had officially died—the *Fountstar* raid.))

{{The Vanguard was quick to reply, his voice building momentum as he talked, "Yes. Probably why they let him research Renegades in the first place. Someone should have seen his interest for what it was sooner.

By the time they did, he'd already infected his Acolyte with his madness."}}

((If their words so far were any indication, they'd be spending the next few decihours venting their feelings about every piece of stray information. The spoken word was so inefficient, so imprecise. He found joy in the act of writing, unfashionable as it was in this holographic galaxy.)) [[The legislation around fusion bomb disarmament: now, *there* was a tightly crafted piece of writing. As was the entire slate of legislation limiting the rules of warfare. They had to be tight; they were the bedrock the Accords were built on. The Torandians wanted war to stay conventional, even intimate—and the first thing you learned as a councilor was that when the Torandians wanted something, they usually got it.]]

He skimmed through Arcus's career as a Pillar, starting with his initial escape and the death of his Vanguard by his own hands. Then his time on the run: sometimes solo, sometimes with others, but always leaving a trail of destruction. There were a few unconfirmed accounts claiming he'd been spotted meeting with Praeters, as well as a lengthy section on a Surolian independent lawkeeper who'd taken up his government-issued bounty. None of it interested him. The best pulp waited below the bark.

{{"How's all this ancient history gonna help us find him?" said the pilot.}} ((She seemed to enjoy the sound of her own voice.)) {{"This stuff's all from over twenty years ago. If it mattered, they'd have caught him already. We should be looking at his associates. Find the friends to find the sape. That's what all my bookie buddies used to say. Nice bunch. Long as you didn't owe 'em."}}

And there it was—the *Fountstar* raid. Like a spider with a meal wriggling in its web, he prepared himself to dig in. He was a fast reader, well practiced from countless hours spent poring over government briefs. ((Many councilors saw the daily briefings as a chore, but he'd always enjoyed them. So much information, delivered in its purest form.))

The attack had been sudden and brutal. Arcus and his onetime Acolyte Amara Vert had disabled the transit convoy in a barrage of fire. Then they'd boarded the ship together, Arcus engaging the guards while Amara herded the children—young Enhancers, one and all—aboard her vessel. Though she had escaped into space, Arcus had supposedly met his end in that battle, his heart ruptured by an Enhanced kick to the chest. ((The description of the damage that kick had done redoubled his resolution to stay on the Renegade's good side. At least, while within striking distance.))

{{From the sound of it, the Renegade was pacing like a bed of thorns had begun to grow under her feet.}} Amara had escaped, taking the children and leaving the body of her former teacher behind. ((There was sense in that. The only way through was forward, no matter how many bridges atomized behind you. Still, one owed a certain enduring respect to their mentor: a debt incurred by the time and effort sacrificed to a nebulous potential.)) Arcus's body had been brought to the morgue on Atraxu Station, subjected to tests to confirm his identity, and incinerated.

Officially, at least.

A series of images accompanied this section: stills taken from the morgue's camera. The first showed Arcus's body, tagged and lying on a metal cot. In the second, his pale eyes were open. By the third, he was standing, blood from the fatal wound he'd suffered still staining his robes. He hadn't moved in the fourth image, but his eyes had found the camera, his face alight with satisfaction.

((Hiding something like this was a matter of cost. Whatever that cost had been, it hardly seemed worth the benefit.)) [[The Galactic Congress's seats—and, by extension, votes—were divided among the Coalition's member species. As such, prospective cosignatories were required to unify their government as a condition of joining. Their share of the vote was based on their share of the Coalition's economy, and if they couldn't lay claim to at least one-tenth of a percent, they had earned no voice in the affairs of galactic governance. The Torandians had earned a very, very loud voice.]]

{{"I think we should start with Amoretta," said the Vanguard. "Ties to Fiurn Hult seem relevant. It was one of their facilities where you… encountered him."}} ((The "him" in question, Teomonious surmised to be Arcus.))

{{"And he killed everyone there." The Renegade's reply came fast and quietly. "Almost everyone."}}

[[He needed to consider his own economic situation; his investment portfolio could do with some adjustments. He had an alvear financial manager—naturally—who kept him apprised of business developments in real time. This did not work outside the Di-ro, so their communication had been markedly disjointed of late. He'd drop a message once he was done poring through Ceowograffach's file; ask Pectorastridus to increase his stake in meal cubes.]]

There followed within the file an enumeration of the classification of everything related to Arcus's survival, as well as the specific codes cited, but what seemed to be missing—at least from this section—was *why*. ((It wasn't immediately obvious what was relevant and what wasn't, but there was plenty of distance between his current position and giving up.)) He scrolled back through, looking for more information about the Acolyte. ((As good a place to start as any.

The Vanguard's organizational algorithm had done its job well. For all that he looked like he was drowning on dry land, he seemed passably competent.)) Amara Vert's subsection was easy to find. A picture of the human topped the information. She was tall, like most humans, with brown hair that hung loosely down to her waist. Her gray eyes were wide, and held a flat intensity.

((Though Teomonious hated to admit it, even to himself, he'd never been particularly knowledgeable about Enhancement. His only direct exposure to it had sterilized much of his interest in the subject.)) <<They had once euthanized their own Enhancers in infancy. The modern solution was less brutal, but not by much: surgical removal of their connection to the Di-ro. It left their minds forever isolated from the greater whole; one entire mental track derailed and replaced with an endless, intruding quiet.>>

|| ... ||

Unlike Arcus, Amara had shown worrying tendencies from the start of her career. She'd washed out of the Agent's discipline due to her proclivity for violence. Her strong interest in fieldwork had led her to become a Harmonizer instead. From there, Arcus had become her mentor. ((Teomonious had mentored several aspiring politicians himself. They'd all distanced themselves when his scandal had broken. Evidence they'd learned well, though the betrayal had still smarted.))

<<The first time the alien power of Enhancement had first warped and surged through the Di-ro, it had flooded a whole world with the memory of an infant's birthing agonies. The memory had been overwhelming—in many cases, fatal. That had been long before his time, but the tragedy of that day lived on in their collective memory, passed down from mind to mind, preserved like a flower caught in a bubble of glass.>>

((Thus, they'd embraced a small horror to protect against a greater one. Where Teomonious listened to hyperchord to dip his feet into the silence, those unfortunate children were forced under—all for the crime of being born with incredible power. On occasion, Teomonious made himself live through those hatchlings' one and only memory contribution to the collective.)) <<It was a flagellant way of grounding himself, to dive into the final moments of connection, the memory of a child too young to even know how to stop their continuous upload to the Di-ro. He lived their fear, their confusion. Most of all, he lived the strange feeling they had; a terrifying tension in every centimeter of their body, seeping out to suffuse the very air around them.>> ((A sensation his own body would never feel. Very few chose to stomach the price of that particular insight.))

{{The pilot scratched out a quick staccato on her beak.}} [[It took a moment of digging for Teomonious to find the associated meaning: triumphant discovery. So many species swarmed the galaxy, each with their own mannerisms and body language. Like many alvear, Teomonious kept references within his stored memory just to keep track of them all.]] {{"There *is* another tie between Arcus and Fiurn Hult.

Check these nordok out. They're just mercenaries, but ones suspected of working for both."}}

{{"What do we have on them?" the Renegade said.

"Not much," said the pilot. "A few possible sightings.}}

{{"I don't think there's a big enough link there," said the Renegade. "Mercenaries take clients from all over. Doesn't mean those clients are related."}}

The remainder of Amara's record was a dead end. Following her retreat from the *Fountstar*, she'd carried out a few minor raids before her eventual death at the hands of the High Warmaster Eternal. A short and violent life, to be sure, but not a particularly interesting one.

{{"We have to start somewhere," said the Vanguard.

"Let's start with the government, then," said the pilot. "We know they know more than they're letting on. No way it ends at just one Renegade's questionable mortality."

"This is what the government knows." The tapping noise of a human fingernail striking metal. "We have it. A few scattered facts on a who's who of Renegades and war criminals."}} ((The Renegade's emotional state seemed to worsen as the excitement of new information wore off. Perhaps the inescapable reality of her situation had at last found purchase.)) <<There were parallels to his own struggle there; on that awful day, it had taken time for the full truth of it to coalesce from vague ephemera into something that was very cold, and very real.>>

{{"Someone's probably penning my file right now," the Renegade continued. "Mine right next to his. Nothing can change that."}}

Arcus's next documented associate was a thrall escapee named Merotte. He read the first few words, frowning to himself. ((Why was he still helping? Perhaps it was professional pride, or perhaps his curiosity had yet to cool, but either way, it had become detrimental to his goals. The time had come to talk his way out. Or just walk away; they seemed distracted enough for it to work. As much as the puzzle begged to be solved, he could always solve it with a penthouse view.))

{{"What about *him*?" The Vanguard's gruff voice came out a little too fast and a little too desperate.}}

[[He'd replayed *Beneath this Blanket of Stone* more times than he could count, but the song's rhythmic clicks always helped calm his nerves. Already, a touch of certainty was spreading across the disparate portions of his mind. Though memories of music never measured up to the original experience, he was thankful for this one, and would be thankful for it many times in the future.]]

{{"Oooh, ugly," came the pilot's voice.}}

Teomonious blanked his omnipad and stood. His eyes went to the trio of outlaws, still huddled around the holoprojector. ((He was already trying to phrase a request to be dropped off in the meekest language he could.)) Then he saw the image they'd stopped on.

"That's the monster they sent Scratch after," said the Renegade. "Five years he's been active. Longer than any Renegade in the past half cycle."

The monster was a wall of muscle and rage, topped with an untended garden of hair so pale it was practically white. He had a proud, jutting chin and a lopsided smirk that crept up toward one ear, though it stopped short of his eyes. According to the holo, the human's name was Viron.

"They're working together?" the Vanguard said.

"Associates, at least."

But it was the words below that had driven his mental track into a tailspin: a list of known aliases. One of them, he'd heard before. Nashafal.

<<He'd been at his Peramit office, hearing the ten-day brief from the investigator he'd hired to look into Ceowograffach. Samson had been showing him a voice recording he'd captured from a distance. Teomonious could have recalled the whole conversation, but there was really only one salient part.

"*He won't let me holo Nashafal,*" Ceowograffach had buzzed. The sound was a little fuzzy, but each word was unmistakable. "*I have to meet him in person. If I'm not back in three hours, send a data core to UNB. Make it sufficiently incriminating.*"

It had been a tantalizing lead, so he'd asked Samson to pursue it. Shortly thereafter, Samson had vanished. It was then that he'd understood Ceowograffach was no lucky amateur, but a conniver through and through. That still held true, but it now seemed possible that a far more dangerous mind had engineered his fall from grace.>>

"I know where to start," Teomonious declared. Any intention of leaving had vanished from every track of his mind. "If I am correct, our interests are still very much aligned." ((And if he was wrong, he would at least be unleashing an angry Renegade on Ceowograffach. Not at all a bad outcome.))

The reaction was almost exactly what he'd hoped for: the Renegade and her pet Vanguard swiveled to face him like a ship's laser seeking debris. The pilot took a longer, more deliberate turn, boredom clinging to her feathers.

"You do?" said the Renegade. Then, just as quickly, "why didn't you mention this earlier?"

[[The song was reaching its crescendo, buzzes intensifying to a roar. A masterful showcase of sound and syncopation.]]

"I lacked critical information," Teomonious said. ((He searched through his stored memory for an appropriate human physical response and settled on a shrug.)) "These files have jogged loose a thread of possibility that I am willing to unspool if you are. All I ask is that I be allowed to accompany you, to see justice done."

The pilot gave him a beady look over her pointed beak. "Do we have to bring him? I say we just beat on him until he tells us whatever he knows. Then we can ditch him on the hillside. Nothing more fun than leaving a sape in the middle of nowhere. Especially if you take their omnipad first." ((Maybe with time and patience, he could convince the Renegade to do just that to the pilot. It would be a fine way to pass the hours, if he really was going to be traveling with them.))

The Renegade and her Vanguard shared a look, Arcus's file still hovering in the air behind them. The former gave a tentative nod. "If you have a real lead, you're welcome to come along."

"So," said the Vanguard, "what do you know?"

"Hold that thought for a moment," Teomonious said, raising one upper arm and turning his eyes back to his omnipad. Done with the conglomerated files' section on Arcus, he flipped over to Ceowograffach's information instead. ((While he yearned to pore over it, there really was just one thing he needed right now.)) Ah yes, there it was: his travel itinerary for the next half year.

His other five arms rose to join their brother in a broad, magnanimous gesture. "I would recommend setting a course for the mining planet of Urgam."

CHAPTER FOURTEEN
DEFERRED MAINTENANCE

"Peace is an ideal," said Frael. He stood by his chamber's wide balcony window, looking out at the Modellus skyline. Even young as Tala was, she loomed over him—at least physically. From their first meeting it had been clear that he had more wisdom in one sagging jowl than she could learn in a lifetime. "Hold it close, but do not aspire to capture it forever. The path worth following is winding, and longer than the span of a day."

Recognizing the reference to the 149th Tenet, Tala bowed her head.

"But walk it you shall," he continued. "And step by step, you will grow into understanding. That you have only begun your journey is no fault. My own steps were slow and halting at your age."

He fell silent. Tala lifted her head to find him staring at one of the many artworks that lined the chamber walls. A man, with a painted expression so serene that she couldn't tear her eyes away.

Seeing that familiar painting tugged at her memory. A long struggle to tease out its meaning. Hundreds of hours spent staring at it, meditating beneath it, delving into the history of its siari artist. She'd *lived* this moment before, though the Central Pillar's fur had been browner, his bulldog face less lined. That she was here again, with memories that didn't match her nine-year-old body—

She was dreaming.

Her mind flopped like a fish in a shallow puddle at that realization, throwing itself at the dry shore of wakefulness. *Not yet.* The world around her was shifting, but she wasn't ready to let herself awaken. Frael's voice probably wasn't one she'd hear again.

"What is that?" she said, the same as she had sixteen years ago.

Frael turned to her, smiling gently. "*Flowerbed*, one of Duna's lesser known projects. A zephyr that parted more than hills and valleys. And a former celestial touchstone, when I held only youth and trouble. You feel its pull as well."

It wasn't a question. Had it been one originally? She found she couldn't remember.

With a wave of his paw, Frael turned off the painting's holoprojector. He lifted it off the table, examining it with dark-pebble eyes. "I still find clarity within its meaning, when the waves can find no safe harbor. Oh yes," he said, tail twitching. "At times, even the Central Pillar cannot dispel the fog of irresolution."

"What does it mean?" The question blurted itself out, born of the combination of a nine-year-old's decorum and an adult's urgency when faced with a fading window of opportunity.

Frael answered with a question, as he often did. "What is a destination without the journey?"

The holoprojector's casing was cold against her skin, but she closed her fingers around it anyway—a rare gift from the most respected Enhancer in the galaxy.

The chamber walls began a rhythmic thumping. She felt her eyelids trying to pull apart. Outside the window, Quarack danced on the *Aquilon*'s wing. If a revelation was going to present itself, it was running out of time.

"The painting is an egg," said Frael. He took three steps closer and looked her dead in the eyes. There was a depth to his own she'd never noticed before, one that spoke of strange stirrings just below the surface. "Crack it, and you will benefit. But allow it to hatch, and you will marvel at what emerges."

Frael and his chamber melted away like a stain in the wash. All that was left was the thumping—the *Aquilon*'s engines—and *Flowerbed* itself. She'd taken to projecting it above the blanket on the firm metal flooring she called a bed, here in the *Aquilon*'s storage sub-bay. The painting was among the last few bright points of familiarity from her days at the Center, when she'd been sure of herself and her position within the galaxy.

While the *Chollima*'s designers had placed its engines directly below the bridge—letting her keep her Enhancement efficient while she commanded her Vanguard—the *Aquilon* had been built with no expectation of housing an Enhancer. So she'd eschewed the "luxury" of her quarters for the sub-bay's harder comforts, all to get as close to the engines as possible without actually being inside the energy shielding. She even sometimes sat against the half meter of metal separating them, all in the name of wringing free a few more drops of efficiency. She was now very well acquainted with the wall: the way it shuddered against her back, the heat that built up whenever Quarack cranked the throttle too hard.

She cast her mind out until she found the engines. Day by day, they grew more familiar, their reassuring *thump-thump* a mechanical heartbeat no less regular than her own. Already the ship flew eighty-six percent faster than when she'd first boarded. Their light brightened in her meta-awareness as her power flowed into them.

Flowerbed was waiting patiently when she turned away from the engines. Just as it had every morning. Her previous efforts to plumb its depths had yielded no revelation, but perhaps this time would be different, with her dream still hovering in the oriels of her waking mind. She adjusted the projector a half centimeter to the right and gave *Flowerbed* a searching stare. The human stared back, tranquil as ever, lit by subtle hues of violet. Siari lightlets glowed violet to indicate sorrow, and art critics agreed that Duna had intended a similar emotional resonance. In Tala, it evoked only frustration. Frael had advised her to "let it hatch," but years later and she couldn't even see a hairline fracture.

Anger's greatest sin is waste, she recited.

Tala isolated the negative feeling and exhaled it into the *Aquilon*'s stale air. That was the proper response to disruptive emotions. As long as she kept her mind clean, she could not lose herself to insanity. No matter what the galaxy decided she was, or what the government lied about.

Another flash of anger. The emotions were coming faster and stronger, and the urge to cling to them was maddening. She exhaled the anger as well, finding a fragile equilibrium. There was stillness there, and peace, and the sort of self-reflection that nudges you away from mental event horizons. But she gave up on the painting for the day; she was too susceptible right now.

Next to the projector was a short stack of plastic-wrapped breakfast patches. Tala unpeeled one and pressed it against her left wrist until it adhered to her skin. Patches weren't a proper replacement for food, but going to the kitchen meant sacrificing speed. While her wrist absorbed the nutrients, she picked up a clothing canister and dressed herself with a few sprays of fabric. By the time she'd finished setting her omnipad's alarm for five hours, the pale yellow liquid had dried onto her.

She started with calisthenics. She'd been neglecting her regimen lately, opting instead to sift through the data she'd recovered—*stolen*—from the GIAB databanks. She'd spent hours upon hours learning everything they held about Arcus Boral, then going back through just in case she'd missed anything. Part of that single-mindedness was a legitimate desire to study her enemy, but more than she cared to admit came from trying to keep her mind busy. She didn't know *what* was going on with her anymore, or even if staying busy was helping, but if there was even a chance it was helping keep her from—

Best not to think about that. It was invading too many thoughts on its own for her to help it along. Far better, more productive, to keep digging through Arcus's file—though it had gotten to the point that she could hold the words and images in her head while her routine played out on autopilot.

She stretched a leg out behind her and dropped into a lunge. It was still hard to believe—ironic, even—that he'd been the Pillar of Devotion, given his lack of it. Once among the Center's greatest luminaries, he'd championed the idea that, as sapients no longer in control of their actions, Renegades deserved sympathy and care—and if possible, rehabilitation. Transcripts of his many speeches on the subject had been faithfully preserved in the GIAB archives, and Tala had read every last one. Multiple times. Enhancers, politicians, the wider public…just about everyone had seen those speeches as compassionate, if naïve. How had so many sapients failed to see the *sympathy* hiding beneath his words?

Whoever he'd been no longer existed. He'd become what he'd dedicated himself to understanding. The proof was laser-etched into her memory.

She could feel where that thought was leading her, but not fast enough to stop. These tributaries all fed back into the same polluted river. All the moments that would never be, all the chances they would never get. A piece of her had never escaped that dusk-lit underground room and the pile of bodies surrounded by monitors. The piece capable of hoping —

"Gooooood morning, crew!" Quarack's voice floated in, far too cheery for the early hour. No part of the ship was safe from her semi-frequent shipwide broadcasts; though the sub-bay didn't have its own etherway, one was installed just outside the door. *"And if you've slipped off centralized time, good afternoon or evening. Whatever's more accurate. If anyone's awake, we're approaching Bartamitraxul, and should be passing through within the hour."*

Tala brought her legs together and started the next stretch. That put them about two-thirds of the way to Urgam. Though the Tenets frowned on pride, she couldn't help but feel pleased with how quickly she'd taken to the *Aquilon*'s engines.

"For anyone who isn't awake..." Quarack paused. *"Well, you probably are now."*

Shaking her head at their captain's audacity, Tala refocused on the engines. Enhancers were accounted for as a general rule, even those currently inactive. If a ship entered Bartamitraxul's scanning range at Enhanced speed without a corresponding Enhancer aboard, that ship would find itself detained for questioning at best. An active Renegade (*me*, she reluctantly acknowledged) had last been seen operating in this cluster, so they might well shoot on sight. She reclaimed energy from the engines in a steady drain, tapering off so as not to appear suspicious to other ships in the vicinity.

Her alarm was nowhere close to going off, but she let herself stop exercising anyway. There was no reason to stay in this room if she couldn't work the engines. She had the next few hours to grab some real food, do her chores, and even shower guilt-free. There weren't many opportunities to do that without slowing down the ship. Once the Enhancement was going, she didn't have to expend any focus or effort keeping it in place, but distance from the engine did sap the strength of her connection. Quarack had brushed away her concerns when she'd brought it up. To the corvid, being a passenger meant pitching in to help keep the ship running.

That it *did* run was almost enough to get her believing in the old religions.

Wiping the sweat out of her eyes with one hand, Tala waved the door open and started through the narrow, winding corridor that led through the *Aquilon*'s essential machinery to the spaceship proper. Strange how so much distance could be packed into such a compact space. Many of her assigned chores concerned this section of the ship; she'd at least been able to claim the ones that kept her closest to the engines. Given what chores those were, it had been an easy sell.

The fuel pipe access point was coming up on her right. The routine she'd fallen into had her starting there, saving the life-support filters for last. But today, she had something that was all too rare aboard the *Aquilon*: time to burn.

A little further down, snug against the wall's scored paneling and exposed wires, was the narrow ladder that led to the upper turret bubble. Instead of passing it, she laid a hand on one of the plastic rungs. For once, she could indulge the urge to climb—it might well be the only chance she got.

The turret bubble was little more than a blister clinging to the upper hull, through which the view in every direction led to space. It hadn't been designed for a woman of Tala's stature. Only about three-quarters of her body made it through the hatch before her head touched the domed, transparent ceiling. She curled herself to fit, drawing her legs up to her chest. Now her knees were blocking the turret controls. After a few moments of constricted wiggling, she gave up. She had what she'd come for: a view.

The gentle curve of the *Aquilon*'s nose directed Tala's eyes to what looked like a dim, flickering star. Unlike the other stars dotting Tala's field of vision, this one was growing larger. She managed to bump the viewing glass's magnification to the highest setting with her knee. When that wasn't enough, she let a tiny bit of Enhancement bleed into her vision. There was no transition, no slow zoom in. One second, she was looking at a vaguely triangular smudge. The next, the details of the massive structure snapped into focus. Three nodes powered the Bartamitraxul gate, each connected to the others by thick metal bands. In the center was the gate itself, a triangle of space visually indistinguishable from the rest. There was no swirling maw of crackling energies, no rippling distortions. Not even a clear demarcation dividing the different slices of galaxy, though light-years of distance separated them.

Beacons orbiting the gate gave off a shimmering glow, blinking off and on in a regular pattern. A visual guide for anyone having trouble with their navigational systems. The light glinted off the metallic hides of dozens, perhaps hundreds, of ships arriving and departing in all directions, shepherded expertly by Bartamitraxul's nav-systems.

She couldn't help but wonder again how the Pathmaker's discipline would have suited her. Pathmakers didn't have to interpret orders or struggle against their baser impulses or make difficult decisions on the fly. They just took off and never came back. Right now, that seemed almost luxurious in its simplicity. Perhaps it would have been enough.

Perhaps it would have saved her from herself.

The familiar patterns of guilt began to cycle, forcing her brain to relitigate conclusions already dismissed from the docket. It was self-defeating and unproductive, but that didn't stop her. The gate grew larger and larger in the glass as the decihours slipped away, one by one...

"*I've been told there's a delay,*" came Quarack's voice from below. Another shipwide announcement. "*High volumes. Plus, they've got some additional security tripe bogging things down even more. They aren't boarding, though, so little blessings. Teo, if you know any top-secret clearance codes that can speed things up, report to the bridge after breakfast.*"

Having seen the *Aquilon*'s control room, Tala thought "bridge" to be a terribly generous term.

"*Actually, anything top secret at all. I'm not picky.*"

Tala somehow managed to uncurl herself and slid back down the ladder into the *Aquilon*'s underbelly. It was too easy to lose track of time watching the ship cut its way through the endless light-seconds. Fortunately, her stomach, tired of subsisting on meal patches, had provided the necessary impetus to move her along.

"*Or embarrassing personal stories. We can trade if you want!*"

The walk to the dining area took her past Ferric's quarters, home to muffled clanging. Since Tarous, the noise was more or less constant; rare was the occasion Ferric could be caught outside his room. Now that some of the distance between them had closed, she'd been looking for a chance to make up the time they'd ceded to ambivalence. If his self-imposed exile was any indication, he wasn't interested.

On several occasions she'd caught him outside, usually while sweeping the corridor. Every time, he found a new way to apologize, and every time, the conversation warped around that apology. Perhaps that was where his reclusiveness stemmed from; Ferric never had enjoyed admitting he was wrong. That explanation didn't feel right—too petty, too simplistic—but it was the best she had.

Whatever it was, it would hopefully be over soon. She wanted her friend back.

There was more noise as she approached the galley—an argument. Since Teomonious's arrival onboard, Tala had heard many such arguments, often interspersed with squeaking cries of *bonus!* and *basket blitz!* from Quarack's omnipad. Some sapients were glued to their games, but never until Quarack had Tala met one who kept playing through a full-blown shouting match. Tala kicked her pace into overdrive.

"We aren't talking about the details of Evelyth Harms's carnal conquests." That was Teomonious, voice colored with a quaver of exasperation. "We're talking about my gun."

"I already said I haven't touched the stupid thing."

"Need I remind you that your testimony was identical the last eight times I—"

"Yeah, yeah. Your point?"

Tala rounded the corner into the dining area.

"And it just so happens that each of those eight times, the gun was later found—"

"Are you tossing pink right now?"

Tala coughed once, boosting the sound to make it audible over the argument.

"What does that—" Understanding bloomed over the alvear's features. "Ah. Yes. I do indeed believe you're lying."

"Hey, Captain." Tala put a little more force into it, and this time, both sapients acknowledged her. Teomonious tried to say something, but she talked over him. "With ninety-three days left on my account, we're on track to reach the Cirasis Nebula ahead of schedule. Once we've rounded the far crest, Urgam will be only a few centralized days away."

This information was easily available from the ship's computer if Quarack cared to look, but Tala had been looking for an excuse to interrupt. If nobody stopped them, they'd be at it for hours.

"Tala, good morning. Would you terribly mind convincing her—"

"Wow," said Quarack. "We just keep getting faster. You're better than a brace of peckin' devastator engines."

"It's only," Teomonious tried again, "the gun will be very difficult to replace. I would appreciate its safe return."

Tala wasn't yet sure how she felt about their newest crewmember. True, his tendency to ramble until someone stopped him was more endearing than infuriating. But for all his eager spouting of information and opinions, something about him kept her on edge. Perhaps it was the way his body language shifted when he thought nobody was looking, or the deftness with which he steered conversations awry whenever he grew uncomfortable with the subject matter. Still, there weren't many sapients she could talk to these days without provoking terror, violence, or both. There were really just two others, and Ferric barely counted these days.

"Quarack," she said tiredly. "It stopped being funny after the fifth time. If you took his gun, give it back."

Quarack shrugged, wings outstretched in a corvid expression of honesty.

"I can't do much more than that," said Tala to Teomonious. "But I'll keep an eye out. It's on this ship somewhere."

The alvear drew himself up to his full height, which would have been more effective coming from someone taller.

"Unless," he hissed, "*someone* thought it would be funny to eject it from an airlock."

He stalked out of the dining area with as much dignity as he could salvage.

"I'd never do that," Quarack said. "Waste of money. That gun could feed a small planet for a deciyear. And I would know—personal experience and all."

There weren't enough calming exercises in the galaxy to handle this trip. Swallowing a reply, Tala allowed herself to be distracted by the galley's food synthesizer. It was hard not to compare it unfavorably to the *Chollima*'s as she selected her species, subspecies, allergies, and current health status. After a few seconds, a loud hiss filled the room and the machine began to extrude something soft, blue-brown, and marginally edible from a fine-tipped nozzle.

"Never seen that color before," remarked Quarack as Tala sat at the dining area's lone table, regarding her plate the same way a Surolian might regard a pit of magma.

"Lucky me," said Tala, with enough sarcasm that even Quarack wouldn't be able to pretend it away.

Quarack drummed her talons against the side of her beak and sat beside her. "So, where's the wind blowing?"

"Where it will." Tala gave the traditional corvid response, a display of manners that Quarack rarely reciprocated. "And for you?"

"If I hear one more cheep from Bugboy, I'm gonna lock him in the smuggler's hold and forget about him. Did you know he listens to hyperchord?"

"Actually—"

"Yeah, it's terrible. He wouldn't stop singing this morning. Well, not *singing* exactly, because you know, hyperchord. But making that weird *shyix-shyix* noise. I don't have the right mouthparts for it. You know what I'm talking about."

"Cries of Grass in the Wind?"

"Yeah! That's the one. It's all over the Network right now. See? He doesn't even like the sub-freq stuff, just overplayed, mass-market trash. Well, it's all trash. But he went on and on. So annoying, wouldn't shut up. You know what that's like?"

"I've got a notion. So you stole his gun? Again?"

"Mere speculation," Quarack scoffed, bobbing her head.

"You know we can read minds, right?"

Quarack blinked twice before letting out a loud *caw* of approval. "That was pretty good. Almost got me."

Tala spooned a chunk of synthesized food into her mouth, gritted her teeth, and swallowed. The oily residue it left on her tongue reminded her of the chores waiting for her—specifically, the dross that kept accumulating in the life-support filters.

"Besides, he still says he won't help you."

Tala stopped trying to suck her tongue clean. "No, he's right," she said. "Congress has too much control over the UNB. Even if he could get the file to a reporter without anyone connecting the two of us, odds are they wouldn't run it."

"So reach out to one of the smaller organizations. Maybe a few professional cranks. This is big enough; it'd spread. We shouldn't be sitting on it."

"Nobody's going to put their name behind a Renegade," Tala pointed out. "They'd focus on the Arcus aspect. Let's say that all comes out, and sapients actually take it seriously instead of calling the evidence a forgery—which they easily could. Then what?" Quarack tried to reply, but she kept going. "Congress issues an apology and we're back to the Advent. They wouldn't clear me. We'd be right where we are, except Teomonious would be persona non grata with the media."

"He's just worried the blowback could hit his precious career."

"Maybe. But that doesn't mean he's wrong. We should still try if this new lead doesn't pan out, I'm just not convinced it changes anything. As Tenet forty-six says, *determination will not fly a ship through an asteroid.*"

"Sounds like good advice for avoiding collisions, but how does it apply?"

"It's metaphorical. The ship represents—"

"Don't care. Moving on." Quarack ran a claw through the gelatinous mound on Tala's plate and lifted it to her beak. Tala couldn't bring herself to care. "What if—not bad—he's part of the cover-up? Maybe we can't trust anything he says!"

"That doesn't seem likely," said Tala for the eighth time. Quarack always seemed to conveniently forget this part of their conversations. "The file was eleventh-tier classified, and councilors default to ninth. I can't find any reason to suspect he'd have extra clearance."

"I dunno. I've been looking through what we got, and this seems exactly like the cloak-and-feather stuff he'd be into. That meltdown on Kennesor? Did you read that part?"

"Yes." Tala had, in fact, gone through it two days ago. A city had entered lockdown three years back following reports that a fusion plant had suffered a catastrophic failure. According to the GIAB file, the meltdown had been wholly fabricated. Arcus had been traced to Kennesor Two and they'd tried to keep him there. It hadn't worked.

Two things were clear from the last twenty-two years of history in Arcus's file. First, the government was still pursuing him with every available resource. And second, everyone involved—including Arcus himself—seemed hellbent on keeping his survival secret. Why this was, Tala had yet to figure out, but they'd been willing to brand her Renegade for it. For a lie. When she thought too long on that, her jaw trembled and the placid waters of her mind gathered into peaks.

"But we have to trust him," she said.

Quarack squawked dismissively. "That's the most midday idea I've ever heard."

"Mid…day idea?" That was a new one, and its meaning wasn't immediately apparent.

"You know what I mean."

Tala shrugged, noticing that Quarack had begun fidgeting.

"It's a midday…you know. Like…" she seemed to be choosing her words with rare attention. "Something you tell your friends you're doing later in the day. Except you aren't actually gonna do it, so you didn't think the details through, so it'd go really badly if you actually did it." She took a deep breath. "*Now* do you see?"

Tala turned this over in her head for a few seconds. "And why am I telling my friends I'm going to do something I won't be doing?"

"I knew you were sheltered, but seriously?"

"And why midday, specifically?"

"Because—" Quarack clamped her beak shut, catching herself. "No. You've gotta be messing with me."

"You'd be able to tell if I was." Tala let a smile through. "Probably."

Quarack spluttered, but her eyes were twinkling.

It wasn't often, but sometimes Tala did manage to get past Quarack's barriers to a moment of genuine connection. This felt like one of those times. So naturally, Quarack decided it was a good time to crank her omnipad's volume up to max and start playing. Tala swallowed the rest of her "food" (at least it went down easily) and rinsed her mouth out at the sink.

"See you," she said on her way out, and got an enthusiastic "*basket blitz!*" in return.

The clanging from Ferric's room had subsided. Was now a good time to knock? Her tongue was heavy with everything she wanted to say, but the struggle of that final push proved heavier still. *Later*, she resolved. *Later*. She had duties to attend to, and it wouldn't do for them to remain unfinished on Bartamitraxul's other side.

Tala couldn't help but feel a flicker of resentment toward the *Aquilon* and its leaky pipes as she dipped a nanofiber cloth in a bucket of aggressively orange cleaning solution. She should have accepted her duty with more grace, as the third Tenet instructed, but couldn't quite think herself into the proper mindset. The fuel pipes needed replacement, not constant wiping. One particularly solid globule of gunk refused to give, so Tala zeroed in on it, wondering how Quarack managed when she didn't have passengers to press into service.

Once that was done, it was time to pay the gravity coils a visit. For reasons Quarack hadn't been able to articulate, they weren't hooked up to the generator. This meant changing their fuel cells at regular intervals or losing gravity, which came with its own slew of problems—problems only slightly larger than Quarack's fuel cell expenses. At least the cells popped in and out easily enough. Replacing them was the only time Tala felt as if the ship weren't actively resisting her efforts to care for it.

Just thinking about the next chore down the list could turn a two-decihour fuel cell change into a half-hour exercise in procrastination. The life support was right by the gravity coils, so Tala would periodically glance over and see the filters waiting for her. Another item for the list of things she was avoiding.

Among them was the last section of Arcus's file, *Possible Sighting on Neea*. It wasn't long. Just a few sentences like *"given Arcus's official status, responded accordingly"* and *"no evidence of Arcus's presence detected on-site."* It always made her want to darken the omnipad rather than read further. Almost two deciyears now, and even the name of the planet could break her chain of thought like a baton to a mirror. Sometimes she could put the pieces back together cleanly. Other times, it took decihours to reconstruct, fighting to control her breathing while every attempt at progress looped back into another bloodstained memory. The center of the spiral was always the same: another protracted internal castigation, well earned, for the way she'd laid on the floor like a coward while her friends died for her. She hadn't deserved them.

She dragged out the fuel cell replacement, but eventually had to screw the last one into place. She checked the tightness, ran a diagnostic (unnecessary; if the coils had stopped working, it would be obvious), rechecked the tightness, and—finally—ran out of excuses. Only the life-support module remained.

Because self-cleaning filters were apparently black magic, maintaining the *Aquilon*'s life support was a manual affair. Tala had experimented a great deal, but ultimately had been forced to admit that there was no better way to scrape out the filters than with her hands.

The filters slid out easily, as if eager to ruin her day. Both of them dripped with viscous cyan sludge. Breath held tight, Tala set them down and slid new filters into place. Then, grimacing, she plunged her fingers into the goop. It wouldn't harm her as long as she kept it away from her mouth, but it *was* revolting. She scraped what she could into the disposal, then put the filters into a tub of water to soak clean. Quarack claimed reusing them was perfectly safe. While Tala wasn't sure this was true, there were only three sets of filters aboard, so it was used filters or nothing.

The gunk never came off her hands easily. No matter how hard she scrubbed, she was used to wearing the last coat of sticky residue for hours. But this time, she didn't have to feel guilty about using power generally allocated to the engines for personal use. She sent some of her reserve into the soap and shoved her hands under the spigot. In record time, she was vacuum-tubing her fingers dry.

Her fingers were clean, but between the morning's exercise, the fuel pipes, and the nonessential nature of showering, the rest of her was less lucky. She was past due for a cleanse. For the first time in days, Tala started off toward her assigned quarters. Perhaps away from the engines' thumping, she could even get some real meditation in. She reached the main

corridor...

And saw that the door to her quarters was wide open.

Tala sent a surge of Enhancement through her body—just in case— and crept forward on noiseless feet. Sharpened hearing picked up the tapping of chitinous legs on metal. *Teomonious*? Why would he be rooting through her room?

At the threshold, she scuffed her foot deliberately against the door groove. Teomonious whirled around, making a startled trill. "What are you doing here?" he stammered as he tried to reclaim his lost composure.

"It's my room. What are *you* doing?"

"Ah." Teomonious glanced about awkwardly, mandibles working overtime. "Of course. It's your—yes. Dreadfully sorry."

"You're saying you didn't know it was mine?" Tala kept her voice even, but the question was no less pointed for it.

"That's—no, I knew, but—" he gathered himself. "Private space. The concept. It isn't intuitive."

From what Tala remembered of the Center's xenology classes, the excuse checked out, at least in theory. Native alvear colonies clustered together in compact warrens. Every centimeter of that space belonged to the colony's hivemother, to be doled out or restricted as she saw fit.

More than any other species, alvear tried to mold themselves to local norms, happily discarding their social structures, mannerisms, and speech patterns upon exposure to a foreign culture. They often succeeded so well, it was easy to forget they were by far the newest species to be folded into the Galactic Coalition. Everyone else—Tala included—just... took for granted that for once, an alien species was eager to assimilate with the larger whole. Nobody really considered whether such things came entirely naturally.

Still, his explanation wasn't perfect.

"And you came in here because..."

"It's that abominable fowl!" Teomonious threw all six arms up in exasperation. "Your captain stole my weapon, and I cannot locate it anywhere."

He put a strange emphasis on "your," as if repelled by the idea of suborning himself to Quarack.

"She wouldn't put it here." Despite the violation of her privacy, Tala was finding it easy to forgive the poor alvear. The Tenets had some things to say about being overly attached to objects—fifty-six, in particular, was uncharacteristically direct—but most sapients hadn't benefited from the wisdom of such an education. Even Tala, who *was* supposed to embody the Tenets, imagined it would be distressing to lose, say, her stuffed koala. "Next time, just ask me and I'll let you in, all right? Actually," a new thought, one she should've had immediately, "how *did* you get in?"

"I didn't break in, if that's what you're implying," said Teomonious with some indignance. "The door was unlocked."

"Hmm."

Tala thought she'd sealed her quarters after her last visit, but it *had* been several days ago. At this point, it was hard to remember. She didn't believe anyone aboard would steal from her—she didn't have much to take, and she could already tell nothing was missing—but the possibility wasn't a pleasant one.

"I... apologize," said Teomonious. "For entering your quarters unbidden, as well as for thinking the worst of you when we met."

"And you don't anymore?"

"I'm not entirely sure," Teomonious admitted. "You don't seem like a Renegade. You value the Tenets, you appear sane enough, and you're remarkably peaceful for someone who's traveled so far with that corvid. Besides, it seems you were right—about that Arcus fellow, I mean. I still find it hard to believe that the Index could contain innocents, but..." He shrugged. "All together, it makes for a compelling case."

Tala held his gaze. "Thank you. Truly."

"Besides, I have seen the quarters you keep in that little storage room. You possess quite an eye for art. Duna is severely underappreciated. A genius with color, even for a siari."

"She was," agreed Tala, thinking back to her research for something intelligent to say. Most art lectures she'd found had slid in one ear and right back out the other side. "Her line work is, uh, it's..."

"So vividly differentiated, yes! And the use of textures to apply a counter-perspective to each subject, sublime."

"Absolutely." Tala was out of her depth, but that in itself was an opportunity. "There's something about that one that just grips me. Does it have any particular meaning to you?"

Teomonious hummed contemplatively. Tala could tell that he was examining some memory of *Flowerbed*. "To me, it speaks of hopelessness lost amid the greater tragedies of the galaxy at large—note the trails of violet woven through the starlight, and within the human's hair. The lack of arms, the submissive posture, there's acceptance there.

You can't be fooled by the face's serenity, not when the textures speak a different language entirely. It's harder to see when you don't have the original, but you must have noticed the roughness?"

She hadn't. "Yes."

"You have no idea how relieved I am that *someone* on this relic appreciates culture," chittered Teomonious, disdain dripping from his mandibles. "It might make the trip bearable." He shook his head, seeming for one odd moment authentically human. "Don't get me started on my walls. They're *covered* in gyrating corvids, and I can't get rid of them. It was enough to make me wonder if this whole endeavor was worth the vexation. I know it will be, of course, but my resolve had begun to falter of late. Even this modicum of intelligent conversation has done wonders for my morale."

"Please, don't mention it."

"I hope we can speak more in the future, about art, and perhaps music. Assuming you listen?"

"Yes," said Tala, surprised by the rawness of his enthusiasm. "Some stuff, anyway."

"A sapient of discerning taste, then. Perfect! You have full permission to enter my quarters whenever you find yourself in need of more sophisticated conversation."

"Thanks, but I won't have too many opportunities for that. I need to spend as much time by the engines as possible."

Teomonious looked like she'd broken his prized gun into a thousand pieces right in front of him.

"Remember," she said, with a consoling smile, "The more time I spend down there, the sooner we'll be on Urgam."

"Of course." Teomonious *did* look a little mollified at that. "I want this wretched business done with as much as you do. I understand. Perhaps I'll come visit you from time to time."

"That would be...an option." Tala couldn't commit to more excitement than that, but maybe some social interaction would be good for her. "Anyway, I was going to take a shower."

"Of course, of course. I won't delay you further."

With an exchange of farewells and a polite bow, Teomonious scuttled off. The door closed behind him, and Tala was alone again, pondering what he'd said about *Flowerbed*. Hopelessness didn't sound right. It certainly wasn't the meaning Frael had taken from it, all those years ago. Nor was it a realization that could have helped her, as the Central Pillar had seemed to think it could. There had to be something *behind* the hopelessness. A hidden dimension that Duna had planted amongst the painting's flowers for only the most astute to find.

The room's shower unit was nestled in the corner opposite her bed, a capsule-shaped half-yellow/half-pearlescent unit mounted on the wall. Her omnipad interfaced with it as she approached, sharing her stored preferences. She set the omnipad down on the glass dome covering her bed, then removed the canister-fabric clothing she'd sprayed that morning. She'd put it in the reprocessor later.

The unit lit up as she entered the shower's boundaries. Then came a low hum that tingled across her skin, everywhere at once, as the device bathed her in hypersonic waves. She lifted her arms to make sure the machine had full coverage. Ten seconds and it was over. Tala stretched appreciatively. When was the last time she'd felt this clean? She permitted a smile to touch her face and retrieved a cream-colored jumpsuit from her cabinet. It was a little more rumpled than she remembered, but it felt much nicer on her skin than a sprayed outfit.

This time, Tala made sure to lock the door when she left. As she trotted back into the belly of the ship, she passed under the turret again, the view no longer as tempting as it had been. The corridor narrowed the deeper she got, until she reached the small hole outside the main storage bay that led to her makeshift quarters. There was a ladder here too, but like she always did, she ignored it in favor of dropping to the floor. Before she could walk in, the etherway crackled to life above her.

"*Hi, sapes and sundry! This is your captain speaking—in case you hadn't figured that out already. Did you ever see that old holoshow* A Brief Injustice? *Apparently, there was a Preeminent who tried to change the Tribunal robes so they'd look more like Hammerson Tate's robes from the show. The vote failed and he got so mad he resigned. Well, he said it was for unrelated reasons, but no one believes that. Also, does anyone want to watch* A Brief Injustice *later? It's really good!*"

Tala had already sealed the sub-bay door. It didn't quite block out Quarack, but it did muffle her enough that she could be ignored in favor of the steady thump of the engines. Tala reset her omnipad's five-hour alarm and dropped into a warmup stretch.

Renegades were often content to leave paths of destruction that could be spotted from space (her thoughts had circled back to Arcus while her body ran through the motions by rote). Arcus was a ghost by comparison, whose activities had taken the GIAB equal parts effort and guesswork to track. Perhaps he was simply smarter than the rest—he'd survived more than ten times longer than the average Renegade's post-turn lifespan— but no amount of intelligence should have made a difference in that regard. Without the Tenets to guide them, Renegade minds were marred by psychosis and megalomania. Arcus's own madness must have manifested differently, somehow. But the madness would still be there, clouding his judgment. If Tala could determine how it was affecting his thought patterns, she could exploit that.

Almost as inscrutable as his movements were his motives. The GIAB had seen a pattern of striking government targets, though never anything large or particularly vital. For someone who'd spoken of dismantling the Coalition, it seemed a nibbling sort of approach—slow, based more on opportunity than deliberation. What was it he'd said, exactly? His words were foggy. What came next was sharp in her memory, but everything before was washed out. Less real. Unimportant.

No, this couldn't amount to the sum total of his goals. But there was nothing in the file to suggest at his larger plan—just a bunch of Arcus-shaped holes. Tala suspected there was more in the archive that she hadn't gotten, locked behind a higher clearance level. Too many wires weren't connecting. She'd never thought it would be as easy as finding a handy map to Arcus's hideout, but she *had* expected some attempt at assessment. It was right there in the bureau's name, after all.

Even the details on his descent into madness were sparse. There was nothing that couldn't be found in public records; one day, he'd turned on and slaughtered his Vanguard, then fled into open space. No warning signs besides an unhealthy interest in Renegades. Simple, sudden, and settled.

An explanation so satisfying as to leave no questions in its wake.

Tala stiffened, aborting her kata halfway through. It was happening again.

How does the fourth Tenet go? 'Disobedience is the precipice, weakness the fall'? Isn't it convenient there's a moral imperative to obey?

"The Tenets inform our actions," Tala said to the voice of her friends' killer. "They don't equate to thoughtless obedience, whatever the fourth says."

You take their words as truth, without even asking the question. Can you deny it?

"You broke from them, and look what happened to you."

Yet for all your adherence to the Tenets, you've done a poor job staving off my fate. Didn't I tell you that you'd be just like me someday?

"Don't pretend you're anything like me. You killed sapients. I'm trying to save them."

If the voice had intended to respond, it didn't get the chance. The sound of Quarack's singing poured through the etherway, leaking right through the closed door.

"Aaaaaand I feel the magic in her eye-eye-eyes.... Iiiiiiii wanna try her on for si-i

-ize.... Reach out, and—oh crumbs, this thing's on." A loud clanging, as if someone had dropped three nested pots onto the etherway's receiver. *"We're through the gate, so you know. Total downflight. Give us a half hour to get clear, then start ramping up the speed, yeah?"*

Tala shook her head, letting out a long breath. This made five times that icy voice had spoken to her. She still didn't know what was happening, or how to stop it. And the conversations were growing more frequent.

The truth was, it frightened her.

Cold sweat streaked her jumpsuit, dripped down her forehead, and played over her eyes. Her muscles were aching—a good, healthy ache. She was getting stronger. But what good would strength be, if she couldn't trust her own mind?

She took a battle stance and fell into one of Scratch's combat drills. As she jabbed at the air, she filled the empty space with the faces of Arcus's associates from the GIAB file. She'd studied their images until they appeared on the inside of her lids before she fell asleep. Those creepy nordok mercenaries. Amara Vert, his dead Acolyte. And Viron, the bloodthirsty Renegade her mentor had been sent to kill. She imagined herself fighting them, taking them down with every little trick Scratch had taught her. Practice for the real enemy.

Practice wouldn't be enough. She'd replayed their battle in her mind more than she could bear. Every stance, every blow, every second. What the memories of that nightmare day told her was that she'd had no chance from the start.

She needed a force multiplier of her own. A flagship play. Something Arcus couldn't plan for, something like the—

The room had changed since morning.

It was incredible that she hadn't caught it before; her thoughts must have been too full for stray observation. In the corner, several supply crates had been shifted. They'd been stacked before. Now they were pushed together in a row, forming a small alcove by the wall.

Those crates had been empty since they'd left Ipwaan. Why would anyone move them?

She approached cautiously and undid the crate seals, one by one. The boxes were still empty. But behind them, in the makeshift alcove, was Teomonious's platinum laser pistol.

Tala heaved a sigh and returned to her workout. She'd put it off long enough, and nothing, not the bickering of crewmates or half-imagined voices, would get in her way this time.

CHAPTER FIFTEEN

CONFRONTING THE EVIDENCE

The first glimpse of a new world had a pull to it, no matter how many you saw. Forests, mountains, plains…even the settlements had something unique about them. Sometimes subtle, sometimes obvious, but always interesting. Every planet was an adventure waiting to be discovered, with its own varied topography, striking colors, and unique native life.

Except for Urgam.

Urgam was a ball of orange dust, flat deserts stretching across the planet without so much as a dune in sight. Aside from the rare gleam of metal denoting a city, or the wind whipping a patch of dust into a rolling cloud, there was nothing to Urgam but barren uniformity.

Single-biome. The term wasn't pejorative, technically, but it was more often colored by scorn than not. Of course, cost ruled supreme and a mining planet only needed to be terraformed so far to be operable.

They were approaching rapidly, though Tala had stopped Enhancing the engines over an hour ago in favor of watching from what passed for communal space aboard the *Aquilon*. Teomonious occupied his usual stool in the far corner of the kitchen, mandibles buried in his omnipad. Every so often, he glanced up at the main holo as if to reaffirm their progress.

"This is your captain speaking…" Quarack's voice came in through the etherway, accompanied by the sound of claws dancing across metal.

That got Teomonious's attention. His eyes snapped up from his projected newsblurb to focus in on Tala. "She is most assuredly not my captain. Under no circumstances would I consider placing myself in a position of subservience to that one."

"…landing on sunny Urgam momentarily. Home of desperate miners and conniving councilors. Come for the dust storms, stay because you died of dehydration."

True to Quarack's words, the flat swaths of dust were now so close that the ship was practically hugging them. Then came a small clang, followed by a concussive thud and an explosion of dust that mantled the outer cameras and made further observation impossible. The whole ship lurched beneath their feet as the landing gear expended the ship's excess kinetic energy outward. Teomonious pitched off his stool, arms flailing. It did nothing to arrest his fall.

Groaning, he grabbed the edge of the dining table and pulled himself up. "Probably made the landing rough on purpose," he said with officious contempt.

"Actually, I had to come down fast to get under the cities' aerial scanners." Quarack had apparently been listening in, no doubt waiting

for a chance to get in a snide remark or two. *"Call me a rough beak, but I thought our two friends here would have a little trouble talking their way past customs."*

Most planets detected incoming ships with an atmospheric planetary grid, but Urgam had no such amenities. In fact, Urgam didn't have much in the way of anything: ten cities supporting a single massive mining complex, large deposits of europium buried in the crust, and a whole lot of dirt.

Teomonious's face went through a number of spasms. He turned to Tala, searching for commiseration. "It's ever the diligent soul that suffers in the name of retribution."

He looked so indignant that Tala had to chuckle. "Growth is the blossom, struggle the seed," she offered. Ferric's favorite Tenet.

Quarack swaggered in a few seconds later, pep practically sparking from her talons. She gave Teomonious a smug look. "We have a long walk ahead. You can complain as we go."

"I hardly need your permission, but I'm glad to hear you'll be willing to listen. I've been assembling a list, and I assure you—it's quite long."

"Can't wait. But watching you bake in the heat will make it all worth it."

They were incorrigible. Tala had seen enough similar arguments to know this was headed nowhere good. "Let's not forget we share the same goal. We're here to investigate Ceowograffach, not waste energy picking at each other."

"Tala's right."

All eyes went to the kitchen door as Ferric walked through. He gave Tala a little nod and took position at her right shoulder. "Cut it out or wait on the ship."

It was her first Ferric sighting in five days. Judging by the others' reactions, that was probably a safe guess for them as well. His face was pale and pinched from long nights with his suit, and the guilt he felt wasn't less obvious for its lack of vocalization. He still wasn't meeting her eyes, she noticed. But he was back at her side, where he belonged, and that was something.

"Thanks," Tala said. The word hovered languidly between them, holding the door open for everything else she wanted to say. She kept it down. This wasn't the time.

"I refuse to miss a moment of this," said Teomonious. "Perhaps Tala couldn't lie her way out of a room full of amnesiacs, but my trust in the rest of you could be measured with a microscope."

Whether an insult or a compliment, Tala elected to ignore that remark.

Quarack ran a claw down her beak in amusement. "You sure you'll be okay? What if you dry out?"

"I—"

"You'll both be fine," said Tala. "We won't be walking long, and we can call a pod once we've gotten some distance from the ship. I can help with the walk if you want—though heat's a bit more involved."

"Do you mean providing us with Enhancement?" Teomonious's mandibles were clicking together with enough speed to impact his pronunciation.

"If you want."

Quarack chewed at her tongue, talons scraping at the metal floor. "I don't know. If it's too much trouble—"

"No trouble at all."

Ferric's mouth was twitching with barely suppressed disappointment. There were rules for when it was appropriate to Enhance others. There were rules for just about everything.

"Let's move out," she said, brushing past the snag of resentment her mind had caught on. "We have a schedule to keep, even if it isn't ours."

There was something strange about wearing someone else's face. Not the act in and of itself, though the stickiness of the mesh mask took some getting used to. It was the forgetting. That if she looked in a mirror, the face looking back would be a stranger's; that if she happened to smile, that stranger would smile for her. Keeping that in her mind was a constant process, because the strangest part of the experience was how strange she didn't feel.

Teomonious had supplied the holoveils, originally procured alongside the cloak to circumvent GIAB security. They'd gone unused, but they would prove their worth now; the hologram they projected was far more sophisticated than that of the spacer-rigged omnipad she'd strapped to her neck on Tarous. The mesh fit over the contours of her face closely enough to fool most security cameras, to say nothing of the scrutiny of random sapients. With her face plastered across every omnipad's wanted list, such measures were necessary.

Though less recognizable, Ferric also wore a holoveil. His new guise had an older look, with a broad, squashed nose—the kind that brought to mind good cheer, or too much barroom brawling. The veil couldn't do much about his hair, so it was a lucky thing that he wasn't the type for distinctive ornamental carvings. In fact, he was more likely to take a carving knife to the chest than the hair.

Quarack wore her own face, but even that had been transformed by a childlike joy. Her wariness at being Enhanced had fast turned to excitement. Tala hadn't even given her all that much—just enough to ease the desert's burdens—but Quarack was running and jumping about, testing the limits of her new energy. Teomonious seemed no less entranced, but he went about it more quietly. Speculative and curious, he kept flexing his grippers one by one, as if feeling each of his muscles move under the chitin.

Given the harshness of the desert heat, Tala was glad for his distraction—if not for that, his complaints would have been ceaseless. The air felt as if she'd been trapped inside a kiln, complete with the smell of burnt clay. Every so often, a parched breeze would send up whorls of dust that gave the light a fractured quality, like water dripping through a sieve. She squinted against the glare, trying to spot Deltor City Six up ahead, but saw nothing on the shimmering horizon but the orange sun.

If the desert was separating her from only another dead end...Tala curled her hands into fists, feeling the skin stretch over the raised bumps of her knuckles. She wanted this whole affair done with. The longer it went on, the more questions she discovered and the more lost she felt.

At least she had Ferric at her side again. Even wearing a different face, her Vanguard was a comforting presence. His stride slotted into place against hers, their rhythm etched out over many long years. Familiarity aided Enhancement, but that was far from its only benefit.

She still wanted a real conversation with him. Dorian's centralized birthday was in a few days; if nothing else, it would be nice to know if they could lean on each other for moral support. But Ferric's omnipad was up and his earclips on. Like everything else, the device was under constant assault from eddies of orange dust. Ferric kept brushing it away, but more settled on the screen whenever he stopped. Competing with the dust, a tiny, holographic Maestervolt lectured soundlessly, occasionally holding up an electron magnetizer or other multipurpose tool. Tala took out her own omnipad. She and Ferric had been friends long enough that she knew he'd be dead to the galaxy for a while.

She looked up her mentor first. Scratch's current whereabouts were officially secret, but the Network had its share of Enhancer enthusiasts. Eyewitnesses claimed he'd been spotted on Vanak. She wondered what he was doing there. Was it chance, or a hunt coming to fruition? After all, Vanak wasn't far—just one cluster over. Though Urgam felt like an edgeworld, it was closer to the bright center of civilization than it had any right to be.

Next, she tried Viron. Still no news of his death or capture, just a small newsblurb from three deciyears ago spotlighting Meftti Sou, Hedegarb, and Castor Cord as the new team taking over the assignment. They were a good group; she'd even worked with Hedegarb before. And no news meant no recent massacres—at least, not since Scratch's reassignment. Tala sighed and refreshed the page, but nothing changed. She hadn't expected it to.

Looking up from the omnipad, she caught sight of the first break in the desert. Ahead in the distance stood a small sheet-metal cottage, an early indicator that civilization might not be far. Beside the ramshackle abode, one lonely tree, amber in color, rose above it. Tala increased the brightness of the Enhancement on her eyes until she could make out tight-closed shutters on the windows. Whoever had once called it home seemed to have left—if not for greener pastures, at least for somewhere less isolated. Between the house and the tree, a driving pod lay flaking in the sun. The pinkish paint had been scoured from the frame, exposing the blue metal beneath.

Where there were pods, there were podpaths. Tala shielded her eyes from the sun with her hand and squinted into the distance. There—about six kilometers away. Infrequent blurs flitted across it, barely visible over the empty desert.

"Podpath ahead," said Tala, pitching her voice over Quarack and Teomonious, who had just started antagonizing each other anew. The mesh caught her voice as it came out, warping it just enough to fool a vocal recognition program. "Should hit it in three-quarters of an hour."

"—molting, or just naturally patchy?" Teomonious turned to Tala before Quarack could retaliate. "Does that mean we've come far enough to summon a pod? I am beginning to reach the end of my patience with this insufferable desert."

"Didn't notice you had any," muttered Quarack.

Tala answered before Teomonious could. "I'd say we're a good distance out. Calling a pod this close to a podpath won't stand out in the transport logs. Let's—"

Teomonious yanked his omnipad from the inside of his robe and opened the Podcaller icon faster than Tala had ever seen him move.

"—do it."

"*Welcome, Cernarvitalimun Teomonious.*" The voice was precise and mechanical, every consonant over-enunciated. "*Thank you for choosing Podcaller. Your account's default order is a deluxe, extra-space gray travelpod for two. Will you be placing the same order?*"

"Yes—actually, make it a pod for four," Teomonious forced out through tired mandibles.

"*When would you—*"

"Schedule pickup for seven decihours from now."

"*All right, I've placed your order,*" the Podcaller voice whirred. "*Please state your destination. If you don't know your destination and would like help, please say: 'help'.*"

"Gray?" Quarack whispered loudly to Ferric. "Who sets their default color to gray? I mean, I guessed it'd be a deluxe something, but this is further proof that if we cut him open, he'd bleed memos."

Ferric ignored her, but Teomonious didn't. "Gray is sophisticated but subtle. You could learn from its example."

202 Δ WEAPONS of the MIND

The service program made a sharp dinging noise. *"That is not a recognized location in our planetary database. Please either repeat your destination, or say: 'help' for assistance."*

Teomonious glared at his omnipad, clicking his mandibles with impatience. "Haymore Mining Transit Station, Deltor City Six."

Another ding. *"Thank you. Your account has been charged and your pod is on its way. Please head to the nearest podpath to await pickup. Remember, with Podcaller, you call more than a pod; you call a way home."*

Teomonious terminated the icon and redoubled his dogged march toward the pickup point. Tala found herself impressed with his stamina—even Enhanced as he was.

As the others sped up, Tala let herself trail behind. Ferric must have been keeping an eye on her because he sent her a probing look, but didn't intrude further. She appreciated that, though she wasn't hiding any big secrets. Just another omnipad search, one more embarrassing than interesting. Looking up Viron and Scratch had been part leadup, part delaying tactic. Now she was out of excuses. She had to see.

"Your footsteps are dragging."

Tala almost stopped dead. It was a voice she knew well, one she could almost mistake for a too-vivid memory. The voice of her mentor.

"Why this weakness when I taught you to be strong?"

"I—" she bit back her retort, remembering just in time that the others could hear her. It was lucky she'd dropped back so they couldn't see her stumble, or cast her eyes about like an injured sparrow. There was nowhere Scratch's voice could be coming from. But by the disciplines, it sounded like he was standing right next to her.

"What holds you back? Are you afraid of me, or for me? The spirits are silent. I can make out their words, but their whispers have been choked off at the source."

"As usual, you're asking the wrong questions." The other voice joined Scratch's, and this time, she didn't bother looking. She knew Arcus wasn't nearby. "Better to wonder why she's still trying when she's already given up this venture for doomed. Why she walks forward at all when she sees no end to the path ahead."

"There is always merit in striving," Scratch replied, *"and in facing defeat without fear. I have demanded nothing from Tala but her best. So long as she gives it, the illusion of failure cannot deceive her."*

Tala quickened her pace—not due to Scratch's words, but hoping to leave the voices behind. She drew long breaths, expelling each one on a count of four. Whether it had worked or not, both Arcus and her teacher fell silent. All intention of completing her search had fled her mind with their departure. She kept breathing and kept walking, the sun overhead, her thoughts an empty pool, and the podpath drawing nearer and nearer.

She would have passed it entirely had Ferric not placed a firm hand on her shoulder, jarring her back to the waiting world. "Thanks," she said. It was all she could muster.

The pod didn't take long to arrive; it came less than a decihour after they reached the podpath. The pod's gleaming chassis resembled a lightly flattened sphere, and was just as gray as advertised. Once all eight wheels had stopped spinning, the same precise voice Teomonious had interacted with issued forth from the pod. "Welcome! The omnipad of registered user Cernarvitalimun Teomonious has been detected. Opening doors now. Your destination: Haymore Mining Transit Station. Please enjoy your trip, and remember, with Podcaller, you call more than a pod; you call a way home."

Speech concluded, the pod's sides slid open, releasing a wave of cool air that made Tala's skin sing with joy down to the last pore.

Inside the pod was more gray. It brought to mind the interior of a cocoon made entirely of imitation-leather couches. There were drink dispensers, a wide holoscreen, and a device at head height that looked like it was designed to spray scented mist. She couldn't remember the last time she'd taken a pod this nice, and guessing by the smugness radiating from Teomonious, he knew it.

Quarack took the seat by the temperature controls, but made no move to touch them—a wise choice, Tala thought, as she might have found herself tossed out of the pod if she had. Tala opted for a chilled bottle of water from the dispenser, taking long sips. Quarack followed her lead, but went with something orange and fizzing.

"Shut doors and begin trip," said Teomonious, collapsing heavily onto an open seat. "Window tint to maximum. Engage privacy mode."

All four windows darkened, dimming the sunlight as the pod's sides resealed themselves. Each door clicked into place and the pod began to move.

"Here we go," said Quarack. "Off on our quest to kill some poor sape's shoes."

Ferric made a shushing noise.

"We should be safe to talk," said Teomonious. "The deluxe Podcaller model's privacy features are very extensive."

"Duh," said Quarack. "I knew that. So can anyone tell—"

Tala frowned. "Does that strike anyone else as a bad system?"

"Yes, yes, very inequitable." Teomonious said, waving all six arms. "To be fair though, most sapients who can't afford the privilege don't tend to have secrets worth the bother of taking."

"I still want to know why you hate shoes so much," said Quarack, already immersed in some game or other.

Tala took another long gulp of water before answering. "We don't hate shoes."

"Part of the plan is to shoot his shoes."

204 WEAPONS OF THE MIND

"With a microstick listener," said Ferric. "Did you listen to the briefing?"

"Let's say, hypothetically, that maybe I only caught around half."

"Well, listening devices don't do well with water, so you want to stick them somewhere that rarely gets washed. And few traveling sapients bring more than two sets of footwear, so shoes are an all-around good target."

"Sounds like an excuse," muttered Quarack. "You can't hide your all-consuming hatred of shoes from me, pal. But as long as we're asking questions, why's *he* here again?"

Teomonious still hadn't adjusted position since his collapse. "Let me answer your question with another: which of us is paying for the driving pod and the tickets? Unless a certain corvid has decided to volunteer to chip in, she should stop relitigating questions well answered."

Quarack actually let his comment lie, in favor of her game. Nobody stepped up to fill the conversational void, so Tala pulled out her omnipad. She still had to make that search, the one she'd only recently let herself even think about. She tilted the screen away from the others. The imitation leather squeaked as she shifted.

"Would you look at that!"

Latching onto the excuse, Tala's eyes followed Teomonious's outstretched arm. Outside the window, a gyrocycle raced along the podpath, keeping pace with their pod. It looked like two whirling pot lids, angled inward and joined by a circle of dark plastic. As Tala watched, the vehicle veered sharply off the podpath, sending a wave of dust into the air. By the time the dust had settled, the gyrocycle was a speck in the distance.

"We should have procured a few of those," the alvear continued. "They would have made the journey across the desert far more pleasant. Not that I wasn't fascinated by the sensation of being Enhanced."

"I've driven one before," said Quarack. "Loads of fun. You can build up a good amount of speed. But it's manual pilot only, so I'm the only one who could steer the thing without eating a face full of dust."

"If *you're* capable of steering one, I daresay I'd find it to be no challenge at all."

They were at it again. She'd heard enough of their bickering for three Torandian lifetimes—even spending most of her time alone in the *Aquilon*'s sub-bay, by the loud, rattling engines.

Outside the pod, buildings started to flick by. Just a scattered few so far; run-down huts like the one they'd passed earlier. Each was uniquely haphazard, so unlike the efficient uniformity she was used to seeing on the more developed planets. The huts bled into larger living complexes fairly soon—mass-produced plasticrete blocks of tenement housing, all company owned. Haymore had gotten its landing grips into Urgam well ahead of the competition. The final mark of their entrance into civilization was a fleet of metal-banded drones dotting the air like buzzing birds.

When Tala had been a speck of a thing, before the Center, she'd chased her share of the little flying machines. She'd run below them, jumping, trying to knock them from the heavens. Not once had she come even close, but that hadn't deterred her from leaping about the perfectly engineered grass like her next jump would be the one that let her scrape the sky. *My little spring,* Mom had dubbed her. That nickname had faded after she'd left home.

The memory stung at her resolve and sent her back to the omnipad in her hand. This time, she followed through. Her mouth was dry as the outside air. There were so many results. She touched one—*Sela Kreeth: A mother speaks on her daughter's crimes*—with a porcelain finger.

"I want to say sorry. Sorry to the families of the victims. Sorry to everyone who was hurt. And sorry to her—Tala. I don't know how this happened, or why..."

There was a rawness to her voice Tala had never heard before, not a hint of the salessape's familiar gloss. Eyelids itching, she reached for her water to wet her throat. That was when she realized the pod had gone silent, and everyone was looking at her.

"...but I am so sorry all the same."

She'd somehow triggered the deluxe pod's screenshare. The interview was playing on the main holoscreen.

Tala seized control of her facial muscles, reordering them into neutrality as she did the first thing she could think of: switch the screen's signal source to satellite with a forceful wave. A gauntlet appeared onscreen; a room of spinning wooden paddles whipped at a sprinting thrall from every side.

"Boring," Quarack said, waving the image away. "Who's got time for those tame runs?"

"—you baste it with the oil and flutegrass. Really make sure it's all covered..."

The screen now showed a green-feathered corvid in a kitchen, looking down his beak at two humans and another corvid who themselves were bent over their prep boards, slathering fish with an oily pink mixture.

"Turn it off."

Quarack was running both claws along her beak in a pattern Tala hadn't seen before, her talons clenching and unclenching as if they kept expecting to find something to grab onto.

"Jemes, your measurements are wrong. Look at—"

Tala waved at the screen again, a quick sideways slice. The program cut out at once. Quarack was avoiding eye contact with Tala. Ferric was trying to meet *her* eyes, but silence was the sound of the moment. She blanked her omnipad and put it in her lap, turned her full attention to the closest tinted window, and tried to give her thoughts over to nothing.

Their pod merged into a line of traffic, fitting perfectly as the grid directed. The sapients on the walkways had no such guiding force. While Urgam's total population was small, its few cities teemed with bodies. Deltor City Six was a plasticrete-metal tangle, skyscrapers clawing at the cloudless sky and casting stark shadows on the walkways below.

All too soon, the pod pulled to a stop. Tala barely had enough time to prepare herself before the doors slid open again, filling the carriage with the outdoor heat. *"You have reached your destination,"* chirped the voice. *"Thank you for choosing Podcaller. Our only goal is to help you reach yours."*

"I'll lead the way," Teomonious said. Tala was already slotting the inevitable generic jab from Quarack into the flow of conversation, but Ferric got there first.

"Bear in mind that we're keeping a low profile."

"I know the rules of this game. *I'm* not the fool in our present company."

With that, he stepped out into a surge of foot traffic.

Quarack tapped Tala on the shoulder. "Who do you think he's trying to convince?"

"Hmmm," Tala replied without conviction, and followed Teomonious out of the pod. After the quiet and comfort of the pod's interior, contending with the crowd felt like going over a waterfall—pulled along in a single direction, and smacked about every centimeter of the way.

A pulse of Enhancement helping her along, she pushed through the crowd until she was in front of Teomonious. The others gratefully fell in behind her as she cleared a path. In a crowd this size, all her instincts screamed danger. Only a thin mesh layer and the disguise it projected kept the sapients around her from trampling each other in a panic.

She only had to bear it for the few seconds it took to reach the transit station. It was a long, enclosed, split-angle building with walls so bright they were almost reflective. The entrance, atop a flight of stone steps, was gated. Built into the ground by the stairs was a sloping cement tunnel through which she could see the orange, flickering light of the workers' substation.

Squeezing free of the press of sapients, they climbed the steps to the gate. On the other side, a Serdin occupied a small security booth. Her thin coat of hair drooped low, brushing against the shoulders of a light yellow uniform that had Haymore Mining's logo plastered in at least eight different places. She looked over their odd group, hair not betraying even a single twitch of interest. "Hello. How can I help you?"

"Yes, excuse me!" Teomonious swelled up, pushing himself in front of Tala. The potential of interacting with someone under orders to assist him had reignited something he'd been missing since Tarous. "I pre-purchased four premier tickets for the seventeen-four gravtrain."

"Your tickets should be on file," said the Serdin with a listless flop of her hand. "Hold your omnipad to the scanner and wait for the yellow light."

Teomonious did so, and the mesh gate swung open.

"You're all fine to go through," said the Serdin. "Have a nice day." It didn't sound like she cared one way or the other how nice their day would be, but Tala accepted the sentiment regardless.

With Teomonious at the head, they walked up another three steps into the station proper. Its decor was clean and minimal, as if the traditional white tile of a wasteroom had been stretched out over a hundred meters or so to four forest-green walls. Despite its size, it was largely empty—their only company was two humans and a smartly dressed corvid talking quietly among themselves, reclining on three of the many retractable chairs sprouting from the station's walls.

A soft voice announced the arrival of the next train. It rumbled as it swept into the station: a sleek, narrow set of five carriages that hurtled along the two-pronged track like a spear in flight. Floating several centimeters from the track, its silver body crackled blue with the arcing traces of powerful inertial dampeners. As quickly as it had arrived, it was gone.

The next one came much like the first, slotting itself into place along the boarding docks. Even fully stopped, it stayed floating. The well-dressed sapients got on, leaving Tala's group alone in the station. While they waited, two more trains came and went without anyone getting on or off. The station's grandiosity seemed disproportionate to its use.

Their train was right on time at seventeen-four, with a now-familiar rumble and a rush of wind. It settled in the arrival zone, and doors whooshed open along four of its five carriages. The last, at the gravtrain's rear, stayed shut.

Tala broke away from her sidelong examination of a waste receptacle. Ferric was closer to the arrival zone than she was, so she walked a little faster to catch up. "You ready?"

"Always," he said, trying for a smile and botching it royally. The result was half grin, half grimace, and all uncomfortable.

Quarack swatted his lower back with a winged claw. "Let's murder some shoes, bone head."

"I'm not—you know what? Forget it."

"So callous. They have soles, you know."

Their carriage was the second to last, the most expensive option available. That last carriage, where their target was situated, was not for sale. Teomonious's money had gotten them as close as possible. The rest was up to them.

"Get it? *Soles?* C'mon, that one was clever!"

Tala passed over the rubber lip of the doorway into the carriage's neat, spacious interior. The walls were programmed with a high-res wood façade that blended nicely with the ornate BevMix in the corner. Next to that, an eleventh-tier food synthesizer had been built into one of the carriage walls. The seats were a blue that reminded her of the GIAB's uniforms, and almost aggressively well-padded. Each was equipped with a set of hanging straps for hands-free omnipad use. Like the station, it was empty of sapients—aside from the two stone-faced nordok in rumpled suits standing at one end. Guarding the door to the final carriage.

The plan was to get a good distance out before making their move. If something went wrong, the further they were from an armed response, the better. Tala sank into one of the seats and activated its massager. Relaxing was as good a way to pass the time as any. Getting too comfortable wouldn't do, but her shoulders held enough tension to drive even a Serdin to panic.

It was Ferric who set the risky part of the plan in motion. When they'd gotten a safe distance from the station, he coughed once, indicating it was time. Then he pulled a maroon blanket from his pack, using it to cover his retrieval of the microstick's firing tube. With the blanket draped over his lap, he started shifting, giving the impression of someone failing to get comfortable. Tala focused on the lights that represented his sight, reflexes, hand-eye coordination, and anything else she could think of that might help him make what would be a very fast, difficult shot.

Quarack was up next. She'd been throwing the guards—and the door behind them—uncomfortable stares since she'd walked in. Now was her chance to do what she did best: aggravate. "Is it true?" she said as she stood, excitement lining every step toward her victims. "Vibe Hat's in there? You have to let me get a pic." For someone with the temperament of a primed explosive, Quarack had crammed an impressive amount of false cheer into her voice.

The left guard, the stockier of the pair, sighed. "Please step away from the door."

"But Vibe Hat *is* in there, right?"

"*Mas'*, I'm not at liberty to tell you who's inside. Now please—"

Quarack let loose with a triumphant cry, vibrating with likely-genuine excitement. "I knew it! You'd only say that if it was them! I've been listening to them since I was two. I want them to sign my eyelids, so I see their names when I sleep."

The taller guard answered her this time. "*Mas'*, you need to back up."

With another loud squeal and the speed of someone well practiced in the art of petty theft, Quarack threw herself between the guards. "Just let me lick their hair!" she shrieked, throwing the door open wide as they pivoted to intercept.

At that moment, with all eyes on Quarack, Ferric aimed the firing tube from beneath his blanket and squeezed. The microstick listener sailed between Quarack's legs, through the open door, and toward a pair of Compax-brand flats on the other side.

Three things happened at once.

The two nordok each caught Quarack by a shoulder and shoved her back.

The owner of the shoes, a squat, effete alvear, made a surprised hiss at the sudden disturbance.

And the sapient next to him, a hooded behemoth whose head almost scraped the carriage ceiling, whipped out a gloved hand like an asteroid drawn in on a collision course. Huge fingers plucked the microstick from the air with the impossible speed only Enhancers possessed.

The hand tightened. There was a soft crunch.

Staring through the open door at Ferric, the cloaked sapient opened his hand and the shattered remains of the device fell to the floor. *"Finally,"* he said. His voice was light and breathy, with a strange musical quality to it, like a reedy flute. "I knew I smelled a good time."

He pulled back his hood. What lay beneath might have been human once. A mouth overstuffed with jagged, interlocking teeth that ended in clawlike points, a nose that was nothing more than two gashes in anemic greenish skin, and slitted, reptilian eyes. His veins stood out like cables across warped, unnatural bulges of muscle. He smiled, and his fanged grin stretched almost to his ears.

Monstrous and twisted though it was, she recognized that smile.

Viron.

CHAPTER SIXTEEN
ENHANCED INTERROGATION

"Everyone back," Tala heard herself say.

Enhancement burned through her body, igniting in the space between instinct and thought. But as she rose, a shadow whispered in the back of her mind. She was a failure, it said. Wasn't her last fight with a Renegade proof enough of that? She and her companions were already as good as dead—

"*Surrender cedes the battle before it begins.*" Scratch's voice poured steel into her spine. The battlecalm came with it, settling her face into an impassive mask. "*Trust your spirit; I've given you all you need. This is your fight to win.*"

"By the black standard," said Ferric. "That's Viron."

But the Viron before her looked nothing like the sneering human in the GIAB's files. He looked like...

Like a Praeter experiment gone awry.

Translucent scales dusted the bridge of his nose. Above it, iris and pupil blended together into a black circle, all surrounded by a sclera of deep gold. His mouth, smiling that familiar lopsided smile, was more shark than man. Given the rumors she'd heard about Praeters, the idea of fighting a Praeter *Renegade* wasn't filling her with confidence.

The taller of the two guards reached for his omnipad.

"Put it down," Viron breathed, pulling off his right glove. Each finger ended in a daggerlike claw. "Remember your orders, no lawkeepers. Killing them is such a nuisance."

He chuckled and took an easy step forward. Tala could see the guard's facial muscles contorting as he tried to keep his fear from showing. He was in over his head and he knew it. The other guard sank back into the carriage, looking for cover.

"Let's abort," muttered Ferric. His shield snapped into existence around him. "We aren't prepared."

Tala squared her legs into a "ready" stance. "He won't let us run. He wants a fight."

Viron's smile stretched at that, pulling up toward his left ear.

The guard seemed reluctant to drop his omnipad. Viron motioned toward the second carriage's other occupant, standing by a food-laden table and wearing the off-white robes of an elected official. "Isn't that right, Councilor?"

"Juh, juh, just...do as he says," said Ceowogreffach.

The nordok re-holstered his omnipad, misgivings evident in every motion. Just as quickly, he and his partner drew and opened fire.

The situation just plummeted past worst-case scenario straight into Urgam's core, Tala thought as she slid between the first few shots. Viron dashed forward in the bullets' wake, moving almost as quickly. Tala spun to the side as he lashed out with a treetrunk arm. Then she threw herself into him shoulder-first, sending them both into the side of the train. It felt like ramming a bulkhead.

She recovered faster. A lucky thing, as the extra half second of hasty retreat kept her throat from being split open by his next blow. He didn't seem at all fazed by the dent he'd left in the metal, but that was all right —she'd diverted his charge. As long as she kept his attention, her squad had a chance.

The guards had retreated into the luxury carriage and were exchanging fire with Quarack and Ferric, bullets striking shields and shredding the faux leather seats. She had no time to check on Teomonious—Viron was advancing again, claws whistling as they bisected the air.

Tala aimed a flying kick at his throat, Enhanced muscles propelling her up and over the giant's strikes. Viron caught the blow on a massive forearm, and as she tumbled to the ground, his other hand scythed down toward her face. Grabbing at an omnipad harness, she yanked her body left mid-fall—almost too late. He missed by a fraction of a fraction, clawtips catching on the mesh that hid her face.

He let her recover, delight lining his jagged features. "And here I thought this would be boring," he said. "He was wondering if you'd find me."

By the sound of it, she'd been recognized. One hand went to her mask, feeling at the gash Viron's claws had torn right down the middle. Tala put a hand to her hairline and peeled the useless thing away.

"You mean Arcus," she said. She sent her eyeballs spinning to the margins of her vision, taking advantage of the lull. "He's been watching me?" *Talking to me?*

Teomonious was safe, thank the disciplines, fiddling with his laser pistol behind one of the padded seats. Quarack had taken cover behind the BevMix, which leaked fluid from several bullet holes. Ferric's shield was gone, and one hand was pressed over a wound in his side, but she couldn't spare any energy to help him through the pain. He gave her a quick nod, as if to say "focus on the Renegade," then sent a spray of suppressing fire into the other carriage.

"Keeping track. You might be one of his favorite projects." Viron chuckled. "Course, I'm still allowed to kill you. He trusts my judgment, after all."

Allowed. Everything this creature said helped her sculpt a little more of the holo. "So he's in charge. What are you then, his pet monster?"

"Stop being useless, Teo!" Tala heard Quarack yell, and in the moment her attention was caught, Viron struck. Tala stifled a shout as a claw sliced right through her Enhanced skin into her shoulder, her dodge a decisecond too late. She managed to catch his other arm by the wrist as it flew toward her face, bracing against the metal floor to keep from being flung back. Energy rerouted into her hand and with a grunt of exertion, she snapped his wrist.

She was tempted to press her advantage, but the stinging pain in her shoulder had shifted into a strange numbness that trickled down her side and into her arm. Not satisfied with three-centimeter claws, Viron had apparently made them venomous as well. Tala had memorized thousands of different poisons, each with their own avenue of attack and a clear Enhancement-fueled defense—but to use that, she had to know what she'd been poisoned *with*.

Leaving her opponent to nurse his broken wrist, she stumbled back, shunting energy into her immune system. Too much and she'd tear her own body apart from the inside, too little and the venom would cripple her. If it attacked her from a vector that bypassed her immune response, it might cripple her anyway. But the numbness did recede slightly—that was encouraging.

Slowly, making sure Tala caught the motion, Viron lifted his right arm. The hand dangled uselessly at the end. He swung it from side to side like a pendulum.

"There are no monsters," he growled, smile gone. If the wrist was bothering him, he didn't show it. "Only those who choose perfection over their natural limits."

"Praeters," said Tala, hoping to keep him talking. As long as she was diverting energy into her immune system, she was slow, weak, and frail.

"No. Oh, no no. The Praeters should *worship* me."

The hand twitched. Then, before Tala's amazed eyes, it rotated back into place with a rough scraping sound. As if to demonstrate the repaired appendage's functionality, Viron curled his fingers one at a time into a fist. The claws pierced his palm, but he didn't even flinch.

He'd fully healed a broken wrist in less than five seconds. Not even Frael had the raw power needed to fuel something like that. Tala would have claimed it impossible until…well, five seconds ago.

"You're starting to realize how hopeless it is. I can see it all over your face."

Despite his words, Tala knew her neutral mask still held firm. Beneath it, her mind was moving as quickly as it could go short of being Enhanced. Something wasn't right. If Viron had enough Enhancement to sweep away a broken wrist, the fight should have already been over.

"That's quite a trick," she said. The poison was weakening every second, loosening its hold on her body. Just a little more and she'd be ready.

"It's more than a trick." Viron spat, and whatever chemicals his saliva contained began eating through the train's plush carpet. The punctures in his palm were already gone. "You can't hurt me. Nothing can."

Deep, slow breaths. Tala cloaked herself in the familiar comfort of her battlecalm, holding fast to it just as she'd been trained. But even as the mental exercise reinforced her focus and stifled her doubts, she couldn't help but notice a difference. The battlecalm didn't feel implacably solid, the way it always had before. Almost as if there was a fault deep beneath the surface. Something not visible yet *felt*, an old wound that hadn't properly healed.

"Get this corvid out of here!" came a shrill buzzing from inside the luxury carriage. Tala turned one eye toward the sound as Viron did the same. Ceowograffach's guards were down. Ferric was tying them to the luggage rail, leaking blood from the graze in his side. Quarack was practically preening, brandishing her gun at the robed alvear. The councilor cowered at the carriage's rear, antennae thrashing at the air. "Do your job and protect me!"

"My *job*," said Viron. He seemed unconcerned with his principal's fate. "I could not have engineered a more boring task. Next time you give me an order, I'll kill you myself and suffer the rebuke without regret."

The last of the numbness bled away. Tala's battlecalm soaked up her relief like blotting paper as she redistributed her Enhancement, setting her limbs alight with power. To her left, Teomonious was still bent over his pistol, wearing a look of intense uncertainty.

"You wouldn't dare murder a sitting councilor. Not when your plan —"

Ceowograffach's goad became a high keen of terror as Viron turned his broad shoulders and charged. Tala moved to intercept, channeling everything she had into speed in an effort to protect what was currently their best lead. A high-pitched squawk mingled with Ceowograffach's keening as Quarack hopped backward onto the table, kicking over a tray of fruit in the process.

Tala launched herself at Viron's waist as he barreled into the carriage, and managed to catch his legs instead. With a quick twist Scratch had spent a pain-filled afternoon teaching her, she sent him tumbling to the floor beside her. Before he could right himself, she kipped up and kicked him in the throat. He crashed back against a luggage harness, rage simmering in his eyes. As he pulled free, Tala approached—but cautiously, well aware of her opponent's venom and claws.

She spread her arms invitingly. He lashed out with an open-palm swipe, but she was already dancing back out of his reach—at least until his arm *lengthened* mid-swing. Before she could react or even understand what had happened, he'd caught the side of her face. Her whole head erupted in searing agony as his clawed fingers clamped around her like a vise, digging in and holding her fast as he started to squeeze.

It was all Tala could do to Enhance her skull's durability, shoring it up against the massive pressure Viron's grip was generating. When it didn't cave in fast enough, he lifted her by the head and swung her against the side of the carriage. The world spun. Several somethings cracked.

Wish we had an oxygen chamber, she thought hazily. Every part of her body was screaming for Enhancement and there wasn't enough energy to go around. *Skull. Neck. Spine.* The rest was unimportant—she could fix it later. Hypothetically.

Her wounds were numbing as the venom entered her system, but she didn't have any spare power to fend it off. Her vision had started to swim and her feeble kicks weren't accomplishing anything.

His hot breath played over her ear. "Tell me I'm perfect."

It took several long moments to register she'd heard something—or maybe she'd imagined it. It faded and resurged in her mind like a half-remembered dream; part of her subconscious internal cadence one moment and then, jarringly, a real thing she'd heard the next.

A series of sharp cracks rattled through Tala's ears like someone had taken a baton to the inside of her head. Someone was shooting. Then the noise cut off. Even in her present state, some part of her understood what that meant. She thrashed helplessly, limbs leaden and uncooperative.

"I want to hear you say it. Say it, or you die right now."

Viron's voice had taken on a strange, echoing quality that made it hard to focus on. It was hard to focus on anything, actually. The pain was drawing most of her attention, lancing through her scalp and cheek, spreading steadily into her neck. It felt abstract in a way pain never had before, as if she was watching it happen to someone else from a faraway room.

I should say something, she thought, but she couldn't remember what.

Then she was falling and Viron roared, blood fountaining from his wrist where his hand had once been. A hand that was still embedded in her head. He whirled in a blur of fury, sending a bloody arc across the carriage. Ferric was right there next to him, already bracing for the blow. Brave, reckless Ferric. He was too close. Much too close.

Her throat found breath deep within her lungs and she screamed, all battlecalm swept away at the sight of a squadmate, a *friend*, once again facing down a Renegade to save her—

Light seared across her retinas, impossibly bright and accompanied by an angry crackle. It existed between seconds and was gone before the next, leaving her to blink the sunspots away from her vision and try to puzzle out the guttural gurgles she was hearing.

The first thing she saw was Viron. He was on his knees, holding himself up with his remaining hand. A smoking hole half a meter across cut through his chest, edges charred black with licks of angry red. She could see his desiccated ribcage and right through to the carriage wall behind, where an intense heat had melted a similar hole right through it.

The gurgles were his aborted attempts at breath.

Framed in the carriage door—and looking immensely pleased with himself—Cernarvitalimun Teomonious lowered his high-powered, platinum-burnished, very illegal laser pistol.

She should have felt relief of some kind, but it was hard to feel anything but tired. The world drifted in and out of focus and her head felt like it was ticking down the seconds to detonation. She pressed it against the cool metal of a Surolian seating frame. It felt nice, but wasn't stopping everything from getting hazier. Somebody was shouting at her, so she burrowed against the seating frame and tucked her head into her elbow. Why couldn't they just be quiet?

Pain jarred her thoughts back into focus, a sudden line of fire across her left hand.

I'm dying, she realized with her newfound clarity. *Poisoned.*

I should do something about that.

She let the power seep out of her muscles and bones, repurposing it to fight the agent that had infiltrated her bloodstream. Her organs grew hardy and began to shore up against the damage that had already been done. Her immune system rallied. The process was easier the second time around; she'd beaten it once and her body remembered what to do.

"Tala Kreeth. Get. Up."

It was Ferric's voice, coming from right in front of her. She forced her eyes open to see his face, lined with concern.

"Great Pillars, you're all right," he breathed.

He held a severed hand. Greenish-gray, slightly scaly, claw-tips dripping. In his other hand was a sharp-looking piece of scrap metal.

Her thoughts were still sluggish, pawing lazily at each other and hoping for the best. She looked at her left hand, which was throbbing, and saw a jagged cut oozing blood.

Ferric grimaced. "Sorry."

Why is he apologizing?

"You can hear me, right? Can you move?"

Right. Movement.

Tala took a deep breath in and drew power through her body, pulling from a deeper well than she'd known she had. Her heart pounded in her ears as she strained against her injuries. *Just a little more*, she told herself. *You chose not to stand once before. Never again.*

With a mighty heave, she lifted herself to a sitting position. The back of her throat tasted like blood and her whole head swam like she'd just done thirty-one hours of training, but she was up. Kind of.

A current of hot air whistled through the carriage interior, drifting in from the hole Teomonious had blasted through the train. All around it, the projected wood pattern had failed, leaving only reflective mesh.

Outside, the unchanging desert landscape continued to fly by. For a hand weapon to make a hole that size, it couldn't be anything but *twelfth*-tier. A flagrant violation of the Accords, which she was willing to overlook given the situation.

"Nice shot," said Ferric to Teomonious. The alvear hummed contentedly at the praise, but his attention was elsewhere, somewhere behind Tala's right ear.

Ferric squeezed her unwounded shoulder. "We did it."

Tala was too focused on burning the venom out of her body to respond. She closed her eyes and let out a long exhalation as feeling returned. Breathing was still difficult, but she could blame her host of other injuries for that one.

Ferric tossed aside the piece of metal. The edge was discolored where it had gone through Viron's wrist. "Sorry again. About your hand."

She patted his leg. That was all she felt up for, but he seemed to understand.

"Good try, but no." Quarack's voice carried across the carriage from where she still held Ceowogreffach at gunpoint. "Who knows where that money's been?"

Viron's mountain of a body collapsed forward, arm buckling in a doomed struggle to stay upright. That he still clung to life was extraordinary, but Renegades often took a while to die. They fought to the end, unable to accept that they too were mortal, using ever-increasing amounts of Enhancement to keep their bodies working just a few seconds longer. It was too bad Viron would be taking his secrets with him, but he couldn't breathe, let alone talk.

His eyes snapped open.

Tala barely had time to shout a warning. The scaled behemoth jumped to his feet with a smile that split his entire face like an axe wound. Through the hole in his robes, Tala could see the rent in his flesh knitting together. *Impossible*.

Beside her, Ferric said something that would have gotten him a contrition shift back on Modellus.

"Funny thing about Enhancement," said Viron, almost gasping the words as his lungs finished reforming. "It multiplies. The stronger you are, the more strength you get. The faster you can heal…"

There was the last piece of the puzzle; his absurd strength wasn't all Enhancement. His baselines were far beyond human limits. And the state of the rest of him even made it obvious where those baselines had come from.

Tala stood. It felt like jumping into a razorwire net, but she managed. "So Praeter gene-splicing gave you some sort of regeneration. Is that standard with the 'monstrous abomination' package, or did you request it special?"

There were definite cracks this time when she dropped back into her battlecalm, where the anger was bleeding through. Anger at the galaxy that had produced such a creature, anger at what should have been a lethal wound, even a little anger at herself for feeling *jealous* when her own injuries flared with pain.

Viron flushed, skin mottling sickly green beneath translucent scaling. "You saw what I just did! What I *survived!*" he half shouted. "You can't deny what I've made myself!" He gave his head a fierce shake, as if to clear it. "Now you'll die like the others. Just another body in the pile."

"Got another shot?" Ferric asked Teomonious.

"Got another ninth-tier power cell?"

"Then get out of here," said Ferric. "That means all of you."

Before Tala could object, he opened fire with his automatic. The microexplosive rounds detonated against their target. Viron's skin bubbled beneath the assault, repairing itself as fast as Ferric could damage it. Then he began to walk forward, leaving a trail of blood and pulverized flesh behind him.

The fusillade of gunfire stopped. So did Viron. He eyed Ferric like a predator deciding how much it wants to play with its prey before eating it.

"Back." Tala's voice was tight with barely suppressed fury, a fury that steadily ate away at what remained of her battlecalm. Ferric blinked, and she couldn't blame him—the way she'd sounded had surprised her too. "*Now.*"

She interposed her protesting body between him and Viron. Teomonious, at least, was long gone. He'd found somewhere to crouch among the seats. She couldn't risk turning her head to make sure Ferric had obeyed, but she could hope.

"Time for round two," she said with more bravado than she felt.

By way of response, Viron spat at her.

It was a viscous, green-tinged wad of bodily fluid that Tala would have preferred to avoid even if she hadn't seen it eat through carpet earlier. She ducked and it hit the floor behind her. On contact with the metal, it sizzled.

Viron was right on its heels and the battle began anew. Tala could barely keep ahead of his claws, which he swung through the air with relentless precision. Twice more, he tried to catch her off guard by lengthening his arm midstrike, but she was wise to that trick now and kept a few extra centimeters between them. That additional margin of safety was keeping her alive, but also heavily restricting her ability to take the offensive. Not that taking the offensive would accomplish much.

And she was weakening as the fight dragged on, losing more blood than she could afford to replace while Viron seemed just as fresh as when they'd begun. His gut wound was almost gone and still closing. Worse, a new hand had started to force its way out of his wrist stump. Staying ahead of one was hard enough—she couldn't imagine keeping up with two.

She'd have to kill him before it regenerated. The problem was, she wasn't sure he could die.

Both of them made sure to avoid the spot where Viron's acidic spit had landed. It had eaten a hole in the floor. Wind howled through the opening, batting at her legs when she got too close. The lip was pitted, brittle-looking. Tala was afraid that if she stepped near it too hard, the whole section of floor would give way and plunge her onto the double-pronged gravtrack below.

How do you kill something that can regenerate a half-meter hole through its stomach? she asked herself again as she pivoted away from a lightning-quick gut punch. She caught Viron's other arm and threw him past her, abetted by his own momentum. *If only I'd brought the—*

Viron's claws impaled her between the ribs. She let the blow move her out of danger, tumbling backward and thudding against the carriage wall. The train echoed with triumphant laughter as she struggled back to her feet, using the wall for support.

"*Never let idle thoughts distract your spirit,*" Scratch scolded her. "*Lose focus and you lose everything.*"

Tala rolled to the side and another wad of spit hit the wall she'd been leaning against. This time she saw the impact. The acid frothed like a living thing as it stripped away the paneling. Liquified metal dripped down the wall in rivulets.

Her energy still burned bright, but her body was failing bit by bit— and the weaker she got, the less Enhancement could do for her. Viron sensed the kill was close. She could tell by the hunger in his sharklike smile.

She was going to die.

The realization was accompanied not by calm acceptance—as she'd been taught—but by more anger. It wasn't right that Ferric and the sapients they'd dragged into this affair die because she'd run headlong into an unkillable opponent. It wasn't right that she meet her end on some single-biome world before Arcus even knew to be afraid. She had to live.

"Should I make you beg?" smirked Viron. "I think I want to."

Looking at it from that perspective, the answer slotted into place like it had been waiting for her all along. An Agent's duty was to end threats to the galaxy. That duty still pulled at her, but she'd chosen another. It was time to commit to it, the altar upon which her old life had been sacrificed. She wasn't here to stop Viron. The goal was Arcus, and always had been.

She stared him down, trying to keep her knees from buckling. "Go ahead and try, you genetic mistake."

His sudden anger couldn't have been more predictable. With a manic yell and murder in his eyes, he threw himself at Tala—almost 150 kilograms of muscle, claw, and rage, suffused with Enhancing energy and practically indestructible.

Her hand shot behind her, fingers curling around acid-weakened paneling. Sharp tingles spread across her palm. She disregarded them and ripped the panels away with one pull. Viron's eyes bulged but he'd already committed to the leap. Tala dropped to the floor with no time to spare and channeled every last spark of energy into Enhancing the force of his impact.

He hit what remained of the wall and tore through it like flame through a spiderweb. The entire train rocked so violently, Tala feared she'd knocked it off the track. Miraculously, the repulsion field held.

If the wind had howled before, it was positively shrieking now. The carriage vibrated beneath the stress, shaking like it was about to fall apart. There was a Surolian-sized hole in the side of the train, through which poured the desert heat. At its edge, a clawed and scaly hand had embedded itself, locked in a death grip around a half-destroyed sheet of paneling.

Tala staggered over to it, head buzzing. No time to rest. She couldn't stop. Ferric called her name and she looked behind her just in time to catch the piece of metal that had taken off one of Viron's hands. With tired finality, she brought its edge down on the other. She was rewarded with a roar, pain and anger mingling together in a ghastly dirge.

Her first blow failed to sever the hand, so she struck again. This time, the metal went clean through. Viron's shouting cut off at once, swallowed by the wind. For all his strength, he was just a whisper in the face of 640 kilometers per hour's worth of force.

Tala peeked her head out, just to be sure. The wind batted at her like a giant's hammer, but she squinted her eyes against it and looked back along the track. There was a dark shape just outside the grav-field, growing smaller by the second. She couldn't tell if it was moving.

It probably was. Even a fall that brutal wouldn't overwhelm regeneration capabilities like Viron possessed. No, he was still loose in the galaxy, and Tala was partly to blame for whatever lives he took in the future. She hadn't beaten him—only saved herself. Barely, at that.

The thought nauseated her. Mixed with the strain of keeping her eyes open and the residual effects of Viron's venom, it set her world spinning. Like magic, a familiar steadying hand found its way to her side, helping her stay upright as it pulled her back into the train.

"You all right?" said Ferric, barely audible over the carriage falling apart. She let him guide her to the door, happy to outsource navigation to someone else. Quarack dragged Ceowogreffach along as well, and none too gently either.

"I'll heal. But so will he."

"You did well," Ferric reassured her.

Quarack extended a gallant wing toward the door as if to say, *after you*. It was wide enough for them to pass through side by side without issue. The luxury carriage's nordok guards still lay motionless by the wall, bound to the luggage rail and breathing shallowly. Tala collapsed into the closest seat and began accelerating her healing. The first-class carriage was blissfully quiet—quiet, clean, and calm.

"All done," said Teomonious. The far door's control box was smoking. "They'll need to cut their way in, and when they do—ah, Fate, to shift our fortunes so!"

His demeanor transformed in an eyeblink as Quarack and her prisoner entered the carriage, from business to pomp and delight. A little too much delight, Tala thought blearily, for someone who'd cribbed his opening line from classical nordok cinema.

"Darfelatulaming Ceowogreffach," he said, each word soaked in satisfaction. "Under present circumstances, I find I'm genuinely happy to see you."

"You can't think you'll get away with this," hissed the other alvear.

Teomonious indicated the luxury carriage with a middle appendage. "*You* certainly did."

"Let's speed this up," said Ferric, interposing himself between the two politicians. Teomonious let out an indignant buzz and tried to scuttle around him, but Ferric's arm swung up and blocked him. "I know you've wanted this for a while, but we can't waste time. You've won, all right?"

"What's he paying you?" said Ceowogreffach, but he didn't sound hopeful.

Ferric glowered at him. "We know you've been involved with the Renegade Arcus Boral. Tell me why."

"I am not accountable to you," said Ceowogreffach. "Only to my constituency."

"*That's* your defense against treason?" said Ferric. "I'd tinker with that one."

"Treason, from the one threatening a sitting councilor." Ceowogreffach clicked his mandibles in frustration. "You will permit me to find that ironic."

"Nobody's threatening you."

Tala found it hard to follow the back-and-forth, given the state she was in. Ferric seemed to be doing all right, but the whole situation made Tala wish she'd picked up some Harmonizer training. As it stood, she wasn't much help.

"Good to hear. I will take my leave, then."

The portly alvear tried to wheel about and collided with the barrel of Quarack's gun. Quarack poked him with it.

"Coerced cooperation at gunpoint isn't a threat? This is barbaric!"

The anger was starting to stir again, forcing its way through the ball of pain Tala's nerves had become. She took a long, calming breath. It didn't help. Finally she'd found someone who could give her answers, and he was stonewalling. How could he pretend at innocence when they'd just caught him with the most vicious Renegade currently active? When he was working with the same sapient who'd murdered her friends?

"Not barbaric," she interjected, lurching to her feet with a smothered yell. "Justifiably harsh."

"Justice has—"

Ceowogreffach froze, antennae trembling. All six eyes had locked onto Tala like he was seeing her for the first time, his face a pageant of terror.

Her heart turned over in her chest.

She should have been numb to it by now, or at least acclimated through experience. Why did she still let it darken her vision with regret? Why did she still flinch away from the truth that had lived in her shadow since Scratch had promised to claim her life with his own hands?

There was no going back. No possible retraction of the title with which she'd been branded. No way to steel against the galaxy's hatred, not when she felt it so intimately within her own heart.

I am a Renegade, she told herself, and for the first time she allowed herself to hear it. *And to be a Renegade is to be feared and hated.*

"I—" Ceowogreffach stammered, pushing the words out past each other with no regard for making himself understood. "Mother preserve me. I promise you, I am worth far more alive than dead. Please, give me the chance to prove—"

His eyes dropped to the shattered BevMix and stayed there.

Compassion, bitterness, and guilt churned her stomach in their fight for dominance, every whimper from the panicked councilor a reminder that this time, *she* was the cause. Yet something stayed steady beneath the uncontrolled swirl of emotions: a clear and pure directive instilled within her by the Center. A sapient was in need—the drive to help was all but instinct by now. *Tenet forty-four: The decision to allow suffering lies within every observer.*

She reached out a comforting hand but Ceowogreffach flinched back, eyes wild. Another icicle embedded itself into her chest. *Feared and hated.*

It was then that she knew what she had to do.

In the strictest sense, it was a lie. A lot of little lies compounded into a big one. Lies of omission. Lies of inference. Direct lies, if necessary. But just as the Tenets did not forgive small transgressions made in avoidance of a larger sin, neither would she forgive herself. No excuses for her actions, just acknowledgement. A compromise, of sorts. A reminder that she could still tell right from wrong beyond the Center.

Tala narrowed her eyes and quirked her mouth into a sardonic smile, reworking her face into a picture of confidence and control. Standing with her legs in a wider, asymmetric stance, she lifted her chin and looked down on Ceowograffach from her considerable height. A slow-burning energy had taken root somewhere just above her pelvis, driving away the pain and fatigue.

"Your only worth lies in answering my questions," she said, and she filled her voice with poison and frost. Ferric started at the sudden change. She didn't acknowledge him. Tala the Renegade considered him beneath her. "Even then, it's a fleeting thing."

She took one slow step forward, maximizing every centimeter of their difference in stature. Ceowogreffach shrank before her advance. His jitters—the alvear fear response—were worsening.

"It wasn't my idea!" he wailed. "It was him, he made me—"

"What is his plan?"

Ceowogreffach whimpered something unintelligible.

"Teomonious," she said. "How much does it hurt when you rip out an alvear's mandibles?"

The ex-politician hesitated. She'd gone too far; her companions' reactions made that much clear. Even Quarack wore some shock, though in her case it was mixed with approval.

Their distaste was not enough to stop her.

"Never mind," she said. "I can find out for myself."

Two more steps and Ceowogreffach had run out of floor to retreat to. She had him cornered now, and she filled the space between them with the implicit threat, the *lie*, of imminent physical harm.

"S-stop!" commanded the portly councilor with his last vestige of authority. "I am protected by the Galactic Accords, and any act of harm —"

One finger brushed ever so lightly against his thorax.

And like fallen glass, the councilor shattered. If alvear had tear ducts, there would have been a river at Tala's feet. He prostrated himself, grabbing desperately at her legs, mandibles twitching and working. His entire body shook, all semblance of control lost to fear.

It was exactly the reaction she'd sought and she felt twice cursed for it.

His words muddled and bled into each other. "Please, please, please," were the only sounds Tala could distinguish. *One more push*, she thought. *A violent motion, a few cruel words.* But she felt rooted in stone: too committed to turn back, but unable to continue. Thankfully, it was the councilor who broke before she did.

"The Legislatorium!" he choked out between gasps. "Peramit!"

Before he could say more, his body fully succumbed to a series of jitters.

Shock drove out everything else, disbelief following after. What he'd implied was too ludicrous, too impossible to consider. But nobody was laughing. All her skepticism drained away, replaced by seeping dread. "You mean he's going to attack it."

The Legislatorium was the seat of the Galactic Coalition's power, and Peramit the sparkling gem at the heart of the galaxy. Together, they stood as reassurance that no matter how different the galaxy's denizens, their shared purpose brought them together. A symbol of everything Tala had vowed to protect.

"Answer me!" she snapped, clamping down with her fingers. The chitin was weaker than she'd expected; she wouldn't even need Enhancement to crack it. But Ceowogreffach stared sightlessly past her, terrified past the point of functioning. His speechlessness provoked a spike of anger that set her teeth against each other, and an impulse to—

The anger was *real*. Tala recoiled from it, in that moment aghast at the act she'd been putting on. The poisonous persona she'd adopted had colored her thought patterns; the line between pretense and reality was far too thin for comfort. It had led her toward anger when she needed calm.

Disobedience is the precipice, weakness the fall.

Breathe.

She'd made peace with pursuing the right thing over rigid adherence to the Tenets-as-written. What she'd just done—what she'd started to *mean* as she did it—went a step beyond that. Several steps.

She would *not* become Arcus in the process of stopping him. The line between peace and chaos still existed, even if she sometimes had to squint to see it. Her gut wound burned in concert with her throbbing skull and she almost retched as she crumpled into the nearest chair, her surge of vigor abating.

"He can't." Ferric's expression had darkened. "Even the craziest Renegades stay far away from the Legislatorium. It's like a fortress inside a vault surrounded by a defense grid. You'd need to get through at least eleven layers of security—"

"Eighteen," whispered Ceowogreffach. His buzzing voice had a quaver to it, but it appeared his tremors were subsiding—though he was still looking anywhere but Tala. "And I told him about all of them."

"Let me make sure this is clear." Ferric said with new disgust. "A Renegade wants to throw the galaxy you swore to serve into chaos. By murdering his way through the legislative body that you happen to belong to. And you justified helping him *how*?"

Ceowogreffach tried to interject, but Ferric plowed right through, voice rising. "They trusted you! And you worked alongside them, plotting—"

"Barely," sneered Teomonious. "This upstart hasn't held the post a year. High treason in one's first year of legislative service is quite an achievement, Ceowogreffach, and it will be your only one. The shameful stamp on a career notable for its ineffectiveness. But then—oh!"

Teomonious's antennae stiffened like they'd been hit by twin bolts of lightning. "Yes, yes, yes," he murmured, mostly to himself. "Of course."

He rounded on his rival with new gusto.

"I should have seen it sooner," he said. "Your mind is a gravepit for political instinct. You shouldn't even have crawled your way out of the preliminaries, much less unseated me. A lot of good investigators disappeared trying to uncover your backers. Now I understand. Even then, from the very beginning, it was Arcus conducting my misfortunes."

"You always did have a conniving cleverness about you," said Ceowograffach bitterly. "I warned him you'd leave half your tracks on me once you were ousted. The fool didn't listen."

"I cannot believe it. You traded the Legislatorium for a chance to discredit me. Oh, this is wonderful!"

Everyone looked at him. "This is terrible," said Ferric.

"Yes, yes." Teomonious waved dismissively. "You are absolutely right, of course. But don't you see? I wasn't beaten on fair terms!"

Quarack was looking between the two alvear like she couldn't figure out which one she had a lower opinion of, and in that moment, Tala found it hard to blame her.

There was only one bright spot to this whole mess: Ceowogreffach's fright had been genuine. He was as clueless she'd been framed as the rest of the galaxy. That was some evidence against a government conspiracy —or at least a widespread one.

Ferric chewed his lower lip. "When will this take place?"

"I can only tell you that it's soon." Ceowogreffach cast a furtive glance Tala's way. "It was easier not to know."

Just then, the train gave a shuddering lurch. The view through the window told Tala they were slowing, and quickly.

"Emergency stop," said Quarack. "Keepies won't be far behind."

"We're familiar with the protocol, thanks," said Ferric. "Time to go, then?"

He looked to Tala for the final call. To her surprise, so did the other two. It felt nicer than she would have expected. Almost like having a Vanguard again.

Outside, the unchanging scenery stopped moving as the train settled into place atop the gravtracks. Something slammed against the carriage door.

"Quarack, call the ship," she said, orders springing from her tongue with the ease of long experience. "Ferric, grab an arrival estimate from PAP observer channels. Teomonious..." she hesitated. "You still have valid omnipad links with other councilors, right?"

"That you even have to ask is—"

"Great. Get in touch with whoever you can. Let them know an attack is imminent."

"Shouldn't we evacuate first?"

Tala considered. Delaying the warning by half an hour likely wouldn't make a difference and their capacity would be better spent on essential activities.

"True."

Teomonious scuttled away, looking relieved.

"You want to save the Legislatorium?" said Ceowogreffach. "I can help you. Just give me some assurances—"

"Gag him," said Tala. Teomonious practically chortled as he tore off a chunk of the councilor's robes. "What's our wait time?"

Quarack consulted her omnipad. "Hovering around a decihour. We *should* be gone before the keepies can get a bite of our tailfeathers, but we don't have any time to dig for wrapworms either. We'd better make sure we're good to go when it gets here."

"I think we'll be safe until then," said Ferric from the door. There were voices behind it, growing louder and more numerous with each passing moment. "PAP estimate is a little under two."

"Great." Quarack winked her central eye. "There's just one more thing, then: what are we doing with him?"

She jerked her head toward Ceowogreffach.

"Turn him over to the authorities under charges of aiding and abetting a Renegade, high treason against the Galactic Coalition, shaming the office of councilor, and accessory to several thousand counts of attempted murder," Ferric rattled off.

"We're wanted criminals ourselves," said Tala. "There's no feasible way to do that without handing ourselves over as well."

"I'll do it!" said Teomonious. The thought of personally delivering his successor into custody was making his antennae vibrate.

Tala took another concerned look at the door. "Doesn't matter who does it. He knows too much. Think, he's seen you with us. So unless you want him telling the lawkeepers that you're associating with known Renegade Tala Kreeth—"

Teomonious waved his arms back and forth in the universal gesture for *erase*, looking horrified.

"Well, I'm not taking the little plucker aboard," Quarack chimed in. "Tolerating *two* annoying bug politicos—"

"I object to that."

"Are you saying we just leave him here?" Ferric's voice rose. "After what he's done, you want to let him—"

"He might alert Arcus," said Tala. "We have to take him with us—"

"I am *not* sharing a ship with that disgrace to my species!"

Ceowogreffach let out a muffled whine, arms beseeching.

"Do you have another idea?" said Ferric, wheeling on Teomonious.

"I most certainly can find a better one."

But if a better solution existed, another half decihour of increasingly heated arguing failed to uncover it. Ferric was just threatening to break Teomonious's legs if he tried to stop Ceowogreffach from being taken aboard when Tala heard a high-pitched humming that grew louder and louder. Her first thought was that the lawkeepers had managed to beat Ferric's estimates. Then she saw the single gleaming speck on the horizon: the familiar purple prow of the *Aquilon*. It was approaching at a speed discouraged by safety advisories and—somewhat concerningly— seemed to be heading straight for the train.

"I hope you aren't telling it to crash into us," said Tala.

"The closer she lands, the less time we waste getting to her," said Quarack. "Don't worry, I've done this before. Everyone ready?"

Tala followed the *Aquilon* with her eyes; it was slowing, but not by much. It looked like the train would end up barely outside the landing gear's shock wave—if at all. "Are you sure—"

"Also," Quarack continued, neatly cutting across Ferric and Teomonious's argument, "time's landed."

There was a single gunshot.

Tala whirled around, knowing what she'd see. Ceowogreffach was still falling. He hit the carriage floor with a soft thud. His limbs were already curling. Deprived of the fear that had animated him, his body looked almost flat. As if he'd sunk into the carpet. The only evidence he'd ever been alive was a slow trickle of dark blue staining the plush.

Quarack met Tala's eyes and reholstered her gun.

"Problem solved," she said into the shocked silence. "No more feather-flapping; aren't we in a hurry? Lawkeepers inbound and all that?"

She gestured with one wing to the *Aquilon*, now thirty meters above the empty desert and closing.

"Quarack..."

But Tala found that she didn't know what to say next. Killing didn't inherently bother her; she'd taken a few lives herself. But always hostiles, in the heat of battle—and never without a heavy heart. The Tenets made a clear distinction between murder and self-defense. Quarack's action wasn't even in a gray area.

There should at least have been remorse. But Tala couldn't see a trace of that either, just practiced defensiveness falling into place like blast doors.

Ferric too was uneasy, and hiding it less than adequately. Even Teomonious, who'd probably fantasized about Ceowogreffach's untimely death many times, looked dazed.

There was a rumbling crack and the whole train jumped beneath their feet. Outside the window, a curtain of displaced dust swept along the ground toward them. Within deciseconds, the train was swathed in the swirling storm. Tiny pebbles tapped against the windows with enough force to leave cracks.

"This the part where we pretend he didn't have it coming?" Quarack's head swiveled to Teomonious, who recoiled as if tapped with an electroprod. If the sandstorm had fazed her, she wasn't letting it show. "You heard what he did. Judge me for giving him what he deserved if you want, but at least admit you're glad it happened."

As quickly as it had begun, the squall subsided. The *Aquilon* was perched at the epicenter of a large dust valley, a crater of its own making. Its landing ramp was already unfolding, and with it, the promise of safety.

"You can't—" Ferric began, but Tala silenced him with a look. That he stopped talking was as due to surprise as anything else.

"Not now." Strength threading through her muscle, she shoved against the closest window, bursting it out of its frame. "It's time to go."

CHAPTER SEVENTEEN

A GLIMPSE OF THE ETERNAL

They left Urgam to its empty deserts.

Tala remembered keeping her feet moving, one arm draped around Ferric's shoulders as he dragged her across the desert. Teomonious turning around to look at her, concern splashed across his features. The *Aquilon*'s ramp closing with them still on it. Thinking that Quarack wasn't wasting any time.

She couldn't remember anything *between* these fragments, but the gaps weren't hard to fill.

Quarack aimed the *Aquilon*'s nose at the sky and didn't hold back on the accelerator. The thrusters sent dust billowing into the air before flash-igniting it. An explosion echoed outside, rattling the ship like marbles in a tin.

Through an outer viewport, Tala saw a cloud of gritty red smoke bloom over the ship, streaming in smooth waves from some hidden source. Up they climbed, shrouded in crimson, until the concept of *up* no longer existed. Pursuit would be fast, so they had to be faster.

This time, Tala couldn't help. All her Enhancement was needed to keep herself upright. Her head was a series of agonizing pulses and it was easier to count which of her bones *weren't* fractured. Her teeth were locked in an iron grimace against the patchwork of pain her skin and muscle had become, from the punctures in her gut to the gash on her shoulder.

As they left the stratosphere behind, she found the presence of mind to redirect a trickle of power toward that shoulder wound. The power took hold and her blood clotted.

Ferric met her as she staggered up the long central corridor, a numbing pill in hand. "Are you critical?"

The old lingo came fast to Tala's lips. "Severe, but noncritical." Then, more colloquially, "Hurts bad."

She took the pill and downed it. It broke apart on its way past her throat, splitting off into tendrils of numbness that spread and multiplied through her body. Relief, even if from a disconcerting source.

Her steps became ponderous as the pill kicked in. Walking wasn't difficult, exactly, but her legs felt like they belonged to someone else.

"He's found a way onto Peramit," Ferric said. "I can't even begin to imagine what kind of damage he could do."

Tala rubbed her scalp with fingers that felt too big for her hand. It was like prodding rubber. "I can. It's the sort of thing that's been rattling through my mind ever since Neea."

The admission slipped out before she could swallow it. She turned away. She hadn't said anything terrible, but obsession and madness were friends fast and old.

Something warm and firm slipped into her hand and squeezed. Her own fingers tightened around it until they trembled, as if she could pull the past into the present if she held it firmly enough.

Ferric sucked in a breath and Tala's hand snapped open.

"Stumps," he said, rubbing his palm ruefully.

"Sorry."

"It's fine. Nothing broken. Probably. Was that Enhanced?"

Tala shook her head and Ferric clacked his teeth together. Nordok accolades, or something of the sort. The sound of voices raised in anger drifted down the hall, killing the moment. Quarack and Teomonious were moving to join them. Ferric's eyes narrowed to slits.

The *Aquilon* must have been safely away because Quarack looked particularly smug. A bad look on her given the day's events. As for the ex-councilor, Tala couldn't tell what he was thinking. Considering he was an alvear, probably a lot.

"What in the six Hells was that?" Ferric exploded. "You just shot him without blinking."

As always, Quarack was more than ready to fire back. "I think you just answered your own question. I shot that scumbag. And I didn't blink."

Tala knew she wanted to say *something*, but the words kept getting out from under her. The room was wobbling like it was slowly being shaken awake. Whether that was due to her injuries or the painkiller, she couldn't tell.

"Speaking as Ceowogreffach's closest relation among us, one could hardly call him an innocent victim," murmured Teomonious. "But we have *systems*. Tribunals. He was to stand publicly and answer for his—"

"Personal feelings aren't an excuse for murder," said Tala, stumbling over the words.

Quarack gave her a once-over, taking in her ragged state. "We couldn't leave the councilor to go squawking and we couldn't bring him along. Even if we'd found a way to get him on board safely, the moment he got in range of a hivemother he'd broadcast what he knew to every alvear in the collective. Our location included. If you can't leave him and you can't take him, what else are you gonna do? Even ol' six-brain over here couldn't think of something."

"Just because it's inconvenient—" Ferric snorted, shaking his head. "I shouldn't have to explain this."

"Tenet…" Tala frowned, trying to remember. The number was right there in her head, but the fog made it hard to see.

"Look, he's dead, all right?" said Quarack. "He won't come back to life if you roast me hard enough. Shouldn't you be more worried about the guy with the keys to the Legislatorium?"

That brought the argument to a halt.

"We have to warn them," Ferric said. "But we aren't done. That's a promise."

"It's a date," snapped Quarack. "You're paying."

Ferric turned his attention to Teomonious. "Comm someone." It was good he'd taken charge, as she was in no position to. "One of the Dauntless Guard would be best. This has to go to the top."

It hurt Tala's mouth to smile, but she did anyway at the thought of Arcus going up against one of those mighty suits of battle armor. Renegade or not, he'd be lit up like Peramit's nightside.

"Alas, I do not even know who they are. The sapients allowed to contact them number in the single digits—"

"A councilor, then? One who could mobilize them?"

"Yes, yes. How does…Moravan sound?"

In the moment that followed, Tala could hear the subtle hum of every one of the *Aquilon*'s electronic subsystems—and that was without doing anything to her hearing.

"Moravan?" said Ferric. "You mean *Eternal* Moravan? *High Councilor* Moravan?"

Few Torandians lived long enough to make a claim on the Eternal caste, and fewer still survived the initiation. Moravan was the most eminent of them all, a legend among legends. He'd helped pen the Galactic Accords during the Coalition's founding, and had carefully pruned them to perfection over the cycles since. Where he walked, history followed.

Teomonious chittered. "We have something of a special relationship," he said, which was sort of like Ferric mentioning in passing that he had Admiral Highwater's personal frequency.

Ferric opened his mouth, but looked to her instead, seeking confirmation. This time, it wasn't the fog that stayed her tongue. If a wider conspiracy *was* loose within the Coalition's upper echelons, Moravan almost certainly had a skeletal hand in it.

But if he was on their side, Tala could imagine no stronger ally. "Do it."

Teomonious clicked his understanding and oriented himself and his screen away from them. Unusually accommodating, Quarack stepped to the side without a word, tension stitched across her face.

The air above the omnipad flashed gold. Within it materialized a skull, shaped and yellowed over seventeen cycles into a narrow, bellicose mask. The High Councilor Eternal was powerfully built, with thick-corded veins of soft blue and only the slightest hunch to his shoulders.

The shadows in the corridor seemed longer, as if the hologram had sucked the light out of the rest of the ship—impossible though that was.

"Cernarvitalimun Teomonious," said the most powerful sapient in the galaxy, pausing as if to consider the name. He accented the words almost beyond recognition before switching to Torandian proper. "My friendling. I thought I'd be hearing from you."

His voice was soft and sibilant, every word polished to a shine. Where Scratch liked to punctuate his words with the loudest clicks he could manage, sometimes even Enhancing the noise, Moravan was content to practically drop them altogether. The overall effect was strangely chilling. Even Quarack shrank back against the wall.

"High Councilor Eternal Moravan." Each of Teomonious's six arms met its opposite, grippers brushing against each other as they separated. He too spoke Torandian, and though his mouth was ill-suited for it, the sounds were well practiced and clear. "There is much to discuss, and little time to spare. I have uncovered a plot against the Legislatorium itself—"

Moravan's tongue lashed the air soundlessly. It was gone before Teomonious's next word.

"—and at its heart, none other than Darfelatulaming Ceowogreffach."

"Interesting." Moravan appraised Teomonious with mild curiosity. "The councilor is discredited, then, as you wanted."

"When the details are made known, I imagine disgrace will be the least of his worries."

"You ought to have given those details time to circulate before you killed him."

Teomonious's mandibles twitched at that, and if Tala could see it, the tell would be as clear as the Erriten sky to Moravan. Nor did he try to deny it.

The menace filling the corridor intensified, raising pinpricks on Tala's skin. "Heed the difference between killing a hound as it walks peacefully beside its owner and when it charges a defenseless child. The second will make you a hero, the first a monster. I hope for your sake that the explanation for your involvement is sufficient."

"He was a traitor, High Councilor. He organized an attack on the Legislatorium, which I believe is imminent. And..." Teomonious hesitated. "This is strange to say; in doing so, he conspired with the Renegade Arcus Boral."

Tala watched for a reaction, but Moravan's features stayed rigid as ever.

"How could Ceowograffach conspire with someone who died before he was hatched?"

"The Index..." Teomonious squirmed, "appears to have been overly optimistic."

But you knew that already, didn't you? Tala thought. *They who stand at the summit see the lay of the land spread out before them.*

Moravan tapped his needles together, considering. Then he turned without warning, shifting his gaze outside the holo's range of replication. His lidless eyes were looking right at Tala. She froze, pinned in place by two lava-bright orange globes in an emaciated skull. *He can't see you,* she reminded herself. *You're safe.*

Teomonious coughed. "If you need proof—"

"Proof is for the Tribunal," said Moravan, still looking Tala's way. Those eyes had her transfixed; the certainty she saw there put reality itself to shame. "You know better than to insult me with a lie. The matter is settled. I will reinforce Legislatorium security at your recommendation."

"The traitor indicated that Legislatorium security could be circumvented."

"The matter is *settled*," Moravan repeated. "Or perhaps you think me incapable of dealing with internal threats."

"No, I—That is—"

"Now explain why you did not take Ceowograffach alive, so we could hear of his machinations firsthand."

"That was an accident, actually." Teomonious shifted with real discomfort. "To secure a confession, I had to hire mercenaries, and…" he waved his arms helplessly. "One lost control."

He delivered the lie with such gloss that Tala almost believed it, even knowing the truth as she did. But perhaps Moravan sensed something, for he turned back to Teomonious—allowing Tala to take a quiet breath, blinking in an attempt to banish the afterimage of his unyielding eyes.

"Unfortunate," he said at last.

"Yes."

Quarack made a face at Teomonious.

"There will be an investigation," Moravan said. "I will be surprised if the Tribunal does not require your testimony, particularly once they obtain a certain magtrain's ticket records. Sloppy that."

Teomonious winced. "I was hoping my involvement in this mess could be handled more discreetly."

"There is a great deal of scrutiny where dead councilors are involved. Remember that next time you hire mercenaries."

"I will, Eternal."

"Good." Moravan's tongue swept across the top of his jaw. "I would speak face to face. If you are not already bound for Peramit, change course accordingly."

"But—" Teomonious flinched, realizing he'd been about to protest to the *High Councilor Eternal*. "At once."

"Keep me apprised of your progress." The command carried no allowance for objection. "I await your return to civilization. Despite your diminished status, you will be permitted to use the Councilors' Hangar."

It hurt Teomonious not to react to that last part, Tala could tell.

"Your actions today will be remembered," said Moravan. "Now, if there is more…"

"No, that's all," said Teomonious. The hologram shut off before the second word had made it out of his mouth. Though the image was gone, the tension it had ushered in hung thick in the air, like the smell of smoke after a wildfire. Even the empty air above the omnipad still demanded attention.

That's that. Tala sagged against the wall. She wanted nothing more than to lie down and not move for a while. Not even Arcus could contend with the Legislatorium on full alert. Whatever he tried, they'd be ready.

The thought wasn't as comforting as she'd thought it would be.

Ferric gave a small shake of his head. "So that's what it's like to see a councilor up close."

"Come again?" said Teomonious.

"Hey," said Quarack. "There was that one I shot. I mean, if you count that worm as a councilor—waitasec. Hey Bugboy, is it specist to call an alvear 'worm' if it's an accurate representation of his character?"

"Why of all the criminals in the galaxy did I have to get stuck with you lot?"

"Gotta be karmic justice," Quarack offered.

"Did that really strike you as anything but a rhetorical question?"

Quarack frowned. "What about that one? Still rhetorical?"

Maybe it was the chemical-induced calm pumping through her bloodstream, but for once the next link in the twisting chain she'd dragged across the galactic map wasn't a struggle to see. Because she knew—it was obvious, really—why the Legislatorium wouldn't catch Arcus no matter what new measures they added.

It was for the same reason one only goes after a tarmoraptor's nest while the mother is out hunting.

"We need to go to Peramit," said Tala.

"Quite right," said Teomonious. "The sooner the better."

"It's your tab." Quarack was frowning again—for real, this time. "He *is* rich enough to make his own way. But if you want to spend it chauffeuring Teo to his meeting, go for it."

"No, I mean *we* need to go there. That's where Arcus will be."

"Tala, I don't know," said Ferric. "As far as security goes, Peramit's a tough crabshell. That fancy landing gear won't beat pole-to-pole orbital scans and double-layer planetary shields. Seems to me like going there ourselves is risking a lot for little gain. Can't we let the Dauntless Guard handle it?"

"No, because he's smart." There had to be a more eloquent way to put this, but the words were floating just outside her reach. "Too much security and he just won't show. But whatever happens, we know he'll be on Peramit. We have a chance to catch him before he bails."

"Not if we get blown out of the sky," Quarack muttered.

"We'll take a hint from Arcus." The thought made her recoil, but none too harshly given her present state. "He's using a councilor for access. Well, we have one too. He should have enough clout to get us through."

Teomonious gave a sage nod. "I *am* a sapient of impressive reach."

Quarack erupted into a coughing fit that sounded a lot like "impressive ego."

"My concerns could populate a cluster," said Ferric. "But I'm not straying from your side. Not again."

"You all assume I'll *let* you use me for access." Teomonious clicked his mandibles pointedly. "It is quite the unnecessary risk for me, you know."

"I can get you to Peramit fast enough to give you a chance of getting ahead of this scandal," Tala said. "Spin it however you want. Make yourself a hero. If I'm caught, I'll even say I took you hostage. But I need this from you. Please."

"I wanna be a hostage too," Quarack interjected.

Teomonious considered. "*And* you owe me a favor?" he said to her, ignoring Quarack.

"Done."

"Now that we're in accord, it strikes me how unlikely it is that I'll be able to collect," he mused. "Ah well. How fast can you get us there?"

Tala did the math. Seven days? No, not with the energy healing would take. "Ten days."

The energy was forming anticipatory whorls in her mind at the thought of what it would soon be asked to do. She'd already been giving the engines everything she had. Where she'd find the power to do that *while* healing from near death, she didn't know.

Perhaps even ten days would be too long a journey. Without a concrete date for the attack, she had no way to know whether her task was utterly hopeless…or just theoretically so.

"We just have to hope that's good enough," she concluded. "I'll go get started. The details will have to wait until I don't need painkillers to think."

Careful not to overbalance, she pushed off from the wall she'd been leaning against and began the walk to the sub-bay. Ferric didn't follow, to her surprise, opting instead to ask Teomonious what security measures they could expect from the Councilors' Hangar. Just like him to weld down the details early. It was Quarack who took up her trail, falling into place at her shoulder with a playful crook to her beak.

"I heard human faces freeze if they hold an expression too long," she said. "Just a warning."

Tala raised an eyebrow in reply, then kept walking. She didn't want to think about Quarack right now.

"Wait!" she heard, alongside the distinctive scrabble of talons on metal. "I have a plan! A way to bring Bugboy down a few branches!"

Tala closed her eyes. "I don't think—"

"You heard him back there." Quarack spoke with the speed of someone running out of time before their mouth seals shut. "After that whole Eternal thing, it's safe to say his smugness has hit critical levels. It needs to be lowered, for his own safety—and the galaxy's. We could have a meltdown on our hands. You'll help save the galaxy, right? That's what you do."

"Great plan," said Tala. "Love to help, but I'm fixed to the engines —"

A claw caught at her arm and she spun around, forcing her breathing into compliance. "I don't want to talk right now," she said.

"Too bad," said Quarack. "Talking's the only thing on the menu."

"Talking, and murder." It was out before she could help it.

"If you were just upset, I'd get it. But no. You're shocked. You all are. Like I *fooled* you." Quarack's claws curled. "Funny Quarack, quirky Quarack. Breaking news, Tala! I don't follow your rules. You seem fine with that when I'm working with Renegades—" Tala's lungs iced over, "—and helping you break into buildings. And yeah, I've learned how to kill people when they back me into a corner. You know what? I bet you have too."

"Never civilians. Never prisoners."

"And if that prisoner had a gun? Mark my beak, that bug was anything but harmless. Just looking for the softest place to ram home the shiv."

"That doesn't make it right."

"I know you think so. And that's why it had to be me. You couldn't have lived with it, but me...I can."

Oh, but her temper wanted to flare at that. She held it in check, barely, feeling it ripple and peak against her muscle.

"If your conscience is so clean," she said, "then why pretend you did it for me?"

Quarack recoiled.

"I thought I knew you." Tala gave Quarack a weak smile. "Silly me, right?"

She turned around and kept walking, deeper into the ship's depths, even as she left a piece of her behind. The ladder to the turret was just a little farther, and she couldn't help but wish she had time to climb it again. To gaze out into the void, the only thing separating them a thin glass bubble. If only life were more like space—unending, peaceful in its emptiness.

"Yeah," she heard behind her as she rounded a curve. "Silly you."

The truth was, it was too late to start wishing. Unlike space, life didn't go on forever—and she'd always known this would be a one-way journey.

CHAPTER EIGHTEEN

THE CHOLLIMA'S LEGACY

The darkness of Quarack's smuggler's hold was deep and unchallenged. The air smelled of old metal and sweat. Worn, unopened boxes cast rough shapes, vague impressions in the dark. Ferric too sat somewhere nearby. She couldn't see him; the gloom had swallowed him whole. Indeed, the only signs of life were the sounds of their breathing and the whispers that she tried to ignore.

Each rise and fall of her chest was quiet and carefully metered, though she knew it didn't matter. Any scanner that could detect her breathing could detect her in any number of other ways.

"Ask yourself, is this wisdom?" Arcus's voice echoed through the sealed chamber. And as it did, something shifted in the shadows. A four-armed silhouette lit with amber rings.

Tala's heart pumped a tingle of frost through her veins. *What you see is a falsehood*, she told herself. *Same as his voice.*

The first shape was joined by new movement, a whisper of ancient bones. "For once, I find us in agreement," said Scratch.

Tala kept her breath steady and let her eyes fall closed, turning the near-darkness total. His words were unfair; she had a plan, undeveloped though it was. They did have a way to slip through Peramit's security, down to the surface. That was at least something. The rest could come later.

She was closing in. The thought held eagerness, the culmination of a long hunt fulfilled. But Scratch's words jarred loose a new realization: he was more right than she'd credited him with. She'd made a plan to get in, yes, but she hadn't so much as thought about getting back out.

The notion of her own mortality wasn't foreign; given her profession, it was a concern well fermented. The Tenets that taught of death's intrinsic nature had not landed well on her ears. No words—not even Mitra's own—could ever lead her to acceptance. No, if it came down to it, she'd rather suffer imprisonment than death. However they held Renegades, it couldn't be worse than the alternative.

"Say you do find me," said Arcus. Her breaths hadn't quieted him this time. "What then? Do you expect you can kill me? You couldn't even stop Viron. What under the pallid sun do you think you can accomplish?"

She felt the ship come to a stop. It must be their turn through the security cordon.

"You see this as a personal struggle. But what about Ferric? You'll bring him right to me. How well did that work out for the rest of them?"

It would *not* be the same. This time, she was prepared. This time...

...she would do what needed to be done. Her jacket pocket wasn't large enough for the answer she'd concealed within it. Its bulky shape pressed against her side. A source of discomfort, in more ways than one.

"Tala."

She squeezed her eyes tighter, willing the sound to wilt to nothing.

"Hey. Tala."

Wait. That wasn't...

Her lids flew open to nothing, blinking away spots that weren't there. "Ferric?"

Ferric's hand reached out, grasping around blindly until it found her shoulder. He gave it a light squeeze. "If something goes wrong, if we're discovered, we could always hide. Peramit's a big place. There are places on the outskirts where we could make our own life. We don't have to treat this plan like a flagship play."

Even in pitch darkness, she was an open channel to him.

"Hard to keep a low profile," she said, trying to give his hand a squeeze in return. She ended up grasping his wrist, but she hoped the feeling was clear.

"We could use the mesh. Put up a face ugly enough that nobody would look twice."

Tala's laugh bubbled up out of her, catching her by surprise—and bringing with it some small solace. It had been too long since she and Ferric had shared laughter. "What would we do in this theoretical life of yours? Our accounts are frozen, and our skill set isn't exactly prime for civilian living."

The ship's engines kicked in. The movement was sudden but not unexpected. Nobody would keep an Eternal waiting.

"We could figure something out. I managed for a year with barely seven under my belt."

Tala stood, hunching her back as she rose to keep her head from smacking into the ceiling. If they were moving again, they'd made it through the scan and the hold was no longer necessary. Whatever time they had left before they made landfall would be better spent finalizing preparations and making her goodbyes.

"Shall we head up?" she said, back throbbing. Her mostly healed wounds hadn't played well with the smuggler's hold's cramped dimensions.

"Probably should," Ferric said. "But remember what I said. I wasn't joking." He rose as he spoke, and pushed open the hatch to the main hold.

Tala let him go first, lingering for a breath in the stale, dusty air. Ferric's idea—his offer—was a non-starter so long as Arcus drew breath. The gray-clad siari was an event horizon, warping any future she might have toward him and him alone. That state of affairs suited her, most of the time. She didn't want to imagine anything else—though for Ferric, she almost let herself consider it.

Almost.

She looked around the smuggler's hold for Scratch and Arcus. They were gone, but some of the fear remained. It would do her no good. Besides, Teomonious deserved a farewell that went deeper than the skin. And, she forced herself to admit, Quarack probably did too.

She focused her mind inward, much like she did when Enhancing, imagining everything around her as mere lights in the void. From that luminous space she let the sparkle of her earlier laugh shine through, brightening and brightening until no fear remained. A grin formed on her face. She was ready.

The real cargo hold's exit was right by the life-support filters. She gave them and the viscous masses they produced one final glare as they walked by. Of all the things she'd miss about the *Aquilon*, its run-down subsystems were not among them. That view from the turret, though—*that*, she'd miss. The short trip through the *Aquilon*'s belly seemed to stretch, a hundred idle musings for each step. Some part of her didn't want to leave.

They moved into the main corridor to a familiar sight: Teomonious grumbling while Quarack laughed all along her beak. Tala froze, contemplating retreat back into the hold. But the twenty-fourth, thirty-first, and seventy-fifth Tenets anchored her in place. She would not run.

"It's not funny," Teomonious huffed. "Why are you even here? In my experience, pilots are supposed to stay in the cockpit for a landing."

Quarack waved a claw. "Nope. We're on remote override. They wouldn't let a ship fly free this close to the city. Sounds to me like your past pilots were just avoiding you."

It was a striking sight—not the bickering, but the viewport behind them, which showed a small piece of the greatest defensive network in the galaxy. The ship was on course to fly through the mouth of a yawning metal ring, one of seven orbiting the planet. Testaments to the cutting edge of planetary shielding technology. They could only trust that the iris was open and the way clear. If it wasn't, the *Aquilon* would smash itself to powder as it collided with an unassailable wall invisible to the naked eye.

Though if the military wanted their ship destroyed, deception wouldn't be necessary. A spread of bristling orbital defense platforms spun languidly through orbit, each covered in more guns than a twelfth-tier warship.

"Look who decided to join us," Quarack said, turning her own head away from the viewport and its daunting display. She still wasn't meeting Tala's eyes.

Ferric closed the distance to his door and waved it open. "No problems?"

Through the open entrance floated a magcase, filled with what could only be the pieces of his Volter suit. As much as he'd always wanted a chance to field-test the thing, he didn't look too excited to take it with him.

"None at all—well, no thanks to this one," said Teomonious. "I'm an old touch at this."

Tala hadn't moved, but her attention had slipped away from the viewport. And onto the ship, which she realized she probably wouldn't see again. At least when she left this one behind, it wouldn't be sent to its destruction alone in the nothing. That was a thought to hold onto.

"Thank you," said Tala to Teomonious. "Very few would have chanced things with me. I know you'll find yourself back in your old seat."

The stout politician leaned back indulgently. "For a dangerous criminal bent on indiscriminate destruction, your company is bearable enough."

Ferric took his position at Tala's shoulder. He'd retrieved her bag along with his, and was carrying them both. While she hadn't asked, she appreciated the gesture. "What you're saying is you'll miss us," he said.

Teomonious gave the nordok a once-over, shrugged, and turned back to the viewport.

"Hey, Tal," Quarack said. She turned her beak downward, her voice almost soft. "Remember you still got seventy days left. Don't have to use 'em, but I'll be around for a bit, and . . . well, you know."

"Right," said Tala, focusing her attention on her own feet. "I'll keep that in mind."

In response, Quarack pulled out her omnipad. She looked as drained as Tala felt.

"Hey, Teomonious," Ferric said. "Wasn't there something you wanted to show me?"

"I don't believe so—"

Ferric grabbed Teomonious by the shoulder, steering him away. "Let me show you something, then."

Quarack looked up as they left, head crooked, feathers bunching around her neck. All Tala could do was purse her lips, searching for a correct thing to say that didn't come. Finally, she settled on "I've been doing some thinking."

"You're into that too, huh? Lots of fun." Quarack shook her head, letting the omnipad drop. "Yeah, that came out wrong. I'm not great at this. My standard move when I don't know what to say is stealing a ship and booking it."

"If you'd like," said Tala, trying to stop the twitching at the corner of her mouth, "I could recommend a few Tenets that—"

GREENWALD / KIVELSON 🚀 241

"Just whatever revelation you were about to share, please. And don't say you're in love with me. I get the appeal and I'm flattered, but cross-species just doesn't do it for me."

"That's definitely *not*—"

"Not prejudiced or anything! Just, human hair reminds me of a pile of worms."

Tala sighed. "I didn't imagine this conversation going like this."

"Skiarawa," said Quarack, nodding as if she'd just said something very wise. "Now quick, get it out before I derail us again."

"I was unfair."

That wasn't what she'd imagined herself saying either. Somehow, between Quarack keeping her off balance and the need to speak quickly, something else had come out. Something a little closer to the heart of the issue. Something a little more true.

"I still don't agree with what you did," Tala admitted. "But you've never been shy or secretive about who you are. I decided to be your friend anyway. Because deep down, I already knew something it took me ten days in that stupid sub-basement to figure out. Everything you've done from the moment we hired you has been to keep us moving forward."

"Part of the job."

"No," said Tala firmly. "Even right before we started fighting. You followed me down there to try and cheer me up with some stupid plan —"

"Hey, it was a wonderful plan! I stand by it!"

"The point is," said Tala, "you see a flightpath and you take it. No hesitation. Whatever it takes. And…everyone needs somebody like that. Everyone should be so lucky."

She pulled the small corvid into a tight hug. She hadn't fully sorted her feelings, but she *really* hadn't wanted to keep things sour. Quarack let out a few indignant squawks before begrudgingly accepting the embrace.

"I wouldn't let just anyone get away with this," Quarack said.

Tala released her. "Friends?"

"I'm insulted you need to ask. Now c'mon. I'm worried about leaving those two unsupervised."

They found Ferric and Teomonious some way down the corridor, staring through a viewscreen at their descent. The ship had just passed through the shield ring, and the view of the planet stopped Tala's breath in her chest. Even from the exosphere, Peramit glowed. The city below painted the clouds blue and green and gold with its light. Long, thin clouds, like comet trails stretching across the globe.

It was her first time here—both to the planet and the city that shared its name.

They'd caught Teomonious fully submerged in a well of words as deep as it was self-indulgent. "—barely a grubling then, but they still recognized my potential. I got reassigned as a staffer to the Galactic Health and Wellness Bureau. . ."

Every so often, Ferric grunted or gave a weak nod as he struggled to pretend he was engaged.

Like frost on a window in early spring, the highest clouds melted away before them to reveal the murky shapes beyond. Buildings as far as the eye could see, tall and broad and so closely placed that they seemed to sway together as a single shifting mass, a packed stadium undulating their hands in an endless wave. Podpaths snaked between them and up their sides. Vert-capable pods anchored themselves on tracks that rose into the sky or sank into the hidden depths of the city. Messages and lights flashed across the buildings as each one tried in vain to stand out among the others. The smallest glimpse at the smallest piece of Peramit held so much life that trying to think about it overwhelmed her.

"Those early years were hard." Teomonious was still going strong. "A mountain made of harsh words and demeaning tasks. I scaled that mountain, I did. Climbed it to the very summit. But even at the peak, I couldn't—"

"We're back," said Tala. "Thanks for the assist."

"And don't worry! You're *all* invited to the wedding. Except Teo."

"I take it everything's back to normal then," said Ferric.

The alvear huffed. "Excuse me! Some of us were discussing matters of import."

They were getting low now, Tala noted as she moved to join Ferric. The tops of the tallest buildings rose above them as they moved into the thick of the city, weaving sedately through the web of inter-building connective corridors, most broad enough to have their own buildings and podpaths within. They passed over the Garden of Unwanted Knowledge, too fast to get more than a glimpse. She saw no sign of the Legislatorium itself, but they had to be close now. Their destination, the Councilors' Hangar, was situated as close as possible without violating the restricted airspace surrounding the Legislatorium—a short drive or flight from the city's heart.

The ship slowed as it angled toward the ground. Below them, a gaudy, gold-hued hangar eased into view. Its broad roof—a glass mural depicting the first signing of the Accords—slid open to receive them. They flew through the opening, the ship still obeying its predetermined flightpath. It drifted into a single bay among many, shuddering slightly as a metal claw locked it in place. The ship fell silent as it powered down. They'd made it.

"Handful of sapes approaching," Quarack commented, eyes flicking to her omnipad. "Anyone order a greeting party?"

"That would be my escort." Teomonious straightened, all six arms patting the wrinkles out of the ornate robe he'd taken to wearing since Urgam. "It would appear I'm to be afforded a councilor's due. The right sapients must be starting to hear what tune the wind is crooning. I would ask that you send my luggage to my personal residence, but that would be a futile gesture, wouldn't it?"

Quarack tapped her beak in agreement. "That's maybe the third sensible thing you've said in the entire time I've had the displeasure of knowing you."

Teomonious didn't even look that annoyed. He just gave Tala a hiccup of a nod. "In that case, if you'll excuse me. My honor guard awaits."

With that, he left, his back straight and his steps measured.

"What if I just kept the bay door shut?" Quarack mused under her breath. "How long do you think he'd stand there waiting?"

"Oh, let him out," said Tala. "He did his part."

Once he had left, so could she.

Ferric must have been thinking along similar lines. "How long do you think he'll take out there?"

"Hopefully he'll keep it to a few hours or less," Tala deadpanned. "If the guards humor him, we might need to stay the night."

"Mmmm. Good thing we aren't in a hurry."

"Don't say things like that," said Quarack with a glare. "You're just asking for trouble. But as long as we're here, I *do* have a list of additional charges incurred..."

Tala nudged Ferric. "Bets on who finishes first, her or Teo?"

"First: a six-star emotional support fee."

"You don't have anything to bet with. Neither do I."

"Favors. First pick of meal canisters. Your suit. Get creative."

Ferric shifted, and didn't meet her eyes.

"Second: three crescents for every use of foul language. I don't tolerate swearing on my ship. Ferric, just the stuff I heard walking by your quarters puts you at sixteen—"

There was a screech then—a long, wobbling call that rang through the thick metal of the Aquilon's hull. It rose and fell, oscillating from sound to silence with a steady rhythm. Despite its volume, it had a far-off pitch, like it was being funneled down a long corridor into their ears.

Quarack let loose with a chain of curses.

Tala squinted, concentrating as she strengthened her eardrums to withstand Enhanced hearing. "I don't think it's for us," she said, pitching her voice over the din. "It's least a kilometer away."

And there happened to be one thing about a kilometer away that would warrant an alarm this loud. The Legislatorium.

"It's him," said Tala. Somehow, she was sure—despite the additional security, Arcus had chosen this moment to strike. There was no doubt in her mind. It all lined up so well.

Maybe too well.

Ferric pulled his bag open. A long shotgun found its way into his hands. "I take it we're scrapping the plan."

"We don't need it anymore. We know where he is."

Quarack made a frustrated noise. "That twice-pecked egomaniac still hasn't left. He was chitchatting right up until this alarm blew our ears off. Now whoever's in charge of his little parade is telling me don't panic, and await further instructions."

"Probably got the panicking covered on their end," said Ferric.

How powerless Tala felt huddled inside the ship, waiting for the all-clear to leave while Arcus aimed himself at the nucleus of the Coalition. The alarm pulsed through her muscle and made resonators of her bones, each beat another lost second. Another second gifted to Arcus. She didn't want to imagine what use he'd put them to.

She found that she was done waiting.

"We're going now," she said, striding down the corridor.

"How?" Ferric called, scrambling to pick up the bags and follow. Her old opsuit was folded away in one. She'd have to change on the way.

"Through the guards. We'll figure out the rest as we go." She readied herself, clearing her mind and letting the battlecalm numb her to other worries. "How many are there?"

"Eight." Quarack bounded down the corridor, keeping pace with three steps for each of Tala's.

All that was left was for Tala to put on the holoveil. She reached into one of her jacket's elastic pockets, fingers pausing on the other bulky object she'd stored there. Her mind shied away from it, but it would be there when the time came. The blaring alarm made it clear that that time would be soon.

Stopping, she gave Quarack a determined nod goodbye. It felt wrong not saying more, especially after they'd only just started speaking again, but she was out of time. Quarack returned the gesture with a roll of her three eyes.

"Good luck," said the corvid—but softly, and only once they'd rounded the corner to the exit ramp. Without Enhanced hearing, or had her words not caught the alarm at its quietest interval, the moment would have been lost entirely.

"I take two, you handle the rest?" Ferric suggested.

Tala slid the mesh over her face. "No," she said. "I've got it. Just keep Teomonious out of the crossfire."

Before Ferric could splutter out an argument, Tala waved the exit ramp open.

The door unsealed, sending a lightly mint-scented breeze across her face. Without that barrier, the sound of the alarm intensified. Teomonious's security detail flanked him, clad in lightweight body armor, casting uneasy glances back and forth as they tried to make sense of the situation. Guns dangled from their hips, but she saw no Irradiators among them.

One stood apart from the rest, leaning against a parked flier. He was unarmed, in civilian clothes. The pilot, presumably.

The others started to turn. Tala launched herself, so fast that she left dents in the exit ramp. The minty air ripped past her face, crackling in her ears. Enhanced reflexes stretched the seconds out, each microsecond of motion its own frame.

The ranking officer—an older woman with a crest of gray hair—was Tala's first target. Either through well-honed instincts or random impulse, she'd started for her gun the second the door had opened. It probably couldn't do more than bruise Tala, but ricochets could be a real danger to everyone else.

The gray-haired woman pulled the trigger and Tala reacted, slapping her right hand down. Bullets were too fast to intercept mid-flight, but she *could* respond to the hand that had fired them. She felt the round thunk against her palm as she smacked it onto the landing platform. Circumstances notwithstanding, Scratch would have been impressed with her timing.

She was on them before anyone else could fire. Her other hand lashed out, strength carefully modulated. *Tenet seventy-seven: Destruction is control yet to be mastered.* She'd always had trouble wrapping her head around that particular Tenet, but as she flipped another of the honor guard through the air, she thought she understood. It was a warning of just how fragile sapients could be when met with an Enhancer's strength.

The guards were good, but they couldn't match her. She downed two more with a few quick blows and a backward kick, spinning between their retaliatory strikes and snatching a gun out of another one's hand. That dependable *speed-strength-speed* pattern kept her in motion, dropping her opponents one by one.

Then it was over, and the only moving sapient left among them was the pilot. He held up his hands, mouth twitching with barely corked fear. Tala took a deep breath and let her battlecalm drain away, checking around for Ferric.

He emerged from beneath the *Aquilon*'s ramp, carrying an apoplectic Teomonious under one arm. The alvear was putting on an excellent act of squirming and ranting about the indignity of being held hostage. Ferric's own expression was stony, but Tala suspected he was enjoying himself more than he was letting on.

"You're not a normal stowaway, are you?" said the pilot.

"No," said Tala.

"Are you gonna kill me?"

"Nobody's dying today. But I do need the flyer."

The mousy-eyed man's eyes darted around the hangar. "This alarm. It's for you, isn't it?"

"Don't worry about the alarm. I'll see to it."

"That's not really comforting to—"

"Get on the ground and stay there," said Tala. "I am sorry," she added as the man sat with a gulp.

Her peripheral vision caught Ferric making his way over—absent Teomonious, but carrying their two bags. He stopped by one of the fallen guards, scooping something up from the ground. A shock stick. As he reached her side, he tagged the sitting pilot with a casual swipe. The man twitched twice and collapsed, temporarily paralyzed.

"Had to," he said, catching what she was about to say before her mouth could open. "He could have reported in after we left. If security learns this flier was stolen, we aren't getting through."

Her thoughts on that were still formatting when she noticed a shape moving down the *Aquilon*'s loading ramp. Her first assumption was Teomonious, returning to protest their theft of his ride. But it was only Ferric's magcase floating its way to its master's side, like a loyal hound.

"He seemed fine waiting on the ship," Ferric said, again intuiting her thoughts. "Ready?"

"To go, yes. For Arcus, not sure."

"We taking the flier?"

"Seems like the most direct route. Can you get it off the ground?"

"I'll manage." Ferric swung the cockpit's saucerlike door up and open. His magcase floated past her and followed him through.

Following his lead, she approached their commandeered ride. It was about twelve meters long and vaguely triangular, with a rounded stern that suggested a heart shape. Row upon row of cold-burning thrusters lined the bottom, like a collection of candles flipped on their heads.

The alarm hadn't stopped. If anything, it had gotten louder.

"How's it looking?" she called as she swung open the passenger door.

"Surprisingly good." Ferric turned around in the pilot's chair. His omnipad was plugged into the main console. "This little beauty's got our course preset. Direct flight to the Legislatorium. No safeguards to speak of. I guess they figured nobody would be dumb enough to steal a government flier."

He was separated from the passenger's section by two meters and a light plastic screen. The rest of the chairs were arranged in an outward-facing imperfect oval, and when Tala took one, she found it almost sinfully soft. The whole interior was so clean, it gave the impression that the flier had come fresh off the assembly line. "Dumb seems right, considering where we're heading."

"It goes without saying," Ferric said, clicking a series of buttons on the dash that made the engine sputter to life, "but I'm not exactly thrilled about this."

She'd known something like this was coming. She hadn't made a decision since Neea that hadn't bothered Ferric in some way. Lately, she'd found that she couldn't even fault him for it. The secret in her jacket was heavier than ever; he had to have noticed the bulge it made.

"Do you trust me?" she said, and she wasn't sure which answer she wanted.

Ferric opened the plastic barrier. His face was set. "With my life."

The flier rose smoothly, a luxury ride through and through. A small hole opened in the hangar's ceiling and they drifted toward it, following their preprogrammed flightpath.

"It's just, we never talked about where you stand. After we learned —" Tala broke off. "It's not the time. I know."

They passed through the roof into open air. The flier picked up speed as it ascended, clearing a small thirty-story building covered in bright green leaves that spilled over every terrace, a vibrant waterfall.

"And that's on me. I'm," he swallowed, "sorry about that. I didn't want to face you, after how badly I'd wronged you."

"You didn't."

"Oh, but I did. Day after day, every time I didn't let myself see you as my friend. Every second I wasn't there to support you. I should have told you all this before, but—" he waved helplessly. "But I do trust you. How could I not?"

Tala sank back into the plush seat. "Then why aren't—"

"Because this is the point of no return." Was that a tremor in his voice? "If we go in there, there's no coming back. And you're still hurt, and—"

"All true."

"Knew you'd say that."

Tala let a soft smile through to her face. "You don't have to come."

"Of course I do."

"If this is just about finally having a chance to use the suit—"

"Right," said Ferric. "About that."

He lapsed into a momentary silence. The flier dipped and weaved, moving through the maze of interconnected buildings. They almost appeared as one organism, their attached points meticulously coordinated.

"I've known this was coming for a long time," he said. "Not exactly this, but something close. And I've been thinking."

"About?"

"I swore my life to you twenty years ago, and that oath stands. If it comes to it, I will stand with you against Arcus. No matter what. But I can't hope to fight him directly. You're the one. You can win. I'm—" he grimaced, "Darkest Hell, I'm a liability."

Other fliers sped through the air around them, heading in the same direction. A chaotic whirlwind of activity, with the distant Legislatorium the eye of the storm.

"But your suit—"

"This isn't some desperate apology, or attempt at atonement. I'm asking you to do something you won't be comfortable with."

Tala waited. Wherever Ferric was leading, he'd get there on his own.

"It's the suit. I pretty much took apart our old ship to rebuild it—you must have noticed. Anora piloted the *Chollima*, but you were the one that drove it. That was our truth, more than any Tenet. We were a bastion against the worst the galaxy had, and you were our heart."

The emergency lights shining on the surrounding buildings reformed into familiar words. *Active Renegade Alert.*

"After I learned the truth, I knew what I had to do," said Ferric. "I can't wear it anymore. It doesn't fit me. It's sized to you now, near as I could get it."

Tala froze, eyes on the magcase. At the forbidden thing inside.

"You should have a connection with it. Mitra knows I've shown it to you often enough. And nobody knew the *Chollima* like you. Every piece, biggest to smallest."

"But the guns," she said. "Weapons. I can't."

"I know," said Ferric. "But I trust you, remember? And having weapons is not the same as using them. Think of it as armor. Like a shield unit. With Enhancement backing it up, you should be able to take a missile to the chest and keep on swinging."

It should have been a no, definite and immediate. But it wasn't. It hadn't been for a while.

"I thought I was building something that would let me fight him with you, as equals. I imagined we'd bring him down as a team. But this isn't about me. It's about stopping him. You in the suit, that's our best shot."

Ferric was breathing hard, like he'd been carrying those words inside him for days. Now his mouth was empty, waiting for her response.

There was shock, yes. But that was fading, and there was no momentum behind it. And in the space it left, she found only relief.

She reached into her jacket pocket and pulled out the weapon she'd hidden within. The weapon that would have been her edge in the battle to come. The weapon she'd taken for herself on Tarous. An Irradiator.

Of all the responses she'd expected, Ferric's wasn't among them. He gave a loud bark of laughter. "This whole time, we've both been stewing in our secrets."

She placed it on a chair between them. Even touching it had sent a chill through her.

"And why is that?" said Arcus. "Because you're forbidden to use it, or because you know you will?"

She didn't flinch, though she was sure that if she turned her head she'd see him sitting next to her. The question didn't matter. She didn't have to think about it anymore.

"I'll wear it," she said, "but you take the Irradiator. Arcus thinks you're not a threat. Let's both give him a surprise."

Ferric stood and joined her. The magcase followed, cracking open as it went. And just like that, all that was left was to put on the powersuit. A suit Ferric had spent years making and a deciyear reworking to fit her. He'd given it a new paint job too. A depthless royal purple, with pale orange lining the joints.

"So, how are we getting in?" Ferric said as he clicked the torso piece to her chest, releasing a blast of compressed air.

"It's a well-defended position and we've got a flier. Only one thing for it. Anora's favorite."

"Going in heavy." Ferric let out a soft grunt of approval. "Well, at least if we get shot out of the sky, it'll be dramatic."

He went back to the console and tapped out a few tentative commands. The flier tilted upward, engines straining as it gained momentum.

"Seventy seconds," he said.

Together, they finished dressing her. For as bulky as the suit was, it was surprisingly easy to get into. And though she'd learned all through childhood that using such a thing invited madness, wearing it didn't make Tala feel evil or insane. All she could feel was the rubbery polymer of the interior coating.

She flexed her new metal fingers. "Are you ready?"

"You know me," Ferric said, pulling a pair of worn heavy boots from one of their bags. They were scuffed and scratched, but the mechanisms locked around his feet like they always had. "I never run from a challenge."

Tala removed her mesh mask so Ferric could slide the visored helmet over her head. She blinked as an overlay activated, augmenting her vision with a series of small readouts.

"I was more asking if you were ready to jump, but good to know." Even her voice came out clear. Amplified, to be sure, but still organic.

"Fifteen seconds," said Ferric. He scooped up the Irradiator, then activated the flyer's door. The alarm was louder here, blasting out from the building below. Wind poured in along with it, hammering at Tala and causing the flyer to wobble. "Smells smoky," he added.

They walked toward the opening together, feet thudding softly with every step. Ferric held at the threshold, hanging onto the rail for support. "This isn't the end," he said. "If they lock you up, I'll break you out. If they try to kill you, I'll have your back. Whatever happens down there, don't count your life as over."

"Tenet twelve," said Tala. "*Every action has its cost, but a good deed is beyond price.* Whatever the galaxy thinks, whatever other Tenets we run up against, hold to that one. Right here, right now, we are doing something good."

The flier came to a stop. It was time. Tala could tell Ferric wanted to say more, but he knew as well as she did what a delay might cost them. So with a nod for luck, she took the last step and flung herself out into the smoke-filled air.

CHAPTER NINETEEN
THE FALL

They fell together toward Peramit, and for a moment, it felt like old times. That feeling of weightlessness, the wind battering at her body, the ground rushing up to meet her. Squad Thirty-Three had drilled relentlessly in the maneuver starting when she was nine, until everyone —even Vigdis—could jump without fear. Until they could twist their bodies to swim through air just as well as water.

A few more seconds of falling soon stripped away the similarities. Ferric's powersuit split the usual rush of wind and kept it out of her ears. The drop, normally cold, was warm if anything—both from the suit's insulation and the Torandian-friendly humidity already spreading steam across her visor. Most troubling was how the suit had thrown off her balance. Instead of the controlled fall she'd spent years perfecting, her feet were fighting to stay aimed at the breach point. She was practically an Initiate again, fighting the drop instead of riding it. An inauspicious start.

She spun. Once, then twice, and then the whole descent became an unchecked tumble. She *had* to regain control. Some targeted Enhancement amplified the weight of her boots and air resistance did the rest, pushing her back into alignment.

She twisted her neck back to see how Ferric was doing. His form was perfect as always. Not that she'd expected otherwise. His eyes met hers and she grinned behind the visor, imagining his delight at finally seeing his suit in the field. If she knew Ferric, it would still sting that he wasn't wearing it himself. She'd have to make it up to him with a good demo.

Guilt fluttered across her emotional landscape; she wouldn't be showcasing the whole suit. The guns would have to stay powered down. She still wished he'd removed them. She was so aware of their presence on the ends of her arms, the way they moved with her and pointed wherever she did. They were impressive, to be sure. Ferric had done good work. But wielded by her, they were marks of betrayal.

The airspace was a hive of activity. Fliers and emergency shuttles flitted through the air, congregating around landing pads and avoiding the wires strung between the Legislatorium's three towers.

She would have missed the first spray of flak if not for her visor's HUD. It detected the bullets deciseconds before they hit, highlighting them in a blue glow. Almost immediately, she felt the sharp *ping*s of glancing hits. The rounds were meant to down shuttles and aircraft, but they slid good-naturedly off her Enhanced armor—though they *did* knock her out of alignment again.

In that moment, she felt invincible.

It was her first time wearing it, but the armor wasn't a half-bad conduit. The result of years of Ferric showing off his work, along with her intimate familiarity with the ship he'd repurposed into it. It was enough that she could flat-out *laugh* at bullets. Even anti-aircraft slugs.

Ferric wasn't in her field of vision, but with a sense cultivated over almost two decades, she could still feel him shifting his position behind her, keeping her body between him and the flak cannons. She moved with him, widening her angle of approach to maximize cover. While she could take those hits, no Enhancement was strong enough to save him from bullets of that caliber.

The Legislatorium loomed wide beneath her, its towers jutting up, talonlike, as if to pluck her from the sky. It was shaped like a cresting wave and textured with a jagged diamond pattern that gave it the impression of having been fit together out of thin slats. Along the wave's peak, the diamonds converged into a spine that ran the length of the roof, tapering into sheets of curved metal that caught the sunlight and cast it onto the podpaths and gardens below. Every centimeter was a uniform whitish-yellow—not a regal gold, but the color of age-stained bone. Still, it gleamed with a newness as impeccable as it was deceptive.

It was also leaking columns of greasy black smoke.

Another two heavy rounds clipped her chest. She Enhanced her weight in bursts to keep the impacts from rocking her. The fliers had to have noticed her by now, what with the anti-aircraft turrets tracking her fall with sustained fire. Still, none moved to intervene.

Knowing Ferric would be watching, she held up a gauntleted hand. Five fingers, less one every second. Time to impact.

Four.

The cannons stopped shooting as she passed below their range of fire.

Three.

She hit a web of wires at terminal velocity and felt a brief tug as they snapped. Without the suit, they'd have sliced her to ribbons. It was hard to assess mid-fall the damage she'd just done to the Legislatorium's electronic systems. Hopefully they'd built in redundancies. The towers surrounded her now; she'd be landing dead-center between them.

One.

The roof exploded on impact in a shower of glass and chromium. Tala felt the collision in her legs as the armor bucked and jerked around her. She hit the floor a decisecond later and that gave way too, imported marshwood planks splintering along with the plasticrete beneath. The hope was that these levels had already been evacuated. Maybe that was true and maybe it wasn't, but she hadn't landed on anyone—yet.

Her momentum carried her through another floor, and then another. Debris filled the air around her, beams and flakes of plasticrete and splintery dust. She plummeted through the Legislatorium like a meteor, barely slowed by each new floor. Then she hit something that didn't give way. A resounding crash shook her entire world, and she dropped involuntarily to all fours. The helmet ate her howl as pain snaked through the hairline cracks in her bones that had yet to heal.

Moments later, the room rocked again at Ferric's landing. He stumbled slightly, heavy boots absorbing the rest of the momentum. Both arms covered his head. The building wasn't collapsing on them, but debris rained down in a steady stream, an expanding dust cloud with the occasional solid hazard.

Tala got back to her feet. The floor they'd landed on was solid metal. Dented but otherwise undamaged. The dust restricted her vision, but nobody was shouting or shooting at them so they were probably alone. In fact, the only sounds came from chunks of rubble hitting the floor and the steady pulse of the evac alarm. "Status report."

"Nothing worth mentioning." Ferric knelt to disengage the heavy boots' braces. He plunged his nose into the crook of his arm to take a dust-free breath. "Thanks for drawing their fire. And clearing a path."

Tala looked up through the ragged hole she'd made in the Legislatorium, past sagging bits of floor, snapped support beams, and sprinkles of powdered plaster to the small patch of sky above. "That's my job."

Given the rough landing, she was grateful for the power armor. Still, with the protection came a disconnect. The galaxy was separated from her by a layer of metal; sensory inputs were filtered and modulated. A series of blinking diagnostics overlaid her vision. There were weapons, actual working weapons, attached to her arms. If the second Tenet's broader meaning was to keep in tune with one's surroundings rather than one step removed, she'd already failed.

"Look," said Ferric.

He tilted his head off to the side. She followed the motion to a small information kiosk, just visible through the swirling detritus.

Slumped against it was a body.

Tala felt herself slip into a combat crouch. As soundless as fifty kilograms of armor let her be, she shuffled closer. The victim was alvear, the back of his pale uniform drenched in blood. All six arms clung to the kiosk's half-open door.

"Light's on a vocal trigger—"

"Lights," Tala enunciated. A bright beam sprang to life above her visor, illuminating the kiosk and the room beyond. The room was larger than she'd thought it would be. Its walls were decorated with a traveling view of Peramit from the perspective of a tour flier. And the floor was strewn with corpses. Dozens of them.

She moved her visor from side to side, casting the light into every corner. Bodies surrounded them, strewn casually about like the aftermath of a child's game. Washed-out splatters of blood emblazoned the walls and dripped from chairs and pooled in different colors, mixing together into the same muddy brown.

"Arcus came through here," she said.

If she'd had any doubts that it was him the alarm was for, they were gone. The scene was Neea all over again, Neea on a grand scale. Except that Tala couldn't see any soldiers among the dead. Clerks, functionaries, visitors. Nobody who could have threatened him or kept him from his purpose—and he'd slaughtered them anyway. For fun, perhaps. Maybe just because he could.

Ferric drew the Irradiator, scanning the wide room's corners with suspicious eyes. His sweep lingered on the front desk, over which its representative had been pulled, throat slashed. Above, holographic signs still displayed directions to other wings of the Legislatorium, or announced appointments with no awareness that the names they displayed no longer lived.

"Not the stealthiest approach," he said, but there was no humor in it.

"Stealth must be losing air pretty fast. They've got alarms going."

Ferric scanned each of the room's six exits, eyes skirting around the dead when they could. The dust was starting to settle now, leaving a few more of the closer bodies half visible. "Which way?"

The visor she'd resented moments before was a benison now; a buffer between herself and her surroundings. She was more accustomed to seeing death than she once had been, but it would never be easy. Still, she had to look. The bodies hadn't fallen randomly. They'd been sapients, capable of reacting to a sudden threat. The fight-or-flight instinct was present in most species, and Tala was sure a Renegade's arrival was enough to push *flight* into the forefront of anyone's thoughts.

So what direction had they been running?

"He came in that way." Tala pointed to an open hallway. "Killed those three before anyone realized what was going on. They ran, he followed. Chasing, but also making his way *there*." She indicated a large, arched doorway bookended by twin granite columns.

"Makes sense," said Ferric, jabbing his thumb at the holographic sign above the door. It read *To Legislatorium Approach* in Universal lettering.

Tala felt a chill pass over her. "Let's go."

She was moving before she finished, trusting Ferric to fall into position. Not running yet—Arcus could be lying in wait around any corner.

The door already hung open. She took in the hallway beyond with a single sweep. It was empty save for two guards, both lying face up with identical holes through the center of their helmets. For a moment, Tala was on Neea and the guards had the faces of Anora and Dorian. A twinge of disquiet later, she was back in the Legislatorium with the lives of the Galactic Congress in her hands and no time to grapple with the past.

"Two-centimeter hole," she said, kneeling beside the guard on the left. The rough-edged pale blue armor covered him like a crab shell. "One shot. Looks like it went right through the brain. Armor damage consistent with a small-caliber bullet, Enhanced to roughly four times baseline. Neither weapon was taken."

It made sense he'd kept his weapon. Probably the same pistol he'd used against her. Arcus would prefer a weapon he'd already built familiarity with.

He..." she hesitated, looking at the guard on the right. "He hit them in the exact same spot both times. They even fell the same way."

The suit pushed her to her feet almost before she'd articulated the desire to stand. No time for a full analysis. Arcus wouldn't stop moving just because she had.

A circle had been cut out of the door behind the bodies, large enough to accommodate a siari. Tala squeezed through with mere centimeters to spare. Ferric, being suitless, fit easily.

"Least he's making himself easy to follow," Ferric said. Further down the hallway, four suppression capsules had been ripped from the wall. As Ferric was still upright, Tala assumed they'd also been defused.

"*And* disarming their defenses," she said. She broke into a jog. Every second counted. "We'll have to thank him."

They encountered another body at the stairwell landing, a kirtian in civilian clothing. Her neck was twisted almost a full ninety degrees, face forever frozen in open-mouthed shock. Tala shook her head, trying to clear the image from her memory as she started down the stairs, Ferric at her heels.

The stairs opened out into a broad hallway, a concourse shaped from blue silver. It glimmered in a strange half light born of evenly spaced cylindrical chandeliers sculpted to austere Torandian tastes. The floor was uneven; flat, circular stretches persisted for perhaps several meters before giving way to small changes in elevation. It reminded Tala of the wide, sleepy river on her parents' estate. Along the walls hung woven tapestries, each emblazoned with a sovereign symbol representing a part of the Galactic Coalition.

This was the Legislatorium Approach, that last crossing before the room where councilors gathered to shape the galaxy. All along the Approach, other pathways converged from every wing of the Legislatorium. It symbolized unity, the galaxy coming together in common purpose.

Currently, the effect was ruined by the broken corpses strewn across it, splatters of blood in all their many colors dripping in long rivulets across the irregular floor. Behind Tala, Ferric sucked in a breath of equal parts shock and disgust. Her own feelings were in agreement, though she kept her face neutral—even hidden as it was behind her visor.

Arcus had left behind an uneven but consistent line of death starting where Tala now stood. Three staffers lay motionless by the stairwell, one still holding her omnipad. Beyond them another pair, and then a guard shot right through the faceplate, body still shielding a Serdin in a Uni-News reporter's uniform. Tala broke into a run as she passed them. There was no shortage of others waiting ahead.

Where was the Dauntless Guard? One would be in the chamber itself to serve as a last line of defense, but that left two unaccounted for. Yet of the legendary unit assigned to protect the Legislatorium and the government it housed, there was no sign. Nor any indication of the sort of fight that would have resulted if Arcus had crossed paths with one. For there would have been a fight. Of that much she was certain. The Dauntless Guard's exact capabilities were shrouded in hearsay, but if even a tenth of what she'd heard was true, they'd be well equipped to handle even an ex-Pillar.

And more than capable of annihilating her if one found her first.

The trail of death thickened ahead, where a security checkpoint had bottlenecked traffic, trapping the fleeing sapients while Arcus slaughtered them. Dozens had died pressed up against the shimmering, semi-translucent blue partition, more like a sheet of light than a physical barrier but no less solid for it. The center panel was plain, dull glass with a ragged rent cut through the middle that revealed the elaborate wiring within. Not far beyond the barrier, Tala knew, was the Congressional Chamber. Arcus could already be inside.

Ferric scrambled to catch up, unable to match her armor-augmented speed. On a normal mission, she would have waited for him. Talked over some kind of plan. Gone through the breach with a clear course of action outlined and ready to execute. But they were out of time. She gathered her weight and sprang like a Numena sablewulf through the opening, glass edges splintering against her armor.

She cleared the barrier—and it was as if the entire Legislatorium had faded from her sight. There was room for nothing but the tall, four-armed figure at the end of the Approach. Arcus stood with his back to her, regarding the imposing emergency door that had shuttered over the entrance to the Congressional Chamber. His faded gray longcoat, splashed with blood, brushed against a lumpy satchel at his feet. Despite the noise she made as she landed, he did not turn.

Tala gritted her teeth against the temptation to fire, calling the Tenets to the forefront of her mind. Calm. Control. They would be her weapons. She needed no others.

Arcus hefted a small dark half-sphere in one hand and stuck it to the emergency door. Tala didn't need her visor's electromagnetic setting to know what it was.

"I wondered if I'd be seeing you today," said Arcus, still facing the door. "One can never be sure."

For a moment, she thought she was hearing voices again. But no, it was him. She just wasn't used to hearing him through her ears. The pitch was off. A little higher than the version in her head.

"But then, I didn't expect you to renounce your teachings so quickly either."

"Step away from the door," Tala ordered. That sterile laboratory smell was back in her nostrils, even through the helmet's air filters.

"I was very proud when I saw you'd been classified. What I imagine a father would feel toward a child who has painted the stars with their destiny."

Arcus's movements were languid, almost contemplative, as he turned to face her. He looked no different from the day he'd left her life a ruin. The same milky eyes, the same slender arms, the same polite apology in his voice.

The same bodies in his wake, killed because they'd stepped between him and something he wanted.

She took a sliding step forward. "A classification based on false pretenses. That *you* engineered."

Of all things, Arcus laughed. "I suppose I did."

Tala couldn't tell whether her shiver was born of excitement or rage. Either way, it stilled as quickly as it came. For him to admit it so openly, he must have already taken care of the cameras. Besides, she had a feeling even a recorded admission wouldn't change anything.

"A flimsy charade, but it was easier than you'd think. You see…" He paused, considering his words, then shook his head. "You're operating on a fundamental misunderstanding. I didn't trick them into finding you guilty. To them, you were guilty before you so much as entered Neea's atmosphere."

There was a momentary weariness, like his many years had wrapped their chains around him at last, lightlets shining a pale violet. "You can't go back. If that's the dream you're chasing, release it from your heart. Nothing will be enough. Not killing me. Not preserving the rot that festers behind this door. You're one of us now, until your last breath."

"Have you…"

Have you been talking inside my head? was what she wanted to ask. But she didn't. Neither possibility was one she could bring herself to hear confirmed.

"The armor *is* an inspired touch," he said, eyes brushing over her. "I approve. The Center wouldn't stand for it, but I don't imagine that means as much as it used to."

From behind her came the crunch of broken glass as Ferric emerged. For the first time, he took Arcus in. The author of their upended lives, in the flesh. His face simmered with unrestrained rage.

"Wait," said Tala. "Don't engage."

This had all happened before. She could see it now, so much more clearly than when she'd handed Ferric the Irradiator. Her against Arcus, with her Vanguard providing supporting fire. The memory of that battle's end grew larger in her mind, the past threatening to overtake the present.

"Like hell." Ferric stepped into place beside her and leveled the Irradiator. "We fight together."

"I can keep up with him. You can't."

Her head throbbed, the echo of a familiar pain. She couldn't lose him too.

"And we have the best chance together. I'm a soldier, Tal. Risk has always been part of the job." He ran his fingers across her shoulder plating with his free hand. "Your loss, your pain—I feel it all too, just as strongly. You understand why I can't let you do this alone."

"Yes," said Tala. "I understand."

And she did. The argument that could blunt Ferric's resolve simply did not exist; she knew it as surely as she knew herself.

It was almost too easy, given how well she knew him. All it took was a minor touch of Enhancement. Ferric had time only for a surprised grunt before his eyes rolled back and he collapsed, out cold. Tala caught him as he fell, pulling him into a corner of the room, hopefully far from the coming battle. Arcus was the pragmatic sort of cruel, and he'd focus on direct threats first. To keep Ferric safe, she'd made him less of one.

That wasn't much of an excuse. He'd trusted her, in the end. The proof of that was wrapped around her body. And this was how she repaid that trust.

She hadn't taken her eyes off of Arcus for a moment, but he seemed content to watch. Amused, even. His face betrayed not even a flicker of surprise at Ferric's fall.

"Dangerous, to show an adversary what you care about. Once I'm done with you, he…" Arcus's slender mouth curved. "Well, I'm a kinder sort than most. I needn't kill him if you're so attached to his life. Shall I take his eyes instead?"

"I wouldn't plan ahead that far." Tala's power was sparkling in her veins like gemstones in sunlight. Everything she'd done had led to this. She *couldn't* squander this chance. "All I have to do is win."

Ferric put up no resistance as she pulled the Irradiator free from his limp fingers. The blocky, rectangular weapon felt small cradled in her gauntleted fist. It held just enough energy to stymie any attempt Arcus might make at Enhancement-based sabotage. With only a moment's hesitation, she straightened and pointed it directly at the Renegade's center of mass. She'd never shot a gun before, but the general principle seemed simple enough.

Arcus's lightlets brightened to amber—amusement. "If you think that little gun will stop me, I suggest you steel yourself for disappointment. The Center's meditation techniques are useful for that, as I recall."

He wasn't quite successful at keeping the bitterness out of his voice.

That voice. The same voice that whispered to her whenever her mind grew silent. The one that kept her up late worrying, poking holes in whatever determination she tried to muster.

"I'm done listening to you," said Tala, and found that it was true. It came out more tired than she'd meant it to, like the sound of a barbell hitting the mat after a workout. Arcus's lightlets flickered once, too fast for her to spot the interrupting color.

She knew what the Tenets would say; Scratch had spent a great amount of time carving the second Tenet into her soul and subconscious. *A life taken by hand is a life taken out of necessity.* Agents fought by hand and hand alone. No exceptions. Yet she held a gun. What was the Irradiator but one more in a long series of compromises?

There will come a day when you look back upon where your choices have led you and realize you've become just like me.

The weapon dipped toward the floor for a single decisecond before she steadied her arm. Arcus watched from six meters away, lightlets projecting a soft yellow calm shot through with that underlying amber. Almost as if he didn't expect her to fire....

Oh. Of course.

On each of the many occasions Tala's thoughts had drifted to fighting Arcus again, she'd told herself not to underestimate him. Yet here she was, treating Arcus like a normal opponent. But Renegades *weren't* normal opponents, and Arcus least of all. Tala had buried her doubts before crashing through the Legislatorium's roof, and it had taken but one casual sentence from him to see them resurfaced. To draw her attention back to the fear of going Renegade in truth, itself seeded in part by his words during their first encounter....

The strings were so visible now that she knew to look for them. She could trace the path her thoughts would have taken. They would have led her to reaffirm her identity as an Agent, throw down the Irradiator, and charge into battle unarmed. And die.

Instead, she did the logical thing and shot Arcus with a beam of concentrated radiation.

Or so she tried. Instead, the weapon let out a sad crunching sound as the entire section her hand was wrapped around caved in. The glow of righteous satisfaction in her chest winked out.

"Admit it," Arcus said. "You knew before you fired that nothing is ever that easy."

Tala managed to keep her breathing steady, but behind her eyes, her brain was buzzing with shock. Even with her own Enhancement protecting the Irradiator, he'd managed to break it. She put it together a moment later. He hadn't touched her *or* the gun directly, but multiplied the force her hand generated as it tightened on the barrel.

As the sheer surprise that her flagship play was a dead box of circuits and lead wore off, the shame fully sank in. She'd given in. She'd pulled the trigger. There was no justification, no gray area; the Tenets were clear in their forbiddance of weaponry. Yet when the test had come, that hadn't mattered. Hadn't been worth more than a few seconds of deliberation.

She lowered her arm, hoping the motion looked more like a tactical decision than disgust at her own actions. What had Frael always warned her? *The path worth following is winding.* She hadn't trusted her ability to overcome Arcus, and so had sought an easy way out. Truth be told, she didn't have much of a chance without it. Higher than before thanks to Ferric's suit, but higher was clusters from good.

If she could at least survive until the Dauntless Guard arrived...

Arcus nudged the satchel against the wall with his foot. The contents made an ominous clink. "Anything else you want to try?"

"You're going to wish you'd killed me the first time," Tala whispered. One by one, the fingers of her left gauntlet curled into a fist.

"I didn't think so."

Tala knew a preliminary to combat when she heard one. Before he could finish speaking, she slipped into the battlecalm.

Arcus went for his gun. Tala burst into motion, powersuit augmenting her run, servos straining to keep up with her. She hurled the broken Irradiator at Arcus's head as she closed the distance. Arcus's upper-left arm moved like a diving falcon, knocking the impromptu missile aside. He was less successful at deflecting the flying kick that followed it.

Every last drop of Enhanced strength, everything she could wring from her muscles, every single repressed feeling of rage and pain and hatred, she poured into the armored boot that made contact with Arcus's chest. The blow stopped his momentum cold and sent him flying back with a choked gasp.

Tala landed with a thud, frustration prickling at the edges of her battlecalm. It could have been her imagination, but the air had felt strangely thick right before she'd made contact, her leap slower than when it began. As if for a single crucial decisecond she'd moved in slow motion, stripping the kick of some of its stopping power. Already, Arcus was climbing to his feet from a blow that should have crippled him. Though his breathing was labored and his stance unsteady, he was still very much a threat.

She pressed her advantage, closing the distance between them with fluid strides. Before she made it even halfway, Arcus had his pistol up and firing. Her visor highlighted each bullet in blue. The first few flattened harmlessly on the powersuit's Enhanced exterior. The fourth, perhaps Enhanced to a higher degree than the last three, pushed its way through the steel plating and struck her chest. She felt it like a kick to the gut, but the bullet didn't have enough force left to penetrate skin.

As this was the same gun that had blown her squadmates apart, she was grateful for her extra armor. The suit had its own shield unit built in, but she didn't activate it yet. Better to save its charge than drain it on a few inconsequential shots.

Arcus fired again. This time, she was ready and slid around the shot, slapping the gun aside before he could get off another. Now he was in striking range. She pivoted, sending her other hand toward his face—but again, the air *tightened* around her, becoming something she had to struggle against. Arcus grabbed her arm as it decelerated, braced against the floor, and with a surge of Enhanced strength sent her flying past his shoulder to slam into the floor of the Legislatorium.

It would have been trivial to bound to her feet and continue the fight, had gravity not chosen that moment to intensify. Fortifying her limbs, she attempted once more to rise, but Arcus was already mid-pounce. He held a gleaming coral-colored knife that her memory told her was supernaturally sharp.

He landed in a crouch beside her, blade arcing down toward the hole he'd shot in her chest plating. Still unable to rise, Tala managed to twist into a half roll. It saved her life, but did nothing to keep Arcus's blade from sliding right through the powersuit into her side. Pain flared like a thunderclap beneath her skin. She thrashed, but Arcus kept the blade steady as he dragged it toward her heart, lengthening the wound he'd made and adding to the already immeasurable pain. Blood pooled beneath the armor, lots of it. Tala could compensate for the loss, but the more Enhancement she needed to draw on to keep fighting, the weaker she'd be.

The knife continued inexorably forward, despite frantic Enhancement of her armor. She struggled, threw punches and kicks that Arcus simply caught or ducked around. Her visor was a panopticon of ill news: system failures as Arcus's knife sliced through vital machinery, leaving only useless circuitry behind—

No. Not useless. Tala gathered her willpower and shoved it into a single loose wire, one that had been severed clean through just deciseconds ago. More specifically, the electricity that was leaking from it and seeking a new conduit.

The Enhancement took. There was a popping, sizzling sound and a flash of light so bright Tala's visor darkened in response. Arcus fell, skin blackened, and Tala brought her fist down with all her might on one of his arms. It was all she could reach. The snap that the powersuit's audio filters ferried to her ears was immensely satisfying, as was his grunt of pain.

Arcus scrambled back, releasing his invisible hold on Tala and letting her stumble to her feet. The long gash that stretched from her ribs to her chest was bellowing in agony and she felt blood trickling down her leg and squishing against her toes. Breathing hard, she focused on scabbing the wound.

But Arcus wasn't about to give her any such respite. Even as he disengaged, cradling his broken upper arm, the air within Tala's helmet grew uncomfortably hot.

Of *course* the powersuit's climate management was offline in the wake of Arcus's knife. Tala sucked in one last deep breath before the air became dangerous to breathe, noting her fogging visor. Already her visibility was half what it had been.

Was there a camera view setting? Ferric hadn't mentioned one, but then, she hadn't asked. She could barely make out a siari-shaped orange glow in front of her through the fogged-up helmet. Only one real option left. Tala lifted a hand to her face and unsealed the visor, sucking down cool air as it retracted. She could see again—and what she saw was Arcus pulling the trigger of his pistol, aimed unerringly at her exposed face.

The powersuit's kinetic shield caught the bullet, halting it a quarter centimeter from her right eye.

Tala let out a shaky breath. She'd barely turned it on in time to save her life.

It saved her life again just a second later, another bullet dropping to the floor. Tala bolstered the shield with energy, but Arcus did not shoot again.

She was so tempted to return fire. To *use* the weapon emplacements bristling from her arms. Her previous attempt only made it more enticing. The yearning intruded on her battlecalm, a pressure that fluctuated up and down but was always present. Of the two battles she was fighting, the physical battle might even have been the lesser.

"You're bleeding out," Arcus said. His voice was even, tremorless. Like she was a mildly interesting bug he'd pinned and left to dry. "Even Enhancement won't keep you going much longer."

Tala said nothing. She was too busy closing the wound through which her life was spilling. A deep injury, but the knife had been sharp and the cut clean. She'd had worse.

"Why do you defend them?" he whispered, stepping sideways toward the door to the Congressional Chamber. "The selfish, bloated bureaucrats who claim themselves best suited to lead. They are a plague upon the galaxy. The last disease, somehow uncured when the remedy is obvious. The galaxy deserves *better*."

"I defend the stability they represent," Tala answered despite herself, her eyes gravitating toward Ferric's unconscious body. "I defend the life of every sapient as precious. I represent a greater ideal than myself: a shield to *protect* the galaxy."

It was an archetypical Enhancer response, the sort Frael would have commended her for. So why did the words feel hollow inside her mouth?

"A shield cannot protect against the rot that spreads behind it. Sometimes, something more…surgical is required."

"Murder."

"They are motes against the backdrop next to such as us. The universe will spare them no violet."

"You're mad."

Arcus's lightlets flashed, anger threatening to ignite his pale blue skin. Perhaps he was a more typical Renegade than he let on. "I'm the only one who's sane. They are *unfit to rule*, Tala. We should be leading them, not powering their ships and chasing down their problems. If you could see it as I do, you wouldn't throw away your life for them in a futile attempt to stop me."

"I don't have to stop you," said Tala, taking an experimental step. As she'd thought, her injury was already less crippling. "Just keep you busy until the Dauntless Guard gets here."

Above Arcus, a circular portion of ceiling simply *vanished*, crumbling away into black flecks that swirled madly as if caught in a cyclone before evaporating altogether into nonexistence. From within the destruction loomed a humanoid suit of power armor at least four meters high and as wide as Arcus was tall. It was far bulkier than Tala's own, modeled in the carapace-esque style favored by the Torandians and burnished in ivory with red veinlike patterns inlaid along each limb. The veins glowed softly, indicating readiness of innumerable weapon systems.

Through herculean effort, Tala kept her face expressionless. "In fact," she said, speaking over the oppressive, low-pitched hum that had settled across the room, "I already have."

CHAPTER TWENTY
CONVICTION

The Dauntless Guard.

Tala couldn't help but feel a shiver at the sight of the mammoth powersuit as it dropped into the room, armored boots thudding against the thick carpet. She'd been raised on children's stories about the Dauntless Guard. The unremitting shield between the seat of galactic power and any who would do them harm. Each suit was unique, built by the greatest minds in the galaxy. Each had multiple Wonders integrated into its design, the inherent anti-Enhancement properties of which carried over to the suit and the sapient beneath, keeping them safe from the deadliest of Renegade tricks. Unstoppable, implacable, they carried enough firepower to hold off entire armies.

Now all that power had been turned against one sapient.

Arcus's body was red-lit, and for once, it wasn't his lightlets: tiny targeting lights showered his head and torso. Warily, he turned, three palms up and splayed in the universal gesture for peace. He couldn't lift the fourth.

In reply, one of the cannons mounted on the Dauntless Guard's shoulder plates spat out a coruscating burst of brilliant green light, aimed not at Arcus but at the space between him and the Congressional Chamber. The light hung undulating in the air like a deadly, wind-tossed curtain. This new barrier also managed to divert Arcus's attention from her, giving her time to start healing her side. Ferric was still out—breathing steadily, but vulnerable nonetheless and worryingly close to Arcus's side of the room. She'd need her strength to watch over him in the chaos to come. In a clash between Guardian and Renegade, no noncombatant would be safe.

"The much-vaunted 'Sentinel of Oblivion'. Such an impressive title." Arcus clicked his tongue. "And yet, all that power cannot break what binds you, Sentinel."

The Sentinel of Oblivion rose a half-centimeter off the ground and floated forward, indifferent to Arcus's taunts. Slow but inexorable.

Amber flashed down the siari's face, mixing with the targeting lights to create an orange glow. "Or do you prefer Merceus?"

The effect was instantaneous—the Sentinel of Oblivion halted as if struck. That had been a name. The Dauntless Guard's personal information was so heavily classified, the barest whisper of it could put someone away for life. And for good reason. A name was a weakness; a point of vulnerability in an otherwise invincible bastion. By naming him, Arcus had just ended the Sentinel's career—and exposed him to a galactic government's worth of enemies.

"Merceus *tor* Garen." Arcus played his tongue over the name, pushing it around his mouth like he was poking at it with a biometric reader. "Stop me if this sounds familiar: human male, age forty-seven, born on Concordon A—"

One of the Sentinel's hands glowed red. The world shifted, and everything seemed to drain away, leaving only a numbing haze. Her aches faded, her side stopped hurting, a stale taste filled the air. Surfaces became drab and dull, colors transitioning into panels of white, gray, and black—and still the pressure built. Tala's breath began to stick in her lungs. She couldn't tell the shade of Arcus's lightlets, but his eyes were firm as he stared down his armored opponent.

Arcus's voice was broken and rasping, as if stretched through a sieve. "Too *late*. You lost before you even arrived."

The distortion vanished with an echoing chime. The pressure let up, freeing Tala to take a long, gasping breath. And as the precious air poured into her lungs, the mighty Sentinel of Oblivion collapsed. A mountain of impenetrable armor toppled in an avalanche of noise.

And then there was silence save for Arcus's soft chuckles and the crackling curtain of light that was already fading.

"He should have realized."

Any moment now, the fallen powersuit would rise and continue the fight. He'd only arrived seconds ago. He couldn't already be—

"Once I had a name, the hardest part of killing him was picking the method."

The Irradiator had failed. The Dauntless Guard had failed. Tala was at the precipice and she couldn't fall again.

"Two down. That leaves the Argent Warden with the councilors," he continued. "Appropriate. And difficult, next to the poor Sentinel. Still, I wouldn't count on her to stop me."

"She won't get the chance." Tala ground out through locked teeth. "Stopping you falls to me."

"You actually believe you're trying to protect them, don't you? I suppose that *is* the most convincing sort of lie. The kind you tell yourself until you no longer believe it to be anything but the truth." He held up an arm, cutting off Tala who'd been about to speak. "Save your breath. Allow me to demonstrate with the help of a few lucky guesses."

His fingers sliced through the air in a dramatic gesture, though Tala couldn't think of a reason for it other than melodrama. In fact, Arcus had been altogether too prone to long, conversational delays for a sapient on limited time. Almost as if he couldn't help himself....

If she was right, she'd just found a sign of Renegade instability. A mental quirk she could turn to her advantage; a flaw in that incandescent intellect. *Prone to theatrics.* Or perhaps something else, call it *hesitance to finish the job*. It could explain why he'd left her alive. Or maybe—

"After our encounter on Neea," said Arcus, referring so casually to the murder of her friends that she could actually *feel* her blood fizzing, "you found yourself reclassified as a Renegade."

"As you planned from the start."

"You still shy away from understanding," Arcus said. "The Coalition doesn't see you as an Enhancer, but as a Renegade that hasn't snapped yet. They clothe their fear in finery and you believe it to be respect."

"What I believe is that you're a monster through and through."

"I don't deny it. But do you think yourself that far behind me? Explain then why you pursued me here from Urgam, instead of simply alerting Congress and allowing them to increase security. You thought of that, I'm sure."

"I—" Still formulating a response, Tala shut herself down cold.

She *had* alerted Congress. At least, she'd been there when Teomonious had, and Eternal Moravan had agreed to take the threat seriously. Had Arcus walked right through the increased defenses without noticing? Or had Moravan's efforts been derailed?

Either way, one thing was clear: for all his power and plans, Arcus had read her wrong. Given that he'd been one step ahead from the beginning, it seemed like a *very bad idea* to correct him.

One faulty assumption could lead to many faulty decisions.

"Lost for words? Here's an easier one. Explain why you picked up the Irradiator. An effective weapon, to be sure, but one that works over a period of *hours*. Not helpful if your goal is to keep me from ridding the galaxy of its current crop of fools, but a good way to ensure I die in excruciating agony."

"It was a deterrent. The threat of being hit would limit your..." But that was another lie. When given the chance, she'd pulled the trigger thinking only to end the pale Renegade's life. And indeed, had she been successful, the Irradiator would have lost all tactical usefulness—for after one shot had found Arcus, he would have no reason to avoid another.

"You told yourself whatever you needed to look past the truth, but there was only ever one reason you came after me. Will you admit it?"

Tala took a deep breath. The answer was there, both resting on her tongue, and scrawled across her thoughts. But to give it life outside of her would make it more real than she was willing to allow.

"Agent Kreeth, your silence will not change what *is.*"

"You want the truth?" The words came slowly, each one dragging over her teeth and clinging desperately to her lips as she spat them free. "Fine. I'm not just here to save the councilors. I didn't flee Neea just because you needed to be stopped. But I *have* been chasing you. I have flown across the galaxy, left behind every trace of the life I knew, and ground my moral convictions into sand to repay the lives you stole. I'm here to kill you."

There was a lightness within her now. As if by expelling the truth, she'd unburdened herself of all the weight it had accumulated. It was not the feeling she'd expected when she began, but it had happened nonetheless, word by word and syllable by syllable. When had she discarded her battlecalm? She found she couldn't remember.

She gave her hip an experimental roll. No bite of pain from the wound, though by no measure could it be called healed. It would no longer hold her back.

Nothing would.

With dawning purpose, Tala slotted her visor back into place. A series of precise eye movements brought the targeting display online. Now that she'd accepted the truth of her motives, she could no longer justify shying away from—

No, that train of thought wasn't quite seamless, but Tala blinked away the confusion and leveled her right arm at Arcus's chest.

"For a Vanguard murdered. For Anora and Dorian and Vigdis. For making me live on without them. And when I'm done, you'll regret Neea as much as I do."

"Preserving an Enhancer's life is never cause for regret. Not when a lesson in power will—"

The rest of Arcus's sentence was stripped away by a fusillade of bullets.

Tala felt the force of each slug as they left her arm, but she held it steady. Her will reached out to each bullet, imbuing them with greater speed and density. Enhanced eyes tracked them as they flew, following each individual shot over the course of an eyeblink. About half a meter out from Arcus, they slowed visibly, some even angling. Arcus's shield sprang up just in time to catch the first few out of the air. The barrier flared beneath the stress, but held. Dozens of missed shots tore into what remained of the security barrier and sent it shattering to the floor. Tala sent some spare Enhancement to Ferric's skin as glass exploded next to his motionless form.

The suit's five rotating barrels sustained a constant barrage, but Arcus's shield refused to break. Worse, the graphic in her HUD representing ammo was depleting rapidly while the metal around the grafted gun went from warm to searing against her skin.

It appeared as though Arcus could actually *Enhance air* at a level that could interfere with gunshots. The idea had been touched on during Tala's training, but dismissed as requiring unfeasible amounts of either power or familiarity to be effective. Yet here Arcus was, robbing her bullets of enough kinetic energy that a shield could hold them off without overloading. Just how deeply did his familiarity run? Or was his reserve of energy simply that vast, somehow?

Some small part of her was still repeating that this was not the Enhancer's way, but it was the same small part that hadn't stopped her attempt with the Irradiator. A part easily overwhelmed by the rest of her, which was trying to figure out how to breach Arcus's shield before her arm melted off.

The answer came in a flash of insight, *there* in her head as if it had only been waiting for the right time to reveal itself. Quick as the thought had formed, she severed her connection with every last bullet. Robbed of that impetus, they grew positively sluggish as they passed through Arcus's impossible barrier of air—

And, now barely faster than an underhand toss, slipped through his shield as well.

A small victory by any measure. Any projectile slow enough to penetrate a shield wouldn't even bruise a competent Enhancer, much less one at Arcus's level. So she picked a single bullet from along them and poured a hundred bullets worth of Enhancement into it. Speed blossomed where there had been none, and with it, power.

It shot forward with new purpose and struck Arcus in the chest.

Arcus stumbled back a full step, flashing a deep, brilliant indigo. Shock. He felt at the wound with one hand, disbelieving, ignoring the other bullets as they bounced away harmlessly. His mouth opened, but instead of words, all that came out was a pained cough.

Her rush of triumph lasted only a decisecond. Arcus's lightlets became unbearably bright, a depthless surge of orange that seared her eyes to look upon. Her visor polarized, but not even that could block out what felt like a glimpse at the core of a star. She turned her head away, shut her eyes, and rerouted energy to her hearing. Arcus was on the move; she could hear him running toward the thick metal emergency door.

Tala threw herself into a blind charge, thinking of nothing but her duty to interpose herself between Arcus and the lives he threatened. A soft *thwish* was her only warning. Searing pain blossomed like a bloody flower in her gut, an impact that sent her reeling even as her momentum carried her forward.

Keep moving. Don't let him win.

She stumbled another two steps and hit the Congressional Chamber door.

"Perhaps this time," said Arcus, "the lesson will persist."

The pervasive light, now tinged a pale lilac, faded. Tala blinked away the sudden darkness, vision slowly returning as her visor depolarized. Arcus stood roughly four meters away, his upper-left palm open. The hilt of his mono-field knife protruded from her armor, blood dripping from the hole it had made.

Tala pulled the knife free, gritting her teeth as her world threatened to turn white with agony. Knees on the verge of buckling, she doubled over around the wound. It screamed at her to lie down like she had on Neea. Cower on the floor next to the Sentinel's body while Arcus murdered his way through the Congressional Chamber. He wasn't here for her, the pain said. She didn't have to die.

But she would, if it came to that. Bitter experience had taught her where lying on the floor would lead. It was death in its own way; the death of the sapient she wanted to be. After all she'd lost, she couldn't lose that too. Until her legs gave out beneath her, she would stand.

Tala's fingers flexed around the handle of the knife and squeezed. Arcus took a step forward as he tried to save it—the handle put up more resistance than it should have. She ground it to scrap anyway. The atom-thin blade flickered once and died.

"As teachers go, I've had better." She gripped the doorframe and pulled herself fully upright, bracing against it to keep from toppling over. Her armored frame filled the space, blocking the door entirely. "The Galactic Congress is under my protection. Do your worst."

"My *worst?*" Arcus smiled, and there was something caustic and bubbling behind it. "I hardly think that will be necessary, even for a student as difficult as you."

"Difficult, I cannot argue with," came a new voice. One raspy and familiar, one that brought forth a maze of feelings that she couldn't even begin to navigate through. "But she is not *your* student."

It's happening again. She whipped her head toward the tall figure standing just beyond the broken security barrier, bones marked with a distinctive map of scars. Again, her mind had conjured up her mentor. Any moment, Arcus's phantom voice would make its rebuttal—

But Arcus too had looked. And Exemplar Scratch certainly *seemed* real. The Pillar of Justice strode across the field of glass, face a motionless ivory rampart. The perfect model of Agent protocol.

The weight of his presence roiled about him like a storm ready to strike. The veteran of a thousand battles, the hunter of Renegades— Arcus could not hope to stand against such a foe. Her worry melted away like ice beneath twin suns, leaving only certainty that everything, at long last, was going to be all right.

"Exemplar," said Arcus. "It *has* been a while. Two decades at least."

"Pathetic." Scratch had abandoned his stately bearing in favor of a full Torandian predator's stance: high-toed, with fingers splayed and shoulders thrust forward. He stepped past Ferric without acknowledgement, took in the fallen Sentinel of Oblivion without visible reaction. "To spend all that time playing dead, only to die for true the day of your miraculous return. The spirits of your victims howl for vengeance, and I will oblige them."

Arcus smiled bitterly. "It's a wonder I didn't hear it before, how foolish you sound. I would have left of my own accord."

"Careful," said Tala. "He's faster than—"

Scratch looked at her, really *looked* at her, and whatever she'd meant to say died a wretched death at the sorrow in his eyes. None of it reached the rest of his face—and perhaps it would be unnoticeable to anyone who didn't know Scratch as well as she did—but it was there all the same, and the sight of it tore at her heart.

"What happened?" he asked, voice at once soft and heavy. "How did my failure burrow so deeply? Tell me, what could I have done?"

"I," Tala swallowed, feeling suddenly like she had at six years old, meeting Scratch for the first time in the Center's gardens, "I wasn't lying. Arcus *was* on Neea, you can see he's been alive all along. It's like I said, I've been hunting him. Couldn't turn myself in, knowing he was still out there, but I haven't lost myself. They made a mistake. It's still me."

"Your claims did carry more truth than I credited them with. But any excuse dries up faced with what came after. Breaking into a government outpost. Stealing classified information and civilian driving pods. Assaulting government employees. Wanton property damage with no concern for sapient life. And now, use of weaponry in battle. This *thing* you wear."

At every new item, Tala's throat closed up a little more and Scratch's face grew another tick stonier.

"He admitted it," she said. "Just now. This is what he wanted."

"What happened that day no longer matters. By your actions since, you *are* a Renegade. Beyond all doubt."

She had known since the day she'd left Neea that the path ahead would be demanding, and not just in a physical sense. The compromises she'd have to make had been abstract then. Easy to take on. Hearing them listed out one after the other…Tala couldn't have picked which hurt more. That or the hole in her gut.

"Listen to me," she whispered. "Please."

Scratch studied her, tongue playing against the rim of his mouth. "I never wanted this for you, little one," he said. "If there is any trace of the Tenets left upon your spirit, demonstrate it now. Surrender yourself into my custody."

He extended a skeletal hand.

A second offer of surrender. Unprecedented, as far as Tala knew. When she'd rejected the first, so long ago it felt like another life, she'd never imagined she'd get another.

"We need not raise our hands against each other. Let the spirits guide you to peace."

And the more Tala thought about it, the more she realized there was no reason to refuse. Arcus had this day revealed himself to the galaxy at large; they could hunt him down without her. Even now, Scratch stood ready to stop him for good.

It could all be over.

All it would mean was a lifetime locked away. An end to freedom. Why should she be expected to give up so much when the architect of her downfall stood but meters away?

Tala took a deep breath. "I—"

"Exemplar, these spirits." Arcus backed away from Scratch, closer to her. She could hear something approaching humor in that soft voice. "You *see* them, yes? They actually speak to you? This isn't some metaphor derived from ancient wisdom?"

"Irrelevant." Scratch matched Arcus's retreat step by step, like a second shadow. "They but pass judgment. *I* am the one you should fear."

Had Scratch misunderstood the question? His talk of spirits was just eccentricity. A colorful spin on the Tenets. He didn't actually…

"You poor fool," said Arcus. "The moment you started hearing voices, you should have known."

He turned his head slightly and gave Tala a smile that sent the room spinning around her. He was talking to *her*. But how did he kn—

"Of course, it's so much easier to listen. Ignore the signs."

"Hold your blasphemous tongue," Scratch commanded, voice hard as stone. "And as for you," he said to Tala, "your surrender will have to wait until this murderer is put to rest."

"It isn't too late. I can still save you. I can *fix* you." Though he said it in Torandian, every word was meant for her. She could feel each one slotting into place around her heart like links in a chain.

Back and forth her eyes went between the Pillar and the Renegade, all while her head pounded a drumbeat of dismay. The implication of Arcus's claims was enough to freeze her in place as she processed. But time was a luxury of those who'd never needed to shoulder a galaxy of burdens.

Scratch took another step and Arcus exploded into motion, leaping to engage the scarred Torandian on his own terms. Tala moved too, running on shaky legs, ignoring the burning in her stomach, and throwing misgivings to the winds. In this kaleidoscopic whirl of uncertainty shone one steady line of conviction: her duty to the Coalition.

Three steps later, the first sortie had resolved in favor of Scratch, with Arcus bleeding from the chin. Then they clashed again, flickering in and out of the bounds of perception, Arcus a light-streaked blur, Scratch a whirlwind of bone and claw. The floor split beneath the intensity of their deadly ballet, shrapnel fountaining into the air around them.

And Tala was barely halfway to them.

She reached out with her meta-awareness, channeling energy into a small area of wooden shards. They swirled with Enhanced velocity, scoring Arcus's body with bloody groves and bouncing harmlessly off Scratch's bone. Arcus ducked back and got a claw to the cheek for his trouble, ripping right down his line of lightlets.

Scratch's face flickered in her direction, impassive expression betraying nothing. For a moment, she worried he'd attack her too. But he took a half step back, falling into a familiar position—one so ingrained from their training together that her body moved into formation before her mind registered the change. This was no flight of fancy. No delusion born of hope. The Pillar who always fought alone stood at her side.

At the Center, she'd wished for nothing more. What a fool she'd been.

Scratch lashed out with a clawed kick. As Arcus raised an arm to block, Tala was there to grab the arm and pull it away. Scratch's foot sank into Arcus's stomach and pulled. Pale blood splattered the carpet.

A heartbeat later Tala found herself tumbling, legs swept out from under her. She hadn't even seen the strike coming. She threw out an arm to break her fall and a Torandian hand closed around it, pulling her back up. Scratch gave her a brisk nod.

Arcus had taken the opportunity to disengage, retreating to the center of the room near the fallen Sentinel of Oblivion. Tala and Scratch advanced as one, each with an eye on the armor in case Arcus tried another of his tricks. With a hand signal to Scratch, she circled back toward the chamber door while he took the front. Together they had him cornered.

They were doing it. They were *winning*. A few more solid hits—

As Scratch approached, Arcus laughed. From above, where a hole had been vaporized out of the ceiling, came a metallic shriek.

Scratch moved like a bolt of ossified lightning, but not fast enough. Down came a roaring torrent of rubble, striking Scratch again and again until he lay buried in a pile of metal and stone.

Any moment, the mighty Pillar would burst free. But a second passed, an eternity in a battle between Enhancers, and no movement came.

He couldn't be dead. Enhancers were hard to kill, Torandian Enhancers doubly so. But he was out of the fight, and Arcus was sprinting toward her.

No, not her. A small satchel by the wall, forgotten in the flow of battle. Arcus snatched it up without breaking stride.

Then the satchel was tumbling end over end toward her and the metal door behind. She knew, somehow, that when it hit the door—or her—the charges within would explode. On the doorstep of the final barrier between Arcus and the Galactic Congress. Then the slaughter would begin—councilors' brains melting, hearts exploding, Enhancement used to its fullest, deadliest potential. Faced with that, her choice was clear, wasn't it?

Just her, a satchel full of bombs, and her resolve. There was only one way that could end. It had been drilled into her since childhood; imprinted on her soul in words as old as the Enhancement Corps itself.

Whatever was happening inside her, it could not change the core of who she was. She was the line between peace and chaos.

Tala Kreeth, Renegade. Tala Kreeth, Agent of the Coalition.

She flooded her limbs with strength, surged forward, and caught the satchel by the strap. It looked almost dainty dangling from her mechanized fist. Already, the contents were emitting a familiar high-pitched whir. Hugging the satchel to her stomach, she folded herself around it. Every last drop of energy she could muster—*every* drop, even the constant personal Enhancements she powered semi-automatically—flooded into the powersuit Ferric had entrusted her with. She emptied reserves she didn't know she had and *brightened* her armor, pushing energy through a conduit forged by familiarity and understanding.

The charges detonated.

A wave of heat and concussive force slammed against her, battering her like a rag doll. The metal screamed and she joined in with it. There was the distinct sensation of flying through the air, which ended with another abrupt impact that felt as if an angry god had slapped her back to the ground, broken and helpless. The powersuit was cracked and shattered, metallic shards shredding skin and tearing flesh in a half-dozen places. Her right leg felt like it had been dipped in molten sulfur. Three different warning klaxons blared inside her helmet, competing with the ringing in her ears to inform her just how few systems were still online. The visor was a blood-splattered web of fractures. She spat more blood into the helmet, noting the numbness in her lower jaw as she did so. *Broken*, her brain catalogued. If that was her only break, it would be a miracle.

But she was alive.

The blast had hurled her some distance from the door. It was barely visible through the ruins of her helmet, but what she could see assured her that it stood unbreached. In fact, she couldn't see any structural damage to the circular door or the carved stone surrounding it—not that her vision was worth much at present.

Arcus didn't Enhance the charges, came the thought, as if through dense fog. If he had, the damage would have been far worse. And she never would have survived.

What *had* happened to Arcus, though? With the state of her visor, he could be about to kill her and she wouldn't know until the blow went through her. She fumbled at her helmet's release—one-handed, as her other arm wasn't responsive—only to discover it hadn't been designed with one-handed removal in mind. She'd have to pass that note on to Ferric.

Thinking of Ferric knotted her chest with sudden worry. How large had the cave-in been? *You'd better be alive*, she thought fiercely. *You don't get to die without hearing your helmet design needs work.*

Without any apparent success on Tala's part, the helmet unsealed with a pneumatic hiss. Relieved, Tala began to tug it off—but someone was already removing it. Her head slid free at last, and any gratitude she felt vanished as she saw it was Arcus crouched beside her. His face was mere centimeters away, milky eyes locked on her own. His pained rictus and slow, uneven breaths ignited in Tala a vicious satisfaction that she once would have chastised herself for feeling. She tried to pull away, but her entire body erupted in protest at even the thought of movement. Arcus placed the helmet next to her and gave a polite grimace.

"Seek out Athrumir Station, should you still desire revenge." The words were a whisper, barely audible to her still-ringing ears. "But this time, you have—"

Tala lurched toward him. She made it a few centimeters before her body gave out.

It didn't matter. Her Enhancement had already taken hold within the jagged twists of metal the explosion had made of her chest piece. Multiplying their momentum even as she flopped forward, the rest of her suit unaugmented.

Not all of them were so tenuously attached that the sudden surge of momentum wrenched them free. But enough were. Arcus raised his arms to shield himself as tattered metal sped toward his face. And one arm, the one Tala had broken, lagged just a decisecond behind, leaving part of him vulnerable.

A chunk of metal buried itself in Arcus's left eye. He cried out and fell back, clapping a hand to his face. Pale blood dripped out from beneath it, running down his arm.

Tala never got to see what he would have done next, because the heap of rubble near the center of the room started *shaking*. Arcus whirled around, shoulders straightening as the pain left him, just in time to see Scratch tear his way free at last, bursting out from the rock.

Arcus broke into a sprint for the exit, Scratch leaping to pursue. But her teacher had only taken a few steps when a puff of flame licked the air between them. Scratch shied back as that brief flash expanded into a blue curtain that bisected the room, scorching a black line along the carpet and lapping hungrily at the walls.

Scratch dropped to all fours, priming to launch himself through. Then, with a low, frustrated growl, he stopped. "No," he spat, clutching at one of his ear holes. "Leave him to me."

He stood back up. The air rippled and shimmered, casting his bones a ghostly indigo. "Very well. But the spirits will not be denied forever. They demand their due." He lashed his tongue, standing tall and still, staring into the blaze as if delving for answers. His distorted shadow stretched the full length of the room and up the wall, shifting in the flickering firelight.

Her mentor. Her confidant. Whose wisdom she now had no choice but to question. A decade of conversations with Scratch flash-fired through her brain all at once. Innumerable morsels of wisdom. Support and encouragement. Chastisement and warnings. His reassurances when she struggled with meditations. His promise not to tell when she'd broken a training sphere in frustration. With a horror that spread through her entire being like acid through her veins, she realized everything Scratch had ever said made a lot more sense if he truly believed he could hear the spirits of the dead. Thinking back, she couldn't recall a time he hadn't referred to the spirits with reverence. With dogmatic fervor.

It couldn't mean what Arcus had implied. But even if the siari had intended to provoke this very response in her, she couldn't stop herself. Because if the Pillar of Justice heard voices, that meant...

She didn't want to finish that thought. Of all the things that had kept her upright, she had so few left. But hiding from the truth wouldn't change it. Admit it or not, she already knew.

From the beginning, she'd had trouble with the Center's teachings. She'd been the disruptive one, always something holding her back from true understanding. Never quite able to set aside her doubts or focus her thoughts. Eventually she'd learned, but that feeling that she was pretending where everyone else *got it* had never gone away.

Over a decade of sustained effort had gone into getting even that far. All that, and the slightest of pushes had sent her stumbling from the Tenets' path. Not even stumbling, at times. When playing the Renegade for Ceowograffach, she'd slipped so easily into the role that it had almost claimed her.

She'd studied the treatises, memorized the Tenets, meditated for hundreds of hours, learned to clear her mind. She'd done everything Scratch had asked of her and absorbed everything he'd taught. Or...she looked at her mentor again, still staring at the flames. Had that been the problem all along?

Stand.

Slowly, with the dogged stubbornness that had never failed her, she rolled over onto her belly. Her right leg hung behind her, throbbing and useless, threatening to intensify in pain with every movement. On one leg and one arm, she began to close the distance to Scratch. The wall of fire was dying, Arcus's Enhancement losing power with distance.

Her leg caught on a scarred bit of flooring and the resultant javelin of lightning-hot agony almost made her pass out. She dropped to one elbow, shaking and panting, taking in the blistering air in sharp gasps. Her injuries were not important. She needed to reach her mentor. Needed to know if his wisdom had been as shallow as a puddle, reflecting only a darker truth. Needed to understand what that meant for herself.

Her gut wound flared, sending her into a full-body spasm. Bile rose in the back of her throat and she forced it down again. Enhancement steadied her shaking arm. She couldn't give up. That was definitely a Tenet, but it wasn't coming to mind. Sweat dripped down her face and found its way into her mouth. She dragged herself another centimeter. Progress. *Steady, soldier. Almost there.*

Footfalls outside her field of vision; the rhythmic click of metal on metal and the crunch of shattered glass.

Tala knew what she'd see before she looked. Lawkeepers were emerging two by two through the broken security barrier. They shouted as they moved, setting up overlapping fields of fire. Preparing for the order that would drown her in bullets.

There weren't too many yet. All she'd need to do was focus on them, turn up the lights representing the temperature within their skull, and watch them cook from the inside out—

No. Not like that. *Never* like that. All the fight left her, and she allowed herself to sink to the ground, adrenaline giving way to a rolling boulder of pain. Nothing left but dead ends. It was almost a relief.

The flow of uniforms showed no sign of stopping. There were twelve now, and Tala could hear thirteen and fourteen rounding the corner. Two stopped by Ferric, securing him with electrobinding.

Then she heard it: the command she'd been dreading. "Open fire!"

"Hold!" The countermand came just as quickly, Enhanced until the sound echoed off the walls.

Scratch had turned away from the wall of fire, which was dying now that Arcus was too far away to maintain his Enhancement. Every lawkeeper stood frozen beneath his scrutiny, unwilling to contradict the order of a Pillar. Tala felt it then, a shadow of the hope that had so briefly ignited at Scratch's arrival.

"This Renegade has surrendered in accordance with the Renegade protocols," said Scratch. "She is to be taken into custody pending trial in absentia."

He gave the commanding officer a withering look until he was sure he'd be obeyed. Then, while they filtered the new order up through the chain of command, he left them in favor of a position at Tala's side. He knelt beside her, every bit the doting mentor.

"You did well, little one," he murmured, uncharacteristically quiet. "No training could have prepared you for such a fight as that—yet thanks to your prowess and bravery, the Coalition lives on."

"Scratch..." Her voice came in a whisper, the mere act of forming words a struggle. What was there to even say?

Regardless, he gave no indication he'd heard. "I cannot yet let myself hope for the state of your mind. But this I *can* say, and I will make sure the galaxy knows it: Renegade or no, your actions here exemplified the Tenets. I can give no higher praise."

Perhaps it was foolish, given the pool of blood and broken steel she lay in. Given the guns leveled on her and her pending arrest and the questions that even now scrubbed what remained of her composure over a washing board made of barbed wire. But hearing Scratch admit that here, now, made the rest of the day worth it.

"And the spirits whisper their pride as well."

Like night creeping across a hemisphere, a sick feeling overtook her burgeoning triumph. There was nothing to celebrate. Nothing at all.

A trio of lawkeepers approached her, one brandishing electrobinding while another held her at gunpoint. The third slapped a gag over her mouth. She wrenched at it, but it stuck fast, stretching with her movements. More lawkeepers lurked in the entrance, still barking into their omnipads as Legislatorium security tried to block Arcus's escape.

It wouldn't matter. Unlike her, Arcus would never have made his move without planning a way out. The day would end with him bloodied but free, already devising a new plan to force his vision on the galaxy.

Athrumir Station. The unfamiliar name he'd whispered still clung to her ears. *Should you still desire revenge...*

She did. Tenets preserve her, but she did.

At that moment though, she would have settled for answers.

WHAT HOLDS US BACK

Moravan's manor had been built to match the wealth and reach of its owner. As such, it was unthinkably vast. Quarack had been admitted almost an hour ago, yet here she was, walking down yet another corridor tall enough to allow four Torandians stacked atop each other to walk unimpeded. Why a group of Torandians would want to move that way, she couldn't guess—but if they tried, they'd find the space more than met their needs.

The walls were polished marshwood, hand-carved with intricate murals of the Eternal performing various heroic deeds. Along the ceiling, a line of metal disks displayed his personal heraldry on repeat: a skeletal hand formed from twisting branches. Quarack couldn't imagine the ego it took to live in a museum of your own deeds; even Bugboy looked humble by comparison. But as massive and ornate as the manor was, the rooms she'd seen on her expedited tour had been almost empty—of sapes and furnishings both. The whole place was practically abandoned. Doubly wasteful on a planet where housing prices were so high, she wouldn't get more than a shed for her whole pecking ship.

Her thrall guide was spry, for all that age had painted her scales a snowy white. She hadn't given a name. In fact, she'd barely spoken as they made their way through the cavernous corridors, her tree-patterned forest green robe trailing on the planks. The most frustrating part was how controlled she was, ignoring all of Quarack's numerous attempts to provoke any change in her stony smile.

In contrast, the three grim-faced Torandians stationed at the front gate had been almost too easy. A few mildly disparaging words about their lord and master, and they'd looked ready to murder her on the spot. They couldn't do anything, of course. Not to an honored guest. But the way their eyes had swiveled in their sockets while their fingers clacked together, that was worth a cackle and a half. That her rudeness would reflect terribly on the sape who'd invited her was the dollop of jelly on a stack of spring biscuits.

The thrall eventually halted in front of a door carved from gold-flecked white marble, split through by vascular jagged patterns. Like everything else in the manor, it was far too big.

"He awaits you inside," she said with a voice like sand in a blender. "Touch the door when you're ready."

Her task seen to, she bowed once and began the trek back up the long corridor. Her back was straight, but her shoulders were hunched tight. Quarack scratched a proper farewell into her beak. Some sapes were worth being polite to.

Just her and the door now. This whole meeting was probably a fool's roost, but where was the fun in life without a little foolishness? She leaned in, brushing her claws against the stone. The door swung inward in response, quiet as a whisper despite its size.

The room behind it was not what she'd been expecting. It wasn't even a room as much as the intricate offspring of an office and a verdant lake. Rectangular rings of polished wood formed three concentric platforms, each connected by thin walkways. Between the platforms, exotic foliage burst up from the ground. Water lapped at the roots of wispy-leafed trees that rose to the domed ceiling. Where the tree shadows fell across the water, small aquatic creatures swam. At the center of it all was an island of wood adorned with a lavish workspace. And at the center of *that*, sitting in a high-backed chair behind the widest desk she'd ever seen, was Bugboy himself.

In front of him was a tray of sponge-wafers and a sheaf of scrawl, which he was flipping through sheet by sheet. As she watched, he frowned at the page in his hand and pushed it off to the side.

"Seems inefficient," Quarack said as she made her way into the room. While the rest of the manor had a wet, oppressive heat, the air was nice in here. Still damp, but more like an ocean breeze than the inside of a mouth. "Someone steal your omnipad?"

"More a point of caution." Teo didn't even glance up at her entrance. "Omnipad security can be circumvented. Physical documents are more secure."

"We're looking at something dangerous, then," Quarack said. She placed a careful talon on the walkway, testing its stability. Falling into the water would be as good as giving Teo the higher nest. Which, given his general...*everything*, wasn't something she could live with.

"*We* aren't looking at anything," Teo replied. "Though I suppose there's no harm in telling you. I've been gathering information on Arcus. His files have gotten noticeably easier to obtain of late—especially with my old contacts swarming to do business once more."

Like roaches from a house fire, Quarack appended. As she reached the middle platform, a section of floor rose unprompted and unfolded itself, snapping together into a seat opposite Teo's own. How many more, she wondered, waited hidden in the ground? Had she walked over a whole theater's worth of seats without knowing?

She took the chair. "So security conscious, yet you're squawking away. *That*'s safe, then?"

"Words can always be dangerous. But we won't be recorded, if that's what you mean. Far too many secrets—and more than a few dangerous truths— are spoken on the premises for the High Councilor Eternal to allow anything of the sort. On that front, we are as safe as safe can be."

"Then I can insult you as much as I want, and nobody will ever know?"

"But it *does* take some of the fun out of it, doesn't it?"

"Takes all the—hey." Quarack glared across the table at Teo's smug little face.

"Have a wafer. They're good."

She ignored the tray and tried to lean back in her chair, only to discover it was still firmly interlocked with the floor. "I guess I should ask why you're looking into him."

"Yes," Teo replied, mandibles clicking in a way that mimicked the corvid beak pattern for agreement. "That is a much better question. But one to which I'd have thought the answer obvious. It is, of course, the same reason I allowed myself to be swept up in this merry little escapade in the first place: *revenge*. It was Ceowograffach who took my seat, but he only ever acted at the behest of another. Now that I know that, do you think I'd let it lie?"

"You let a lot of things lie. Like your mouth."

"No," said Teo. For all he was pretending otherwise, she knew he'd heard her. "No rest until that creature regrets the day his broken mind decided crossing me was a profitable decision."

And that was the only thing she respected about the old bug: his vindictive streak. By the Nine Winds, she still wished to this day that she could get a holo of Dad's face upon discovering a melted tower made of his beloved pots and pans where his ship was supposed to be.

"If anyone learned even half of what you've been up to lately, they'd be calling you a criminal too."

Teo waved her reminder aside. "I've dispelled any possible notions of impropriety on my end."

"You mean, you pretended you'd been held hostage. Then you complained at the keepies about how badly you were being treated until they let you go, and slipped away while they were still dealing with the fallout. Turns out you're less important than some monster of a Renegade."

A light-winged shortbeak alighted on a pink lily pad as it floated by. The bird had probably never been let out of this room, nor would it be for the rest of its short life. Fed, cared for, and trapped.

"Never thought I'd have to qualify Renegade with the word 'monster'," she mused, watching the bird peck at the pad's flower. "It always seemed inherent."

"It did."

The shortbeak flew up from the pad and landed on a nearby tree. It strutted along a long thin branch, trilling as it preened. If it came any closer, she might be able to nab it and smuggle it out. A trial run of sorts.

"It *is* a shame that Tala has been locked up," Teo continued. "I imagine she'd be all too willing to assist me in getting my chunk of chitin from Arcus's shell."

"Truly, you are the most sentimental of us all."

He actually laughed at that. A small chitter, but no less surprising. "You really are more palatable in small doses."

If he really thought that, she was losing her touch.

"Not that I imagine you care," Teo said, "but the situation has developed very well on my end. Ceowograffach dead and disgraced, and myself the champion of justice who uncovered his plot not a moment too soon. Hivemother Kitik has indicated the emergency election will begin within the next few days."

"Glad I could help." She hoped the sarcasm was clear—when it came to his own ego, Bugboy was liable to miss the joke.

He shrugged all six arms. "Yes. Grim business, that, but the deed is done and buried."

Quarack resisted the urge to drum discomfort against her beak. Right as he was, burying the deed had taken ten days longer than she'd expected. Not that she was about to let Bugboy see that. "Deeper than a paranoid kirtian's treasure pit. So, why'd you call me here? 'Cause I have other things to do, so unless you're planning to pay me for my time…"

"Quite right," said Teo, shifting through the scrawl on his desk anew. "We should keep this interview brief; I've another engagement scheduled for twenty-five sharp."

"Yeah?" She leaned forward, placing her claws on the desk. None of the sheets of scrawl were in grabbing range, but maybe if she faked a seizure…. "A meeting with one Grex Hamul, perhaps?"

Take a small dose of that, she thought as Teo spluttered semi-coherently. "And how, exactly is it," he demanded, "that you know that name?"

Quarack tapped her beak with amusement. "As you said, omnipad security can be tricky. Especially if someone's had physical access. Why, they could install all sorts of programs."

"You know I could have you arrested for that?"

"Maybe." Quarack flapped a shrug his way. "But the same authorities who nicked me would be interested to hear you've been bribing a prison architect. All those maps—mighty suspicious, no?"

His seething silence alone made the trip worth it.

"What's the plan? Gonna stage a heist? I hear the soap they give the inmates is really nice stuff. Just think of the resale value."

"Enough," said Teo. His voice was disappointingly measured—but then, he wouldn't be a proper politician if he couldn't master himself. And she wouldn't have found him nearly as insufferable. "Bluster aside, I am well aware that our interests overlap in this regard."

"I've got plenty of soap."

"No one would know it, given the state of that ship of yours."

Quarack wasn't offended. The *Aquilon deserved* every square centimeter of filth it had accumulated.

"Ohhh," she said, trying to make her face light up like she'd just solved the mystery of the century. "You're springing Tala, aren't you?"

"Well, I couldn't—"

"A dangerous criminal like her?" Quarack added a sprinkle of mock indignation. "I can't believe you're even considering this. Sorry, Bugboy. We had some good times, but this is a flight too far. I've gotta take this to the keepies."

For a single sweet moment, Teo's face swam with shock—but all too soon, it faded. "If I could trust anyone else with this, I'd take great joy in never talking with you again."

"Admit it," said Quarack. "I had you there for a sec."

"I will admit to no such thing."

Quarack reached over and took a wafer. It looked decent, and her standards were not low. She actually wanted to try a bite. But this snack was destined for greater things. Keeping her claw low, she waved it enticingly toward the shortbeak. It took notice at once, beady eyes locking onto the wafer she held.

"You know," she cawed, drawing out the moment, "I've decided to let you help me. Always good to have a patsy, just in case."

"In the time-before-times, when the seed-shoots of the new had not yet parted the ashes of the old, on a sunswept planet not yet named, walked a young siari."

Central Pillar Frael beamed out across the assembled body of Enhancer Initiates and their Vanguards from his usual position atop the assembly chamber's simple dais. The chamber was a high-domed room, large enough to hold a thousand young, inquisitive minds beneath one roof. The entire left wall was a single unbroken window, a pane of glass overlooking the edge of the mountain into which the Modellus Center had been built. The sun was just vanishing over the horizon and scattered lights had started flickering on across the farmsteads below. In the distance, Teldeesi City glimmered. Though change spread across the fields with the coming of night, the city's lights never went out.

There was a lesson in that.

The Initiates were still settling in at the back of the room. Some had just come from dinner. Ripples across a lake of faces—yet they awaited his address with respectful silence. How blessed he was to share their company. The years had pulled at his jowls, taken the spring from his whiskers, and thinned his fur, but they had given him so much more.

"The siari had no memory of beginning his journey and no conception of when it would end," continued Frael. "He knew only his destination, and that if he walked in step with the world, it would lead him where he needed to go. Thus, he traveled as slowly or as quickly as his preference suggested, leaving a winding trail through the wind-scoured plains while the sun grew larger in the sky. The landscape was harsh and barren, but he loved it all the same.

"So it was that he came to a small cottage in the shadow of a lone coruda tree. His instinct was not to hurry by, but to admire the tree's twisted bark, the pastel blue of its leaves, and the dappling of sun and shadow beneath its spreading branches.

"The siari's hunger and thirst had swelled expansively as he walked. He first looked above, at the branches overhead, but this particular tree was entirely bare of fruit. Then he looked below, but found nothing but the dust of earth untraveled. Finally, he looked ahead, at the cottage, and imagined what nourishment whoever lived within might share if he but asked. So he knocked against the orange-painted door. When no answer came, he knocked again. A third time he knocked, and still there was nothing.

"But he did not turn away, for while he was virtuous, the gnawing in his stomach had driven him to desperation. He opened the cottage door and peered within, trying vainly to see what lay ahead. In the end, he took those last steps over the threshold."

The addresses were among his great joys. He didn't think he would tire of them if he could live another hundred cycles. Just as food hoarded would only rot, so it was with wisdom. It had been granted him so that he might disseminate it, and plant the same seed in others that had grown so tall within the loam of his mind. He would not get to see this new crop reach the fullness of its height, but it held weight even in abstraction.

"The door swung shut behind him. The cottage was a single room, barren and devoid of nourishment. And when he turned around, he found that the door he'd come through was now a wall. With no windows to let in the light, he could only see by what shone from his own body.

"He battered against the walls until his hands were raw and bruised, but to no avail. When he realized the futility of his efforts, he shouted for help until his throat was sore, but heard no answer from without. Having no other flightpaths open, he cried until his eyes and lightlets each echoed the other's violet, but when his tears were exhausted, he was just as trapped as before."

Frael paused. The throng of onlookers waited in silence as he worked his throat, his mouth bone-dry. The fatigue was setting in—again ahead of schedule. His own personal sunset was near; he would be a fool not to admit it. Every day his back grew a little more stooped, his bones were a bit louder in their protests, his tail lost some of its elasticity. Not even the incredible power of the Central Pillar could hold back the advance of time.

That same power hovered even now on the edge of his meta-awareness: a shallow lake of energy wider than his mind's eye could take in. Infinite in scope, limited in possibility. He required more and more Enhancement to keep everything functional, a constant drain. Most days, he was content to venture out only ankle-deep while the rest lay in reserve, unneeded. He was knee-deep now, and it still was not enough.

The mental construction of his self took another few steps into the lake, spreading ripples through the glassy surface. As it moved, he felt his head lighten on his neck and new strength push weakness from his limbs. The water now brushed up against his middle. It would not be long now before the depths claimed him.

"But with the clarity of time came acceptance." His voice, too, had found new strength. "For while the cottage walls kept the siari from his journey, there was peace to be found even within their confines. If he had trusted the world to lead him before, what reason had he to doubt now? While nothing within the cottage could slake his hunger or thirst, there was nothing *without* that he was being kept from. Whence, then, did his anguish originate?

"Only from himself.

"And when Mitra grasped that truth," Frael's reedy voice reached a triumphant note, "the cottage walls could not imprison him. They melted away and he sat alone upon the dusty plains. The freedom to resume his journey and the freedom he had found within were one and the same."

He took one step back along the dais, let his arms fall to his sides, and fell silent, letting the Initiates digest what they had heard. They spent a few seconds in contemplative silence, then turned to their neighbors with whispers of discussion. Frael watched it all from above, lips still crooked in a benevolent smile.

Tucked away in one of the Legislatorium's lesser-used wings is a small room, modestly furnished. Casual inspection could see it mistaken for a poorly placed lounge, though anyone seeking to use it as such would be turned away by the *Under Construction* signs that seem to plague the area. These signs have become a running joke among the Legislatorium's staff, a commentary on the inefficiency of bureaucratic construction efforts.

Less casual inspection reveals that the room is soundproof, the door magnetically sealable, and the walls resistant to thermal sweeps and electroscans. None of these features are mentioned in the Galactic Information and Assessment Bureau's files, or the Legislatorium's floor plan, or the records of the Block By Block construction company.

The councilors meeting within this room have reluctantly put aside their usual debates over gate locations, tax exemptions, regulations on shield generator reprocessing, and the other thousand thousand issues that demand the attention of a galactic ruling body. Matters more worthy of their consideration have reared their heads in multiple clusters, and their presence has been requested—or perhaps *ordered*—by High Councilor Eternal Moravan himself.

The High Councilor Eternal has had an interesting day. He has lived through enough of them that for one to stand out as interesting is a feat in and of itself. One worthy of special attention from the preeminent politicians of the era, the few trusted with a view behind the veil carefully woven about the galaxy. That veil will suffer now that Arcus is no longer content with playing dead, but such things are unavoidable. The Renegade always held the power to end that particular lie the moment it suited him. Events will proceed as planned, with feigned surprise at Arcus's return and an extra degree of caution when appropriate.

Most of the committee is concerned with the attack on the Legislatorium, their focus on supporting a multipartisan effort to eliminate the security flaw of the private hangar. That is to be expected. Huddling together in the Congressional Chamber with only a single door separating them from a Renegade was a bitter shock. The mortal councilors are in disarray, the transient nature of their existence brought to the surface by Arcus's actions. If Moravan is disgusted by their lack of vision, he manages to hide it. Small-mindedness is a common enough flaw of the mortal species that encountering it even among their foremost speakers is unsurprising.

Some, though, glimpse small facets of the larger picture. Councilor Awawk has launched an independent investigation into Arcus's role in the siege of Haven. Councilor Master Dartooth is more worried about whether the Biostabilization Matrix lost there is sufficient for Arcus's purposes—and, if so, whether his resources are sufficient to make full use of it. Moravan finds these questions infantile in their naiveté; surely Arcus's recent activities adequately highlight the resources at his disposal. Reconstruction will be already underway in some remote corner of the galaxy, all but unfindable. Yet despite their shortsighted line of questioning, Awawk and Dartooth at least grasp the danger. That is progress.

In one corner of the austere chamber, Councilors Foguin and Simaphorniun argue heatedly over the purpose of Arcus's attack. Both frequently cast beseeching looks toward the main body, hoping to coax support from an unresponsive audience. Councilor Martin, a spectacularly myopic specimen of humanity whom Moravan has considered having killed, scoffs that the attack was entirely unsuccessful;

that no councilor, and only two high-level staffers, were so much as scratched.

"By its very nature, the attack could not have succeeded," Simaphorniun buzzes. Norinnythmocalic Simaphorniun possesses a self-awareness that is rarely found coexisting with a politician's temperament. Moravan finds this refreshing; far too many mortals overinflate their importance to the march of galactic history, willfully ignoring the likelihood that their names will not merit so much as a footnote. This is, of course, foolishness.

"Even the successful murder of every sitting councilor would have caused only a brief period of instability before proper succession protocols were followed and our positions were filled," Simaphorniun continues. "In the long term, he would have accomplished almost nothing at all."

It is a good point, one Moravan has already considered. Arcus is patient in a way no other Renegade is capable of, the methodical mindset of his scholarly years attuned to his new anarchic agenda. Twenty-two years, and Moravan is no closer to learning what Arcus has done with the Center-bound children he appropriated.

"If Arcus was hoping to change—"

"Do not presume to know what Arcus hopes!" The stress of the day has inflamed Councilor Foguin's temperament, though it has not dulled her wits. "If those flaws are obvious to you, imagine how obvious they are to *him*! Isn't it clear he wanted something else? And by the Churning Chaos, I have to assume he got it!"

Her translucent bristles sway, as if caught in a storm. None of the others dare interrupt.

"This was no mad whim! Arcus must have spent years on it! How long must it have taken, to groom and install a willing sapient to high office? Not a mere planetary governor, but a *councilor!*"

Councilor Jimac, who was once seated next to the late Ceowograffach and worked with him on several legislative efforts, shudders at the allusion to the traitor councilor. His bone tresses rattle uncomfortably. Disgust, Moravan concludes, and guilt for not having noticed anything amiss.

Foguin has lapsed into near-silence now, taking raspy breaths. The curse of mortality is upon her; soon, she will die a shameful and inglorious death. The legislature's collective intellect will suffer as a result. It surprises Moravan—as it always does with those mortal few who gain his respect—that the thought of Foguin's death is a sad one.

She is close, tantalizingly close, to organically deriving Arcus's one weakness. Moravan once believed he had none—the Renegade is devastatingly intelligent and impossible to second-guess, though he reads his opponents like omnipads. The consequences of his actions are not readily apparent; you could look back on a power coupling he tripped

over twenty years ago and realize how instrumental that moment was to the plan unfolding before you. Every detail, however insignificant, has purpose. Every action, however minute, contributes to the whole.

This strips Arcus of some of his opacity, more than he realizes. Once it is given that Arcus's every move leads unerringly toward a chosen destination, a keen mind can examine what happened, follow causality to its conclusions, deduce Arcus's preferred outcome, and so divine his ultimate goal.

Eternal Moravan has begun to do exactly this.

Arcus's recent maneuver has given him plenty of data to sift through. Yes, Moravan could have heeded Cernarvitalimun Teomonious's warning and secured the Legislatorium in the face of the impending attack, but the extra security might have warned the Renegade off, and Moravan would be no closer to predicting his opponent's next move. The lives lost in Arcus's attack are nothing to the information it has given him.

For he has glimpsed where Arcus's flightpath will lead, at least partially. And so he mulls over the most important question of all, which no other councilor has noticed through the murk of their petty distractions.

What steps are to be taken in the event of an uprising?

APPENDICIES

AN INCOMPLETE HISTORY OF THE GALACTIC COALITION

The highest governing body in the galaxy, the Galactic Coalition is made up of seventy-two different signatory species across ninety clusters. The Coalition has held power for almost sixteen cycles, replacing the Eternal Autocracy (a Torandian empire that imposed its will on a much smaller slice of the galaxy, keeping "lesser species" as subjects). In its current incarnation, the Galactic Coalition is an ever-expanding "nation", relying on Enhancers and new Gates to find and claim new territory—regardless of the willingness of any native species. Theoretically, these species can join the Galactic Coalition and have their voices heard in Congress. In practice, as seat allocation by species is determined by economic share of GGP (galactic gross product), newly discovered species very rarely have the production capacity to match the interplanetary financial muscle of established species and fail to meet the minimum benchmark to qualify for representation—as such, much of the legislative warfare within the Congressional Chamber involves trying to bolster the economic output of one's own species while diminishing the rest. Though independent planets (and occasional star systems) do exist within Coalition space, each of these exceptions is the result of special circumstances.

The galaxy being a *very* large thing for a single central governing body to run, much of the decision-making is left to more local governments (planetary, cluster, species, etc.). As such, schisms can often arise even between ostensibly allied clusters—the most pertinent example being the issue of slavery, which is legal under galactic charter but banned in almost half of all galactic space by various local governments that see it as a moral atrocity. These different groups are forbidden from warring, but often interfere with each other in less direct ways.

PRE-CONVERGENCE—The Eternal Autocracy began on Torand and spread first to the stars, then—with the emergence of Gate technology—to other systems. Torandian battle prowess and superior technology crushed any species they came across, such as the peace-loving siari. Expansion was slow, lacking Enhancers with which to efficiently navigate the distance between stars, but the Torandians were ageless and focused on conquest.

One fateful day, Torandian Gate ships opened the way to a new system, already occupied by two warring species: the corvids and the Serdins. When the Torandian army arrived to stake their claim, the war became three-way—and then two-way again as the corvids and Serdins made truce to battle the invaders together. Thus began the Cluster War, the first major challenge to Torandian hegemony.

The Torandian fleet was unscarred from endless battle, superior in conventional warfare, and possessing a natural, easily defended beachhead in the form of the Gate. But the concept of impersonal warfare, of efficient destruction, was new to them. So focused were they on personal conflict, bloody struggle, and honor through victory, that they had never pursued particular destructive paths that were well mined by corvid and Serdin scientists. Never before had Torandian warriors contended with planet-killing superweapons, endless armies of self-sufficient drones, self-replicating nanobombs, emergent artificial intelligence, and other such cataclysmic weaponry. The Torandian army found its entire philosophy of war upended, and as momentum shifted against them, they were forced—for the first time—to contemplate their utter destruction: Torand itself annihilated by weapons larger than they had ever conceived of using.

But cunning as they were, they adapted. Leveraging conquered species as well as their native thrall population as hostages and shields, the Torandians made continued warfare morally unpalatable to their enemies until at last, no side possessed a will to fight. A peace summit was held, with Serdin and corvid diplomats passing through a Gate for the first time to lay the groundwork for a grand new system of government: the Galactic Accords.

THE NEW GOVERNMENT—Over the course of peacetime negotiation, it soon became clear that nothing less than unifying the three warring species into a single collaborative government would do. Thus were the Galactic Accords conceived, and as their scope grew, so too did calls to include other species, those the Torandians had already brought into the Eternal Autocracy. After much negotiation, the siari alone were admitted. When the Accords were complete and agreed upon, the Torandians managed to keep a substantial share of power for themselves. The Galactic Accords also forbade many of the most destructive weapons unleashed over the course of the Cluster War, conceding to Torandian pressure that idealized warfare as sapients meeting each other on the battlefield, proving themselves through personal prowess alone.

The Galactic Accords' signing ushered in a new, more peaceful era, known by historians as *Convergence*. The Accords themselves are a nightmarishly complicated document split into six separate "articles".

Article I details the formation of the government itself: how species may achieve representation, the schedule by which representatives will meet, the process by which laws will be passed, the specifics of the judiciary, etc. Article I also establishes Peramit as the capital of the Galactic Coalition.

Article II details the government's powers and sovereign authorities over aspects such as trade, currency, taxation, regulation, gate placement, etc.

Article III details the organizational structure of militaries, the rules by which they engage, and the limits on their authority. Article III has since been amended to make explicit the right of the Galactic Congress to assemble, pay, outfit, and maintain a standing army beholden to the Coalition itself.

Article IV details the rights that all citizens of the Coalition are entitled to, as well as the rights, privileges, and responsibilities of local governments (including a provision granting local governments authority over any issue that the Galactic Congress does not explicitly have control over). It also contains a generalized rubric for solving internal disputes among local governments.

Article V details the process by which new species may enter the Galactic Coalition. It also contains the clause by which the Galactic Accords may be modified in other ways.

Article VI contains a list of "inalienable crimes", those so important that they have been woven into the Accords to make the process of removing or altering them far more difficult. All local governments must adhere to these laws exactly, where with other galactic laws there may be wiggle room. It details the range of punishments for these crimes, all of which are particularly harsh. This article is the most often amended.

The formation of the Accords is legend within the Coalition, the main players in the achievement revered in folklore. Though in reality, it was a joint effort of many thousands of sapients, those most remembered by history are Eternal Comizzat, Clarla, and Varov 21200. Over many cycles, the story of the signing of the Accords has been told, re-told, dramatized, deconstructed, and woven into galactic myth. The most famous of these adaptations is a holoseries called *Before Unity.* The most esoteric is a Belrosen sensory performance called *Scents From The Nonth Cycle.*

The final draft of the Accords had over 1,200 signatories, and this number grows every time a new species joins the Coalition. The total number currently hovers at almost 2,000.

LEGISLATORIUM—The capitol building of the Galactic Coalition, known as the Legislatorium, is one of Peramit City's great landmarks. Of Torandian make and design, the Legislatorium is host to the meetings of the Galactic Congress—as well as other numerous, less important tasks.

The current Legislatorium, boasting three jutting towers and a wavelike roof made from zigzags of thousands of interlocking diamond-shaped tiles, is not the original building constructed in the wake of the Galactic Accords. This second Legislatorium, built in 290 Cycle 14, is larger and grander, reflecting a bloated galactic bureaucracy and a newer, more ostentatious architectural style taking root in Central Cluster. Much of the old building was repurposed into the new to symbolize continuity. In its current incarnation, the Legislatorium supports 3,300 galactic councilors and their support staffs, offices representing the interests of local governments and constituencies, vendors, dedicated lobbyists and other influencers, and a "spine" of low-ranking but hardworking bureaucrats who keep the infinitely complex organism that is the Galactic Coalition running.

Access to the three towers and many of the upper levels of the structure is either restricted or off limits, but the lower levels are open to the public, including the Legislatorium Approach, the famous promenade that leads to the Congressional Chamber. Access to the chamber itself is limited by several layers of security—in fact, the Legislatorium itself is home to some of the most stringent security measures possible, and heavily guarded against infiltration or betrayal in order to foil even Renegades. Perhaps the most famous of these measures is the "face" of Legislatorium security, the Dauntless Guard.

Within the Congressional Chamber meet the 3300 galactic councilors—the current maximum specified in the Accords. This number is vanishingly small for a galactic civilization, but civic-minded sapients can find many powerful (and lucrative) opportunities to serve in planetary and clusterwide governments.

Councilors are divided by species, with each species claiming a number of seats in proportion to the percentage of their contribution to the galactic economy— but it is left to each species to determine how these councilors are chosen, the length of their terms, the possibility for reelection, etc. Councilors are called upon to serve on individual committees within the wider body of councilors, such as the Committee for Spacelane Protection, the Committee for Enhancer Relations, or the Committee for Robotechnological Safety—to give a few examples. Councilors chosen to chair these committees (based on a combination of seniority and favor-trading) are called high councilors. One high councilor can chair multiple committees.

UNITS OF TIME—Peramit time is also known as "centralized time", the standard-setter for a universally accepted system of time measurement as required by the Galactic Accords. Individual planets will run on "local time" (meaning, a system based on the planet's rotation/travel around the system's sun/seasons), but for interplanetary commerce, official Coalition business, megaferries, space stations, and other such circumstances, centralized time is conventionally used (and in the case of interplanetary businesses, required by law). Thus, galactic citizens often must observe two different times simultaneously.

For species that celebrate birthdays, they will often have two: a birthday in local time (the time, specifically, relating to their birth planet) and a birthday in centralized time. Even in places where centralized time is the default, keeping local hours—or even "innate" hours, referring to a species' biological needs—is socially acceptable. Often, sapients are born on planets with a day/night cycle at odds with their physiology.

Centralized time uses the following units:

Cycle (a span of eight hundred years). Cycles are omitted from any date within the current cycle.

Year (a span of four hundred and twenty-three days)

Day (a span of thirty-one hours).

Hour (a span of two thousand, five hundred seconds)

Second (equivalent to a count of one; the passing of a moment)

The units "year", "hour", and "second" are often broken up into ten to make new units. A decihour (very commonly used) describes a tenth of an hour, while a deciyear describes a tenth of a year. Deciseconds are less commonly used, though they are sometimes employed for dramatic emphasis.

UNITS OF CURRENCY—One great political battle during the signing of the Galactic Accords was the matter of one unified currency. Species are not required to abolish their own forms of currency when joining the Galactic Coalition—and for almost a cycle after the Accords were signed, other species' currencies were commonly used within their territories (and several enterprising moneychangers got very rich). However, for the purpose of galactic business, Torandians managed to institute their currency as standard.

Galactic currency comes in three denominations: crescents, stars, and nova. The first two are named for the traditional minted coins used among Torandians in the pre-Coalition era, named for their distinctive shapes (Torandian coiners would produce metal disks, which then had a crescent shape sheared off of it to create a crescent-shaped coin and a circular coin). The nova has less historical background; it was created after the purge of physical currency and has thus only ever existed in an all-digital economic ecosystem. The nova was introduced to accommodate species that lack the capacity to work with larger numbers, requiring a unit of currency that represented many stars in order to do business on a galactic scale. Ships, planetary shields, large-scale construction projects, space stations—these command prices calculated in nova. One nova is worth twenty thousand stars, and a star is worth twenty crescents. One crescent will purchase a pen at most Central Cluster retailers.

All currency exchange is done through omnipads, and all currency is tied to the omnipad holder's account. These accounts automatically invest the holder's money, choosing which economic sectors to invest in based on algorithm. This innovation has led to a surge of economic growth, as well as several galaxy-wide riots when the economy shrank and sapients found their accounts losing money. Thanks to protectionist legislation passed in Cycle 4, the risk of this has been largely curtailed, and sapients are protected from the worst effects of economic downturn.

Standard currency is not universally used, however. Various holdout species cling to their own currency, particularly if they are new to the Coalition. Planets too remote to have ready access to omnipads will often barter, or mint crude currency. The broader trend of Coalition history, though, skews toward acceptance.

KEY AMENDMENTS: GALACTIC INFORMATION AND ASSESSMENT BUREAU—Among the first amendments to the Galactic Accords, sixty-four years after their signing, were those establishing the Galactic Information and Assessment Bureau (GIAB). Since then, the bureau has become perhaps the most powerful and influential bureau beneath the umbrella of the Galactic Coalition.

The GIAB employs the brightest academy graduates and puts them to work gathering and sifting through data. Their central archive is the largest repository of information ever assembled, containing everything from the smallest detail to the greatest of secrets—though of the latter group, knowledge is limited even within the GIAB itself, parceled out based on a multi-tiered clearance system. The archive also contains a sophisticated filing system specially conceived and designed such that no information is buried or lost. It is guarded by state-of-the-art security features, most of which are kept secret from the general public.

GIAB employees fall into several categories: those that collect data, those that manage data, and those that interpret data. The last group is by far the most influential—not a government decision gets made that is not run through the GIAB, and they are often called upon to estimate the effects of proposed new legislation. Because of this, the GIAB is a go-to scapegoat, boogeyman, and pariah among civilians and other bureaus alike. Even the military is known to grumble when a GIAB number-cruncher countermands a high warmaster. Still, the GIAB is far too useful (and far too powerful) for most to do more than grumble. Even then, every grumble makes it to their desks.

The GIAB is run by Torikov 98443, a particularly dour Serdin with a penchant for pedantry, stationed at Headquarters on Peramit. However, he has less influence than one might expect with regards to other facilities—individual GIAB outposts are more or less autonomous (though coordinating). Across the galaxy, these outposts number approximately three hundred.

KEY AMENDMENTS: GALACTIC ARMED FORCES—Two cycles after the Coalition's formation, the existence of the Galactic Armed Forces (GAF) was enshrined within the Accords after the Accords' limitations became clear. Originally, the Accords called on each signing species to maintain its own army. Semifrequent clashes between these armies necessitated the creation of a unified force strong enough to cow multiple armies simultaneously.

The Galactic Armed Forces is centralized under the jurisdiction of a special committee within the Galactic Congress. Clusters often maintain their own peacekeeping force, but those lack many of the powers and responsibilities of the GAF, and cannot lay claim to the name. Despite their centralization, the GAF does a good job of maintaining its presence across the galaxy (except at the fringes, where lawlessness rules the day).

Sapients of all species can join the GAF by signing up at a recruiting station (there are many on each planet) and then catching a one-way shuttle to the nearest military academy (the one on Peramit being the largest). Graduates are given an armored uniform decorated to evoke the look of a Torandian and scattered across the galaxy to guard spacelanes, garrison undefended planets and stations, hunt Fiurn Hult and other enemies to the Coalition, or keep peace between warring tribes. Individual units of soldiers can be hired by private employers during peacetime (subject to a stringent oversight process), and there have been occasions when the GAF found itself doing battle with its own troops as a result. Such situations are not particularly discouraged; the Torandian ethos of proving oneself through combat thrives within GAF culture.

GAF ranks are styled in Torandian tradition, with twelve separate tiers. Recruits start at the third tier and may work their way up to twelfth through distinction. Poor performance in exercises and simulations, or writeups by superior officers, result in demotion to the second or first. These unlucky souls are the scutworkers in peacetime, and the first wave of cannon fodder in times of war.

The highest tier, high warmaster, is held by only five (technically four) individuals at the moment. Admiral Highwater is the fifth, a decorated tactical mastermind who refused promotion until she was granted the defunct human rank of 'admiral' instead of 'high warmaster'—but in practice, their position within military hierarchy is exactly the same. Those below the tier of high warmaster are referred to as warmasters. Each high warmaster keeps several warmasters beneath their command. The majority of warmasters, however, operate without a specific high warmaster above them.

The GAF numbers roughly 1.5 trillion soldiers and boasts a fleet of over 200,000 devastator-class capital ships. Soldiers are paid well, though not handsomely. Living on a more modest planet, the average GAF servicesape can expect to support a three-sapient family by themselves.

Torandians consider the GAF the perfect place to climb their species' caste system—to "War-Marked," at least, and beyond if promoted into the higher echelons. As such, almost every Torandian has some amount of military service in their record.

KEY AMENDMENTS: NETWORK—As the creation and maintenance of a galaxy-wide communications and file-sharing network progressed, the Galactic Coalition inevitably moved to bring it under their control. The Network (as it is called) is classified as a utility, and access to it is subsidized—but on the flip side, the Network's content is heavily monitored and controlled. Laws surrounding the Network have changed many times over the cycles to accommodate the Network's own changes; it is an ever-evolving interplay between multiple systems, and its current iteration only recently came into being.

During the Coalition's first few cycles, the Network did not spread across multiple planets—each planet maintained its own separate and independent infrastructure. (This infrastructure still exists on many planets and, now decommissioned, is sometimes used by criminals to avoid surveillance.) In Cycle 5, a complex system of peer-to-peer nodes and relay stations was unveiled and rapidly expanded, allowing for some semblance of cross-planet connection. Signals are beamed from node to station to node at lightspeed, and these signals can pass through Gates without interference. Using this system alone, a signal can travel from Peramit to the galaxy's fringes in just over three deciyears.

This system was improved with the invention of the modern omnipad in 288 Cycle 9, in tandem with the golden renaissance that came with the Advent (first appearance of Enhancers) in 782 Cycle 7. Each omnipad functions as its own Network node and relay station, and stores its own local copy of the entire Network—allowing space travelers to access an "old" version of the Network while avoiding long load times and poor communication. With Enhancers finally allowing spacefarers to break the FTL barrier, the transport of omnipads at faster-than-light speeds allowed the Network to be updated that much faster. As a result of this, omnipads themselves became classified as both vital infrastructure and as a utility in their own right.

The discovery of the Universal Signal in 540 Cycle 15 led to the next significant improvement in Network function. This Wonder, held by the Universal News Broadcast corporation, will project any electronic signal it receives to the entire galaxy simultaneously. Thus, updates to the Network (such as the latest news) only has to reach the UNB's headquarters on Peculain in order for the entire galaxy to know. As Peculain is located in Central Cluster, this lets news from the center (such as active Renegade alerts) reach the galactic fringe much more quickly—though the reverse is still not true.

The latest iteration of the Network comes as a result of recent advances in communication technology made by studying the alvear brain. Newer omnipad models have incorporated this research, the result of which enables limited peer-to-peer instantaneous sharing of information. Sharing is limited between two omnipads which have "entangled" each other in person (omnipads cannot handle more than three simultaneous entanglements). This is a closed channel of communication, which means it can't be used to share data with more than one other omnipad at a time. The amount of data that can be shared at once is also quite small, so scaling up such that the entire Network is updating in real time across the galaxy is far beyond the reach of current technology. Still, this technology is very new (less than a quarter-cycle old), and the prospect of further improvements to the Network is exciting indeed.

ADVENT—Despite their integral nature to all aspects of Coalition life, Enhancers have not always existed within the galaxy. The Coalition first tracked the appearance of sapient beings with powers that seemed to defy physics in the year 782 Cycle 7. Little was understood of them or their abilities, but it soon became clear that this new phenomenon was both a blessing and a bane to the galaxy. The sudden appearance of Enhancers marks a the start of a new era in galactic history called *Advent*, and had a transformational impact on day-to-day life. At first, these empowered beings seemed invariably dangerous, often turning rogue without warning. This prompted the Coalition to draw up rules of engagement, something of a precursor to the Renegade Protocols. Slowly, galactic opinion turned toward extermination.

All that changed thanks to a wise siari Enhancer named Mitra—called by many the First Enhancer (a bit of a misnomer, as many came before him). However, Mitra was the first to fit the modern concept of an "Enhancer": one who follows the Tenets and devotes themselves to service. Faced with the Enhancers' destruction, Mitra secluded himself in nature and meditated, pondering the truth of life and his own experience with the power manifesting within him. He wrote down his conclusions and observations, then shared them with the galaxy—a document known simply as the Tenets. Mitra's influence directly led to the formation of the Center and paved the way for Enhancers to integrate fully with the Coalition, leading to the present-day system in which they are indispensable.

It is difficult to overstate the Advent's impact on the galaxy. Trade, exploration, travel, energy, philosophy—all sectors of life were swept up in an economic boom, a cultural renaissance, a golden age where everything seemed possible and nothing could be taken for granted. Worlds became interconnected, families spread out across different planets, and power started to further centralize on Peramit.

KEY AMENDMENTS: RENEGADE PROTOCOLS—The Renegade Protocols themselves went on to be introduced into the Galactic Accords, building on the original hasty rules of engagement put forth by High Councilor Master Thalix. These rules had been meant to stem the flood of catastrophes echoing in the wake of the Enhancers' arrival, but after Mitra's wisdom and the Center's formation in 012 Cycle 8, the famed diplomat-professor Reein refined them into a series of directives called the Renegade Protocols. The vote to codify them was almost unanimous.

The Protocols are comprehensive, laying out the proper response to a Renegade threat on a galactic, local, and individual level. First, the process is outlined by which a Renegade is added to the Renegade Index. From there, the Protocols lay out the comprehensive playbook for engaging a Renegade from a military perspective, taking into account their extensive capabilities and unconventional offensive options. Acceptable losses, financial and otherwise, are outlined here. The Protocols specify that Renegades are to be taken in dead unless they surrender and cooperate (a rarity), at which point they are to be given over to the care of a secure black site. There is a full section on what sort of surrender to accept, written after it became a known strategy by Renegades to surrender as part of a larger, last-ditch plan to deal maximum damage before they are killed.

The Renegade Protocols also detail the expected civilian response to a Renegade threat, from evacuation procedures to the longstanding, reinforced policy of NEVER listening to, obeying, or trusting the word of a Renegade. Renegades can be cunning, and even the simplest, least threatening interaction can be part of an elaborate plan. The safest policy for the galaxy is zero engagement under any circumstances.

The Renegade Protocols' final section outlines the legal framework under which their guilt can be/has been established, and the laws allowing them to be faced with eternal imprisonment or death, as well as what resources can be requisitioned, how the efforts of independent lawkeepers may be integrated, etc.

The language of the Renegade Protocols is remarkably similar to Reein's original text, having survived with minimal amendments for more than eight cycles.

LANGUAGE—The Galactic Coalition has two official languages: Torandian and Universal. The latter was developed surprisingly late in the Coalition's history— early Cycle 10. Though many attempts to develop a common language had been explored previously, human linguists at last managed to consolidate the galaxy's different dialects and weave elements of each into one language designed to serve as the galaxy's shared tongue.

Torandians do not condescend to learn Universal; those who wish to function in the upper echelons of galactic society must learn Universal *and* Torandian. Luckily, the two are somewhat similar (a concession to the Torandians in exchange for the enshrining of Universal in Coalition law).

Human capacity for linguistics and linguistic science was leaps and bounds beyond all other developed species—which they used to their advantage when constructing the language, biasing it heavily in favor of human linguistic structures and patterns of communication. This is among the reasons that humans have been able to carve such a foothold for themselves in the Galactic Congress, and influence Coalition law to the extent that they have. While no laws forbid the use of other languages, humans hold a firm advantage in the greater galactic arena of business and politics.

The human most credited with Universal's development is Tatu Onoro, a Mars-born linguist with a dazzling understanding of the circular relationship between thought and language. Though his team was equally impressive, Tatu ended up with the lion's share of the credit. His frequent verbal sparring matches with Eternal Moravan on the Congressional Chamber floor when defending his decisions are the stuff of legend, study, and dramatization.

The official adoption of Universal was among the grievances used by Eternal Atrex to justify his assault on Peramit in 212 Cycle 10, a conflict now known as the Butcher's Revolt.

KEY AMENDMENTS: DAUNTLESS GUARD—Established in 213 Cycle 10 in the wake of the Butcher's Revolt, the Dauntless Guard is charged with protecting the Legislatorium and the councilors therein. Though not the Legislatorium's only line of security, they are its staunchest, giving pause to rebel and Renegade alike. For the sake of tradition (and budget), the Dauntless Guard maintains a vigil of three: no more, no less. Each wears a bulky, top-of-the-line powersuit with weapons and shields comparable to fifth-tier military spacecraft. Their capabilities are further supplemented by Wonders integrated into their suits, making them unpredictable and deadly combatants.

The suits themselves have been modified over the cycles as each generation's finest engineers iterate upon the previous design. A notable contemporary collaborator is the celebrity power armor engineer and Network personality known as Maestervolt.

While the suits remain constant, the sapient within is regularly rotated out, allowing for continuity of service. Prospective members are handpicked from military service backgrounds and screened for competence, intelligence, and loyalty. Their identities are hidden to prevent blackmail, bribery, or other subversion; this knowledge is considered a matter of Galactic security. Instead, they take on the name associated with the powersuit they wear, subsumed by the suit's own identity and mythology. The public knows these suits as the Sentinel of Oblivion, the Argent Warden, and the Sable Vigilant.

The Guard rotates its traditional vigil between its three defenders. One is stationed within the Congressional Chamber, one guards the Legislatorium, and one watches over Peramit City. These posts are not set in stone; one of the Guard may be requisitioned for bodyguard duty within Peramit City limits, so long as the Congressional Chamber remains under guard. The full extent of the Dauntless Guard's capabilities remain largely unknown—the potential threat they pose has proven deterrent enough to keep the Legislatorium safe for many a cycle.

INSURRECTION—No government exists without opposition. Organized resistance has ebbed and flowed over the Galactic Coalition's nearly sixteen cycles, sometimes causing a significant threat to the galaxy's stability. At present, the Insurrectionist group known as Fiurn Hult represents the greatest organized opposition to the goals of the Galactic Coalition.

The current Fiurn Hult is thirty-odd years old, though they took their name from a much larger rebellion several cycles earlier. *Fiurn Hult* is derived from Old Urdish, meaning 'torchbearer'—but with a connotation of the Torchbearer role in ancient nordok armies, who would lead the advance at night. As Fiurn Hult maintains, the galaxy is in darkness, and they will lead the way through it to victory.

Fiurn Hult is a 'big tent' organization by necessity; separately, the different factions that make it up would stand even less chance than they do together. As such, their tactics, goals, and grievances vary widely from cell to cell. These cells are led by a fierce nordok named Amoretta, whose cleverness and paranoia runs as deeply as her hatred for the Coalition. She does her best to keep the cells in line and their targets acceptable, knowing that some level of public sentiment is all that keeps the Coalition from taking their gloves off and stomping them out for good. Yet she never stops searching for some sort of edge that would allow a fight on more equal footing.

Any attempt to quantify the resources or guiding principles of Fiurn Hult would fall short due to the extent of the variance from cell to cell—and cells rarely stay ahead of the Coalition for long. Yet however many cells the GIAB and GAF liquidate, more always pop up to replace them. Some within the Coalition suspect that victory will only come when they take Amoretta dead or alive, thus depriving Fiurn Hult of the closest thing it has to a unifying factor.

Notable Species of the Galactic Coalition
(Defined here as possessing five or more votes within the Galactic Congress)
Presented in order of discovery

TORANDIAN—A species originating from the planet Torand, and one of the four founding species of the Galactic Coalition. Torandians were the first species with expansionist inclinations to achieve normalized spaceflight. This combination led to the establishing of a hungry inter-system society built on the subjugation of other species. Only when they encountered Serdins and corvids did they find themselves forced into a new, collaborative form of governance. Torandians are still by far the most influential species in the Galactic Congress, holding 43% of the total seats and chairing more than half of the committees.

Torandians are bipedal and fleshless, a tall, gaunt bone frame with muscle-like "cords" allowing the bones to move. They are efficient hunters and terrifying combatants: difficult to harm due to their near-indestructible bone sheathing, and possessing remarkable strength and speed. These advantages make Torandians the most physically imposing sapient species in the galaxy, rivaled only by the Surolians). Their diet is liquid; fluids are carried from their long, needle-like fingernails through their snaking vascular muscles and into the sac of organs kept within their chest. The fingernails run triple duty as sex organs and excretors. Unless killed, a Torandian will live forever.

Torandians have a proud culture that glorifies battle and struggle. Nowhere is this veneration of struggle more clear than in their rigid caste system. Torandians have twelve castes that they work tirelessly to ascend—though not all begin their lives in the same one. Torandian names include their caste, appended to the front of their "individual name"; an advancement (or demotion) in caste changes one's name in turn. The final caste, Eternal, can only be claimed by first living one thousand, seven hundred and twenty-eight Torand years, then surviving the accompanying twelve-day celebration, during which all other Eternals attempt to have the claimant killed. One can refuse the name by deferring the ceremony, though this is seen as cowardice.

Torandians are self-serving, obsessed with image and power, and pride themselves on their physical prowess and economic might. Their brains handle their indefinite lifespans by lacking emotional permanence—their memories eventually lose the emotions associated with them and become mere factual knowledge. Thus, Torandians cannot be counted on to act out of sentiment, obligation, or sense of duty, for the emotions that would compel them cannot be guaranteed to still exist. To a Torandian, the greatest insult is to be called a coward, and the greatest honor victory in battle. It is due to Torandian values that the most destructive weapons (as well as artificial soldiers/drones and advanced targeting computers) are banned and illegal to possess. Battles must be won through prowess, or the battle is worthless. On a more practical level, Torandians use conflict to cull their surplus population through bloody attrition, as no Torandian will ever die a natural death.

The closest Torandians get to religion is a near-universal veneration of the Eternals, whom they view as epitomizing Torandian values (as evidenced by the fact that they survived to claim the title). Eternals command the loyalty of all Torandians by fiat, but even if fealty were not compelled, they would have it nonetheless. Impressing an Eternal with dutiful service is a great way to attain a higher caste, after all—and moving against one is all but doomed to failure, given what they already survived.

"Name Day" is the largest annual Torandian holiday, which each Torandian celebrates in accordance with their name. Those on the upper end of the caste system throw lavish parties; the least fortunate have their own bleak celebrations.

The Torandian economy is enormous and has its fingers in everything from construction to mining to conquest to gate technology (of which they are the sole proprietors). The Torandian population is too small to maintain such productivity; their economic dominance is largely built on the backs of thrall slaves. In a just galaxy, these slaves would be given the share of political representation their labor entitles them to—but Torandians claim that labor as their own.

SIARI—A species originating from the planet Vinasel and one of the four founding species of the Galactic Coalition. Preceding the Galactic Accords, siari were a vassal species under the Eternal Autocracy. They were alone among the Autocracy's vassal species in being allowed to sign the Galactic Accords as a founding member (more have since followed in their footsteps). To this day, siari remember their debt to the corvids and Serdins, whose stubbornness at the negotiation table won their independence.

Siari are bipedal, with four slender arms. Their skin is pale blue and hairless, peppered with small bioluminescent disks (known as lightlets) that change color to denote their current mood. Lightlet body patterns vary based on genetics, but the most common arrangement is a V-pattern on the face, starting just below the ears and progressing down the cheeks, meeting below the mouth. Rows of lightlets also speckle the torso and trail their arms, stopping at the wrist. Siari are tall but slight of frame, and light on muscle mass. Their eyes are cloudy, off-white orbs. Siari have an average lifespan of ninety years, but some very healthy siari have lived to 135. Their bodies and minds stay sharp well into old age, but their lightlets start to fade and eventually become inert.

Siari society values cooperation, trust, and social harmony. Decisions are made with a collective, utilitarian good in mind; selfish actions provoke judgment. Due to the difficulty in hiding one's true emotions, social defectors are often spotted early on and shunned or chastened. There is, however, a technique by which siari can mislead each other. Called *domn* in their native tongue, it is the practice of calling to mind a specific past memory and using that memory's emotional response to overpower one's current feelings. The greatest of siari dancers have mastered this skill, not to mislead, but to control the light of their bodies as they move. In competitions among siari, whoever is glowing more strongly with admiration at the other's achievement is traditionally the loser.

Siari are synesthetic, some to a higher degree than others. Colors *are* emotions and vice versa, making a siari's mood easily affected by their environment. As a rule, siari are calm, polite, and accommodating, quick to forgive and forget. Truth is second nature to siari; all but the most practiced liars will give themselves away. Likely due to their affinity for color, siari possess an infatuation with visual art. Many of the galaxy's most prominent artists have been siari.

Siari are more spiritual than religious, and their spirituality revolves—again—around colors. The "true manifestation" of each color, which also represents a corresponding emotion, drives much of those beliefs. Siari will often swear by the "Pallid Moon", a mythological location/entity that is said to have given all of its color to grant emotion to the galaxy's living beings (and thus turned gray as a result).

On the darkest night of the year, siari gather on their rooftops and look out over their community in a ceremony called the Day of Reminder. Traditionally, they do not go back in until everyone they can see is shining the same color.

The popularity of siari creative output has kept the species' economic output at a level to claim a small but relevant portion of seats on the Galactic Congress. In the business sphere, their difficulty in hiding emotion as well as their general tendency toward openness, honesty, and trust have put them at a marked disadvantage.

SERDIN—A species originating from the planet Serd 01, and one of the four founding species of the Galactic Coalition. Serdins and corvids are from the same star system, and discovered each other long before the arrival of the Eternal Autocracy—indeed, when the Torandians encountered them, they were already at war with one another. To combat the sudden Torandian invasion, both sides signed a truce and formed an alliance, eventually forcing the Torandians into the Galactic Accords.

Serdins are bipedal, broad in the waist and shoulders, and covered head to toe with thick, coarse black hair. They stand a little over a meter high and can be described as squat. Serdins have rough, rectangular teeth, and small dark eyes. Serdins enter adulthood quickly, and most die by around age seventy.

Serdin culture is repressed and repressive. Showing emotion of any kind is discouraged. Every Serdin's life has been carefully mapped out in advance by the Moral Protectorate (the most powerful Serdin government agency) and deviation from the course is punished. The Serdin legal system is a confusing morass of oppressive paradox, in which proclaiming innocence proves one's guilt, and bureaucracy and paperwork rule the day. Not all Serdins welcome the nature of their government, however. There are pockets of rebellion all through Serdin space, including on Serd 01 itself. These groups often do not get along, sometimes to the point of turning each other in. By and large, their goals are to overthrow the Moral Protectorate, reverse the cultural trend towards emotionlessness, or dismantle the totalitarian horror their species has become. Increasingly brutal crackdowns have thus far cowed any threats to the Moral Protectorate's rule.

Serdins tend to be methodical and risk-averse, with little regard for ornamentation or creativity. Unlike most species, emotion is a voluntary process for Serdins—they can suppress their brain's emotional responses at will. Indeed, the Moral Protectorate encourages them to do so at all times. Before the rise of the Moral Protectorate, such a practice was infrequent at best; now, few have even met a Serdin who is open to their full emotional spectrum. Serdin family units are not rigidly defined, with whole warrens acting as family to each other regardless of blood ties.

Religiously inclined Serdins worship law and order above all else and find divinity in the bureaucratic, the tidy, and the methodical. The closest their religion gets to an Adversary is something called the Churning Chaos—not *sapient*, so much as a force of nature woven into the fabric of the universe in a similar manner as the laws of physics— the cause of all things that fall into disarray. Serdins combat the influence of the Churning Chaos in all aspects of life, without assigning any moral weight to its actions. In a Serdin's mind, the Churning Chaos is fulfilling its purpose, and there is no blame in that.

Serdins observe no regular holidays. More unique or individual traditions are discouraged—or in extreme cases, stopped. Celebration would run counter to the Moral Protectorate's goal of stripping the disorder of emotion from the Serdin species.

Serdin space largely exports lawyers, staffers, product testers, and other workers for roles of similar disposition. The amount of bureaucracy needed to keep a galactic civilization running from day to day is staggering, and Serd fills those positions as fast as they appear. This niche in the galactic market has granted Serdins a small-but-respectable bloc of seats in Congress. Some less scrupulous Serdins (perhaps dissidents and revolutionaries fleeing Serd 01) find employment as guards due to their tenacity and general toughness.

CORVID—A species originating from the planet Corvaar (reclaimed after the ancient Reclamation War) and one of the four founding species of the Galactic Coalition. "Corvid" was once the name for a subspecies of the broader avian inhabitants of Corvaar—dark-feathered, large, and clever. However, long before the time of space flight, the corvids managed to conquer and subjugate the rest of the planet during the Reclamation War. In the aftermath of the conquest, the other avians began to refer to each other as corvids as well. By the time they made contact with Serd, the original name for the species had passed from living memory and been replaced with the term "corvid".

In the short but brutal war against the Eternal Autocracy, corvid ingenuity and Serdin technology found common cause. This alliance was not popular among the corvids, and by the time the Autocracy had been dragged to the negotiating table, Corvaar was embroiled in civil war. Emboldened by the good news from the front, the pro-alliance faction triumphed.

Corvids are a bipedal, avian species with an average height of 158 centimeters. They possess vibrant plumage in varying colors, including a feathery comb across the top of their head. They have three beadlike eyes, with the third set between and slightly below the other two. Clawlike hands tip their wings, wings which at this point are capable of little more than gliding between the cliffs of their steep and rocky homeworld. They live an average of sixty-four centralized years.

Corvids are born rebels. Their history is a tale of revolution, with famous revolutionaries overthrowing the powerful and being overthrown in turn. Since joining the Galactic Coalition, these impulses have been largely curbed, but they are still a free-spirited lot; famously irreverent, but also shrewd. The individual is at the core of corvid society—with predictably colorful results when individuals clash.

The typical corvid mind values freedom: freedom of expression, of choice, of authenticity. They are daring, preferring to seize a fleeting moment over waiting for the right opportunity. Vanity is common in corvids, as is an overdeveloped sense of humor. Corvids often put their emotions on display by scratching, stroking, or drumming on their beaks.

Another major pillar of the corvid psyche is their defiance of conventional wisdom and social norms. No better example of this can be found than in the corvid response to Universal—which they still refuse to fully switch over to. While species-specific idioms are something of a social faux pas, corvids will use them far more commonly. Similarly, corvid names are loud avian cries that cannot be adequately translated into Universal phonetics or its alphabet.

Corvid mythology has a proud oral tradition. Among their most pervasive cultural touchstones are the nine winds of Corvaar. These winds are identifiable by their characteristics (Kiraa, the wind of destruction, is hot and dry, first felt in the lowlands, and smells of clay), and are said to herald their associated quality (e.g. Kiraa heralds destruction). Corvid myths can have hundreds of variations, but stories of the nine winds are startlingly consistent in their retelling.

Corvids have more holidays than there are days in a year, most of which celebrate the birthday of a famous historical corvid leader. The choice of which days to observe is an important social signal denoting a particular corvid's political views and sympathies.

Corvids make tenacious business-sapes, and their drive, adaptability and cleverness has kept them afloat in the great game of galactic dominance. Many a high-powered executive is corvid, but they can be found in every area of the galactic economy, plying their talents with all the brazenness and subterfuge taught by the ancient game of *krukki*.

HUMAN—A species originating from the planet Earth, discovered in 097 Cycle 10 and the fifth major species to join the Galactic Coalition—the first since the four main signatories who were able to claim a meaningful amount of political sway. When the Coalition made contact with humans, humans already had a developed interstellar empire of their own several systems large, capable of enough economic output to deliver them a foothold in the galactic government. It is no coincidence that the discovery of another major species occurred soon after Enhancers opened up avenues of exploration and gate placement—with the rapid mapping of uncharted territory, it was inevitable that these previously separated fiefdoms would find each other. At the time the

Coalition discovered them, humans lacked the Tenets with which to curb the sadistic impulses of their own Enhancers. Thus, they faced constant threats to their stability. While some among the Coalition proposed withholding the Tenets to use as bargaining chips to keep this new species in check, this never came to pass. Instead, the information was leaked to the humans by an unknown (possibly thrall) sympathizer.

Humans were largely less advanced in their understanding of the universe than the Coalition. However, they were quick to learn their comparative advantage; the area of knowledge that vastly outstripped the Coalition: linguistics. Humans worked inside and outside the government to push for a new universal language, playing on anti-Torandian sympathy. Following the adoption of Universal, human power in the Galactic Congress increased at a steady pace, marking the first great human power grab. The second occurred as a result of the discovery of the nordok, who with the humans' help became a powerful species in their own right, largely aligned with human interests. The human-nordok political alliance holds strong to this day, the second largest concentration of power within the Galactic Congress.

The human origin planet, Earth, once served as humanity's capital. But it is poorly placed for gate travel, not being close to any gates or clusters, and so it slowly has withered over the years as commerce passes it by. Earth's population is a fraction of its former highs—though some humans do make a lifetime pilgrimage to Earth, hoping to connect with humanity's shared heritage and history. Their new capital, Concordon A, is much better situated for humans' central role in galactic politics.

Human beliefs speak of gods—pantheons, even, each governed by their own (often incompatible) spiritual philosophy. Some pantheons have one member, others are uncountable, but most fall somewhere in between. Religious humans worship some small fragment of this divine cornucopia, or—in very rare cases—all of it. Regardless of the pantheon they choose to venerate, their practices are steeped in tradition and ritual.

Many humans observe Dovalle, a celebration of light with roots deep in their species' past. Human artisans are at their most creative for Dovalle, playing with the medium of light in breathtaking ways. The light is venerated as a symbol of hope, freedom for all sapient beings, and a reminder that though the universe is large and dark, there is brightness within it.

The human economy is diversified, though weighted toward specialized labor and middle management positions. Humans have a knack for logistics and advertising that keep them competitive in most industries. Human pop culture also tends to spill across the galaxy, sparking trends and changing paradigms—despite the Torandians' best efforts to curb this.

NORDOK—A species originating from the planet Urd, discovered in 395 Cycle 13, and the sixth major species to join the Galactic Coalition. When nordok were discovered and folded into the Coalition, they did not meet the minimum requirements for representation in Congress. Humans saw kinship in them, though—kinship and opportunity. Over the next several decades, humans spent political capital helping the nordok: modernizing their economy, funding nordok colonies on other planets, and providing massive loans of vital technology. Humans and nordok have similar brain chemistry, and as such, while the two blocs do not always agree, they tend to approach problems in a similar way. The human-nordok alliance in Congress is comparable in influence to the Torandians, forming two great powers that jockey for favor with the other, less powerful species and keeping each other in check. The emergence of new political landscape marks the start of an era of history known as *Equilibrium*.

Nordok are characterized by their reddish complexion and the patterns of bone that breach their skin, forming protective plates over portions of their limbs and torso. Nordok are bald, but strands of interlocking bone sprout from their heads that give the impression of hair. Their features tend to be sharp, and their eyes glitter in a way that evokes metal. Aside from this, nordok are almost identical to humans; indeed, this resemblance persists all the way down to the genetic level. No explanation for this has been found despite much research on the subject. Nordok tend to be slightly taller and more muscular than humans, though with a slightly shorter lifespan (nordok bone plates put stress on elderly bodies).

Nordok have a fierce and savage past, once glorifying barbarism and brutality. Though they left these days behind long before the Galactic Coalition discovered Urd, there are some on the fringes of nordok society that have kept the ancient ways alive. These nordok shun technology and "easy living" and raise their children into the same harsh lifestyle. These extremists have given nordok something of a reputation within the galactic community as brutes and savages, a stereotype kept aloft in part by the number of nordok that work security or become career soldiers. In truth, this is a misconception; nordok have no particular inclination toward violence.

Nordok are dedicated and determined, with stubbornness that can be endearing or irritating depending on how it manifests. Honor is of particular value to them, especially verbal promises: once a nordok's word is given, it is not easily gone back on. However, these promises are sometimes given internally, without outward acknowledgement, and so it can be difficult to know what promises one has elicited from a nordok. They will honor their self-proclaimed commitments to the letter, holding themselves accountable—another manifestation of nordok stubbornness. Nordok do not shy from conflict, whether physical, social, or mere friendly competition.

Religion is a touchy subject among nordok, particularly that of the species' fringe communities. Nonetheless, its influence remains evident in modern nordok aesthetic and vocabulary, and those who keep the ancient ways still practice. The dominant strain of belief involves a series of six Hells to be traversed on one's way through the afterlife, which get darker the farther one goes. The more accomplished one is in life, the further down they start. The farthest one can get on the strength of their deeds is the Dark Hells of Bloody Battle, the penultimate Hell before the Darkest Hell. This final Hell is home to a creature called the Gimmerüsk, who evaluates each soul based on how long it took them to reach the bottom. The Gimmerüsk gives one final task, to be carried out in pitch darkness. The particulars of this task are a source of debate among nordok theologians, and their answers range from "retrace every movement in your life from memory" to "find a specific soul hidden somewhere in the Gimmerüsk's vast castle", to "defeat the souls of every creature you've ever killed in your life, all at once"). When the task is complete, the Gimmerüsk makes its final judgment and either traps the soul for part of his collection, or allows it to pass onward into oblivion. Oblivion is as good as it gets in the nordok afterlife, though some philosophers argue that persisting as a collector's item in what may or may not be eternal torment is preferable.

Saykan, the nordok harvest festival, is a three-day affair filled with music and feasting. Family units come together as a community to celebrate, though the spirit of competition is alive and well as families try to out-cook, out-eat, and out-perform each other. In the distant past, eligible youths would be paired up for winter as part of this celebration, but this is no longer practiced—except by those who hold to the ancient ways.

The nordok economy is manufacturing/service-based, mostly centered around the model introduced to them by humans all those generations ago. Their economic output has risen steadily thanks to the nordok-human alliance, and while some species command a larger share of the galactic economy, there are a great many that joined the Coalition before them, yet lack comparable power and influence. There are those who resent nordok for the nature of their rise; the gifts bestowed freely by humans while other species were left to struggle by themselves. So long as nordok are backed by humans, though, none speak their discontent too loudly.

ALVEAR—A species originating from the planet Vye, discovered in 509 Cycle 16, and the seventh (and most recent) major species to join the Galactic Coalition. Though only recently discovered, alvear have spread through the Coalition at an astonishing rate. Their rapid breeding cycle led to a population explosion after they were introduced to space travel. As the galaxy opened up before them, their shared memory let them adjust more rapidly than any other species before them and they soon—despite being planet-locked upon discovery —had a massive industrial *and* service-based economy, catapulting them into the halls of the Galactic Congress. This rapid proliferation has worried many (particularly Torandians), and led to a major stalling in the original "Hivemother Ambassador Program" by which new alvear hivemothers would be sent to hiveless planets to bring them into the alvear information network and make them fit for alvear migration. The program is still ongoing—but very slowly, in the face of Coalition attempts to slow and limit what many fear will end with alvear dominance over the galaxy.

Alvear males are short and insectoid, with a thick bronze carapace and six spindly arms—three pairs, each pair with their own purpose: the top, thickest set for lifting, the middle set for fine manipulation, and the bottom set for grooming. They have six eyes too, each of which can focus separately. They are equipped with small but serviceable mandibles and two stubby antennae. Alvear females (called hivemothers) are fleshy cocoons that grow outward into the contours of their hive, communicating with others exclusively through a mental link known as the Di-ro and relying on caretaking to survive. Despite the authority hivemothers command among the alvear, they rarely venture into galactic society, leaving the task of representing their species to the males. When spawning, hivemothers have limited control over the physiology of their young. Hivemothers can live up to two hundred years if properly cared for; alvear males rarely live past age forty-five.

Alvear settle in colonies, with a single hivemother serving as that colony's sole female. While within range of a hivemother (roughly 2.2 light-years), alvear are connected to all other alvear within range through the Di-ro, forming a hive mind through which they can freely share in each other's memories. Each alvear chooses what to share, and with whom—though excessive privacy is considered a signal of untrustworthiness. While alvear promote the interests of their hive above others, there is little competition or jockeying between hives—the hive's males are united in support of their hivemother and the hivemothers are united in support of the greater alvear species. Despite what their hive structure and community-focused mores might suggest, alvear value individuality. Those who stand out among their fellow alvear find themselves celebrated, their memories circulated to ever-greater swaths of the alvear population.

The alvear brain can maintain up to six separate thought processes (one being their connection to the Di-ro), which can be used to experience multiple shared memories at once. This allows for a speedy growth period in youth (a necessity, as alvear lives are short and galactic society fast) and lets them multitask without the requisite division of attention. An alvear can—and will—maintain a conversation with their focus split across five other areas. This can lead others to label them aloof, snobbish, or even untrustworthy, but nothing could be further from reality. Alvear are earnest, cheery, accommodating, and helpful, the model of a good galactic neighbor.

Alvear have no gods but the hivemothers, which they serve and venerate but do not worship. They attribute no divine powers to the hivemothers, but do see value in dedicating their lives to their service, spreading their influence, and looking to them for guidance. Sometimes, the First Hivemother is invoked as an oath, but even she has no specific divinity attached to her.

Alvear are somewhat unique in that, rather than adhering to their own customs or species-specific quirks, they make an effort to mimic those of nearby species. Their shared memories and multi-track brain let them call this information to mind while still devoting their full attention to the conversation at hand. This mimicry makes it easy for alvear to ingratiate themselves to others, despite their off-putting appearance. As such, alvear throw themselves wholeheartedly into others' traditions while ignoring their own.

Alvear have exploded onto the galactic economic scene, quickly acquiring a significant market share of manufacturing, agriculture, quality control, and—above all—education and academia. It helps that alvear tend to work with each other due to the advantages the Di-ro provides. For example, an alvear business-sape will hire alvear workers, retain an alvear financial manager, and eat at restaurants where alvear waitstaff can find his order in the Di-ro without him saying a word. Thus, the alvear economy is remarkably insular—but always expanding.

Notable Subordinate Species of the Galactic Coalition (incomplete)
(Defined here as possessing fewer than five votes within the Galactic Congress)
Presented in order of discovery

THRALL—A species originating from Torand. Thralls were conquered and subjugated by the Torandians long before the Eternal Autocracy—so long ago that the oldest Torandian historical texts take thrall servitude as a given. Since those days, through countless cycles, the thrall species has been enslaved. The vast Torandian economy depends on thrall labor to function, with tens of billions of thrall slaves mining ore or working in factories on unnamed industrial planetoids. If thrall economic output was counted as their own, they would be among the most represented species in Congress—but the Torandians claim that output (and the accompanying representation in government) as their own.

Thralls are a reptilian, gray-scaled hybrid of bipedal and quadrupedal, with long, muscular arms serving as legs when necessary. Their arms and legs end in sharp claws, and their teeth too are sharp. Thralls have a low center of mass and are thickset in stature, with a wary hunch to their shoulders. Their blood is gray and thick, clotting rapidly. They have long tongues that can taste the air, and heads that can rotate 360 degrees. Thralls possess the common, light-based sight shared by most Coalition species, but can also see thermal radiation. Cycles of Torandian eugenics programs have rendered thralls stronger, hardier, more fertile, and more accepting of harsh conditions. Thrall lifespans are short, generally topping out at thirty years—though the stress of their brutal working conditions is almost certainly a contributing factor.

Despite the Torandians' best efforts, the spirit of rebellion still lives on within the thrall population. Most of the more openly defiant thralls get beaten down or killed, but a few manage to escape—and some areas of space will offer sanctuary to escapees. "Free thrall" communities are often overlooked by law enforcement in clusters that oppose the practice of slavery.

Thralls, as a species, are resistant to religious belief, but often find meaning and hope in the screeds of other species—when in a position to learn of them. Some of the less rebellious thralls buy into Eternal-worship.

KIRTIAN—A species originating from the planet Storrel, discovered in 673 Cycle 5.

Kirtians are diminutive, bipedal mammals. Their bodies are covered in short fur colored white, brown, black, or some combination thereof. Their faces are wrinkled, with a short muzzle and large, sagging jowls. They have a tail roughly half a meter in length, which possesses some elastic properties. If not trimmed, their claws can grow to an intimidating size. Kirtians reach old age in their forties, and rarely reach their fiftieth year.

Kirtians are a communal species, living in tightly knit large groups. Business is settled through democratic consensus, and children are raised by groups of adults. Kirtians have a strong genetic predisposition that manifests in one of two ways: roughly two thirds of the population is predisposed toward simplicity. These stay within their community, living in bucolic huts within forests, along riverbanks and in the shadow of hills. The remaining third are ill-matched for this lifestyle and strive instead for complexity. It is this third that ends up leaving their planet and representing their species to the rest of the galaxy.

Though kirtians are considered a less intelligent species by Coalition metrics, the occasional kirtian possesses a remarkable mind marked by an immense capacity for learning and deep, almost instinctive wisdom. Kirtian wisdom is in fashion at present due to its association with Central Pillar Frael, who is much beloved by the galaxy. Kirtians tend to be agreeable and mild—almost to a fault—and so tend to be disproportionately employed in customer service.

Kirtian religion involves a creator deity who created a barren universe, then sacrificed herself while weaving her essence into all things, allowing life to flourish. Adherents are taught to nurture that divine light through kind acts, and to see the interconnected oneness of all life. These days, truly religious kirtians are rare, but the species is still influenced by its cultural trappings.

The Kirtian economy is small, though not insignificant. Few kirtians are high earners, and only a third of them directly participate in the galactic economy. Though Frael's appointment as Central Pillar has done good things for their image in recent years, their representation in Congress fluctuates between two and three seats.

CTASIL—A species originating from the planet Akarest (literally "Interwoven Orchestration" in their native language), discovered in 135 Cycle 8 as part of the galaxy's golden renaissance.

Ctasil are relatively large by galactic standards, a little over two meters tall and just under half as broad. They tend to stoop, for though bipedal, they rely on their single, well-muscled arm for support and balance. This arm also holds a vulnerability; just beneath their shoulder, a major organ sits close to the surface of their skin. Their heads are rounded and hairless, eyes large and uniformly muddy green. Their rubbery, slightly damp skin is a muted purple, but begins to droop and gradually mottles black as they age (usually around their three hundredth year). Ctasil can live to be almost four hundred years old.

Ctasil possess a special relationship with sound and music, and many of their names evoke musical concepts. For the most part, they are content to live on Akarest, eking out full, humble lives and devoting themselves to their pursuits. Their diet is largely vegetarian, as they cannot digest meat. They live with their family unit, and only rarely gather in large concentrations. Ctasil bond with each other by practicing the *hanrine*—a two-handed string instrument. As ctasil have but one hand, successful playing of the *hanrine* requires two ctasil working in synchrony. Approximately ninety-five percent of ctasil suffer from space-sickness; they cannot rise into even the upper atmosphere without suffering crippling fear, nausea, or discomfort. The five percent that do not are often elected as ambassadors or to other necessary interplanetary roles.

Ctasil are often docile and nonviolent, with a deep appreciation for (not just visual) beauty. They are highly intelligent, but often get lost in their own thoughts. They have a deep appreciation for the night sky, and many are proficient astronomers. As their native language makes no differentiation between sentient beings and objects, ctasil prefer to use "it" pronouns regardless of their gender.

Ctasil religious teachings once stated that the beasts of Akarest had been given multiple arms but no capacity for music, while ctasil had been blessed with an understanding of music but given only one arm. The two blessings could not coexist. When ctasil made contact with the Coalition, they were confronted with species that possessed both blessings—leading to a religious schism and eventually, widespread atheism.

Space-sickness and a low drive to reproduce are major barriers preventing ctasil from claiming a larger share of the galactic economy. Since their discovery, they have never held a seat in Congress. They do not seem bothered by this.

SUROLIAN—A species originating from the planet Surol, discovered in 566 Cycle 11. Integrating Surolians (who call themselves Surol's Children) into galactic civilization came with difficulty due to their stubborn disdain for cooperation. Eventually, trade was established using a system of goods dropoffs with plausible deniability on the part of any Surolian who participated, which led to a slow weakening of Surolian standoffishness until they assented to participate in galactic politics.

Surolians are easily identified even at a distance; their thick, massive frames composed of frozen rimace and rock are unmistakable. Though much of the galaxy thinks of those craggy bodies as Surolians, the truth is far less imposing. Surolians are, in fact, clusters of red-gray strings of flesh that construct icy shells around their vulnerable bodies for protection and movement. Surolian shells are similar in form, built following a common genetic instinct (usually four sturdy legs supporting a torso with two craggy arms) but there is room for variation: some build heads, for example. Once a body is complete, the Surolian extends themselves through it and controls it like a puppet. Surolians have a hole in the top of their body through which sound emerges and nutrients are occasionally poured; this hole also serves as a quick escape for the internal flesh if necessary. Surolians can live for almost a full cycle or—more commonly —until they decide to reproduce, at which point they leave their body and split into two or more newborn Surolians.

Surolians possess no ocular organs (though there are surgeries to implant them). Instead, they make sense of their surroundings through the vibration of sound waves against their outer layer of rimace. The flesh cocooned within picks up these signals and constructs a mental image based on the received information.

Surolians are independent to a fault. Each believes themselves to be a fragment of the "First Among Surol's Children" (a semi-mythological ancestor of the entire Surolian species, from whom all reproductive splits can be traced), and considers it an imperative to carry that responsibility well. As part of this imperative, Surolians shun assistance and rely only on their own abilities—total self-sufficiency is the Surolian ideal. Surolians generally do not associate with each other, or with other sapients. Even transactional relationships are distasteful, performed as seldom as possible; as a result, few Surolians ever have occasion to leave Surol.

Surolians are stubborn and goal-oriented. They prefer isolation or small groups—not just because of their beliefs; crowds can overwhelm their ability to process their surroundings. Surolians function best in quiet, slow-paced environments. They are quick to pass judgment on others, but that judgment rarely affects their actions. As their constructed bodies have difficulty conveying emotions, Surolians have a language that uses runes to denote emotion. These runes sometimes feature in the works of other species.

Surolians do not worship, but they idealize the First Among Surol's Children as the only "complete" Surolian. They see themselves as fragments of this whole, but nothing about this spurs them toward collectivism; quite the opposite, in fact. Each strives to prove themselves worthy of the fragment they have become—for to do otherwise would suggest that the First Among was anything less than exemplary in every way.

Due to their lack of cooperation and desire to trade, politick, or even expand, the Surolian economy is largely nonexistent. However, their iceball of a planet is rich in rare metals and other compounds necessary for high-quality ship construction. This incredible windfall of natural wealth has, through several loopholes in the Surolian ideas about trade, enriched the Surolian species to the point that they have a tiny share of representation in Congress—and thus, a begrudging say in galactic politics despite their disdain for collective action.

Settled Planets Within the Galactic Coalition (incomplete)
Presented in order of distance from Peramit, closest to farthest

---

PERAMIT—The shining jewel at the heart of Central Cluster, capital of the Galactic Coalition. "Central Cluster" is something of a misnomer when it comes to Peramit's spatial location within the galaxy, yet none can deny its central nature in galactic affairs. This massive planet technically lies within Torandian-controlled space, but charter defines it as neutral territory—though the world's topography favors Torandian preferences (as it happens, many aspects of the Galactic Coalition favor Torandian preferences). Once home to lush, tropical forests, the remainder of Peramit's natural landscape has been turned marshy through terraforming, and is muggy and hot by the standards of most species. Its gravity can be unpleasant to species such as alvear and siari, but this is partially mollified by a spaceship's ability to gradually alter its gravitational settings over the course of its journey—thus, new arrivals on Peramit have already had some time to adjust and acclimate.

Peramit is home to the Legislatorium, the massive building/complex that houses the government of the Galactic Coalition. It also boasts such galactic landmarks as GFMB Headquarters (Galactic Financial Management Bureau), the Palace of the Eternal, the Grand Peramit Zoo, the Garden of Unwanted Knowledge, Panegyr Military Academy (the largest military academy in the galaxy), and many more. Peramit's marshes have been urbanized to the point where "megacity" is its dominant biome, though undeveloped areas still exist in rare locations.

The planet has seen war and prosperity both, and now stands at the heart of the galaxy, protected by a unique double layer of planetary shielding. Though

Peramit City has grown to encompass almost a continent and other cities continue to expand outward, upward, and downward, real estate prices remain sky-high. Yet from all over the galaxy, sapients flock to Peramit, planting themselves next to power and possibility. The vast number of natives combined with the unending flow of tourists from all corners make Peramit's population centers hopelessly overcrowded.

Orbiting Peramit is one of the GAF's major shipyards. Ships are constructed free of the planet's gravity, their great size preventing them from ever touching down.

No fewer than five Gates open in close proximity to Peramit, one of the reasons it was chosen as capital. This makes it accessible, more or less, to the rest of the galaxy—a trip to Peramit from the furthest settled planet, without Enhancer assistance, takes just under a year.

MODELLUS—A prosperous planet within Central Cluster, with varied topography and gravity at 93% of the Peramit norm. Modellus's vast diversity of terrain and temperature makes it a comfortable home for almost any species looking to settle there. Modellus has many large cities as well as an active rural population, but many of the planet's points of interest are outshone by the Prime Center. A decent chunk of the planet's economy comes from capitalizing on its presence. (While the Pillars may not be happy about the Prime Center's monetization, it *is* perhaps the most popular tourist destination in the galaxy.)

The Prime Center is located high in the Mantru mountain range, on a wide plateau with enough space to land and dock ships (though the full Enhancement Corps fleet is housed within a hollowed-out mountain nearby) and a climate favorable to the Center's extensive gardens.

Modellus boasts no fewer than fifty-two megacities, one of which was built as an artificial island in the middle of its largest ocean. These megacities host the galaxy-wide businesses that make Modellus their home—financial firms, patent offices, data farms, think tanks, omnipad program development, etc. Two megacities, Zanium and Filafor, are home to Modellus's manufactuaries—and therefore looked down on by the rest. Just outside Derios City is Diffido Spaceport, famous for being the first spaceport to offer commercial intercluster travel (in part due to the influx of Pathmaker Enhancers from the Center).

The large corporate presence on Modellus is motivated mostly by the Prime Center's presence. Just about every galaxy-wide business wants to be situated near such a large concentration of Enhancers, so as to increase their chances of poaching one.

URGAM—A planet of dust, rare minerals, and little else, Urgam is a miserable planet on the outskirts of Arot Cluster that would see few settlers if not for Haymore Mining's presence on the planet, providing jobs and opportunity to anyone seeking to chase a living stripping the planet of its europium. Its gravity is 87% of the Peramit norm.

Before its terraformation, Urgam was inhospitable to sapient life. It mostly remains so after terraformation; the heat is bearable, but only just, and Haymore must import every drop of water it wants its workers to have access to. They use this as an excuse to keep water prices high—prices workers pay out of their own meager wages. Haymore and its ten company cities are the only game in town, and there is a government contract keeping it that way. The cities and mines are connected by gravtrains, whose tracks snake across the desert dust.

Urgam is a recent addition to the Galactic Coalition. The Gate linking the newly discovered Arot Cluster to Greens Cluster was built just seventy years prior. As Greens Cluster links directly to Central Cluster, this made Arot Cluster valuable real estate for anyone wanting to set up shop near Peramit. The few habitable planets in Arot Cluster received a flurry of attention, allowing Fleetway to collect samples of Urgam's soil with relatively limited competition —and subsequently lose the mining contract to Haymore. Urgam is the bitter sporefruit of Arot Cluster: surrounded by wealth and opportunity, but itself nothing more than a dry ball of dust getting drier every day as Haymore extracts what wealth it can.

TAROUS—A small planet on the inner periphery of Forres Cluster, far removed from Peramit (though spatially nearby). Tarous is temperate and mild, with a soft, dim sun and a lavender sky through which the stars are always visible, day or night. Tarous sunrises and sunsets transform the sky into a breathtaking display of light and color. Its gravity is only 62% of the Peramit norm, but the planet was habitable to most species prior to terraforming (a rarity).

Despite its relatively disadvantageous position and lack of importance in galactic politics, Tarous is technologically developed, with a population loosely scattered through the countryside and almost six hundred large cities. Part of the reason for Tarous's development is that its local tax laws are unusually lax, leading some companies that can afford to be far from gates—and a fair number of wealthy individuals—to settle there. Noted Tarous-born councilor Jarod Hammry successfully won a bid for a new GIAB facility by pointing to this concentration of wealth and implying very heavily that it needed some kind of supervision. As a result, Tarous is among the least important planets with a significant GIAB presence.

Due to its distance from major spacelanes, Tarous has learned self-sufficiency and has a remarkably stable planetary economy—though infrequent trading vessels do pass through.

RITJI—A small, once-insignificant planet along the outer periphery of De Cluster. Most of Ritji is iced-over oceans, with small strips of cold, farmable land around the equator. Based around these islands are Ritji's three major settlements: Fesna, Colub, and The Cask. Ritji's population lives mostly on tubers and fish. Its gravity is 71% of the Peramit norm.

Ritji was an afterthought to the galaxy until the Ritji Blockade incident brought it into the spotlight. The nordok warlord Dulvar Galoron attempted to claim the planet for himself, laying a siege that was broken by a task force under the command of Admiral Highwater. Over the course of that siege and battle, much of Ritji's crop land was devastated. Since then, Ritji has been reliant on the goodwill of the Coalition to sustain itself. Charitable endeavors from other planets have helped Ritji stay afloat—and even thrive.

Further opportunity came to Ritji when the GAF discovered Galoron's war manufactuary on a nearby moon, and promptly moved to secure it. Military bases soon followed, and then a military academy in Colub, where Ritji's harsh climate is leveraged to toughen soldiers and create endless training opportunities. Ritji's newest governor is an ex-military minor hero. He received the position partly to reinforce and favor the planet's new military identity, partly as a cushy reward for a job well done.

Each of Ritji's major settlements is home to a large fishery. Fesna's is largest, but Colub, with its new military academy, has recently dethroned Fesna as the largest settlement. Considerable quantities of GAF money flows into Colub, but little of it reaches other settlements.

IPWAAN—On the outskirts of Gyfor Cluster, far from any semblance of civilization, Ipwaan is about as removed from Peramit as one can get before entering the lawless fringes. Ipwaan's gravity is 76% of the Peramit norm. The rays of Ipwaan's red sun light the particulate-heavy atmosphere in odd patterns, sometimes making it appear as though the sky has caught fire. While this is an optical illusion, Ipwaan's air is far from safe. Small mineral deposits can catch and build up in one's respiratory system over time, leading to a condition known as "stoutlung".

Ipwaan was only recently settled and has six total cities, with almost no rural population. It gets little traffic from the rest of the galaxy; the majority of visitors come to Colony Four to visit the planet's gauntlet saloon.

Ipwaani citizens are proud and headstrong; the sort who willingly shed galactic protection to tough it out on a hellish, far-flung world. They are fiercely independent—so much so that, when Fiurn Hult sent agents for recruitment, the Ipwaani rejected the notion of throwing their lot in with *anyone*.

Selected Curiosities and Marvels of the Galactic Coalition
(Meeting a threshold of cultural, sociological, or historical importance)

WONDER—Wonders are small pieces of technology of unknown origin and design. These devices are rare and possess a varied range of uses, though no two are exactly alike. Whatever their function, they tend to bend—or outright break—the laws of physics as currently understood. They are compatible with Coalition technology, but resist all attempts at replication. Any attempt to reverse-engineer a Wonder's workings has met with frustration at best, and a broken Wonder at worst. However Wonders came to be, they have since been scattered across the galaxy, seemingly at random.

Sapients who hunt Wonders are known as acquisitionists. Aquisitionists can be publicly or privately funded, though the Coalition tends to buy up those found by other organizations. Every so often, though, one finds its way into private hands.

Not all Wonders are equally useful—one speeds up hair growth in a small radius around it, another retains every scent it has ever been exposed to—but the most impressive ones tend to have equally impressive names, and legends of their own. The weapons used by the Dauntless Guard are some of these, but there are others, such as the Universal Signal employed by the UNB, or the Knowledge Well. Wonders cannot be Enhanced, and extend this property to any device into which they have been integrated.

Theories abound as to the nature of Wonders. Are they remnants of an extinct, galaxy-wide alien civilization? Are they connected to the Advent? Are they pieces of technology from the future, forced back through time? Many will claim to be sure of the answer. All are lying.

GATE—Gates are massive installations that maintain rips in space, by which immense distances can be traversed instantaneously. A ship in the process of passing through a Gate exists in two different parts of the galaxy at once.

After thousands of years of searching the stars for life, Torandian scientists discovered abnormalities in space-time, which they referred to as grooves. Further tests led to the theory that these grooves represented points at which two separate sections of space were *connected* through some hyperdimensional means. More than half a cycle later, the first working Gate was built and connected with a point in space seventy-two light years away. This scientific triumph sparked a resurgence of Torandian exploration under the banner of the Eternal Autocracy.

Gates are triangular, with three large nodes at the triangle's points and a hole through the center. This hole is the Gate itself, and the stars visible through the empty middle are far, far away, their light passing through the Gate without any disruption. Gates are equipped with bright signal lights to alert lost travelers of their position. Gates cannot be "closed" without permanently destroying the Gate's infrastructure, but they are heavily guarded and have sealing protocols in cases of emergency.

Gate placement is a frequent subject of debate in Congress, and the process is not a simple one. It begins when Pathmakers discover a new groove, which indicates a potential Gate location. Next, that groove's parallel location is calculated, at which point surveyors determine whether the new Gate would be beneficial enough to justify proceeding. Few potential Gates make it past this stage. For those that do, Gate infrastructure must be built on both ends—so more Pathmakers are dispatched to the parallel location with a build team. Construction time often surpasses five years from time of arrival, but once the Gate is complete, the new territory is officially folded into the Galactic Coalition.

The most vital Gates are those that link star systems where habitable planets are particularly dense. These densely packed groups of planets are known as clusters. Chains of Gate-linked clusters form travel routes called spacelanes: the trade-dominated veins through which flows the lifeblood of the Coalition. The result is a galaxy in which distance cannot be accurately measured with a map. Star systems thousands of light years from Peramit (but connected to Central Cluster via gate) are considered "closer" to Peramit than systems one hundred light years away with no convenient access point. This makes star charts a nightmare to read, and coming to understand the complexities of Coalition trade routes and scheduling is the work of decades.

HAVEN—The space station known as Haven is a hotbed of illegal activity, an eighth-tier artificial habitat carefully hidden from the Coalition where criminals can ply their trade without fear of (government) reprisal. It has an arid, somewhat cool climate, and maintains a gravity level of roughly 80% the Peramit norm. Its projected sky is evocative of multiple species' origin planets at once, cleverly designed to appeal to as many as possible. It runs on centralized time.

Haven is sandwiched between the floating remnants of a great battle bound by weak gravitational attraction to a planetoid base (long since rendered unusable), and a trio of large asteroids that have created a permanent electrical storm between them. It was once a research outpost constructed to study the storm. The planetoid base served as the scientists' permanent quarters, from which they would commute to the station for limited periods of time. The outpost was decommissioned, leaving the station abandoned until a group of pirates moved in.

The pirates enjoyed good fortune until a smuggler gang traced them back to the hideout. The debris field from the resulting battle litters Haven's airspace to this day. The smugglers triumphed and took up residence in the station. As they grew in wealth and influence, the station became a place to do business (and hide their profits). It continued to grow over the years until the smugglers realized they could transition into "legitimacy", putting their smuggling days behind them in favor of overseeing this growing community. The gang's higher-ups became the first members of Haven's council.

Haven's growing population has necessitated multiple expansions. Its current shape is a lumpy cone, with the cone's interior as the docking bay. Criminals from all over the galaxy flock to Haven: gangs, fences, black marketers, hit sapes, even a few magnates fleeing taxation. Haven is independent of the Coalition, with its own government, its own laws, and even its own hidden Gate. It does not collect taxes, but instead imposes dozens of fees on visitors and residents alike, by which it maintains its revenues. The two current power players in Haven are Citizen Duzzat, the Torandian leader of a local gang called the Talons, and an enigmatic but ruthless human woman known only as 'Slims'.

Haven is one of the galaxy's few criminal communities—and the only one that can call itself truly independent, as the others are run and regulated by their syndicate. They believe their location to be secret from the Coalition, but this is less true than they know.

UNIVERSAL NEWS BROADCAST—Also known as the UNB, or Uni-News, this news conglomerate is by far the largest in the galaxy, verging on a monopoly. It is the only network operating on a galactic scale, a feat made possible by their access to the Wonder known as the Universal Signal. Using the Universal Signal (secured within the heavily fortified UNB headquarters on Peculain), a Network signal can reach every part of the galaxy at once—and possibly every part of the universe, though this supposition is (obviously) quite difficult to test.

Local news does its best to compete (though the UNB often buys out influential local outlets), but most sapients get their galactic news exclusively through the UNB. And Uni-News has its fingers in more than headlines: its programs include music and entertainment, public interest programming, advertising, and more. Whatever the Universal Signal receives, it spits back out, and Uni-News has wholeheartedly capitalized on their advantage.

In 540 Cycle 15, the company that would become the UNB relocated to Peculain, a largely uninhabited planet perfect to hide on while building a Network apparatus around a newly discovered Wonder. Their unveiling quite literally changed the galaxy overnight. Peculain has become an entertainment powerhouse, with hundreds of thousands of producers competing for UNB distribution contracts. Even Peculain's local government unofficially answers to the UNB; rare is the decision that does not first get run by the desk of Barry Rolk, UNB's head administrator.

The government, recognizing the Universal Signal's power, worked quickly and covertly to establish a working relationship (and an understanding) with Uni-News. The UNB is not *quite* state-run; the company is largely allowed to operate freely, but the government does sometimes step in to dictate the framing of a particular story. The UNB also does its duty in relaying vital galaxy-wide announcements, such as updates to the Active Renegade Index. This incestuous relationship between the Coalition government and the UNB is among the galaxy's worst-kept secrets. Because of this, the UNB is sometimes mockingly referred to as the Universal News Bureau.

Uni-News has the honor of being the Coalition's most successful recruiter of new species. Their signals are picked up by many an undiscovered world, whose residents then seek out or contact the Coalition. After the first few times this happened, the UNB began to include in their broadcasts an informational segment on the Coalition: who they are, how to find them, how and why to join, etc.

Notable UNB personalities include Poppy Cartwright, Jalen Urr, Srawraak, Joseph Derringer, Estrafolrudginnud Formuralicut, and many more—there's always more news to cover and a cadre of headline combers making sure the most sensational stories float to the top. Some reporters have their own fan clubs. But as popular and omnipresent as the UNB is, it's not without enemies. Local news companies, for example, would like nothing more than to see them brought low.

Enhancers and Enhancement: An Abbreviated Primer

ENHANCEMENT—A flexible but little-understood art, the usage of which imbues objects or sapients with an Enhancer's energy. This energy magnifies aspects of the subject's being, such as density, velocity, heat, or acidity (though Enhancers are by no means limited to those four examples), as chosen by the Enhancer when the Enhancement is made. Enhancers possess their power from birth and cultivate it for the rest of their lives; one cannot *become* an Enhancer through any known means.

An Enhancer's energy is undetectable and has no physical presence, seeming to exist only in the Enhancer's mind. Enhancers channel this energy through a process of mental conceptualization that seems to differ from

Enhancer to Enhancer. Energy may be reclaimed and redistributed freely. An Enhancer's energy pool is limited; the pool's size varies with the Enhancer. As Enhancers practice and grow into the fullness of their power, they become more efficient with their energy usage.

The difficulty and efficiency of an Enhancement is dependent on several factors:

Distance: Physical proximity to an Enhancer increases the efficiency of their Enhancements and decreases the time it takes for an Enhancement to take effect.

Familiarity: The Enhancer spending time with, understanding, or having an emotional bond with the Enhanced subject increases the Enhancement's efficiency and decreases the time it takes for an Enhancement to take effect.

Size: The larger the Enhanced subject, the more thinly spread the Enhancer's power. Thus, smaller, more precisely targeted Enhancements are more efficient.

Enhancers-in-training meditate, study, and practice to maximize the strength of their Enhancements, and to anticipate and limit an Enhancement's unintended consequences. An Enhancer's most efficient subject for Enhancement is usually themselves, as distance and familiarity are at peak efficiency. Enhancement is multiplicative—the same Enhancement that barely brightens a dim bulb will turn a flashlight blinding.

An Enhanced subject cannot be further Enhanced by another Enhancer. Nor can an Enhancement ever diminish its subject.

Enhancer minds are uniquely at risk of succumbing to violent madness, a risk that increases the more they Enhance. To stave off the side effects of Enhancement, Enhancers follow the teachings of Mitra, a wise siari Enhancer who, through meditations in nature, gained insight into the very essence of Enhancement.

ENHANCEMENT CORPS—Mitra's advocates spread through the galaxy, bringing these new revelations to every Enhancer they could find. But some Enhancers were more ambitious and had an eye toward the future. These founded a school where Enhancers could come to learn the ways of Mitra, and receive support from an Enhancer community. In less than ten years, this school had expanded far beyond its original scope.

The Coalition, still reeling from the sudden introduction of Enhancers to the galaxy, saw an opportunity to benefit themselves and the Enhancers at the same time, and worked to incorporate this school into the government. The school would receive government resources and backing, and would be authorized to find and bring young Enhancers to be taught. In return, graduates would be fully incorporated into the Coalition, using their powers in the government's service. After much deliberation and consultation of Mitra's Tenets, the fledgeling school agreed, and the Enhancement Corps was officially established in 037 Cycle 8. Since then, it has significantly expanded in scope: every Enhancer child is now expected to attend one of the galaxy's seventeen Enhancer schools (now called Centers) and the Enhancement Corps' duties extend to interplanetary commerce, agriculture, diplomacy, exploration, special operations—and beyond.

The Enhancement Corps is structured as a partnership between two bodies: the internal body (the Enhancers themselves, led by the nine Pillars) and the external body (Coalition staffers and representatives).

ENHANCERS—Children who display the power of Enhancement are brought to a Center to learn control, mastery, and duty. New classes arrive at Centers twice annually, staggered such that no Enhancer must wait long to arrive after being discovered. Enhancers are taught a broad range of subjects from an early age, focusing on topics relevant to building familiarity for Enhancement such as biology and mechanical engineering. They also receive education in morality and ethics, meditation, philosophy, and the Tenets. Later on, their education diverges. Occasionally, a young Enhancer will receive special attention and mentorship from a more experienced figure.

Enhancers are portrayed in popular media as noble, wise, and morally pure —or even as divine, inscrutable beings. Some of fiction's greatest heroes are Enhancers, just as many of the darkest villains are Renegades. This depiction is encouraged by the government, which supplements these portrayals with its own propaganda.

As children, Enhancers are called Initiates. Once they choose their discipline, they become Acolytes. Upon graduation, they are referred to by their discipline. There are four disciplines: Pathmakers, Agents, Aides, and Harmonizers.

PATHMAKERS—Colloquially, "Ship Enhancers". Pathmakers derive their name from those assigned to ships that push outward from the known galaxy, charting new space and searching for more space-time anomalies that can support Gate construction. The discipline is much broader, however; duties also include positions on military vessels, merchant or supply ships, or megaferries. Pathmakers serve on the same ship for life, gradually building familiarity (and therefore increasing the top speed they can achieve through Enhancement, even beyond light speed). Enhancers with the most raw power are often given a nudge toward the Pathmaker's discipline, and then placed on exploratory vessels to cross between solar systems in search of habitable planets and convenient Gate locations. Pathmakers are always in demand, no matter how many the Centers train.

AGENTS—Colloquially, "Combat Enhancers". Agents are warriors, trained and equipped to bring the Coalition's enemies to justice. Together with their Vanguard, they form mobile units that can be dispatched wherever they are needed. Armed with Enhancement, they are all but impossible to guard against. Agents most often handle threats not under the direct purview of lawkeepers or the GAF (such as Renegades), though they do work in tandem with those groups. The Agent's discipline is competitive—its allure outshines the Coalition's needs, so many disappointed hopefuls are turned away each year.

AIDES—Aides are the least glamorous of the four disciplines, but perhaps the most important, responsible for Enhancing individual cogs in the machine of galactic society. Aides Enhance crops on breadbasket planets, output from power plants, the speed at which factories can churn out machinery, and much more. Due to Enhancement's relationship with familiarity, Aides are assigned early to their specific task and cannot easily be reassigned. Occasionally, circumstances will dictate a transfer—new technology obsoleting the Aide's assigned factory equipment, for example.

Aides are the most numerous discipline, yet new demand far outstrips supply. It is sometimes said that their ranks are made up of the Enhancers who weren't good enough for the other disciplines, a sentiment with some truth behind it.

Aides can be requisitioned by private enterprises. The application process is competitive, with innumerable businesses vying and jockeying for the trickle of new Aides coming from the Centers. The stakes are high; even a single Aide in a key role can catapult a business ahead of its competitors. Bribery and corruption run rampant.

HARMONIZERS—Colloquially, "Social Enhancers". Harmonizers are the diplomatic wing of the Enhancement Corps, employed as peacekeepers, mediators, and negotiators. Their training focuses on the bodily cues and tells of the Coalition's many species. This includes facial tics and body language, but also subtler cues that might only register to Enhanced senses, such as changes in heartbeat or specific scents associated with certain states of mind. Their skill in this area has led to the (false) belief among some that Harmonizers are capable of mind reading. Harmonizers are expected to uphold the Tenets in any resolutions they have a role in shaping, but aside from this, are given a great deal of freedom in how they approach their duties.

While Agents and Harmonizers are useful, Pathmakers and Aides play an irreplaceable role in galactic society. Through their efforts, trade and travel are feasible on a galactic scale, energy is cheap and renewable, and fields and factories can keep up with a galactic population.

VANGUARD—As children, Enhancers are assigned three to six companions of similar age and species. These companions are referred to as an Enhancer's Vanguard, sworn to accompany and assist their Enhancer at all times. The group becomes inseparable over the course of twenty years of education and training— the best the Coalition can supply.

Prospective Vanguards are chosen as children from a pool of volunteers (though the ethical question of whether children *can* meaningfully volunteer remains). Starting training in childhood is crucial for an Enhancer to build familiarity—and thus Enhancement efficiency—with their Vanguard. The emphasis on familiarity is also why Vanguards are matched to an Enhancer by species.

Vanguards are put through an intensive training regime, which varies somewhat based on their Enhancer's discipline. An Agent's Vanguard will receive full military and special forces training, for example, while a Pathmaker's Vanguard will specialize in spacecraft mechanics and hyperdimensional mathematics. Regardless of discipline, each Vanguard receives the same theological training as Enhancers. They are not required to fully follow the Tenets, but *are* expected to honor (and memorize) them. When a squad is field ready, Vanguards are assigned numbers based on their relative performance in simulations and field training, with the coveted call sign of Vanguard One being given to the top performer. Prospective Vanguard Ones are identified early on.

Vanguards—like Enhancers—are often larger than average for their species. Enhancers are encouraged to Enhance the squad's constructive metabolic processes as their bodies grow and develop.

CENTER—Centers serve as headquarters for Enhancer activity. There are currently seventeen active Centers, but the first and largest Center is located on Modellus. Twice per year, ships arrive at these Centers bearing young children from all over the galaxy who have exhibited the ability to Enhance. Centers are fully funded by taxes.

Centers are designed as all-in-one living spaces, meeting the needs of every sapient sequestered within. The goal is to limit their contact with the outside world until they have mastered their abilities and committed themselves fully to the Tenets. As such, Centers are equipped with living quarters, eateries catering to a multitude of tastes, recreation centers, simulators, a laboratory, a fully equipped holographic library and art gallery, a gymnasium and training facility, and expansive gardens. There are no shops, but residents can requisition anything they need. Enhancers, holding to Tenet Fifty-Six, prefer to minimize their personal belongings and therefore rarely use this privilege.

Centers also have their own shipyard and armory. Enhancers receive a ship and a rack of military equipment at a young age. This is again done to cultivate familiarity as early as possible—but Enhancers are kept under strict supervision when handling dangerous equipment until their age of maturity.

BATTLECALM—Among the Center's lessons is instruction in the mindset of battlecalm, first written of by Mitra in his fourth and final treatise on stillness of mind. Employed when an Enhancer is called to violence, battlecalm is meant to curb negative emotions associated with Renegadehood and filter all impulses through a rational lens without impacting instinctive movement and quick reactions. It is not, by any means, an easy mindset to master. Though this training is most relevant for Agents, all Enhancers learn the ways of battlecalm, in case bad luck and circumstance force them to fight.

Agents in particular are relentlessly drilled in achieving battlecalm, until their calmness inhabits all three levels of awareness (also called the three layers of being): skin, muscle, and mind. They are trained to watch for "cracks" in their battlecalm; moments where emotion leaks through. Within the battlecalm, there is to be no fear, no hate, no pleasure, no desire for glory or gain. Battle is a necessity, an uncomfortable means to a regrettable end. To treat it as anything else invites the dangers of Renegadehood.

PILLARS—Administrative power within the Enhancement Corps is divided into two groups. The first group is made up of Coalition representatives, bureaucrats and elected officials who hold power over things like Center locations, Corps funding, recruitment, and logistics. None are Enhancers, and approach running the Corps as they would any other government agency. The second group are the Enhancer leadership (though they would prefer to be thought of as guides), true believers in the Tenets and their associated quasi-religion. This internal governing body numbers nine, and its members—called Pillars—are revered for their wisdom within *and* beyond the Enhancement Corps. Pillars have individual responsibilities, but vote as a body on important issues under their purview. Beyond their usual duties, Pillars serve as spiritual leaders for their community. Each Pillar has a title relating to their responsibility within the Enhancement Corps, as follows:

Pillar of Justice: This Pillar holds purview over Agents and related matters: receiving missions from the Enhancement Corps officials on Peramit (the Pillar of Justice technically has veto power over these assignments; in practice, it is not used), assigning missions to active Agents, etc. They also have limited influence over Agent training regimens. The position is controversial among Enhancers due to its focus on combat and violence, which runs contrary to many of Mitra's teachings.

Pillar of Unity: This Pillar serves as liaison to the Enhancement Corps' Peramit office and as the Center's representative before Congress should one be needed (in practice, this duty is often shared with the Central Pillar). Outreach and publicity also falls under their purview.

Pillar of Devotion: This Pillar manages Aide and Pathmaker affairs, matching Enhancers with assignments, always with an eye to where the greatest need is to be found. Due to the endless, desperate demand for Aides and Pathmakers, the position is under constant pressure, and is known to be thankless.

Pillar of Wisdom: This Pillar holds purview over the history and stories of Enhancers through the cycles, deciphering and disseminating the wisdom of the past, and meaning encapsulated by parables. They are also in charge of studying and interpreting the Tenets, constantly studying Mitra's original texts for new motes of meaning. Care of the original writings, preserved within the Modellus Center's entrance hall, falls under their responsibility. Though not involved in Center curriculum, the Pillar of Wisdom reserves the right to address an assembly of students for the purpose of imparting a valuable lesson. Due to their nature and reputation, the Pillar of Wisdom is often the Central Pillar.

Pillar of Beauty: This Pillar ensures the continued maintenance of the Centers and their gardens, as well as holding authority over renovations, aesthetic adjustments, and new plantings. The Centers' projector wall and window programmers ultimately answer to the Pillar of Beauty. Most Pillars of Beauty are reluctant to exercise their power, seeing it as a form of vanity that the Tenets do not look well upon.

Pillar of Truth: This Pillar sets the Center curriculum and has some influence over lesson plans. They also may set Enhancement Corps policy with regard to laboratories and libraries—though as with the Pillar of Beauty, this power is rarely used, ceded to the facilities' local caretakers.

Pillar of Humility: This Pillar runs Vanguard affairs. Their most prominent duty is processing and evaluating each year's volunteers, then selecting matches for the year's Enhancers. This is but one duty, though—the full list is long, and includes items such as medical care for wounded Vanguards and adjusting

Vanguard field-ready benchmarks. They also act as a mouthpiece for Vanguard issues when necessary.

Pillar of Compassion: This Pillar serves as the Enhancement Corps' charity arm, identifying high-impact causes and deploying Enhancers (usually students) to assist. They work closely with the Pillar of Unity, but while the Pillar of Unity is more publicity focused, the Pillar of Compassion's foremost priority is making the most positive impact in the lives of as many sapients as possible.

Pillar of Duty: This Pillar heads requisition logistics, setting policy for what requests can and cannot be considered, tracking trends and budget, and submitting formal requests to proper parties for rare or otherwise problematic goods. Those denied a request can appeal their case to the Pillar of Duty.

CENTRAL PILLAR—One Pillar also holds the title of Central Pillar, which denotes a further leadership role, with limited influence over all aspects of Center management. The Central Pillar is the face of the Enhancement Corps to much of the galaxy, and their statements carry unofficial weight (what some might call soft power). The position is a lifetime appointment, as with the more specialized Pillar positions.

The title is bestowed in a process that is partly a vote among Enhancers, partly a vote among Pillars, partly a vote among the Galactic Congress, and partly luck. The Central Pillar is not necessarily the most powerful in terms of Enhancement, but there is an observable bias toward powerful Central Pillars that cannot be denied. Officially, though, an Enhancer's command of their power is not to be considered when selecting a new Central Pillar.

Each newly elected Central Pillar is given the opportunity to record their own Tenet, adding it to the list for future generations to follow. Plenty turn down this honor, believing that the Tenets are perfect as is. Some, though, take the responsibility upon themselves (Tenet subject to approval by various offices of the Galactic Coalition) and so the Tenets' numbers grow.

Central Pillars tend to slightly "reorganize" the structure, goals, and ideals of the Enhancement Corps based on their other Pillar duties. For example, a Pillar of Compassion who held the title of Central Pillar would likely influence the Corps more toward charitable endeavors, compassionate acts, philosophy rooted in compassion, and so on during their tenure.

During votes, the Central Pillar abstains and moderates discussion. In the event of a 4-4 tie, the Central Pillar casts the deciding vote.

The current Central Pillar is Frael, Pillar of Wisdom. He inherited the title from Reece Fillomar, Pillar of Compassion.

Pillar Spotlight: Frael

The current Central Pillar of Wisdom. Frael is a kirtian native to Nybea, and well past the average kirtian lifespan at the age of seventy-two. Abnormal lifespans are usual for Enhancers, but even the power of Enhancement does not fully account for Frael's longevity.

Frael came to the Center at age three and quickly developed a reputation for troublemaking, a trait made more frightening by his immense pool of energy. Many instructors lamented that such talent as only comes along every century had been wasted on such a free-spirited rogue. However, Frael received guidance from Reece Fillomar (Central Pillar of Compassion) and Exemplar Scratch (Pillar of Justice) and with more years began to cast aside his youthful ways. But it wasn't until a training mission proved deadly for two of his Vanguard that he fully committed to the Tenets. That event changed him forever.

Formerly of the Agent's discipline, Frael requested a change to the Harmonizer's—and in a stunning breach of tradition, the request was granted. Frael attended to his duties diligently, and in time became known for his measured approach to diplomacy and his talent for refocusing bitter enemies on the truly important parts of life. It came as very little surprise when he was nominated to the position of Pillar of Wisdom. He found the position a perfect fit, letting him pass along the guidance he had received to students who needed it as he had.

When his colleague Arcus, Pillar of Devotion, was exposed as a Renegade, the scandal rocked the Center, reverberating for almost two years. During this time, Fillomar abdicated her position, blaming herself for the disaster and unable to stomach continued authority. In the resulting election, Frael was voted in as Central Pillar at the age of forty-three.

Though Frael's adventuring days are behind him, he possesses enormous talent and power as an Enhancer. Yet he is better known for his deep and abiding empathy for all things, his piercing insight, and his dedication to teaching young Enhancers the way of the universe. He does so with cryptic nuggets of wisdom and strange puzzles meant to help them discover the truth for themselves. Frael is fond of addressing initiates just before dinner, in assemblies generally called with very little warning. He uses this time to recite a parable, letting listeners come to their own conclusions about its intended meaning. Though some are more opaque than others, all Enhancers know that a parable from Frael is to be meditated on, its wisdom revered.

It is often suggested that Frael return to the field and use his incredible power in service of the Coalition, but he has deflected all such attempts—particularly in recent years, as much of that power goes to maintaining his failing vitals and keeping him active. There are lessons to be taught, and not many years left in which to teach them.

Pillar Spotlight: Exemplar Scratch

Born Citizen Vixam, Exemplar Scratch has held the title of Pillar of Justice for over two hundred years, and his record of service to the Coalition is written upon his bones.

Many Torandian children struggle and fight for survival and recognition, but many Torandian children are not gifted with the power of an Enhancer. Once that power was recognized in Vixam, he was whisked out of the crucible of Torand and sent straight to the Modellus Center. They didn't force him to wait for the twice-annual shuttles or have him seek placement at one of the lesser Centers; Torandian Enhancers are so rare and so powerful that exceptions were made to fast-track his training and to ensure its quality.

Vixam's star rose quickly. Even before Enhancing his natural aptitudes, he was a fearsome combatant; afterward, he was untouchable and all but indestructible. He struggled with the Center's philosophy, which ran counter to much of Torandian culture, but with the endless patience of the Pillars of the age, Vixam grew in wisdom as well as power. He was watched by what sometimes seemed like the entire galaxy. A Torandian Enhancer was a celebrity by virtue of his very existence, and to many, he was more than that: he was a tool waiting to be wielded. The Center protected him from what they could, but the interest of all manner of powerful patrons could not be fully set aside.

Vixam's best friend was a proud corvid named Avwrak. They pushed each other to excel, and Avwrak was desperate to keep up despite being utterly outstripped by Vixam in physical prowess. In time, Avwrak was approached and lured by those who found his connection to Vixam useful. Insecure and jealous, Avrawk was made to feel special and wanted by his new friends, who used this opening to its fullest.

When Avwrak's compromised nature was discovered, the scandal enveloped the Center. Such a public straying from the Tenets was unprecedented; no rules were in place to deal with the situation in any way less drastic than life imprisonment. Many believed this punishment to be too harsh, and Avrawk apparently agreed—for he fled before his final punishment could be determined. Now a Renegade, Avwrak was hunted by none other than his old friend Vixam, who volunteered for the duty. By the time Vixam caught up to him, he had slipped further from the Tenets, doing terrible things in an effort to stay one step ahead of his pursuers. When they fought for the last time, no mercy was left in Vixam's heart.

Vixam soon found himself in a position to strike the killing blow. But rather than defend, Avrawk knew he could not hope to win, and so instead poured all his power into his claws for one last strike, to finally land an injury on his rival. Even this was not enough—all his claws did was leave three long scratches on Vixam's arm. For his victory, Vixam was granted a new caste name: War-Marked.

Though shaken by his friend's death, those emotions soon faded away to nothing—as happens with Torandians. Indeed, Scratch found new purpose in the hunting of Renegades. Whenever a new Renegade threatened the galaxy, Vixam petitioned the Pillars to be assigned the task of hunting them. Being so suited for combat, his petitions were often successful. With Vixam on the hunt, Renegades lasted about as long as they could stay ahead of him. Vixam's reputation grew with each new triumph, and his collection of war marks increased. Nobody knows who first called him Scratch, but the nickname slowly spread through the Center until it was all anyone called him. (He certainly never seemed to mind.)

Scratch had never been particularly cruel or closed off, but as years passed and the intensity of his missions diminished, he grew more affable and started placing himself in more mentorship roles. Between Renegade hunts, he enjoyed searching the ranks of new initiates for signs of promise only he could see and taking satisfactory candidates under his wing to train them in the arts of wisdom and battle. He became not merely a figure of awe and veneration, but also beloved—particularly for his eccentric and unique spirit-based philosophy.

Due to his prowess in battle, many thought him a natural candidate for Pillar of Justice. Many others resisted, believing him more focused on fighting Renegades than on exemplifying the Tenets. But as Scratch mellowed, his detractors numbered fewer and fewer—and indeed, when the previous Pillar of

Justice retired, Scratch was nominated and confirmed as her replacement. Upon receiving this honor, he was granted the caste name of Exemplar.

Scratch is not yet fully retired; he still chases down any Renegades he identifies as worthy prey. But he considers his primary responsibility as an ageless being to be the preservation of forgotten teachings in each successive generation.

RENEGADES—Enhancers who fail to uphold the Tenets invariably lose themselves to paranoia, destructive delusion, and hatred. These dangerous sapients are called Renegades.

The surest and fastest way for an Enhancer to turn Renegade is by Enhancing their brain. Such an act is verboten; the ultimate betrayal of the Tenets. Renegades have no such qualms and can freely Enhance their own intellect to a dangerous degree. They build plans within plans, and are impossible to predict—and the more they Enhance their brains, the deeper into Renegade madness they sink.

Renegades discard most Enhancer limitations, but often inexplicably cling to some, such as limiting themselves to hand-to-hand combat. They are prone to volatility and let their emotions run wild, but this makes them no less crafty or quick with a lie. Galactic citizens are taught to *never* trust a Renegade's word, or cooperate with a Renegade's orders. Even the most innocuous request can have devastating impact on the galaxy. The proper response to encountering a Renegade is outlined within the Renegade Protocols.

Once identified, Renegades are added to a registry called the Renegade Index and the galaxy is placed on high alert. No expense is spared in ending the immense threat they pose to sapient beings by any means necessary. Fortunately —or unfortunately, depending on one's point of view—Renegades don't hide for long, and can be easily tracked down by the destruction in their wake. Renegades are hunted unceasingly by teams of Agents, as well as by any independent lawkeeper willing to risk their life. (A hefty bounty awaits any independent lawkeeper who succeeds, enough to tempt many otherwise-sensible lawkeepers to their deaths.) On the rare occasion that a Renegade is taken alive, they are placed in suspended animation and taken to a high security Torandian blacksite. Here, they are subjected to vigorous scientific experimentation in an attempt to better understand Enhancers and their powers.

TENETS—Tenets are short aphorisms, generally one to two sentences, each of which contains a piece of the code by which all Enhancers live. In many ways, they are the most important part of an Enhancer's education. The Tenets were written by Mitra to preserve Enhancers' minds from the sanity-cracking weight of their own powers, and have been passed down and added to by generations of Enhancers since. However, the Tenets are not merely a series of warnings, but beneficial advice in their own right. An Enhancer who embodies the Tenets not only avoids becoming a Renegade, but leads a blessed life.

There are 154 Tenets at present. The first twenty-seven hold the distinction of coming directly from Mitra, and thus contain his wisdom. The other 127 have been added by generations of Central Pillars, one Tenet at a time. Mitra's

twenty-seven are informally considered to be the most important to follow,
though any Pillar will say that all the Tenets are equally important.

A partial list of Tenets has been reproduced below:

1: To breach the sanctum of the mind opens the door to madness.
2: A life taken by hand is a life taken out of necessity.
3: Duty is not the means, but the end.
4: Disobedience is the precipice, weakness the fall.
5: Emotion must never be a maze.
6: Lies are no less contagious than other diseases.
7: Efficiency is duty done well.
8: The first and final enemy is the Self.
9: Wishing for water brings no rain.
10: Any Enhancement is only as great as its foundation.
12: Every action has its cost, but a good deed is beyond price.
13: Beware nourishment that leaves you empty.
15: Growth is the blossom, struggle the seed.
17: From rot, life.
22: The worthiest revenge is forgiveness.
24: Fear is courage waiting to step in.
28: When luxury becomes necessity, excess and waste follow.
30: Though sunset will come tomorrow, marvel at its presence today.
31: The source of your shame is unworthy of asylum.
32: Treasure what is freely given; the rest holds no value.
33: Contentment is humility's reward.
35: Responsibilities postponed are weeds well-watered.
37: Waste is anger's greatest sin.
38: Company kept is the most truthful mirror.
40: Persistence is the nucleus of success.
41: Though the traffalar is proud and noble, the reed survives the storm.
44: The decision to allow suffering lies within every observer.
46: Determination will not fly a ship through an asteroid.
48: One cannot crawl free of darkness without exposure to light.
55: From each acorn its own tree, from each tree its own fruit.
56: Freedom from objects is freedom from hindrance.
58: Beneath the cosmos, we find equality in insignificance.
61: The weight of inaction carries as much force as any choice.
62: The wise listener turns their senses inward.
65: Water is easily parted, but not easily held.
67: Follow with purpose; blind steps will lead you astray.
68: The choice is yours to freeze or tend the flame.
72: Poison contaminates the bearer as well as the victim.
73: Wisdom frowns on haste.
74: The seed begets the harvest.
75: Fleeing is as easy as failure.

77: Destruction is control yet to be mastered.
79: Without calm, truth cannot flourish. Without quiet, truth goes unheard.
82: Wisdom is not seized, but built.
86: Death's lone balm is acceptance.
90: Gently beats the content heart.
97: Beware the path unburdensome.
98: Remembrance is the duty of the living.
103: Hesitation is the enemy of necessity.
108: Enhancement is not moss, or rock, or water, but all three at once.
115: A forest is the work of cycles, perfect in its imperfection.
127: Idle thoughts breed foolish minds.
129: Still water can hide deep currents.
134: To abandon a friend in need is to abandon yourself.
136: Three things, the galaxy cannot fail to hear: Pain, truth, and conviction.
149: The way forward may wind.

ACKNOWLEDGEMENTS

Writing a book is a collaborative process—and not just when it comes to cowriting. The author is but one of many people who work to bring a story from concept to bookstore. Here are some of those who we'd like to recognize for their efforts in helping *Weapons Of The Mind* reach its final state.

Ted Greenwald and Steven Kivelson, who gave exhaustive sentence-by-sentence feedback across every stage of the project, from the first draft to the query letter and beyond. Their edits and suggestions elevated the story beyond what we could have reached without them.

Pam Davis Kivelson, who pushed us to keep querying and refused to give up on our dream. Her championing of our work on our behalf was tireless and made all the difference.

Our beta readers, who offered feedback at every stage of the process and helped us see when our intention matched our execution—and when it didn't. These readers include Cory Greenwald, Willa Gruver, Merrill Gruver, Mike Griffith, Mary Griffith, Sophia Kivelson, Margaret Kivelson, Valerie Kivelson, Tom Hill, Jake Weber, Gabe Hall, Miles Holland, Thors Hans Hannson, Leila Hofer, Larissa Klein, and Nina Auerbach.

Our other readers, too numerous to name, who encouraged us (and assured us that they would still buy a copy if we sent them a draft now).

Jenna Griffith, who drew the first *Renegades* series-inspired artwork, wore the first *Renegades* series-inspired costume, *and* created the first *Renegades* series-inspired celebratory chocolate centerpiece. The joy she found in Tala's story made our own all the stronger.

DJ Hoffman, whose many creative and insightful questions about the nature of Enhancement gave us a greater understanding of its possibilities. The number of loopholes and edge cases he discovered solidified Enhancement's identity and worked it more smoothly into the world we created, no doubt preempting numerous argumentative internet posts.

The team at Will Dreamly Arts Publishing, who worked around the clock to bring our manuscript into physical form. Special thanks to our editor Michael Koep, for his guidance, hard work, and design expertise. Michael understood our vision from the beginning, and enthusiastically supported us through the publication process. Special thanks also to Andreas John, who saw the potential of our story and fought to make sure we could share it with the wider world.

Herb Leonhard, our cover artist, whose stunning artwork may have contributed to your decision to read this. We are humbled by the majestic, gripping scene he created from our words.

The Soft Shoe Writers Workshop, whose feedback, advice, and commiseration were invaluable.

Thank you everyone, for your effort, love, and support.